CIVILIZATION

CIVILIZATION

❖

AND ITS PART IN MY DOWNFALL

PAUL QUARRINGTON

Vintage Canada
A Division of Random House of Canada

Canadian Cataloguing in Publication Data
Quarrington, Paul
Civilization and its part in my downfall
ISBN: 0-394-22445-0
I. Title
PS8583.U334C58 1995   C813'.54   C94-932126-5
PR9199.3.Q37C58 1995

Printed and bound in the United States.
10 9 8 7 6 5 4 3 2 1

Toronto, New York, London, Sydney, Auckland

And he carried me away in the spirit to a great and high mountain, and shewed me that great city, descending out of heaven from God, having the glory of God; and her light was like unto a stone most precious, even like a jasper stone, clear as crystal.

I gratefully acknowledge the assistance of Lynda
Robbins at the library of the Canadian Film Centre.
I promise to return the books shortly.

Chapter 1

I am damned, all because I wanted to be in *Civilization*.

I have received to myself damnation, as my mother would have it. She used to stand on the streets of The Confluence —especially the streets of commerce and trade — and level a pointed finger at passers-by. "If ye resist His Word," she'd sizzle, "ye shall receive to yourself damnation." My mother was too well-known a crank to truly frighten people (despite her flame-red hair, hacked off to render her head near-bald and nappy) and her conversion rate back then was pretty poor. Several times drunkards crumbled to their knees in front of her, but I am sure they were affected more by her strange beauty than her preaching. No one paid much attention to my mother, except for me, standing nearby holding a sign that read, "Man does not live by bread alone, but by every word that proceedeth out of the mouth of God."

Yes, what I learned at my mother's knee was grim news indeed, and compared to what I know lies in store, the Cahuenga Federal Penitentiary is a cakewalk. To tell the truth, this prison is a cakewalk by pretty much any measure you care to employ. For example, it was only last night that I mentioned to The Warden that I wanted writing materials, and early this morning he obliged in grand style. In the middle of my cell is a huge desk, tilted and ornate and full of hidden drawers. It is a desk such as God must sit at as He plots our course. It is piled high with blank paper, and I have a choice of fine pens.

I am a little unsure as to how to set out, being but a neophyte at this authoring business. (The Warden also gave me a book called *Hartrampf's Vocabularies*, which has already raised the tone of my efforts.) The Warden, who has been eager to accommodate me in every way since my arrival a few days ago, has offered some advice. "First off," he maintained this morning, "you've got to grab their attention." The Warden lit a cigar and commenced wandering about the cell, bumping into my furniture. I am fond of the Warden, although he is in truth a frightening–looking man. He lacks hair, right down to not having any eyebrows or, I noticed the other night over supper, hair in his nostrils. The Warden is over-sized, and this capaciousness refuses to be contained by the blue suit and starched shirtfronts. Whatever tortures may exist within these prison walls — and I do hear men lowing late at night — they must pale beside the horror of his necktie, a thin black affair done up in the Western manner. It threatens to pop The Warden's head like a champagne cork; his eyes bulge and the skin surrounding his collar is mottled. "Chapter One," he suggested. *"I watched Thespa Doone as she rose nakedly from the bathtub. Her breasts etcetera her velvety, um, velveteen etcetera her firm buttocks which I saw when she rotated after having risen nakedly etcetera.* What do you think, Thom?"

"I'm afraid not, Warden. Thespa was none too keen on bath-tubs."

"Hmm?"

"Thespa believed that in a bathtub dead skin cells would find their way back on to her body. This she did not want, sir, being as she was on a quest for incandescence. Thespa preferred bathing in large bodies of water. Preferably salt water, preferably wind-whipped. Always at dawn, owing to the quality of the light. Thespa would scrape her body raw with lye and holystone."

"But," The Warden seemed consternated, "she would be naked?"

"Oh, yes, sir. Buck naked."

"Ah!"

And after The Warden withdraws, I lie down on my bed for a while and think about Thespa Doone.

Although, you know, The Warden may be right, at least about grabbing people's attention. I am tempted to commence the story of *Civilization* in some manner such as this: *C. W. Willison pulled out his Bird's Head Colt and shot the horse between the eyes.*

On the other hand, it is important that you understand how I came to be watching Caspar W. Willison shooting out the horse's brains. It is important that you understand the strange look he'd always give me afterwards, half-amused, half-deadly, his eyes a strange light blue. I would be smacking dirt from my clothes and, more often than not, checking my own body for broken bones. Once I rose up on a twisted ankle, and, as Willison killed the horse, I gimped around and gave out sharp little breaths of pain. I did this as I heard the blast of his pistol, I did this until I heard the sound of it being cocked once again. I looked up and saw that Willison had levelled the Colt at me. Billy Bittner the crankman, Theo Welkin his oily young assistant, the other cowboys and actors, they all watched in silence. Only Thespa Doone made a sound, one which I could not identify, although I had heard it before during our lovemaking. Then Willison lowered the gun and laughed, a laugh too loud and strangely girlish. "I wouldn't kill you, Mess," he said. "At least not until the climax."

So it is important that I start the tale before all that took place, and I believe I will begin as many fine books have, *I was born, etc.*, which I was, in The Confluence, although do not be fearful, I don't intend to take a running start from the day I first entered the sinful vale, naked and purplish. I propose to just sketch in my early days and then Foote and I shall light out in search of adventure.

The Confluence, Ohio, lies in a small plain nestled among the hills, shadowed by two mountains (Mounts Uriel and Sariel, which are not much by world standards, but mountains all the same) where no fewer than seven creeks, streams and runlets come together to form the Petawa, a stately, even sluggish, river.

The earliest maps of the area have *The Confluence* neatly printed on them, and when the town was founded the fathers apparently lacked the imagination to come up with anything new. There is not much by way of industry in The Confluence, Ohio. There are several dairy farms and corn fields. There is The Asylum, a grim building standing just outside town like an errant schoolboy sent to the corner. The Asylum resembles a castle from a book of fairy-tales, but one wherein dwell ogres or pale princes laboring under a witch's curse.

My father was named Walber Moss. He got this strange name from my grandmother, who died as my father entered the world. It was the last pained word that passed her lips. There was much discussion as to whether she'd meant *Wilbur* or *Walter* or even *Walker*, but in the end they honoured her memory by sticking with *Walber*, and although my father campaigned throughout his life for various nicknames, he remained Walber or *Walb*.

Walb Moss was renowned as Captain of the Nine Men From The Confluence. It would seem as if people from my hometown have a definite difficulty in coming up with catchy tags. The Nine Men From The Confluence were, of course, a baseball team and, due to my father's pitching arm, they were virtually unbeaten. The reason history has not honored them is that they continued to play their local brand of town–ball long after other teams had adopted Cartwright's Philadelphia Rules. The chief difference between the two was that The Confluence game retained plugging as a method of outs, that is, hitting the runner with a thrown ball. Walb Moss was a legendary plugger. He once almost killed a run-ner, bouncing a ball off the fellow's temple and dropping him like a sack of rocks. The man complained ever after of a ringing in his ears and a numbness in the extremities, and his head failed to return to its previous shape.

My mother you have already met, if only briefly. I think she could not tolerate being beautiful, which she was despite her shorn head and flour–bag dresses. I am physically like her, in that my own face appears to have been chiselled (by a talented artist, but one in a hurry — at least, there is something angry and violent about my aspect) and I own my mother's eyes. They are large and green and long–lashed, and when I bat them in the Flickers grown women have been known to giggle.

✤ ✤ ✤

Nolan Tweed, Itinerant Shakespearian, came to The Confluence
in the summer of 1892, the year before my birth, with all of the
Bard, the Compleat and Entire Shooting Match, locked inside his
lumpy head. Nolan Tweed was a handsome enough man, but
oddly dwarfish, stooped and lame. He appeared always to have
been newly beaten up, lumps and bruises adorning his body. What
he was was a bleeder, and Mrs. Moorcock (Thespa Doone's
mother) reported to me how Tweed ended his days, opening a large
gash on his foot in between towns. He is said to have delivered all
of the great soliloquies and most of the sonnets as he waited for
Life to drain from him.

    Nolan Tweed would approach a town with the following propo-
sition: let us mount one of the Plays — the mayor or town coun-
cil was welcome to name it — and then split the admission
proceeds straight down the middle. Next, local amateurs were
invited to participate. This was done on a first-come, first-served
basis, which I believe led to some odd pieces of casting — how
about the young Walb Moss as Claudius, killed by a stepson more
than twice his age? Now, from time to time there weren't enough
keen players to make up the *dramatis personae*, but it was part of
Tweed's agreement that he would pick up any slack and do the
remaining roles himself. Once or twice *nobody* was forthcoming,
everyone either lazy, stage-frightened or just in the mood to watch
a play, and little Nolan Tweed was forced to do the whole thing
himself, keeping the characters separate using a variety of wigs.

    So he came to The Confluence in the year before my birth, and
he put forward his offer, and someone came up with *Hamlet*, and
the local bushes were beaten for actors and actresses. Walb Moss
and the Nine Men From The Confluence showed up, taking a real
bite out of the male parts. My aunt Lacky became Gertrude, a part
she delivered with a flushed and breathless quality — Lacky was
stout and tended to perspire freely — which I understand was
somewhat compelling. Soon every part was filled except for that
of Ophelia. Which is when the seventeen-year-old Virginia Maybray came forward.

    At the time her red hair flowed well past her *dorsal region*, Mr.
Hartrampf and I being a little bit fussy as it is my own mother
we're discussing. During rehearsals — and now I'm relating things

told to me by my father, for every so often he would wax sentimental on the porch, waving the Old Bell's in the air, his mind
clouded by memory — Virginia Maybray delivered her lines in a
whispered mumble and would look no one in the eye. Which is
remarkable as those of you who have seen her lately know. She
stomps about, gesticulating grandly, her eyes illuminated as if by
fire. It was during the rehearsal period that my father fell in love
with my mother. I'm sure that all Nine Men From The Confluence did so, but they stood gallantly aside and allowed Walb Moss,
their star pitcher and soaker, first crack at courtship. His first
words to her constituted a proposal of marriage. Her response was
inaudible, followed by a disappearance so quick as to seem magi-
cal.

At any rate, *Hamlet* was mounted in the Town Hall, and sched-
uled to run a total of five performances, which is how many it
would take for everyone to see the thing at least once. *The Chronicle of Daily Events*, The Confluence's newspaper, reports that
opening night was something less than a stunner. The Nine Men
From The Confluence got giddy and giggled throughout the play.
Aunt Lacky fainted three times. Nolan Tweed himself received
only tentative praise; *The Chronicle* recorded that he was easy to
hear, and made much use of the stage, which I suppose meant that
he tramped up and down a fair bit. Still, he was not the ideal
Young Prince, being forty-five and all hunched over. The worst of
it, though, was my mother, who, for her first two scenes, refused
to come out from behind the scenery flats. When she finally ventured on to the boards, she trembled and all her lines were moaned
or sobbed.

Things got better over the next few days. The Nine Men From
The Confluence settled down, Aunt Lacky acquired a fortified
constitution, Nolan Tweed covered his physical shortcomings
with fancy brow-furrowing and ominous "To be or not to be"s.
Everyone made up ground except for my mother, who improved
only to the extent that she actually appeared on stage when she
was supposed to. Until the last night, that is, when my mother
gave the performance of her life. She was particularly effective
when Ophelia hits the skids. Virginia Maybray flew on to the
stage and gave a stunning portrayal of lunacy. The long red hair
had been hacked off, her clothes were torn, she was bedaubed with

dead leaves and cow dung. All of this inspired Nolan Tweed to one of his great performances, but mostly people remember the cold and dreadful recitations of the doomed Ophelia. The Confluence was terrified, none more so than my father, especially when Virginia Maybray told him bluntly that her whispered answer to his marriage proposal had been a *yes*.

My father had no profession other than baseballer. He was a strong and powerful man and often found casual employment in farming and construction, but mostly he sat on the porch, a glass of Old Bell's in hand, and imagined the future. Walber Moss loved to envision how the world would be, say, in the year 1920, although, as that year creeps ever-near I am duty-bound to record that the old man was wide of the mark. Walber Moss failed to see the coming of the Automobile, for example, a fact which has an especial bitterness in that just last year he failed to see the coming of one particular one down Main St. in The Confluence. Instead, Walber put his money on the bicycle, and imagined a world where-in everyone was up and pedalling most of the day. He sometimes described to me special bicycles; transcontinental journeys would be made on enormous contraptions, machines with wheels as tall as trees. Even as a small child I understood that my father was standing a bit shakily on the grounds of Science, but I dutifully imagined this world. Walber Moss was also a bit misled by the fact that the Wright boys had operated a bicycle repair shop in Dayton, and to his mind flight was achieved with a wingèd two-wheeler. My father's confusion was compounded by the fact that when he was growing up, the most popular players for the Cincinnati Red Stockings were the Wright Brothers, Harry and George, so I think he also pictured baseballers aboard these peculiar vehicles.

Walb Moss was mostly a peaceable man (except when Old Bell's and bitterness combined into a foul mood, but every man gets into a foul mood now and again) and in his foretelling there was no great devastation which is going on even as I sit in my prison cell. The newspapers are currently full of stories of how Caspar Willison is in Europe photographing the War. Apparently he stands between the trenches, cranking the wonder-box, as mortar shells explode all around him.

This morning the Hollywood *Megaphone* quoted Willison as

saying that he's almost got all the footage he needs. "Willison hopes that this will mean, finally, the end of *Civilization*."

My father, Walber Moss, made monthly bicycle trips to Cincinnati, mostly to wager on horses, although he also made a regular stop (at least he did until my seventh year of life) at the managerial offices of the Red Stockings, where he pleaded for a tryout. One day they acquiesced, mostly, I'm sure, because my father had a rather likeable manner. His forward thinking, even if a little off the mark, lent his eyes a certain brightness and informed Walber Moss with enthusiam. Walb hurried down to the field and threw batting practice. His usual competition were mere Ohio farmboys, but even the professional baseballers seemed to have trouble with his pitches, I suppose because his style was unorthodox. In the middle of the wind-up my father would jerk his head backward and stare for an instant up at Heaven. He'd stick out his chin, bite his lower lip, and roll up his eyes until nothing showed but the white. Then he'd curl out frontward; his right arm would come high over his head and the bean would skitter toward homeplate. Enough of the Red Stockings whiffed that the front office wrote up a short-term contract and gave my father a uniform.

My father was given a shot in the lower frame of a double header. My mother and I were sitting in the stands that day, at least, I was sitting, my mother was up on her feet with the Bible raised above her head, fielding lightning bolts. "But His Word is in mine heart as a burning fire shut up in my bones!" My mother was a very young woman then, which made her easier to ignore. These days, she has become quite manly in appearance. Her jaw has squared, she's jowly and thick about the neck. She's put on weight, mostly through the belly, her waist remaining small, her legs so thin you'd think they'd snap under the added burden. Of course, her hair remains fire-red, shorn so close that the scalp shows through. And she has followers these days; since my father's death she has forsaken The Confluence and accepted a Grand Mission, tramping about the countryside preaching the Doctrine of Muscular Literalism to the lost and lowly.

"Are ye not," she demanded of the people seated nearby, "children of transgression, a seed of falsehood?"

The opposites, that day at League Park, were Louisville. My father pitched a strong game, surrendering a run in the fourth inning, a solo circuit clout. The Colonels, however, were just as good, and the ninth inning found the teams deadlocked at one.

My father walked out to that mound feeling like he'd grabbed hold of something. (This figure of speech comes from my rodeo days. In bull–dogging, there is a moment after you fall from your horse when it feels like you've jumped off a cliff into some gigantic emptiness — my father's life, I fear, was this instant enacted again and again — and then you grab hold of the steer.) He hustled his beans between pitches and slapped his buttocks, a far cry from the man I later knew, who mostly sat motionless drinking Old Bell's, dreaming of a world of bicycles.

My mother was still saving souls, but I think her mind was at least half on the game; she was going on at some length regarding the cherubim of glory which shadow the mercyseat.

The first man popped up shallow, and Claude Ritchey circled underneath the ball and then swallowed it, and my father sang out, "Thank you, Little All Right!" The next Louisviller was the catcher, Billy Wilson, and some of you fanatics may remember that he was a hard man to strike out, but my father accomplished this. Along with his odd wind-up went some sort of intuitive grasp of physical science — the balls would curve like shooting stars, dance and hover like hummingbirds — that was lost, along with everything else, when the center fielder came to bat, John Peter Wagner, a short and stocky rookie with hands the size of shovel scoops. My father balled up, rolled back, snuck a peek at Heaven and unfurled, hurling a smoker, which this Wagner summarily drove toward right field. Doggie Miller cautiously allowed the ball to meet the ground before trapping it in his mitt. Taking first, this Wagner appeared to run in a mechanically unsound manner, pushing off the outsides of his feet, his huge fisted hams tracing large opposing circles in the air.

Next up was the veteran Charlie Dexter, and my father worked him to a full count — ignoring the strange young man over there on first, who was rocking back and forth on his huge legs as though the world meant to buck him clear — before tossing a grudging strike that Dexter bounced back toward the mound. Walb Moss deftly picked the ball out of the air. That was the last graceful thing he would ever do. My father became suddenly aware of young Wagner bounding toward second base. This was my father's Moment, and he mishandled it. He wheeled around, hurled with all his might, and soaked Wagner. The ball bounced off the lad's head with a small sound that somehow filled League Park. To his credit, Wagner wavered but slightly, and allowed unconsciousness to overtake him only as he collapsed upon second base. It was this sort of grit that made him the player he was. John Peter, known as Honus, became the finest shortstop ever, playing for Pittsburgh, and as his fame grew, so did my father's humiliation.

The Colonels stormed the mound, full of righteous indignation, which I have recently viewed at close quarters and know to be as dangerous as bullets in a campfire. Some of the Red Stockings took to stoning the old man, angry as though he had transgressed some consecrated code writ on stone. As he fled the ballpark, my father was reviled.

We returned to The Confluence.

Chapter 2

Foote and I decided to seek adventure in the world.

I will tell you about Jeff — Jefferson — Foote by writing what my aunt Lacky said about him, that he had "the look of a poet." Leaving aside what this says about Jeff, it reveals a lot about my aunt Lacky, namely, she liked to shine the best possible light on people. "The look of a poet" translates into Jeff Foote owning huge eyes that seemed to be melting, dark ripples cascading over his cheeks. His eyebrows were too heavy for his forehead to support, they sank down wearily and any attempt to raise them resulted in a sea of wrinkles and crosshatches. Foote's mouth, like his eyebrows, was almost too much for his face to bear, due to thick lips so pale as to be almost invisible. And so Foote walked around frowning, and he topped this morose mien with a head of black hair so limp it appeared to have given up the ghost and was merely waiting for the rest of Jeff to catch up. So, by "the look of a poet" my aunt Lacky meant that Foote could ruin your day just by nodding at you in the street.

But he was my best friend, and so, when we were nineteen and twenty years of age, we decided to seek adventure.

The Confluence train depot was a small shack about a mile out of town. The Station Master had, to my memory, no name other than that; he wore a hat labelling him the "Station Master" and was never seen other than at his post, standing by the tracks with an enormous gold watch in the palm of his hand.

He and Foote were alone on the platform when I arrived that morning.

My leave-taking had been pretty painless. I had not lied, but somehow conveyed to my mother the misinformation that I was embarking on a soul-saving crusade. She considered me her ally in the Good War. My mother had presented me with my own Bible, and she had highlighted passages throughout. These were meant to serve, I suppose, as general counsel, but it is uncanny how neatly they seem to comment on the tarnishing of my soul. One example that leaps to mind is this passage from Ecclesiastes, heavily underscored and adorned with brutal little checkmarks: "Be not hasty in thy spirit to be angry, for anger resteth in the bosom of fools."

My father had not risen from his chair on the porch to bid me farewell. I console myself with the fact that he had occupied it early in my honor, that he already held a glass of Old Bell's as a balm for the ache in his heart. My father, I think, had been up all night, and my hunch is that he'd spent it trying to come up with a prediction of such force and accuracy that I could bear it thence as a shield or talisman. But the old man looked ahead and saw only shadows and vapors. "Be good," he offered lamely, and I set off in search of adventure.

I had dressed, in so far as I was able, for the City, although the shelves of The Clothing Store didn't offer much in the way of sophistication. We of The Confluence tended to dress alike, in tans and beiges and shades of grey. I managed to find a polka-dotted bow tie, and hidden near the back was a velveteen top hat, which I convinced to remain half-sprouted so I wouldn't look to be putting on such great airs.

Foote had never been one to pay any attention to his personal appearance (his teeth were yellow, his face covered with pimples and peach fuzz) so I was not prepared for the figure who stepped forward on the platform to meet me. He was wearing an enormous black hat, with a flat wide brim that plunged most of his face into shadow. Around his neck he'd tied a bandanna, the ends left long to dangle over a grey cotton shirt and waistcoat. The waistcoat was made out of some sort of animal, but it seemed like whoever rendered it was not properly schooled in hiding and tanning. Little tufts of fur sprouted — even from a distance of ten feet it smelled foul — and it had attracted most of the area's flying vermin. Jefferson wore denim pants, and over them leather chaps. He completed this outfit with a pair of high-heeled boots, and it was obvious he'd been awake all night polishing them. Foote stepped forward and spat at my feet. It was very strenuous spitting. First off Foote pulled his mouth away over to the side of his face, snuffed and dislodged something from his nose, then hooked a big shiny oyster near my shoe.

"Watch it," I said, because I'd spent a little while with a buffing cloth myself.

"Look at you," snarled Foote. "Damn pretty boy."

"Look at you," I retorted. "Who the hell do you think you are, Bronco Billy Anderson?"

Foote's eyes narrowed. He attempted to spit again, but I guess there was nothing forthcoming. Foote pushed the brim of his hat back, and smiled a little loopily.

"Oh, no," I said, for that was exactly who Foote thought he was, Bronco Billy Anderson.

Foote had long been fascinated by the West, by what he called "men with the bark on," a phrase he got out of the nickel novels he read constantly (most of which were written, incidentally, by J.D.D. Jensen). Bronco Billy Anderson had brought his show through The Confluence when I was eleven, Foote older by a year. There we had seen an exhibition of Wild West artistry, calf-roping and bull-dogging, etc., and Foote and I were both suitably impressed, although I can with hindsight tell you that the cowboys were nowhere near as skilled as I became during my brief career. As a matter of interest, I will report to you that taking part in that show was none other than Bill Pickett, the fellow who, according to legend, became so exasperated with an unmoving steer that he jumped down from his mount, grabbed the animal by the horns and threw it over on to its side. He then bit its lower lip, which is why the activity is called *bull-dogging*, because apparently bulldogs do this when locked in combat, although I've seen no evidence of that. The only creature I've ever heard of biting on lips was Bill Pickett, who repeated the stunt in front of us Confluencers, throwing the steer down disdainfully (a small and docile thing) and then kneeling beside it, pressing his dark face in close and chomping down. A little bleat filled the air.

At a little table nearby Foote went a bit foolish, purchasing an armload of books with titles such as *Cowboy Life in the Wild West, Last of the Great Scouts, Old Glory Round Up* and *Buffalo Bill, His Life and Stirring Problems in the Old West.*

But impressed as we were by the rodeo, we were left open-mouthed — *dumbfounded,* suggests Hartrampf — by the Flicker, the galloping tin-type that they exhibited in a small tent. Inside were some parson benches, a strange machine that looked much like a birdhouse, a sheet stretched out upon a wooden frame. Foote and I had crawled under the canvas nearish the back, avoiding the ticket booth, not because we had no money but because my mother stood five feet away from it, the Good Book opened in her hands. She had managed to assemble a little crowd, mostly the elderly, halt and lame. "For if the Word spoken by angels was steadfast, and every transgression and disobedience received a just recompense of reward..." My mother bent forward suddenly, startling her little gathering. "Then how shall we escape?"

Inside that tent, a man turned a crank on the mechanical birdhouse and a shaft of light exploded out and splashed all over the sheet. Shades and shadows began to dance upon it, and the man made adjustments to his strange machine and Foote and I saw fellows with wide-brimmed hats set out on horseback after a train. These desperados robbed that train, which is why the Flicker had the name *The Great Train Robbery.* I will tell you two ironical things: one being, I was to meet the man that made that motion picture, Ed Porter, at a celebrity baseball game, the Hollywood Stars versus the World Lightning Bolts. Porter's career had not gone the way he'd hoped, and none of his subsequent efforts made either the impact or the money of *The Great Train Robbery.* I suspect that Porter had inaccurately assessed what people liked about it, because he'd turned such Flickers as *The Little Train Robbery,* which is the same story except with all the parts taken by children. The second ironical thing: Caspar W. Willison, then a struggling actor, portrays one of the train robbers. His eyes are bugged open and his eyebrows arched, his mouth is pinched into a smile, and it is an odd expression Willison thereby achieves, much like an idiot child at a birthday party. Willison does not change this countenance throughout the film. Contrariwise, the rest of his body is in non-stop action. His arms are particularly busy, waving shooting irons in the air and, although Willison's desperado poses more of a threat to passenger pigeons than railway passengers, it does convey a certain menace. Caspar Willison portrays a man willing, even eager, to use his guns.

I see the trick to this authoring is to keep the engine car on the tracks. I seem to keep getting shunted off, especially whenever I mention Caspar Willison. Even now I am tempted to relate Willison's acting career, even though he was a come-to-naught. I suppose that's why I want to do the recounting, to tell the truth. From what I gather (chiefly from Mrs. Moorcock, Thespa Doone's mother, a lady well acquainted with the stage) this combination of stupefied expression and skittish physical gesturing was the basis of Willison's style, for which he suffered great humiliation at the hands of the theatrical critics. Mrs. Moorcock was able to quote one reviewer with accuracy, savoring the turn of phrase, that Willison's Such-and-Such-a-Character seemed "at once benumbed and possessed of the St. Vitus Dance." All this, of course, is at odds with the direction he gave to me. "Keep your fess in a state of flex," he'd say. "Let us read your thinks, as piltry and halting as they are. Let your eyes blosoom like flowers. Let them shrivel anew. And for God's sake, Mess, you great biboon, *stand still.*"

Willison's failure as an actor led to his trying his hand at playwriting, his triumph being an overlong production entitled *War*, which Foote and I had the opportunity of sitting through in Atlanta, Georgia. Now, I see how to get the train of authorship rerouted without even backing up, because this was on the first leg of our adventures, and all I am really leaving out is twenty-some hours of excited sleeplessness, during which Foote talked non-stop and consumed all our food. The basic plan was to head south and then westwards, Foote having got it into his mind that there was adventure aplenty near the Gulf of Mexico, even the prospect

of being kidnapped by pirates. That plan involved changing trains
in Georgia, so we decided to treat ourselves to a hotel and (this
was my idea) a play. Well, according to any number of broadsides,
the only play in Atlanta worth seeing was called *War*, written by
one "Charles Wilson." Both Foote and I thought this likely to be
an excellent production. The poster had the word "WAR" in such
large letters that you were sure the Colonel had decided to have
another go at Spain. Smaller print underneath proclaimed this
work "An Investigation Into Man's Baser Instincts."

"Which War do you think they mean?" I wondered.

"I suspect it's just general War," Jefferson opined, and correctly.

The play *War* began in Heaven, or more properly, some
vaporous Waiting Area just outside. The curtain rose — a somewhat old and occasionally moth-eaten curtain, the play being held
in the Temple Theatre, an old Masonic Lodge — and standing in
front of a painting of the Pearly Gates were forty-odd men. They
were all bandaged and tourniquetted, but dissimilar beyond that;
one wore the uniform of a Rebel soldier, another the sheet and
sandal of the ancient Roman. There was a man from most every
major War and Revolution. They were a weary and bedraggled lot.
Some missed body parts, and even those who had all their limbs
leaned upon wooden crutches. They advanced on the audience,
moaning platitudes about the hellishness of War. I believe I was
nodding off at that point, when a woman pranced on to the stage.
She was wearing a blindfold, but little beyond that, a thin piece of
material wrapped around her to form a tunic. "I am Justice!" she
told the men. "And you all have served me well." (Foote giggled
here, don't ask me why.) "You!" said Miss Justice, levelling a finger at a Crusader. "When the dread Saracen rode out of the desert,
filled with heathen blood-lust, how valiantly you defended me!"
Now if, like me, you had no idea what Miss Justice was talking
about, the backdrops shifted, curtains fell, and thereupon followed
a five-minute or so run-down of the Crusades. The commentary
and dialogue was a bit hard to follow, going something like this:

*I, Bohemund, son of Robert, do take up my arms against
thine enemies, and vow to return the aforementioned towns
to the sceptre of the Romans, moreover, I will make War
upon my nephew Tancred if he does not deliver unto me*

these towns, this I swear by the passion of Christ, by the
crown of thorns and the bloodied lance!!

But, I will say this, it was a lot of fun to watch, because every
tableau used about fifty actors, they appeared on stage in appropriate historical garb to bash and/or shoot at each other. Then
Miss Justice would prance on stage in her little tunic. She would
fan her arms, raise herself up on tip-toe, and then she would suddenly become as still as statuary. The soldiers would freeze, too,
even those bounding headlong into the fray, even those in the very
act of dying. The men were betrayed by their humanity; you could
see their nostrils flicker, their eyes blink; you could watch their
chests heaving in a subdued manner. Miss Justice, on the other
hand, was brushed by the hand of death. Miss Justice was portrayed by Lily Lavallée, the Mistress of the Tableau.

Lily Lavallée is important to the story of *Civilization*; amongst
other things, she was Mrs. Caspar Willison. There were three long
years between seeing her in this play *War* and encountering Lily
again, the circumstances of this second occasion being as I will
now set forth.

We were photographing a thrilling gallop across the Flats, a section of The World measuring about a hundred acres and lying to
the east of the mountains, its situation making it dry and wind-
whipped, and, through the eye of Billy Bittner's camera, indistinguishable from the desert. We were making a drama entitled *She
Was Innocent*. A young girl, referred to in the Fat Man's scenario
as "Brown Eyes" (although it does not do credit to the sooty quality of her eyes, the way they would give off neither light nor
warmth), is to be hanged for a murder she did not commit. Her
husband sets off in search of the real culprit, confronting the cur
on a mountain-top. There is a fight; both men pull out large
knives. Eventually the husband hurls the bastard to a rocky finish,
leaps upon his horse, heading back for the town, hopefully before
they tighten the noose around Brown Eyes' thin neck. Along the
way he picks up a group of fellow chargers for added excitement,
a group that included me.

They had the camera set up away down at one end of the Flats, and our little group came down upon them full bore, at which point we were supposed to pull up abruptly, whereupon the main actor would leap from his horse and stop the hanging.

Our main actor was Manley Wessex, a famous Tragedian who, for one thing, drank too much, and for another, hated riding. Manley claimed it made him feel queachy, and I suppose it did, because when he pulled up in front of C. W. Willison and the camera, instead of leaping from his horse, Manley slumped over and vomited on to his saddle pommel. Then Wessex passed out and tumbled off his mount, although he was too drunken to even do this correctly; his feet got caught up in the stirrups and he remained hanging, upside down, his knuckles resting on the ground.

"That man," said Caspar Willison, "has pooked. That man—-" Willison lifted his finger now, and aimed it at poor Manley. "That man has ruint the story."

"Well," returned my friend Jeff Foote, who, because of his impairment and general appearance, rode at the back of the posse, "it was sort of a foolish story."

Willison's head jerked like it was filled with electricity. "Hmm?"

"No offence," returned Jefferson. "It's just that if he really wanted to stop his wife's hanging, it was probably a poor idea to toss the truly guilty party off of a mountain. I mean, what was he going to say at this point, sir? *Don't hang my wife. Hang that pile of mush over there on the rocks?*"

"Do mine eyes deceive me?" demanded Willison suddenly and harshly. "Are you a *unidexter*?"

Usually in situations like this, Jeff would tuck the empty sleeve behind his back, but now he held it out in front and allowed the material to sway in the breeze. Foote said nothing.

"It is true, what you say," said Willison. "Although we apparently are creating within a framework of fection that allows such incongroolies. We seem to have a cowboy who lacks a right hand." I am not setting down with any great accuracy the manner in which Willison spoke, nor could I. A lot of people thought Willison was simply pretending to be English. For example, "cowboy" came out with languid, powdered elegance, "cawbaw." I believe that Willison thought of language as his own personal whipping boy, that he tortured vowels for the sheer selfish hell of it.

"I can ride fine, Mr. Willison."

"And what if you should be called upon to exchange gunfire whilst astride your negg?"

"I'd put the reins in my mouth."

"You are ulso," pointed out Willison, "exceedingly ugly. How many of my little Flickers have you appeared in?"

"I came on about a week ago. Me and my friend — Thom Moss over there — set off from The Confluence, Ohio, in search of High Adventure. We have found naught but ruination and misfortune."

They would finish this discussion — over French cognac and Cuban cigars — later that evening, upstairs at the White Owl (whilst down below, Thespa Doone was displaying her *glutei* and beseeching me to search for imperfection). Willison and Foote were interrupted at this moment by the arrival of Lily Lavallée. I recognized her immediately as Miss Justice, although the intervening three years had been cruel. Her face was wrinkled now, cracked like a useless mirror. Her body was puffy and chalk-white. She appeared in evening wear, with a liquor glass held daintily 'twixt her thumb and middle finger, taking small and tentative steps, as if she had just wandered out from a soirée with potentates and dignitaries and was looking for a powder room.

"Hello, Caspie," she said. "I've come to see you hang Thelma Doom."

Thespa Doone awaited her trip up the makeshift scaffolding, buried beneath linen sheets. I heard her mutter something from beneath her cover — I could not make it out — but beyond that Thespa remained stone-still and silent.

"Lookie, Lil," said Willison, and he began to walk in large, lop-sided circles. "Manley has pooked and keeled from the negg. I am cross with him, so I shall destroy him, and the firmament shall want a new star. Pick one for me, Lil. Pick one of these odorous bummies."

Miss Lavallée did not give it much thought. "That one."

Thespa Doone now allowed the sheets to drop. Sweat had beaded on her face, her cheeks were flushed, whorls of red so deep that she looked somewhat like a circus clown. Thespa Doone wanted to see who Miss Lavallée had chosen, which was me.

Caspar Willison wrinkled his nose, which had an effect on his whole face, drawing the eyes downwards, the mouth up in a little pursed vee.

Which gives me the idea of how to end off this chapter. (Tomorrow I'm going to start on how I met Jensen, lost my fortune and way in the world, and began the bumpy ride to damnation.) Caspar C. Willison — or Charles Wilson as he preferred back then — had not altogether abandoned his career as actor when *War* brought him success as a playwright. No, he insisted on playing a small — *small* in terms of time spent on stage — but pivotal role. You see, all of those goomers missing body parts, those withered warriors, were standing outside of Heaven, awaiting some kind of judgement. It was bruited about that because they had broken the letter of the Lord's Law — "Thou shalt not kill," said He, without caveat or proviso — Paradise shall ever be denied them. Miss Justice seemed to think this was stickling, she pranced about in her tunic and assured them they were shoo-ins, but after four hours the question still remained unresolved. Miss Justice disappeared briefly and then skipped back on stage, blindfolded now, carrying a small set of scales. The tunic had fallen off of one shoulder, leaving a breast out on display, so pale that it held a bluish tinge, the nipple pale and indistinct. Miss Justice assumed her classical pose and froze. The soldiers did likewise.

That's when God appears, floating down from On High, waving open the Pearly Gates and saying a single line, "Eternity is yours."

The skin of God's face seemed to be too thin, stretched tightly across an oddly triangular construction, all brow and almost no chin, save for a small thing, sharp as a garden spade. His ears were large and distinctly pointy, his nose hooked and bent toward the right. God's hair was blond and bristly; it bolted upwards and did not appear to receive much care or maintenance. And God's eyes, even from the loges, were a blue that I have not seen before or since. It was a light blue, light as a robin's egg, but I am stymied to explain the force and power of these orbs. (Mr. Hartrampf suggested orbs, which I think is useful in describing God's eyes.) Everyone in the theatre picked up their programs to look up the actor's name, *Charles Wilson*.

Leaving the theatre, I turned to my friend Jefferson Foote and noted, "It takes a certain type of fellow to play God."

"Especially," added Foote, "without make-up."

Chapter 3

The Warden read the first two chapters after dinner last night. This was an unexpectedly nerve-racking experience. Occasionally he would demand to know the meaning of a word, almost always a word supplied by Mr. Hartrampf. Sometimes he would pause and wrinkle all the skin on his hairless head. The Warden would lift a hand and smooth it out like a bedsheet, asking me to clarify some point, such as, "Why the sheets?"

"Hmm?"

"Thespa Doone was underneath linen sheets, and looked out from under them only when Lily Lavallée pegged you for vast fame and public adoration."

"Got you."

"Why the sheets?"

"It was her thinking that sweat should not be squandered, that the human corpus contains only so many essences and humors, that air should not be allowed contact. Therefore, when we were filming outside, on hot days, she would spend much of her time buried underneath a sheet."

"Would she be naked underneath the sheet, Thom?"

"Not as a rule, no sir."

A little while later, The Warden smacked a page with the back of his hand. "Ah!"

"Ah?"

"This I find very interesting. The exposure of a mammary gland in a public place."

I shrugged, and persisted in my authorly composition.

"I despair," The Warden told me, "for humankind. We shall see more and more of this, and the effect upon the morally weak shall be profound."

I made vague noises of agreement.

"It is Miss Lavallée's utter inactivity that makes such a thing legal," The Warden continued, meshing his hands together. "A body not in motion becomes a work of art." He snorted disdainfully; his nose, lacking all hair, produced a musical tone. "Although," continued The Warden, "you seem to imply that she pranced about at least momentarily with the mammary gland exposed. Did it bounce, Thommy? Did it jiggle provocatively?"

"Warden, you seem to get bogged down in details."

"Thespa Doone is naked in *Civilization*." The Warden got up and crossed over to the huge desk, gingerly touching the pages that began: Jensen, the famous fat author, brought about my Downfall and subsequent career.

"How would you know? Nobody's seen *Civilization*. It's not finished."

"I've heard."

"Anyways, I'd have thought," I ventured, "that you might wonder how Foote lost his arm."

"Foote lost an arm?"

"Sure. Did you miss that? That's what Willison was on about, *unidexter* and so forth."

The Warden pushed out his lower lip, squeezed it between his fingers, blanching it. Thus was the Warden totally without color, excepting the two black pebbles that served as eyes, much like something you'd discover under a rock. "I forgot to tell you, Thom. There is to be an execution."

"There is?"

"John Murtagh. He killed his wife, Thom, he took a knife to his wife, over and over and over again. He is to be hanged for this. I was wondering if you'd like to attend the event."

"Thank you, Warden. I'll give it some thought."

"Do."

Jensen, the famous fat author, brought about my Downfall and subsequent career.

Foote and I continued on to New Orleans. There we spent a few days, expecting to be kidnapped by pirates at any moment. We kept the company of odalisques, Mr. Hartrampf suggests. They were, for the most part, young girls with no more experience than Foote and I. This was very pleasant, still, Jefferson and I decided to seek adventure elsewhere, so we once more boarded the train and headed westward.

Jensen was on that train. He'd had them remove the arm rest between a pair of seats, and he'd settled his hams onto those cushions, and he sat there smiling with his strange pale hands locked together and resting on top of his belly. He wore a bowler that looked to be at least three sizes too small. Jensen, as perhaps you know, was the owner of a magnificent moustache, an ornate construction that required much care and wax, and it was the sight of this that made Jefferson Foote falter in his tracks. "That's J.D.D. Jensen," he whispered.

"Who?"

"J.D.D. Jensen. The most famous novelist in America."

Foote was whispering and Jensen sat thirty feet down an aisle, but the fat man immediately roared, "In the *world*!!" and started to laugh. "Come, boys, have a seat. I'll tell you tales of giants, djinies and cunnies that weep."

So Foote and I claimed the pair of seats across from the fat man.

"I am headed," said Jensen, not that we'd asked, "for Hollywoodland. They need me there, and they are willing to pay bushels of clinkers."

"How's that, sir?" asked Foote. "Why do they need you?"

"Historical expertise," nodded Jensen, and he laid a finger alongside his nose and tapped lightly. "Historical fucking expertise, my lad. Also, I am to pen the few precious words that make sense of the ghostly photographs."

"Sir?" asked Foote. "What's Buffalo Bill Cody really like?"

"Ugly. Grim-visaged, buck. Indecd, when I first encountered

him he was known as *Duck* Bill Cody. But, said I, that will never do. Jensen took up his pen and history was rendered."

"I've read all your books," said Foote.

"No, you haven't. Let's," said the fat man, "have a tug at the witch's nipple." He reached inside his jacket — he wore a cream-colored suit, then again Jensen wore only cream-colored suits, with fabulously ornate waistcoats, the seams and buttons strained by his enormousness — and withdrew a pewter flask. He took the first sip, a long one, and then thrust the liquor toward Foote.

Jefferson took a small sip, and considerately wiped the neck clean for me. I drank and handed it back.

Jensen reached back inside his jacket, exchanging the pewter flask for a deck of playing cards. He made no mention of the cards, and I concluded that Jensen simply liked to play with them in his hands, the way that some fellows like to work coins across their knuckles. Jensen's hands, now that I'm half-on that subject, were fat, in keeping with the rest of the fat man, and the fingers were short and so puffed out that they seemed to lack joints. Aside from the fingers, however, his hands were huge, so they resembled the flapping appendage you might see on a walrus or sea lion. It was therefore surprising that Jensen could work the deck at all, but the fat man showed himself remarkably dextrous in this regard. He started out with a few one-handed cuts, so quick that I could but barely follow with my eyes. Jensen shuffled the cards then, waterfalling them like he was playing an accordion, or, riffling the edges and making a *whirring* sound that was machine-like. As I say, Jensen made no mention or note of the cards in his hands; instead, he kept up a largely one-sided conversation.

"Furthermore," said Jensen, "he was a murderous bastard, Duck Bill was. Liked to kill things. He liked to kill buffalo, of course, and he liked to kill Indians, and if the law would have been more accommodating I'm sure he would have been tickled pink to kill a few white men. I will further say this, young sirs, had he not been a dolt of the highest order, Cody would have been one of the most dangerous men that ever lived. I can see that you are disappointed," the fat man said to Jefferson Foote.

"No," said I, "that's what he looks like pretty much all the time."

"The boy has something of the poet in him. And it's always messy when a poet's dreams are shattered."

Well, I have run into writerly difficulty here, because it was just as Jensen spoke the word *shattered* that a certain thing happened. But it did not happen for a couple of hours after we'd sat down, so let me try to cover over significant ground. Firstly, it was not solely Buffalo Bill that Jensen talked about, although Cody is the one that sticks best in my memory. No, all of the heroes of Jensen's novels, from Thunderbolt and Lightfoot to Francis Hare, the Prairie Highwayman, were revealed to be knaves and rascals, invariably stupid and cruel. Beyond that, they all had their particular and individual faults, whether it be a weakness for alcohol, oriental stuporifics, women, or in the case of Thunderbolt and Lightfoot, *each other*, in what Hartrampf suggests be called the *greek style*. And the other important thing is that we took many more sips from the pewter flask, in fact we emptied it. Jensen then took down his battered suitcase from the carriage rack overhead and produced a bottle of sherry, which we similarly disposed of, although Foote claimed to not like the stuff, leaving the imbibing to Jensen and myself.

"A good sherris sack," quoted the fat man, "hath a two-fold operation in it. It ascends me into the brain, dries all the dull and cruddy vapors..." Jensen popped his fingers, trying to stimulate his memory, except his fingers were too fat to produce anything audible, "and fills it full of nimble fiery and delectable shapes."

"Yes, sir," said Foote and I in unison.

The fat man sprayed the playing cards from one hand to another, the ducats flying in precise formation. He tilted his head and stared at Foote, who was sulking about the sullying of his story-book heros.

"I see you are disappointed," said the fat man. "It's always messy when a poet's dreams are shattered."

As Jensen said "shattered," the deck of cards exploded. He was simply holding them, keeping his hands still to import gravity to his "poet's dream" speech, when suddenly the cards flew off in all directions, and with remarkable force, too, into our laps, into the seats behind, some even bouncing off the ceiling. "Ah," said Jensen, with evident pleasure. "Do we have any poker players amongst us?"

"No, sir," said Jefferson Foote.

"I don't play, other than my father and I would occasionally play for matchsticks."

"Then, Thom, you do indeed play. Because the stakes are no more germane than the color of the felt that covers the table. Whether it be for matchsticks or gold, the game of poker is always the same. Would you care to play the game of poker now?"

I should mention that I had discovered myself to be rather partial to sherry. I still am, and The Warden often brings along a bottle. My point in mentioning it is that I was at that moment light-headed and the prospect of doing *anything* out of the ordinary was exciting. So I shouted, "Damned if I wouldn't care to play that sumbitch game!"

"I know where we could find a game on this train. The ugglesome bit is, the players are a closely knit, rather insular fraternity. They are not likely to admit a stranger. But if I were to claim that you were related to me — perhaps a nephew — all opposition to your participation would evaporate."

"Huh?"

"He wants you to pretend to be his nephew," said Foote.

"Hey, what a fine idea *that* is."

"Moss is drunk, sir."

"I am neither, Foote. You *bastard*."

"He is imbued with the enthusiastic ebullience of youth," said the fat man. "Let us go." We all three rose, although Foote and I were the only two to stand up as such. The fat man pumped his arms and waggled his feet, and in some strange manner he elevated like a hot-air balloon and caught some upright purchase. The rocking of the train knocked him back and forth, bouncing him off seat backs. "Oh!" Jensen tsked his tongue. "I don't think I could explain *two* nephews."

Foote's face clouded over with hurt and confusion. "Why not?" he demanded quietly. "Lots of people have more than one nephew. I myself have eleven."

"Indeed. But two such dissimilar nephews? Is that not stretching the bounds of believability?"

"I don't think so, sir."

"Tell you what, Jefferson, my lad. I have in my travelling bag several scenarios."

"Several...?"

"Scenarios. Deriving from the greek *skene*, that is to say, tent. There's irony there, if you scratch at it. From tents to stages to huge theatres and now back to dingy little tents. Scenarios. Briefly, stories written out with such mind-numbing simplicity that even the dunderheads that make Flickers can understand them. I had a thought that you might care to read them, Jefferson. It would be of great assistance to me, because you could tell me which appealed most to a fellow of fine and rarified sensibilities."

"Well..."

"Hey!" came my suggestion. "Maybe I should read the scenarios, and Foote should go on to the poker game."

"No," said the fat man.

"I'd be very interested to read the scenarios," judged Jeff.

"Fine and excellent." The scenarios were gotten out of the travelling case. There were many of them; the yellowed, smudged sheets stacked up about a foot high. Foote began to read, and immediately chewed off all of the skin around a thumbnail. His too-heavy eyebrows knitted together.

The fat man and I bounced from car to car and found the game. It was in a very stately Pullman, the walls and all of the furniture rendered out of strange and glorious wood, a burnished red that seemed to give off more light than the lanterns. In The Confluence we had only one sort of wood, a very dull pine that gave off nothing except slivers.

Around a huge table sat five men. I cannot remember all of their names. The truth of the matter is, whilst I can recall that wood very vividly indeed, the poker game itself is a bit vaporous, particularly as it progressed into the night. I cannot remember how it ended, although I understand that Jensen carried me off to my seat. The main reason for all this is that there was in the corner of the Pullman a bar that would put most saloons to shame, every brand of eau-de-vie and blue ruin you could think of.

"This is my nephew Thom," said J.D.D. Jensen to the men. "The one I was telling you about."

"Thom! Thom, have a seat! Have a drink!"

I accepted some strange foreign tipple and plopped down at the card table.

"Thom," said one of the men, a fellow almost as large as Jensen. "You are making a Grand Tour, we understand, just prior to taking over your father's company." I watched as cards flew about the table. A neat stack of five fell in front of me.

"Well, I'm off to find adventure. My father doesn't have a company, though."

"No," said Jensen, laughing as he lit his cigar. "The word *company* hardly serves us well, does it, Thom?"

"No, sir. It's not the right word."

"*Empire!* That's the word."

"And just what," asked another man, "does your father do?"

"He imagines the future."

"He is a Visionary," said Jensen.

The men chuckled at this. I picked up my cards and saw that I had nothing much at all. The first bet was a two-dollar bill, and I would have blanched and gasped audibly if I hadn't been drunk, but I did throw in two of my own dollars on the off chance I could pair something up. For the next few hands, I was too excited *not* to play, every set of five cards seemed full of wondrous possibility. So I lost perhaps twenty dollars, putting a small dent into my personal fortune.

I am aware that it is part of my writerly task not to drag you people around by the nose and in the dark, so let me explain about my personal fortune. Foote's uncle Maxwell was a dairy farmer and owned a sizable operation in the shadow of Mount Sariel. Jefferson and I conceived of the idea of adventuring some five years before our departure, whereupon we both got hired on at Maxwell Foote's place. The significance here is two-fold. One, we learnt to ride, although the horses were doleful nags, and as fast as we ever got was only fast enough to goad milchcows around a small corral, still, when Mr. Oglesby asked, "Can you boys ride?" we were able to answer yes and not look too shame-faced. Second, Jefferson and I had saved one dollar per week each, which, if you do the necessary calculations, amounts to a tidy personal fortune.

So I was not unduly upset by the loss of twenty dollars, especially when I perceived a chance to regain it all, namely, I picked up three aces and a couple of low singletons. "I'll take two," I said softly, hoping that the men remembered that often I took two cards in order to make up a straight or flush, a tactic that never yielded results. J.D.D. Jensen worked the deck with his fat flippers, tossing me what turned out to be a pair of queens. "Hmm," said I, and I tried to tinge my countenance with mournfulness, lest I arouse suspicion. When it came my turn to bet I spent a long moment in obvious ponderance. "Hmm. Three dollars." I tried to speak it with all the emotion of a land surveyor, but the next two men both threw in their cards hastily. "Bah!" roared Jensen, throwing bills in with mine. "You've got nothing, Thommy! It's one of your damn bluffs!" Well, this encouraged the remaining men, they all saw the three bucks, in fact one of the fellows raised it up to five. Well, I saw his bet and slyly upped it fifty cents. "Hell's bells!" screamed Jensen. "Let's play *poker!*" whereupon the first ten-dollar bill hit the table. We lost one of the other fellows with that, and I came close to folding myself, but, you know, a full house, aces over queens, that's some hand, and I went with it until the money in the center of the table totalled about a hundred and fifty dollars, at which time it was me, Jensen and a third fellow.

Jensen had a miserable two pair. What he was doing in the betting is beyond me, at least it was back then. The third fellow had a straight to the King. And you know what I had.

So I pulled in that money, lit a cigar, ordered another goblet of foreign tipple and settled back to play cards.

And I woke up squeezed into the train seats, the heels of my boots hooked through the open window. In the seats across, Jefferson Foote sat staring at me. "Look at you," said he.

"Foote," I returned, "even if I *could* look at myself, I amn't about to open my eyes. How about pulling down that window-shade?"

"It was a sorry day when our fates became entwined."

"Is that so?"

"I rue that day."

"Foote..." I kept my eyes screwed shut, but I swung my legs around and shot upright, "why the hell are you so damn mad at me?"

"Oh, for no special reason," he said, with what Hartrampf nails as *execration*, "unless you want to count losing all our money at cards."

"Losing!" Now I did pop my eyes open, and the sunlight came in like icepicks. "If that's what's bothering you, pal, you'd better just simmer down." I began to slap at my pockets. "I had a little run of luck at the gaming table. As a matter of fact," I slapped at my trousers, I slapped at my jacket, "Lady Luck was with me last night." I felt in the band of my half-sprouted top hat. "It was just one of those—" I tore off my jacket now and inspected the lining. "One of those rare, beautiful—" I hauled off my boots in case I'd slipped it all down there for safe keeping. "—beautiful nights."

"What are you looking for?"

"Money. Bushels of clinkers."

"Now, let me ask you this, Moss. If you have money, for what reason did you ask to borrow my personal fortune?"

"I never."

"Mr. Jensen conveyed that message to me. I gave him my money to give to you. He said you were a desperate man."

"This makes no damned sense, Foote. I was pulling cards like a little girl pulls daisies. I could hardly see my opposites for the lucre amassed in front of me."

"When Mr. Jensen deposited you in that seat — dead drunk — he reported that you had failed miserably at the gaming table. He said your luck, at first merely rotten, had worsened with each passing moment."

"I do not understand what goes on." Fortunately — or what looked like "fortunately" at first glance — the poker players came striding down the train's aisle at that precise moment.

"Hey, fellows," I called out. "Didn't I win big at poker last night?"

"You did," they muttered. "And your uncle told us how you did it."

"There!" I said to Foote. "Now, that money..." I was going to posit that we needed only to look around and find our fortune, newly multiplied. I had various observations to make, all of this sunny and optimistic nature, except that the men grabbed me and Foote and threw us off the train. We were not at a station, no sir, nor had the train even slightly slowed, so we bounced off the siding, rolled down a scarp, found ourselves in a strange land where the sun filled too much of the sky.

"Peachy," said Foote.

Mr. Oglesby appeared on horseback. He galloped over to us — we struggled to our feet — and demanded, without pleasantry or preamble, "Can you boys ride?"

I said yes.

Chapter 4

I even proceeded to tag on a report concerning the artistry of our equestrian talents, but Foote dug an elbow into my ribs and silenced me. His reasons for doing this have to do with Mr. Oglesby's appearance, which I shall now describe. I would not embark on this endeavour without the company of Old Man Hartrampf. It's not so much that Oglesby was ugly; his features were even, proportioned and well-sized. The disquieting thing was the skin itself. Much of it was white, absolutely colorless, although a bright purple band of St. Anthony's Fire splashed across his nose and mouth. And everywhere there were black- and white-heads, papulas and pustules.

When Oglesby demanded if we wanted steady work, I answered *yes* one more time.

We walked for the better part of that day, across a flat piece of the earth where God had just run out of ideas and made do with furze and brutish cacti. Oglesby sat on his horse and said not a word to us. Foote muttered bitterly under his breath. Now that the excitement for the day was over, it came back to me that I was saddled with a truly monstrous hangover, so I lumbered along and suffered grievously for my sins. Actually, I thought, it was that

Jensen's fault, he was the one insisting I try every kind of rare and wondrous potation. I spent the hours under the sun trying to piece together the night before, although the foggy patches were too dense.

Mind you, I did manage to crack the nut of the thing. Jensen — liar, alcoholist and cheat — was feeding me cards. It was around high noon, the sun at its meanest, when I figured that out. When Jensen dealt, I was getting ladies and knaves, twins and triplets, and when I cashed in the leftovers I got more of the same. Feeding me cards with his pale little sausage fingers, and feeding me kill-grief and caper-juice, and then when I was stupefied he carried me back to the seat, relieved my pockets of all lucre, and left me to be thrown off the train into a strange and barren new world. I said aloud, "I'll stick that fat man like a trussed pig. I am going to have satisfaction."

Foote made one of those little noises he used to make.

Three years later, when I saw J.D.D. Jensen again, I did, in fact, pull my knife and place it to his belly. That drained the blood out of his face, leaving nothing but grey ashes and a walrus moustache. "B-b-but..."

"Don't give me no buts, Fat Man. You stole my personal fortune and set me on the road to ruin. Look at me now. I am a penniless wretch, a drunken and lowly hunter of tule rooters. Look at poor Foote, my companion. He has been shot in the butt, scarred every which way, he's got white hair, melted ears and he's lost one whole arm. Why shouldn't I push this blade into your stinking belly?"

"Well..." Jensen's tongue came out of his mouth to lick around the moustache. It looked like a little grub. "Well, I could get you a job in the Flickers. I am a close personal friend of the renowned Caspar Willison."

"If he's a friend of yours, Fat Man, I want nothing to do with him."

Those were among the wisest words I'd spoken, although of course I paid no heed to them.

It was late afternoon when we reached our destination, which was the O-Gee Ranch, which consisted of three buildings, all in varying degrees of ramshackletry. There was the main house, where

Oglesby lived alone (although he did return from one of his mysterious trips with a fat, flushed wife in tow). There was the barn. There was the cabin for the hired help, which numbered about twelve when Foote and I were added to it. The bunkhouse was some ten feet high, and the only reason I mention that is that when I first laid eyes upon it, King Palmer was diving off it and landing on his head.

Oglesby spoke his first words since that morning. They did seem to be called for. "Palmer," he said, "why the hell are you diving off of there and landing on your head?"

The other hands were spectating, but with Oglesby's arrival they started moving back into the bunkhouse. King Palmer was picking gravel out of his hair and scalp. "Well, Mr. Oglesby, the men and I had a bet."

"Mm-hmm."

"They thought that a drop like that would crack a man's skull like an egg. I knew better, sir. The head — like all of the human body — was designed by the Lord Almighty Himself to withstand all but the greatest of blows."

"Palmer," said Oglesby, and there was a wearisome tone to his voice, "the men just think of these things to see you do them. You shouldn't—"

"Sir, I would not miss an opportunity to demonstrate the Lord's Superb Engineering Feat!"

Foote asked, "How much did you win?"

"I beg your pardon, friend?"

"You had a bet. How much did you win?"

"Stranger, I won the satisfaction of being a heralder of God's greatness."

Oglesby nodded down toward us, a touch disdainfully, I thought. "These men claim they can ride."

Palmer grinned, stepped forward and extended his right hand.

"Kingsley Palmer," he said. Palmer had a chubby face, and a pleasant one despite a few little trickles of blood. He looked to be a touch on the fat side, but that night, when he came to us naked, I saw that he wasn't fat at all, he was ballooned with muscle.

King Palmer came to us naked because it was his practice to say an evening prayer and address a few points of a theological or philosophical nature whilst in a denuded state. "Revel in the glory of the human body!" King Palmer would buckle his hands on his hips and do a slow rotation, so that everyone might do this revelling. "This is a house not made with hands," he'd tell us all. "It was designed by the Great Architect and Engineer of the Universe! It was planned and erected to withstand every strain and blow, thus to give utmost comfort to the spirit that dwells within it."

When Palmer appeared naked the men mostly kept on what they were doing. Those that could read did so (the nickel novels of the bloated cheat Jensen were very popular), the others largely lay on their pallets and stared up at the ceiling, drawing slowly on cigars and cheroots.

"Man invented clothes to rob his skin of sun and air!" Palmer possessed a remarkable body. You could well imagine God at work as if with mud, packing and tamping. This made quite the impression on me, because, I think, of my mother. I was a very small boy when my mother hit upon her notion of Muscular Literalism, so it had long been my understanding that if you didn't pay exact obedience to His Word, why then, you were headed straight for the lake which burned with fire and brimstone. And given that the Good Book was full of words, hundreds of thousands of them, such observance seemed a bit unreasonable. Even my mother held no great optimism for mankind, and over the years spent more and more time proclaiming the punishment promised in the Good Book than preaching adherence to it.

Kingsley Palmer's point was, amongst the things the Lord hath fashioned, all of them beauteous marvels, the human being stands foremost. And this to me made sense. It was from King Palmer that I got my ideas about physical exercise; I still undergo the Rigors several times a day, the application of appositional force to the voluntary muscles. For example, I link my hands in front of my chest and pull hard in each direction. I imagine that from my elbows shoot long bolts of lightning, swords of light that will brook no opposition, neither from mountain nor man-made temple. Or, I tug my head earthward, imagining that a great weight is pulling it down to the blackest ocean depths; at the same time I push back, swelling my neck, telling myself that Paradise itself could be seen if only I could raise my eyes high enough. I learned these techniques of bodily reconstruction from King Palmer. He would offer Prayer as he went through the Rigors, and at the outset I whisper thanks and praise, but there is always something about the physical exertion that makes me remember Thespa Doone. Then I stop praying.

For it was the Rigors that drew Thespa and me together.

Remember, Lily Lavallée tagged me, after a brief, drunken and disdainful survey of the ragtag carnival boys. That would include Foote, now sheepishly tucking the empty sleeve behind his back, and Bodnarchuk, who never understood why he wasn't bigger in the Flickers but never thought to shave off a peculiar moustache-goatee thing that made him look like an ancient Chinaman. That would include King Palmer, who sat up in his saddle and exuded good health, and was very disappointed when Lily Lavallée moved her eyes away from him. That would include Robert F. Kincaid, the first man I'd ever met with a middle initial, and Lonny Onley, who was a sexual deviate and still has a career in motion pictures. I am forgetting a man or two, for there were often strange faces at The World, transients and hoe-boys who worked for their two-dollar wage and then lit out, satisfied with that, men with no capacity for dreaming.

Lily Lavallée picked me as the best of a sorry lot. Her husband, Caspar W. Willison, wrinkled his nose. "Oooh, Lily. Not that one."

"Caspie," wailed Lily, "you said I could choose."

"Yes, but I absolutely lied, dear heart. I am the director, after all. I shall make a re-opt."

"Oh, Caspie. You enormous turd."

"I want him," said Thespa Doone, and covered her head once more. For a moment I thought Caspar Willison was going to do physical violence. He threw one of his long bony hands toward her, but then pulled back his whole body, and he looked for a moment like his strange train robber from the Flickers. His limbs spasmed and his face washed with twitches. Then C. W. Willison calmed down. "Helloo?" he called gently. "Helloo, Thespa, dear gill? Why did you say this? Just to make Mr. Willy angry?"

"I don't care if Mr. Willy is angry or not," responded Thespa, without dropping the sheet. "Emotions are written on water. I second the choice on account of believability. It is believable, if only but barely, that this young man and I would mate."

"I see." Willison now put his hands on his sides, the thumbs pointed toward his flat belly, the fingers laid out prissily to the rear. "But why weary about believability in the Dream Palace, Thespa? Do you think for one instant that I care whether or not people *believe* any of this? Horsepills. I care about palpitations and scrotum-shrivelling. The clutching of buzooms. Incontinence. You!"

"Me?"

"What's your name?"

"Thom Moss."

"Mess, are you capable of replacing Mister Manley?"

"Well, sir, I can jump off a horse better than that."

Caspar W. Willison barked, a hoarse bolt of dry laughter. He turned his face toward the sun and stared at it for a very long time. "The light is turning yella," he muttered, dismissing us.

It was that night that Thespa Doone and I had our first conversation. We did this at the White Owl Hotel, which existed in the Center of The World. The White Owl sat among three or four edifices, which would change location from day to day; the General Notions Store in particular was, as Hartrampf suggests, peripatetic, popping up beside, then kitty-corner to, the White Owl Hotel.

The building itself was seven stories tall, and I shall start at the top and work my way earthward. I shall commence, indeed, upon the very roof, for on warm nights I would go up there, and lie in wait for whatever breeze might blow in from the ocean. I could see the water, at least, at the edge of The World, darkness in motion, moon-kissed and cloud-draped. The World itself was an improbable assortment of terrain: desert, grassland, forest and mountain, not to mention the odd mesa and butte. It was this very variance that made The World ideal for the turning of Flickers, particularly of an outdoorsy nature. At any rate, that's what you'd see as you looked out from the roof of the White Owl Hotel.

On the top floor lived the Fat Man, in a room filled with books, cigar smoke and empty sherry bottles. Willison had a room up there as well, except that Caspar W. Willison did not appear to need or crave sleep, so I don't think he ever spent any time in it. His wife Lily may have used it, I'm not sure. She, too, was most often awake at all hours, floating throughout The World in white robes that she could never keep modestly sashed.

On the floor below there were more rooms, mostly used for the storage of theatrical costumes. There were two that were occupied: one by Mrs. Moorcock (and a number of tiny dogs, rats with stylish crops), the other by Thespa Doone. Thespa lived in a room without windows, because she was at odds with the manner in which the sun tyrannized time.

On the three floors below were various people in various smaller rooms: Billy Bittner the Crankman, Mr. Boyle the Builder, Manley Wessex the Inebriated Tragedian. There was a high turnover, as people made their mark in motion pictures and moved on. So, for example, Foote lived on the fourth floor. And I lived on the third, once I was elevated from the ranks of the carnival boys, who shared a faded circus tent in the middle of an abandoned cow pasture.

The second floor was given over to the Salon, whilst the ground floor was a saloon, variously named and decorated, depending on what they needed for a particular Flicker. Sometimes it would be called, say, The Red Dog Inn, filled with felt-covered gaming tables, adorned with velvet curtains and gold brocade. The next day the same place would be called El Spectro, and the service would be provided by dark women in loose-fitting clothing.

After a day's work, the carnival boys would hit the Saloon with unseemly enthusiasm. We would consume liquor and play cards. We would lust after the barmaids, although they remained unattainable to us, the lowest of the low. We would make bets, either with each other ("I bet you a dollar you can't eat one of these." "What is it?" "I bet you two dollars...") or with King Palmer ("I bet you a quarter that if I hit your head with this chair leg it would mush up like a grey ghost squash." "You're on, oh ye of little faith!").

Meanwhile, those upon whom Lady Fortune had smiled, the Stars and Main Players, amused themselves in the Salon upstairs, a soft blue room with genteel decorations, although the goings-on were often far from genteel, and sometimes (especially when Willison was drunken) the Salon would sound with angry shouts and screams. And this is where Thespa would spend her time, mostly upon the bench at the Pianola, working the pedals with all her might, drawing breathlessly on a Sweet Caporal. But on that night, after my future was rather off-handedly altered by Lily Lavallée, Thespa Doone appeared in the Red Dog Saloon — or whatever it was called that night — and touched my shoulder.

And, just so I don't forget this aspect of the proceedings, whilst Thespa made the journey downwards, my friend Foote had ascended. He was, at the moment of which I am now writing, sitting in the Salon with Caspar Willison, bolting fine cognac. Although there had never been any evidence of a literary side to Jeff (other than my aunt Lacky's blithe assertions regarding his poetical aspect), in the morning Jefferson Foote would be a writer, a scenarist, and he would swagger about The World with an off-putting jauntiness.

At any rate, I was talking to Bodnarchuk, a man not given to high-nosed airs. "It might interest you to know," Bodnarchuk was telling me, "that cows have four stomachs." Very little of what Bodnarchuk had to report was what I might blue-ribbon as *interesting*, but he was an agreeable sort, until about the tenth drink, when Bodnarchuk would decide to have a fight, usually with the largest fellow he could find.

Also at the bar was a man who has an important part to play in the story of *Civilization*, even if I paid him no particular mind on this occasion, nor, truth to tell, many of the subsequent occasions on which I saw him. I mostly saw him in this one place, the Saloon at the White Owl Hotel. He always sat at the long bar, hunched over, all of his limbs oddly bended and folded. He affected nicely tailored suits, but the material was always spoiled by smudge, blot and stain. This man was bald, and looked as though he took wax to his pate, for it gleamed in a manner that could blind. His face was creased by drunken crying jags; after a few drinks this man would begin to sing, wail and blubber. He would fumble for the pony in front of him, squeezing it between his palms to raise it to his quivering lips, for he lacked fingers, owning instead blackened, charred stumps. This was Mycroft, the explosives expert.

"Grass from the first chamber," Bodnarchuk droned on, "is regurgitated. This we call *cud*."

I'd made the mistake of telling Bodnarchuk that I'd worked on a dairy farm back in The Confluence. He'd worked on one as well,

in his native Kentucky (Bodnarchuk seemed to have had most jobs
at one point or another) and this bond, he seemed to think, lashed
us together forever. "Did you ever taste cud, Thom?"

I felt something on my shoulder. I cannot think, right now,
what exactly it felt like, but my last guess would have been a
woman's finger. I spun around and found myself looking at Thespa
Doone.

"Hello, Mess," she said.

"It's Moss, actually."

"Pretty bland fare."

"Shut up, Bodnarchuk."

"I wanted to ask you," said Thespa, "about your body."

"Uh-huh?"

"You see, I want to exaggerate myself."

"Uh-huh?"

Thespa leaned in close to whisper a confidence. Her lips
brushed against my ear. "I am to be naked in *Civilization*, Mess.
It's a secret, don't tell anyone. I want to exaggerate my body."

This was the first time I'd heard of *Civilization* (still largely in
Willison's head) but I made no note of it, caught up as I was in trying to figure out what she was talking about. "Oh! I get you.
You're interested in bodily reconstructionism. Well, you'd want to
talk to that man right over there, King Pa—"

"I don't want to talk to him. He's a religious man. I'm more
comfortable with the godless."

"Life is movement. Death is stagnation."

Both Thespa and Bodnarchuk nodded, although there was a
world of difference between what she did — moving her head
slowly, keeping her deep-brown eyes trained on me — and what
Bodnarchuk did, which was to bob his head like it had been
hacked off and thrown out to sea. "Nail on the head there, Thom-
boy," said he.

"Muscular movement is Nature's greatest therapeutic agent,
and the scientific application of natural physical movement to a
weak or deformed body part rebuilds any organ or system of better material and enables all the cells of the body to carry out their
functional duties."

"Look." Thespa Doone turned her head back and forth a couple
of times, making sure no one was paying attention. Everyone was.

She spun around. Actually, she pirouetted, for many of the movements Thespa made, even the simplest and most basic, had the grace of Grand Ballet. Now, I see I've made a huge writerly mistake here. I have not told you that she was wearing trousers, trousers and a sweater that rendered her body indistinct. When she was not before the camera, Thespa dressed like a newsboy, and not a very prosperous one either, one that was trying to hawk gazettes in a land where nothing much happened.

So, she was wearing trousers, and now she unbuttoned them and let them fall to her knees.

Chapter 5

"Consider the classic ages of Rome," said Kingsley Palmer, rampaging nakedly in the bunkhouse back at the O-Gee spread, "which showed not only the highest intellectual average, but also the finest physical types which the sculptor ever committed to marble. So long as Rome had its amphitheatres thronged with gladiators and its gymnasia full of young athletes, that state flourished in every art and science."

"It's too bad," said I, "that we don't have gymnasia anymore. I could do with a good romp in a gymnasia." As usual, I was the only one paying attention. Moreover, I was naturalistic, which is to say, buck naked, sitting on my bunk and listening to King Palmer. In the cot above me, Jefferson Foote was reading another of J.D.D. Jensen's little books. Did I mention, those books were becoming increasingly strange? I paid no attention to them, never had when I was younger and was certainly not about to now that Jensen was also the author of my Downfall, but I had noticed an odd trend in the titles of the volumes clutched in Foote's veiny hands. Whereas a few years previous one might find Buffalo Bill *Alone on the Plain* or putting the lid on a *Red Man's Rampage*, these latest books featured Cody *Amongst the Chinese Warlords* or adventuring *On the Ocean Floor*.

"No gymnasia?" exclaimed King Palmer, his eyebrows flexing upon his forehead. "I ask you this. What is a rodeo?" Palmer gave it the royal treatment, pronunciation-wise; he rolled that r around on his tongue and sang out the day-oh.

"Foote and I saw a rodeo back in The Confluence. You know who was there? Bill Pickett himself."

"Uh-yeah," grunted one of the men. "The bull-dogging negro!" Pickett was, indeed, a black man — many of the carnival boys were — but I disremember him ever being billed that way.

"Well, boys," said King Palmer. "I have just received word from Mr. Oglesby that we are to deliver three hundred head to Silver City. And we are going to be there on July the fourth."

For the first time I saw the boys perk up their ears. A couple of them even swung themselves into a sitting position. That would be, incidentally, the two most talented (I was but a tyro at this point), Wild Horse Charlie, a man who grew up breaking horses near Fort Laramie, and Charles Wild Horse, an Oglala Sioux who'd spent a few summers in New York City with Buffalo Bill's Wild West Show. Wild Horse Charlie was a big man with a face that had been kicked in by an Appaloosa mare, giving him what Hartrampf and I are going to call a *disquieting mien*, disquieting to the extent that children would start hollering for their mothers when Wild Horse Charlie was still a hundred feet away. Charles Wild Horse was much easier to look at, but his eyes appeared to serve separate masters. They were always fixing on different places and you could never be certain if Charles Wild Horse was addressing you or the fellow across the room.

Kingsley Palmer buckled his hands on his hips and paraded himself up and down the bunkhouse. His thighs were so swollen with muscle that King had to keep his legs wide apart and swivelled at the hips in order to plant one foot in front of the next. "Yes, boys, we'll be there in time for the big Blow Out."

The men gave out a huge hooray, and King Palmer took advantage of this enthusiasm. He clapped his hands together and began to do Deep Squats, an exercise that was excellent for leg development but not particularly pleasant to watch. "Let us undergo the Rigors, boys!" To my vast amazement all of the men clambered to their feet, all except Foote, who had paid scant attention to the entire proceedings. Jeff Foote continued reading his book, more tripe from the pen of the Fat Man. If memory serves, the book he was reading at the time (Foote would relate much of the story to me — unbidden — and often huge big chunks of the dense verbiage) was *Buffalo Bill and the Nihilists*, in which Cody protects a visiting Russian Grand Duke from assassination.

"Doff clothing!" shouted King Palmer. "Let the cells breathe!" The men pulled off their clothes, and naked we performed the exercises, the apposition of voluntary muscles, our sullied, sinewy bodies nourished and developed in harmonious balance.

"Ah!" says The Warden, raising his eyebrows, except he has none, so all he does is fold up the skin on his forehead. "And you feasted your eyes upon her pulchritude."

"Sir?" What has happened is, while I was working on this fifth chapter, The Warden has been reading the fourth. He clutches the final sheet in his too-white hands, he has crumpled the edges, his eyes have become hard.

"And you feasted your eyes," he repeats quietly, "upon the pulchritude of Thespa Doone."

"No, sir. She'd turned her back to me. I feasted my eyes upon her *glutei*."

"Ah."

The Warden nods, sits down heavily on my bed. He seems, these days, to have no prison duties beyond bringing me food, cigars, liquor and newspapers, beyond reading my pages and offering advice. He places his elbows on his knees, and rests his chin upon a bed of pale hairless knuckles.

"I am currently writing about my first ever Old Glory Round Up, which I think you'll find very diverting."

"Hmmm."

"Though it was my first, I still managed to win two competitions, steer undecorating and wild-cow milking."

"He's a very interesting young man. Perhaps you would care to meet him?"

"Who's this now?"

"John Murtagh. The fellow who murdered his wife."

"Why would I care to meet him?"

"The two of you are not dissimilar."

"I murdered no one, sir."

"Well..."

"I was not found guilty of murder, sir."

"He came home from his place of employment, which was the meteorological department at the University, Thom, Murtagh was a forecaster of weather. He found his wife and a stranger locked in carnal embrace. He took a knife to his wife, Thom. The stranger he spared. Indeed, the stranger he ignored. As the brutal deed was done, the stranger calmly put his clothes on, disappeared into the night."

"All this is very interesting, sir—"

"Yes! Yes, it is, Thom. That's why I'm telling you."

"*From Alamagordo to Silver City*," I speak aloud as I write the words, "*is two hundred and eighteen miles, and the drive took a whole week.*"

"Chicken."

"Sir."

"Tonight's dinner is chicken." The Warden raises his overly large body from the bed. "I'll be back."

From Alamagordo to Silver City is two hundred and eighteen miles, and the drive took a whole week. There were two reasons why it took so long, the first being weather, the second being that we took time out every now and again for rodeo practice. King Palmer would cut a steer loose, haze it into the furze, and one of the men would light out after it. The men taught me — and Foote, who had grudgingly looked up from his dime novels — some of the basic and fine points about the Art I was now taking up. Actually, Wild Horse Charlie covered the basics, Charles Wild Horse the fine.

"Do not," instructed Wild Horse Charlie, "loop the reins around any part of your body."

"Especially," amended Charles Wild Horse, "the fingers."

"Don't stand directly in front of your horse," said Wild Horse Charlie, spreading his arms to indicate the general sagacity of this precept.

"Nor behind it," added his friend, Charles Wild Horse, raising a single digit with delicacy and precision

"When your horse's forelegs come up even with the barrel on the steer," said Wild Horse Charlie, whose words tended to be indistinct due to the impression of horse-hoof where his face should have been, "that's when you jump."

"Except," said Charles Wild Horse, his eyes moving about his face with autonomy, "you don't jump. You fall. Lean and fall gently."

Basic and fine points notwithstanding, the first time I attempted to wrestle a steer I just plain missed. I felt the thin bony tail run through my fingers, I caught a whiff of something horrible, and the next thing I knew I was face-down in the dirt and a particularly matronly old bossy was licking my head. The second time, I grabbed hold, but did not have the hang of the putdown, which of course has to do with timing and leverage rather than strength. I dug in my heels and it seemed like a mile later that I finally abandoned the animal. The third time I executed a perfect Hoolihan, though this is not something you wish to do. The steer and I turned a somersault and popped up right-side. I was on my hands and knees, wondering how such a thing took place, when the steer took the opportunity to kick me in the chin. When I came to, the cowboys were still laughing. They could not be accused of having overly genteel senses of humor.

Mind you, consider Foote's first attempt. Foote had received as much, if not more, tutelage than myself, even though he evidenced no enthusiasm. After spending his lifetime dreaming about cowboys, Foote did not care to become one, and would have been more than content to continue his book-reading. But the boys persisted. Foote was an especial favorite of theirs, which was not true of me, seeing as I was allied with King Palmer. Palmer was a good and fair boss, all the men conceded, but he was perceived as strange if not flat-out addled. So, the cowboys talked endlessly with Foote about the nature, philosophy and practice of the rodeo, and Jefferson nodded sombrely as this was done.

When his time came, Foote screwed the hat upon his head and his face clouded over with manly purpose. He mounted his horse, hawked a beauty onto the ground. They cut loose the steer and Wild Horse Charlie hazed it, keeping it inside to Jefferson.

Now, I had noticed clouds coming across the mountains to the west, in fact, I paid more attention to them than I did to Foote. They roiled like a nest of black serpents, folded into themselves and exploded outwards again, and they brought with them a rumble like drunkards beating on marching drums. As Foote set off after the steer, I noticed that my own horse's forechuck was standing upright, and I further noted that the other men's animals were similarly affected. I asked Charles Wild Horse what he made of this. He only had time to shake his head in a mournful way.

Jefferson Foote was just getting ready to lean and fall when he was struck by the lightning bolt. It snapped him upright and bulged his eyes. A huge lick of flame jumped out of either ear and his hair was blasted clean off his head. The horse's head jerked upwards with a look of great surprise and then it tumbled, although the horse tumbled a small moment after Foote passed out, so Jefferson ended up with the full weight of the horse upon him.

I was the first man to reach Foote, and it is my opinion that he was dead. He certainly looked dead, and he had the bluishness of a dead man, and the stillness. The blueness and stillness could be attributed, I suppose, to the fact that he had a horse on top of him. About the horse there was no doubt, the nag was (Hartrampf suggests) exanimate. I took hold of Foote (one arm and a shoulder weren't covered by defunct nag) and pulled. For many long moments Foote did not budge, and when he did it was all at once, he popped loose, and we both fell over backwards. When we hit the ground there was a "pop" like a champagne cork (I don't know what that was, bone or lung-bellows or perhaps even the spirit making a reappearance) and Foote was sucking air greedily.

His ears were somewhat melted, indistinct at the edges, the whorls and ridges taken away. His hair would grow back white as bleached bone.

When we arrived in the railhead of Silver City, on the third of July, elephants and camels were parading down the main street, ridden by members of the Order of Ancient and Lucid Druids, an association of mystical merchants. (I thought then that the animal-perchers were merely oddballs, ancient men who wore strange clothes, hooded robes emblazoned with celestial images. However, the Druids would both save my frosted carcass and contribute to my Downfall.) Silver City was an assemblage of trust companies, taverns, dry-grocers, purveyors of hardware and tinware, a town designed to accommodate the visiting cattleman and wrangler. There were few true residents beyond the dance-hall girls and piano players. But on that day the streets were flooded with carnival boys getting ready for the big competition on the morrow, which they did by getting blind drunk.

We did likewise. The boys from the O-Gee pushed into the tavern at the Commercial Hotel, and we got as close to the bar as we could, which was about thirty feet away. Somehow drinks were conveyed to us.

Foote's recovery had been remarkable, although he seemed to have lost some hearing, and spent much time rooting around in the melted, scabbed flaps with his little finger, trying to loosen some plug. It had only been four days since the mishap, so no new hair was showing, but Jefferson's scalp had taken on an odd, luminescent quality, snow-white stubble prickling up the pink.

It embarrasses me to record that too much liquor was consumed by all concerned. Chiefly, me. Cowboys in general like to suck back the ignorant oil, I in particular have a wet tooth, even here in this prison there are some nights when The Warden over-brings me bottles, and I drink and cloud over and wake up in the middle of the night with a hole where my brain used to be. The Warden has never mentioned these episodes, although I often wish he would. I suspect I say things, I have the vague memory of awful words ripping out of my mouth.

But back then, I was only liable to get liquored up and do foolish things, for example, piss in somebody's hat, or shoot off a gun in the middle of the tavern. I had never fired a gun before, had never had need or occasion to, but I'd heard that cowboys often did this when drinking heavily, so I pulled the gun out of somebody's holster, fired it toward the rafters, whereupon the fellow whose gun it was tried to yank it out of my hands, so I coldcocked him, laying him out flat on his back, whereupon I pissed in his hat.

It was Foote who suggested that it was time for bed. I argued for a little while, finally gave up and said goodnight to my friends barside. Foote and I fought our way out through the front door. We found the other men from the O-Gee, actually, I did that, by stepping on Charles Wild Horse's head. We lay down and I stared up at the stars, and as tired and as drunken as I was, I could not fall asleep. I had the same thought I'd had ever since I was a child, and that was this: if there is a Heaven, shouldn't I be able to see something of it, might I not even be able to catch a glimpse of God himself?

Perhaps I slept briefly, perhaps I didn't. The stars began to disappear, washed away by the dawn.

My only point being, I was still piss-drunk when I hit the rodeo. Even my horse knew it. He gave me a series of worried and disdainful glances as I cinched up the gear. I gave him some reassuring pats on the neck, but I do not think he was reassured. But I will say this, my horse performed well all day long, quick and precise on the rollbacks and pivots, explosive on the breakaways, and perhaps this was to make up for his rider's liquored-up state.

I had my moments that day. There were the two events I actually won, steer undecorating and wild-cow milking, although these are not among rodeo's élite events. Steer undecorating is: they tie a red ribbon around the beast's head, bowed as on a schoolgirl. The cowboy rides after the steer, leans down, tries to grab the standing end and pull the ribbon free. Wild-cow milking is more fun, especially for the spectators: there is a corral full of a few wild cows, and twenty-five cowboys with empty whiskey bottles. The first man out with a little blue milk in his bottle is the winner. Needless to say, a wild cow's dugs are all pouched and parched, but I scrambled around on my hands and knees pulling at leathery teats, and I was lucky enough to be the victor.

I managed a third, behind Charles Wild Horse but ahead of Wild Horse Charlie, in the bull-dogging. I was just then going to write *despite my drunkenness*, but my drunkenness brought with it a huge advantage, that is, I didn't truly believe I could be hurt or killed. So when my horse's forelegs came up even with the barrel on the steer, I leaned over without a thought and fell, and there was that instant that I've written about, which for some reason feels large and long, and then I grabbed hold of a horn, a wattled neck, I dug in and flipped the creature, and this performance was good enough for third place and started my reputation as a cowboy of talent and flair.

I sobered up near the end of the day, which is when they began the bull riding. Whoever thought of this activity was not a well man, that's my opinion. Bulls are not creatures to be toyed with. Listen, in the Book of Isaiah, the fury of the Lord is likened unto

a wild bull in a net, and Isaiah was not a fellow who favored flip-
pancy. Bulls are huge, far too large for the world, and so deeply
black that it's more purplish, a strange color for a living creature
to be. At any rate, some fellow had the idea of riding the beasts. A
poor boy would get set on top, slip his fingers under a leather
surcingle, the behemoth would be discharged into the pen. The
most optimistic outcome was to get thrown clear after a few seconds of having your fingers ripped off and your gonads smashed
like peppercorns. I declined to partake. Indeed, throughout my
career I left that bull business to the few carnival boys even more
foolish than myself.

Kingsley Palmer had the idea of costumes for the local Round Ups
and six professional Rodeos we competed in that year. Those of
you who read the Hollywood *Megaphone* will no doubt be surprised to find out that my rodeo career, as notable and distin-
guished as it was, only lasted the year and a bit, from that July
Fourth up until the incident with Sophia Oglesby. Part of my
renown, I must admit, arose from the way I dressed, in an outfit
Kingsley made for me. It consisted of a short jacket and tight
pants, every square inch bedecked and festooned with glitter and
thread. I wore a white hat, the band implanted with ostrich feathers and peacock herl. My boots were rendered from snakeskin and
polished until they blinded. If you never saw me in this get-up, it
might be hard to imagine just how much a marvel I looked. The
other fellows were very jealous, and would therefore childishly
torment and jeer at me.

Chapter 6

I was on Mount Angelina well before dawn, that first day of my new career as a Star Player in the motion pictures, because I had not slept whilst with Thespa Doone in her windowless room. Neither had we spent the night locked in carnal embrace. Not that strange night, at any rate. We'd gone upstairs to her room at the White Owl, she'd pulled off the greater part of her mannish clothing, and we had undergone the Rigors. We'd commenced reconstruction of the glutei, because Thespa felt there was flaccidity there, although truth to tell, I could not detect it. But I showed her the requisite exercise, exhorted Thespa with great zeal, in the words of Kingsley Palmer. "The important factor," I told her, "is the speed and vigour of contraction. Squeeze! Release! Squeeze! Release! It is perhaps helpful to think of pythons and anacondas, small rodents locked within their musculature. Try to hear the soft whimpers; try to silence them."

I also made attempts to engage Thespa Doone in general, everyday conversation, but nothing came of this, not that the woman wasn't talkative. She simply had her own areas of interest, which she would address at length, and it didn't much matter to Thespa if the listener was on board or not. She discoursed

endlessly about the nature of light, the undiscovered benisons of
light, also, the insidiousness. Her windowless room was candle-
lit, just barely enough to save it from pitch blackness. Thespa
clung mostly to the shadows, although when a thought occurred
to her (and thoughts occurred to her with frequency and force)
she would come forward and allow the weak flickering to wash
over her body.

"Do you think we were meant to be diurnal, Mess? Myself, I
have my doubts." Thespa then placed her palms together, making
her breasts rise solemnly. "Am I doing this right?"

"Yes," I grunted.

"Have you read Darwin?"

"No, ma'am. Impulsion, then scission. All life is balance. Link
your fingers, draw your arms apart. Ideate forces such as the wind
or tides. Forces that will brook no opposition. Like so."

"We descended from the Great Ape," Thespa informed me, the
new exercise affecting her *serratus magnus* and making her
breasts bob much more playfully, "and they're nocturnal. *So...*"
When Thespa Doone said *so*, you felt like an idiot, for there never
seemed any *so* to be seen. "So, moonlight is better for us than sunlight. Sunlight burns skin cells."

"Let's do a little work on the *pyroformis*. Lean against that
wall."

"Yet moving pictures couldn't be made without sunlight."
Thespa had decided to take a break, which she indicated by lighting a Sweet Caporal and planting, with some care and precision,
the cigarette in the mathematical center of her mouth. "They
don't have lamps big enough."

"Come on, let's go. Never stand still. Remember, great rivers
which rive—"

"—remain pure and sweet, yes, yes, yes."

"Yes'm. Sluggishly moving streams become contaminated with
fermenting and poisonous matter."

The air was thick and moist with our perspiration. It held an
odd odor, as well, not just from our exertion, a pungency, ancient
and woodlike, as though some dark-robed priests had held a
strange ritual.

Sweat beaded up on Thespa like she was made of hot metal, tiny
little droplets which rolled away in all directions. She herself

never wiped it off, Thespa did not like to squander sweat. We worked through that whole night, concentrating mostly on the large muscles, the flexors, the *obliquus abdominus.* Toward the end we started fine-tuning the abductor muscles, the *psoas* and *iliacus*, which is to say, the inside of the thigh, and here it was necessary for me to help out, to slip my hands in and supply appositional force, and the skin was surprisingly cool to the touch, and I think I'm going to go lie down on my cot for a little bit, and then continue with this chapter, which is about the first day of my career as a star in the Flickers.

As early as I was on Mount Angelina, Mr. Willison was there before me, leaping from crag to outcropping. "Helloo, Mess!" he sang out when I was still many yards beneath him on the slope. "We have had a wonderful idea, your friend and I."

"Jeff?"

"Jefferson. Brilliant man. I trust you had a pleasant evening with Miss Doom."

"Sir?"

"Oh, I know all, she told me all. Thespa is bathing over yonder. Stark nekkid in an old tin tub. Lovely bubs on that gill." Caspar Willison leapt onto a boulder just above me, he crouched down and grinned over the edge. "She's a little insane, you know, Mess. Moonstruck."

"No, sir."

"It's the dregs."

"How's that, Mr. Willison?"

"Gladys Moorcock, the Wonder Whistler. So was Thelma Doom yclept when first she came unto me. Brought by that enormous sow that calls itself the mother. Gladys was beautiful, sure. But that is a common and chip commodity, Mess, remember that. One acquires massive disdain for beauty. Look. Whilst you two were doing the grunts, I had a poke-poke at one of the most exquisite critters ever wrought. And what does it mean to me now? *Nada.* Mess, do me a favor, jump over the side of that cliff and dangle off the edge there, hmm?"

"It looks like about a hundred-foot drop."

"The stuff of high drama."

"Not much to grab a hold of."

"The fingers slip away, the nails frantically search for ridges and crannies. Close-up! I shall make an iris and dilate, mimicking the action of the human eye when confronted by danger. Then, you see, leave the scene abruptly, cross-splice, *boomp!* Back to the scaffolding. Same iris width, only this time, close-up, Thespa. Brown eyes. Wan face. He's a genius, I think."

"Who's this, sir?"

"Jeffie."

"Foote's a genius?"

"Look, if you're not going to do this, I shall." Caspar Willison slid down the boulder like a snake, he leapt off the side of the mountain and caught hold of the ledge. His feet dangled, his fingers blanched, Willison grinned up at me, very pleased with himself. "Excellant," he hissed.

"If you should let go," I pointed out, "you're sausage meat."

"Thet's why I ain't going to let go." Willison craned his neck this way and that, much like he was at a county fair and trying to find a purveyor of meat pies. Whatever he was looking for, he found it, because he finally looked at me and said, "Give me a hand up, will you, Mess?"

I pulled him up and was surprised at how light he was, the man seemed almost to lack substance. C.W. Willison blinked at the eastern horizon. "Here comes the light," he whispered. "And there shall be..." Willison leaned in so that our faces were inches apart. I suppose that what I smelled on his breath was stale brandy, but it reeked, like a rat that had died in the wall. "...upon every high mountain, and upon every high hill, rivers and streams of waters in the day of the great slaughter, when the towers fall. Moreover, the light of the moon shall be as the light of the sun, and the light of the sun shall be sevenfold."

Billy Bittner and his assistants appeared on the mountain. Bittner was a large and well-built fellow (he'd played football for the championship Stanford side), so he did much of the actual labor; his assistants huffed along behind. One was an exceedingly old man named Georg, a man who had cataracts over his eyes and, so far as I could tell, spoke not a word of English. Georg was likely hard of hearing as well, given the amount of hair growing in his ears. Billy Bittner's other assistant was a fifteen-year-old boy named Theo Welkin. Welkin was an extremely tall individual, six-foot-five or something, which is the main reason he was hired, because this attribute aided in mark-setting, his main duty. He was acne-ravaged and a little unsightly to begin with, his face consisting of a large nose, eyes and mouth thrown in as mere afterthoughts. Theo — he preferred Theodore, but no one ever called him that — made up for this by immaculate pomading of his straw-blond hair; he split it down the middle and then fashioned curls on either side of his forehead that looked like quote marks. He lusted after the women at The World, Thespa Doone in particular. While this might be expected from a fifteen-year-old boy, there was something unseemly in it, because Welkin was almost always hobbled by an enormous erection, which he took no pains to mask from our view, his trouser-fronts preceding him wherever he went. He was a favorite of Caspar Willison's, so much so that once, when Theo spilt a reel of exposed film out of the black velvet bag, Willison refrained from murdering him on the spot. He merely slapped the boy across the face and then laughed for the better part of two minutes.

"Come along, you arse-whips!" screamed Willison. "We're wasting the fugging light."

Thespa came, a blanket wrapped around her, shivering in the morning chill. Her hair was cowlicked, her skin a pale blue.

"The light! The light!" ranted Willison.

The cowboys stood in a small circle beneath us, and I did not go to join them.

"So here it is," Caspar Willison said, to me, to Thespa Doone, to poor Manley Wessex. "This is Jefferson's brilly idée. You–" meaning me "– are the pus-leaking prick who's done the dirty. Hmm?"

"What exactly did I do?"

"I dunno. All's we know is, Thespa here is found to be guilty of the crime. But really her crime is to be a free-minded young woman! The townspupple cannot accept the fact that she fornicates copiously."

"Oh, Caspar," muttered Thespa.

"Subtext, beauty mine, subtext. Right. Now, Manley sets off in pursuit of the scoundrel—"

"Indeed!" exclaimed Manley Wessex, who exclaimed everything.

"I confront the cur on the mountain-top and dash him to bits!"

"Nay. It is Jefferson's idea, which I think wonderful, that — *surprise!* — you lose the fight."

"What?" exclaimed Manley Wessex.

"Well, think about it. Thom here is young and massively constructed. You are middle-aged and poodgy. I know where I'd place my money."

"But I," exclaimed Manley, "am the star!"

"Look, Manley, you lose the fight, over the edge you go, and as you dangle above certain death, you beseech the cur, *save the gill.* You see? And this bit of altruism moves the hard-hearted wretch. *Save the gill.* Redemption! That's the stuff of art, fugging redemption. Thom flees the mountain, on to his horsey, thrilling gallump, arrives at the scaffold, *I'm your man, Mr. Ellis,* rope around neck, and then — this is the part I like — as the platform drops, you—" meaning Manley "— drop as well. The two men become one in death."

"Don't like it!" exclaimed Manley.

"You lie amudst the rocks, shattered except for the heart. That battered orgoon becomes as a beacon to the finer instincts, even as life departs."

Jefferson stood some feet away. He had acquired a large, wide-brimmed hat which he used to cover his bone-white hair, to shield his eyes from the sun. The hat shielded his eyes quite effectively, because it kept slipping down over them, largely because his melted ears did not act as effective stoppers. Jefferson smoked a black cigarette, but instead of holding it curled up inside his hand — we'd both become cigarette smokers during our days as rodeo boys, and this is how you kept the ember out of the wind — Jefferson had adopted a new style, the cigarette gently nestled between his second and ring fingers, the hand held right beside the mouth for easy access.

"Let's prepare for the fight," said Caspar Willison.

Manley Wessex scowled and walked away to put on some make-up. He had a huge theatrical suitcase, which opened away to reveal all sorts of unguents, pastes and creams. Thespa hooked her finger in the air, waggling it just the tiniest bit, and I followed her over to her own cosmetic chest. It contained only a couple of powders and a few dark pencils. Thespa puffed chalky stuff all over my face, then she drew heavy lines above and below my eyes. She traced around my lips and then smudged the black, her fingertips rubbing gently on my flesh.

Manley Wessex was full of ideas for the fight. "Let's say Thom draws a knife, and without batting an eye, cool as the proverbial cucumber, I smash it out of his hand."

Caspar Willison looked over at me and raised his eyebrows.

"Well, when you draw a knife," I opined, "you tend to have a good hold on it. It'd be more likely that I'd rip your arm open when you tried to smash it. Then I'd cut your throat. I suppose."

"Shall we give it a try, Wessex?" asked Caspar.

"Mano-a-mano!" exclaimed Manley. "Bare-handed combat. Love it, Caspar, love it to pieces. Let's work it out. Thom, I'll strike first."

"Do not," said Caspar Willison, "work it out. Light is too precious. Billy-boy, crank away at your contrumption. Come on, fellas! Away ya go!"

Manley did get first licks, popping me on the nose before I'd even put up my fists. It was a weak blow, and stung more than hurt. I gave Manley a small shot to the stomach which somehow crumpled him like yesterday's newspaper. He fell to his knees and made a series of small retching sounds. I surmised Manley had not yet commenced his daily drinking, because he just dry-heaved a few times and then whimpered.

Caspar Willison appeared beside us. "We can do better than that," he said darkly. "Manley, I like the gentility you bring to the role. A civilized man, reduced to violence. It is, however, more than apparent to the camera's unblinky eye that you are a bungy nancy-boy. And Thom, you practised thug, let us see what you're doing. Exaggerate. Exaggerate!"

"Tell him," gasped Manley Wessex, although it was still partially exclaimed, "that he doesn't have to hit me that hard."

Willison turned away and slapped his own bottom a few times. Willison was forever slapping his buttocks, hustling his testicles; in those rare moments of repose Willison was likely to stick his hand down the front of his jodhpurs and curl his thin fingers around the one-eyed snake. "Come on, Billy! Work your wonderbox!"

Manley Wessex got in first licks again, this time he threw a strange overhanded wallop that might have hurt except I moved my nose out of the way, and his fist landed on my cheek-bone. Then, with Willison's stridulous cries of "Exaggerate!" ringing in my ears, I circled my own fist in the air over and over again (a manœuvre I pride myself on having popularized, although let me be the first to tell you, don't try it in a real fight) and then gave Manley a shot to his own beak. His head jerked backwards, his eyes glazed over momentarily ("Beauteous bit of acting there!" sang out C.W. Willison encouragingly) and then Wessex recovered enough to pick up a big rock. ("Ooh, lookee! Civility must have had a train to catch!") Manley advanced on me with this raised aloft, as though his intention were to crush my brains, and it might well have been, but he presented a fairly large and inviting target doing that, so I gathered up a punch from somewhere near my feet (exaggerate!) and delivered it to his solar plexus. Manley Wessex's entire system seemed to be more finely tuned and fragile than normal. With this blow he voided most of the air in his body. His fingers trembled briefly and then let go of the rock, which bounced off Manley's head and then fell away down the cliff-side. Manley reeled toward that brink himself and if I had not reached out and taken hold of him, I'm pretty sure he would have gone over.

Caspar Willison was very pleased with all this, but I only know that in retrospect (thank you, Mr. Hartrampf). When he was pleased, Willison would act with greater and greater vigor; and if he was extremely pleased his state would be indistinguishable from fury. So now Willison launched himself up the mountainside, he claimed a flat outcropping above us and shouted for Billy Bittner. The crankman began to lug the equipment upward. His ancient assistant Georg, on all fours and groping with his bended fingers for nooks and crannies, began to follow. Theo Welkin took two giant steps and then stumbled on a rounded rock, bouncing back down the mountain and opening a huge gash on the side of his head. He did this sort of thing quite often, his uncommon height rendering him lubberly.

Caspar Willison, with too much energy to contain, raised his arms high in the air and shook his white fists in God's face. Seeing that I was watching, he turned this into one of those stretch/yawn combinations and grinned at me, childlike and innocent.

✧ ✧ ✧

The next thing we filmed is a very famous scene. In the movie —
which had been retitled *Redemption* as per a suggestion of Foote's
— it lasts but a few seconds, but it took the better part of an hour
to film. This is because of the innovations photography-wise. For
one thing, the camera view is straight down, so some time was
given over to figuring out just how Bittner could work the thing
on the horizontal and high in the air. I can tell you that Bill
Bittner and the camera were lashed on to a long plank; this plank
was spun out over the abyss and some cowboys were conscripted
to stand on the other end. Then there was not enough light on
what Bittner was trying to photograph. Willison and Bittner stood
off to one side, their foreheads almost touching. They each tugged
on a bottom lip and tried to think of what to do; they each jerked
up their head when they heard an odd voice say, "Mirror."

The voice — it belonged to the gangly satyr Theo Welkin — had
not changed completely, and it splintered and cracked and was
both angel's and bullfrog's.

"Mirror," nodded Willison.

Someone produced a large mirror from the costuming department, and this was tethered and sandbagged to cragface, where it
caught the sunlight and hurled it down the side of the mountain.

By the time all this was worked out, the better part of a half-
hour was eaten away, which is, as Manley Wessex would tell you,
an awfully long time to be dangling over the edge of a cliff.

"Why," he'd scream, although it was still half-exclaimed, "don't
I come up there while you get all this settled?"

"Won't be a minute, Manley!" returned Willison.

"He's been fooling with that mirror — ow, now the damned
thing is blinding me!"

"Perfect!"

As the time passed, Manley turned more and more frantic, and
toward the end his voice was filled with raw fear — "Hurry,
please!" — and then white-hot terror. "For the love of God, Willison, I'm going to fall I'm going to fucking fall I'm going to die I'm
going to fucking die..."

"Make the shot, Billy," whispered C.W. Willison.

When they raised up Manley Wessex, he was trembling in every
part of his body and appeared to be made of clay. He wobbled

toward Caspar Willison, who calmly awaited his arrival and then socked him in the face. Wessex was so spent he didn't even bother reeling backwards, simply collapsed where he stood.

"What did you do that for?" I asked.

"He was going to hit me."

"What makes you think that?"

"Human nature. Come on, let's git to the gallows!"

Mr. Boyle was the man in charge of all the construction. If he had a first name, I never heard it, Boyle was what he was called by one and all. Boyle the Builder owned the hands of a giant; he was, it's true, a large man, perhaps six-foot-two, broad-shouldered and pot-bellied, but his hands still seemed oversized. The nails were always purpled, whorled and rippled by mishap.

Boyle had erected the gallows just outside of The Town, and like all of his handiwork, they gave the illusion of solidity. As soon as I started mounting toward the noose, of course, the staircase swayed back and forth, the air was filled with muffled howlings. Bodnarchuk had been given the role of the hangman, and he awaited me with a dark hood pulled down over his small pinched face.

The thrilling gallop had gone very well, if I do say so myself. My heart filled with redemptive power, I'd leapt upon my mount and spurred it up into a stand. Then I'd galloped into town, arriving just as they slipped the noose around the neck of Brown Eyes. Her bosom was heaving. I pulled up in front of the gallows, dismounted without whoaing the horse, a stupid bit of business that photographs well, I said, "I'm your boy!" and now Bodnarchuk dangled the deadly loop in front of me and said, "Come along, Thom."

"Keep a lid on it, Bodnarchuk. Can't you see I'm acting here?"

"Hurry up, Mess!" screamed Willison, so I walked a bit more lively, although why a man would pick up the pace on the way to his doom is beyond me. Bodnarchuk threw the noose around my neck and went to man the lever that would drop the platform.

So I stood there and stared straight ahead and tried to convey the impression that I was inwardly regretting a life misspent, and then Willison spoke quietly, "Get on with it."

"See you, Thom," said Bodnarchuk from beneath the black

hood, and he threw the lever. The semblance of serenity vanished from my face as the platform fell away. I hit and bounced and the rope dug into my throat. I kicked and thrashed in an undignified manner and then the rope snapped up in the uppermost beams, which is where Willison had cut it almost through, and I fell on to my keester.

"Veddy gude," said Willison.

Chapter 7

Mr. Oglesby, you'll recall, was possessed of a mottled and carbuncled complexion, and this accounted in my opinion for his sour mood. He was, Hartrampf suggests, introverted and unclubbable. Well, I expect I might be the same if my skin were so ravaged. Thinking back on it, I cannot recall one truly mean-spirited thing Oglesby did; mind you, I am discounting the shotgun blast he fired at our retreating backsides.

It was Oglesby's wont to make monthly trips away, and it was our assumption that these absences — which never lasted more than two or three days — had to do with his cattle business. This was not in fact the case, as I was to discover whilst sitting over breakfast with Thespa Doone, who was my one-and-only, although she never truly comprehended that. I opened the Hollywood *Megaphone* and read how a man had drownded in mud, and it was reported that he'd been taking the mud-bath treatment for years, owing to his (what the papers called daintily) *skin condition*, and when they gave his name as *William Oglesby* I laughed out loud, causing Thespa to spill orange juice down the front of her satin robe. I have known men with foul tempers (I myself own one, as did my father before me) but Thespa outdistanced us on this front. And whereas men tend to explode in all directions, Thespa's anger would be as sharp as a stiletto blade, and she would quickly find the best place to make the incision. On this occasion, as I guffawed over Oglesby's demise (which was unseemly and not very Christian on my part), Thespa stared at the orange juice staining the satin and then turned her dark eyes upwards. "Do you know what, Thom?" she near-whispered.

"Hey, remember I told you about Oglesby who owned the O-Gee ranch?"

"Bad news."

"Hmm?"

"I have bad news. Caspar told me yesterday. There is no part for you in *Civilization*."

Regardless of the purpose of these trips, what is significant is that Mr. Oglesby returned from one of these trips with a wife in tow. His bride Sophia was, at least by comparison, friendly and outgoing. She was a plump woman and did not enjoy the local climate, which was hot to say the least, and she often went about with clownish red circles on her cheeks, and she was always blowing out air through a pursed mouth and waving her chubby hands like little fans and reaching down the neckhole of her blouse to mop up her bosom. Sophia was forever realigning her skirts, tugging up her hose and adjusting whatever she wore as undergarments. Kingsley Palmer identified her problem as a universal one, namely, she was uncomfortable in clothes because clothes were contrary to God's wishes and plans, that she would be a much more contented woman if she would divest herself of them altogether. The men, though not sharing this philosophy, sensed that Mrs. Oglesby was a likely convert. They waited until Mr. Oglesby was away on business, and then they effected a plan.

The Warden pushes open the door to my cell with his enormous fanny, because he is laden with victuals and bottles of wine. I remain hanging upside down from the bars of my high, useless window.

"Undergoing the Rigors?" the Warden demands. "Good, good. And what are you imagining?"

"Weightlessness. I suspend myself in the atmosphere like the filmy wisps of high-cirrus cloud touching the very vault of heaven."

"Look," says he, "I've brought lunch."

"Now, elevation. I imagine I am a hot-air balloon. I push my way through the scud of approaching thunderstorm."

"That's very interesting, Thom. Cheese." The Warden's tie is done up so tightly that his face is purplish. He lays the food stuffs on the small table, arranging it all very neatly with his pale hairless fingers. I find this all very interesting to watch upside down; also, I'll confess, I've become infrequent in my undergoing of the Rigors, and am experiencing sharp twisting pains in my belly, so I take the time to enjoy a little respite.

"Thom," he says quietly, "I found something in Chapter Six very disturbing."

"Hmm."

"You glossed over one thing. There would seem to have been a moment during which your death seemed imminent."

"Yep." I curl upwards again, slowly, like a dead thing drying in the sun.

"You do not describe it in any detail."

"It was here and gone."

"You recall nothing of it?"

"Well... it was mostly anger."

"Ah!"

"It's funny, Warden, but when you see the movie — do you know that one, *Redemption?*"

"Alas, no."

"When you see the movie, when you see my face, it is filled with fearfulness. That is, after all, why Willison pulled the prank in the first place. That is why he let Manley dangle over the side of the cliff, too, because he wanted pure emotion imbuing our countenances. So it's there, in the Flicker, it's there all over my face, terror, but all I recall is this white flash of anger that spread like wildfire through my body."

"You sought no vengeance?"

I curl upwards once more, accompanied by undignified huffings and grunts. I grip the iron bars and extract my feet. Slowly I lower myself to the ground. The Warden busies himself with the preparations for our meal; he avoids looking at me in my naturalistic state — it is best to undergo the Rigors whilst denuded. "Hey, Warden?"

"Yes, Thom?"

"I think I'd like to meet that fellow you're fixing to hang."

"John Murtagh?"

"Yeah, that's right. Johnny Murtagh."

I imagine Sophia Oglesby was more than a little surprised that morning she rang the gong and threw open the doors to receive the men for breakfast, because we filed in one by one and buck naked. Incidentally, not only the hair on Foote's head had turned white on account of the lightning, but the hair adorning his pubis, too. Another incidentally, Wild Horse Charlie had the ugliest scar on his belly. It looked like a garden slug, all white and welted up. Wild Horse Charlie claimed that a bull attacked for no good reason and had then rampaged about for a matter of minutes before anyone could calm him down, Wild Horse Charlie skewered on top. I just mention this because there are some people, Apollo Greenling and the Society for Peaceful Speciate Co-Existence, for example, who maintain that bulls, like all other animals, are docile creatures when left to their own devices.

Kingsley Palmer was beaming, because he believed he was having one hell of a day on the conversion front. Actually, it had started the night before, during one of Palmer's little talks. "I wish to discuss physical and muscular morality!" he'd said, and two or three of the men shouted, "Hell, yes!" and stripped off. The men were too canny to mass-convert, so they left about twenty-minute intervals before shouting, "Hallelujah!" or "Praise the Lord!" Some even waited for the following morning. Charles Wild Horse, who did have a spiritual side, claimed that God had appeared in a dream and demanded that he doff his outerwear. The men knew that this semblance of outstanding success would fill Palmer with irresistible zealotry.

"Mrs. Oglesby," Kingsley began as soon as he entered the kitchen, striking his oratorical pose, "The Lord Almighty is a discerner of the thoughts and intents of the heart. There is no creature that is not manifest in his sight. But all things are naked and opened unto the eyes of Him!"

"Eggs?" asked Mrs. Oglesby.

"Yes, please!" said Kingsley Palmer, and he sat down, and we all sat down, and Jefferson Foote received a splinter that plagued and tormented him for months. "Mankind, Mrs. Oglesby—"

"Yeah?"

"Mankind has done many things contrary to God's wishes. For example, God gave us horses and nether limbs, but Man got rebellious — I don't believe *uppity* is putting too sharp a point on it — and invented the wheel. Think how unnatural the bicycle is!"

"Hey, now, Palmer! There's nothing wrong with bicycles."

The men hushed me sternly.

"Man invented clothes to rob his skin of sun and air. We have noticed, ma'am, that you are discomfited by your garments. We have come with God in our hearts to urge you to rid yourself of them."

"Oh. All right." Sophia pulled away at her vestments, tugging things every which way, loosening ties and unfastening stays. After this preparatory work was done, the clothes flew off her body like birds off a fat tree. I don't believe the men had counted on success, certainly not two minutes into the battle, so they sat there stunned, taking the occasional peek at the naked Sophia, and carefully spooning scrambled eggs into their mouths.

"What the hell is going on?"

Evidently Mr. Oglesby had returned home sometime the previous night. For the most part, the men folded their hands together and laid them over their privates; they dolefully lowered their eyes. All except Kingsley Palmer, who was not about to let up now. He leapt from his seat. "Mr. Oglesby! It is my belief that your malady is a complaint of the very skin itself! *Unshackle me*, it shouts. See how happy your wife looks!" And it was true, Sophia was merrily serving breakfast, and she even looked up and chirped, "I'm happy, Bill!"

Kingsley Palmer adopted the stance, the grinning loin-tilt. He swivelled himself back and forth, allowing Oglesby a view of all the muscular facets. Palmer had perhaps too much faith in this method of silent persuasion. Oglesby punched him in the face. The men decided it was an appropriate time to leave the household, and we stampeded through the front door, lighting out for the horizon.

Oglesby — I know this because I turned around to make sure

King Palmer was with us, which he was, a hand covering his nose, blood spurting out from between the fingers — ran out on to the porch with a shotgun. He raised it and fired into fifteen butt-ends. He managed to catch only the skinny, flaccid one belonging to Jefferson Foote.

The Warden shoulders open the door to my cell, his hands full of weaponry, Bird's Head Colts, the firearm favored by C. W. Willison. The Warden backs in, throwing me a quick glance and a smile before returning his attention to the captive.

John Murtagh enters with a sort of splay-footed waddle, much like the Little Fellow that is so popular these days. His hands he holds before his face, thick manacles encircling the wrists, a short section of chain connecting them. Murtagh is a sandy-haired individual, and beyond that, I'm not sure what to say, and even Mr. Hartrampf is a bit stymied, offering up *even-featured*, which is right on the money but likely doesn't conjure up much of a picture. Besides, I did not check to make sure Murtagh had the requisite number of eyes or a well-rendered nose. I was struck, and made thoughtful, by more intangible things. For example, the curious way that he comported himself, his head canted slightly to the right, as if he had just received a blow and believed another might be forthcoming. And Murtagh's eyes had an odd way of moving, very slowly, and they did not light upon anything, so our eyes did not truly meet, but during their brief encounter Murtagh nodded his head, and even mustered up a smile. And I'm going to leap upon that in my authorial role here, because his teeth were bad, brown and rotted and testament to years of neglect.

"John Murtagh," said The Warden, "meet Thom Moss. Thom Moss, this is the young man I told you of, John Murtagh. He murdered his wife."

"Let's have some of these sandwiches. There's egg salad and, um, cucumber."

"I've enjoyed your performances in the Flickers." John Murtagh spoke softly, as if the world were a huge library with a mean-tempered dowager lurking nearby. "The one I enjoyed much was *Southern Honor*, in particular, the famous Battle scene. It truly fired my heart. Tears spilt forth.

"Mind you," the murderer proceeded, "I am a Southerner. I come from Valestes, Georgia, originally. But I have travelled a great deal. The incident took place in Santa Cruz, but before that I lived in twenty-four different cities and no less than nine different states. We have a joke in the meteorological trade. *You have to go where the weather is.* Ha-ha." Murtagh flashed his smile again, the flash coming entirely from a cap and some fillings.

"When Murtagh says incident," put in The Warden, "he is referring to the brutal murder of his wife."

"I know, Warden. But John and I are getting acquainted."

The Warden shrugs and sits down at the food table. His hairlessness cuts through the shadows. The Warden stuffs food into his mouth and stares at the two of us.

Murtagh and I remain standing, three or four feet apart, our shoulders thrown back a bit, and as I try to take the measure of him, I realize that he is trying to take the measure of *me*. We both start prowling around the jail cell.

Murtagh notices the pile of inky second sheets, by now almost an inch thick. "What's this?" he asks.

"Book. Book about a moving picture called *Civilization.*"

The Warden's mouth is full, three or four dainty cucumber sandwiches crammed in there, so his words are a little indistinct. "It's very good, John. A very interesting account of what goes on in The World. Although, we are still waiting for something to happen."

"What do you mean?" say I, but my question is drowned out by The Warden's eating sounds, huge wet mulches. He raises his own voice and speaks over them. "However, there is much about the lovely Thespa Doone." He grins and morsels of food tumble out of his mouth.

"Oh, yes?" Murtagh responds, genial enough, but then he swings around and stares at me, and he points with his manacled hands at my nether parts and I believe he winks. This meeting was not a good idea.

"I want to write a book," he informs me. "But it wouldn't be about me. It wouldn't be about the incident. It would be about the prediction of weather. First of all, a historical overview. Augury by entrail, and so forth. The priests used to rip open animals, doves and such, and they felt that an examination of the offal would offer clues as to the weather. Oneiromancy is another."

"Presagement through dream," mutters The Warden. "Nothing to it."

I want to ask The Warden whether he means the theory is empty and foolish or the practice is dead easy, but John Murtagh barges on before I'm able. "I would contrast that with the more modern methods. On the surface it would appear to be very scientific. Cumulus clouds mount on the horizon, for instance. They pile on top of each other, they fill the welkin. We predict a storm. But, my book would say, this is, in point of fact, nephomancy. In ancient times the priests might have said that the clouds were the gods forming an army, you see, and that they therefore meant to attack, and that that was what a storm was."

"And," asks The Warden, "what exactly might your point be?"

John Murtagh responds with bitterness. "It would be a book about the prediction of weather. There is no point to the prediction of weather. The storm either comes or it doesn't come, you either find shelter or you don't."

"I see. Thom?"

"What?"

"A penny."

"Well, sir, Charles Wild Horse would regularly tell us what the next day's weather would be, and when we asked him how he did that, he'd just laugh and say, *Isn't it obvious?*"

The Warden cups and raises up both of his white hands, and they became the two sides of a scale. As one lowers, the other ascends. "You see, boys. We have the two sides right there. On the one hand, such things are unknowable. On the other, they are self-evident."

"I'll tell you the truth," says John Murtagh quietly, and I see The Warden inch his buttocks closer to the edge of his seat. He places his elbows on his knees and cradles his chin thoughtfully. "The truth is," Murtagh continues, "I wasn't much of a weather predictor. Not that I was often wrong, no, I just usually required more data than was available, so I would decline to make predictions, which got me in trouble with my superiors. I feel I would have been fired even if I hadn't of killed my wife." Murtagh makes a sheepish grin and joins The Warden at the table. He picks up a cucumber sandwich with his hands, raises it up and takes a small, fussy bite.

"My father made predictions," I tell them. I don't know if they're listening or not, they are too busy consuming little sandwiches. "They were not often on target, in fact, I can't think of one presagement that made itself manifest, but you know, it was important to my father that he make the predictions. He'd sit on the porch and consume Old Bell's, and he would stare at the mountains, Mount Uriel and Mount Sariel, and he would squint at them, and render himself meek before them, although they were in truth just pipsqueak mountains, and he would try to divine the future. There would be nothing but vapors, but my father would stare into them and then speak, and that gave him pleasure."

"So..." The Warden wipes his lips with a napkin, the tiny piece of linen lost in his large pale hands. "The act of prediction becomes more important than the actual prediction."

"I suppose so."

"Proceeding logically," proceeds the Warden, "the act of faith is paramount, more important than the object of reverence, more important than the truth, or lack thereof, of any credo."

I shrug. John Murtagh wipes his lips on the back of his sleeve and says, "Mind you, I had some idea that she was up to no good. You get hints, but — I liked that word Thom used — they are vapors. There is something in the eyes, they are averted a fraction of a second early, or late, and inwardly this twists you up, but you cannot act, you have no information, no data. Your life maintains a semblance of order. Day-to-day existence seems unchanged. You even make love on a regular basis, but again, there are vapors, *did she seem not as passionate, did she seem too passionate?* Insufficient data. You cannot act. So I came home early, I threw open the door, and I was not surprised by what I saw. And on the dresser was a knife, and I wondered, *How did it get there,* even though I knew, I had put it there that morning. Without thinking about it, although when I saw it, I knew I had put it there because I had seen this. I had seen her with another man. I had seen their limbs entwined. I had seen them humping, and her eyes were turned up and buried under the eyelids, so that she looked empty, mindless, already dead." Murtagh picks up another sandwich, looks at it for a long moment, throws it into his mouth. "Much was made, at my trial, of the fact that I stabbed her repeatedly. As if that made me especially beastly. But, you know, I wanted to make sure she was dead. I owed her that much. She was my wife."

Chapter 8

There we were, naked in the desert. It hadn't dawned on me previously that we inhabited a desert. I knew it was hot outside and that if you were looking for a tree to piss on you'd walk around all day with a bloated bladder, but until Mr. Oglesby expelled us nakedly into that world, we hadn't realized it consisted of nothing but sun, sand and wind. As the sun rose, the wind picked up, and blew grit into all our unprotected cracks and orifices.

We splintered off into two main groups, those that were willing to remain with Kingsley Palmer, those that were not. King thumped through the dunes like a man out on a constitutional. "The seed of mankind was planted first in arid soil," Palmer orated. "We come from the desert, as surely as fish come from the sea." He breathed in through his nostrils, as if filling them with the cool air of evening. Palmer's nose soon became filled with sand, he was forced to stop up either nare and discharge grainy plugs. "The wilderness and the solitary place shall be glad for them; and the desert shall rejoice, and blossom as the rose. It shall blossom abundantly, and rejoice even with joy and singing!"

"Fuck you," said many of the men, and they disappeared to the

east. I remained with Kingsley Palmer. Jefferson Foote remained
with me. (I was the only one allowed to pull buckshot out of his
arse-end. Now that I think about it, I was also the only one willing to.) Wild Horse Charlie was tempted to go off with the others, but Charles Wild Horse elected to stay with us, so Wild
Horse Charlie remained, although he thought King Palmer was,
and I quote, *crazy enough to eat shit and call it chocolate ice
cream.* So we headed west, and I guess if we'd been tiny specks
on a map of the area you would have seen us move away from
the relative safety of the desert's edge (those eastwarders, I
understand, found clothes and shelter some time in the afternoon) into the center, and I guess the assumption you'd draw is
that we were tired of the earthly vale and seeking an open door
to Paradise. About five o'clock in the afternoon, even King
Palmer's optimism began to fail. "For he remembered that they
were but flesh," he sang out mournfully, "a wind that passeth
away and cometh not again."

"Oh, lord," muttered Wild Horse Charlie, "I'm going to burn up
like a cinder."

"Oh," said Charles Wild Horse, "don't worry about that."

"No?"

"No, no. You won't be hot once the sun goes down."

"That's true."

"Mind you," pointed out Jefferson Foote, "we're all likely to
freeze to death."

"There is that," said Charles Wild Horse.

When the sun set, which it did with unseemly haste, the tem-
perature plummeted, and our dry skin heaved up with goosebumps, and vultures gathered in the star-dappled heavens. There
seemed little sense in continuing the journey. I think we had
accepted the fact that we were goners. Wild Horse Charlie turned
quite philosophic. "I always figured it would be *something,* a bull
or a bullet. I never counted on what'd eventually do me in being
nothing."

"It is ironic," acknowledged Charles Wild Horse.

Something occurred to Wild Horse Charlie. "Hey! Don't you
know any Indian tricks?"

Charles Wild Horse rubbed his chin. "We could lie on top of
each other."

"Good thinking!" said King Palmer, whose muscled body had turned a bright blue.

"Only," I mentioned, "we can't *all* lie on top of each other. Somebody's gonna be odd man out."

Jefferson Foote took a small step toward us, and I think it was that — a movement made without hesitation or rancor or regret — that calmed us. Jeff raised his hand and touched King Palmer lightly. I see now the logic behind this, King was one of the few men who could support a six-hundred-pound blanket. Next he touched Wild Horse Charlie, then Charles Wild Horse, then me, because, although I had taken up my regimen of Rigors and bodily reconstruction, I was still a fairly scrawny fellow. Then Jefferson Foote climbed on top.

We talked into that night.

About nothing much at first, just a sort of quiet muttering. I believe I said, "I'd like to get my hands on that fat fellow."

"Mr. Jensen?" said Foote from on top.

"Yes, sir. I have a scenario in mind, although I don't believe he'd care for it much."

Jefferson laughed, although it was hard to hear for all the teeth-chattering.

"Hey!" I said, possibly I should even put *exclaimed*, because I over-enthused in the frigid, empty night. "Mary Billings. Did you love her?"

"Yes."

"Thought so."

"But she didn't love me. She loved you."

"Yeah?"

"Thought of you as very handsome."

"She was flat-chested."

"Why would you say something like that?"

"Just mentioning it. Large nipples, however."

"Shut up, Moss. I'm trying to make my peace up here."

"How large?" came a voice from two men below, which would be Wild Horse Charlie.

"How's that?"

"This girl. How large were her nipples? I am partial to a large nipple myself."

"I don't know. Quite large is all. Hush now. Jefferson is trying to make his peace."

"Is he praying?" The voice was muffled and seemed far away, so I concluded it belonged to Kingsley Palmer.

"No, sir, he is not."

"I've just decided," confirmed Foote, "that I'm an atheist."

"Say, Jeff," said I, "if there was a chance that time was running out on me, I don't know that I'd jump on that particular horse."

Jefferson decided, "I am a Free Thinker."

"I'll pray for you," said Palmer down below, "lest you languish in eternal fire and brimstone."

"At least it would be warm," noted Charles Wild Horse, and we all mustered a little spirit, and our pile of naked humanity chuckled in the void.

"Well," I said, "it's not as bad as all that. We'll all be fine. Jefferson's even stopped shivering."

"Actually," Charles Wild Horse said, "that's not a good sign."

"How are you feeling, Jefferson?"

A word was spoken into the night, a tiny word that fell weakly from up top.

"You know what?" I said. "I'm *too* damn hot! Jeff, let's you and me change places."

He answered with groans and fragile bits of breath; he didn't move. I pushed up, Foote slid to the ground. I picked him up easily. Even when he became a famous Hollywoodland scenarist and drank cognac and ate raw oysters, Jefferson remained a frail boy, all sinew and bone. I laid Foote on Charles Wild Horse, then I climbed on top of the pile.

"That's better," said I, even as a devilish wind blew right up into me.

"In a while," said Charles Wild Horse, "I think I'll be too hot. I'll want a turn up top."

"Okay, well, when you get too hot, you let me know. Hey, Foote's started shivering again."

"Good," said Charles Wild Horse.

And Wild Horse Charlie called up, "Yeah, and I'll have a ride on top, too. I'm getting nervous that someone might try to poke me with his pork-sword."

And that is how we made it through the night, rotating top man.

Kingsley Palmer did not take a turn, for the somewhat extraordinary reason that he managed to slumber peacefully through it all, filling the night with stentorian snores.

We awoke in the morning to this wondrous sight: the desert was filled with camels and elephants. On top of them perched little old men wearing velveteen robes, the material bright with silver half-moons and golden suns. The cowls were pulled up, plunging their poppled and plicated faces into shadow. I had seen these men before, and you'll remember where, parading through the streets of Silver City on July the Fourth, that auspicious day of my first Round Up.

We jumped to our feet, full of hurrahs and hosannahs. We shouted for a good long time, until it became clear that the wrinkled little bastards had absolutely no intention of stopping for us. They stared straight ahead, their eyes weak and cataracted. The old men ignored our pleas for help, they refused to see or hear us, and not only that, they couldn't be bothered steering their elephants and camels around us, so we were dodging behemoths and cursing the sourpiss fossils, nearly a hundred in all. The air was filled with strange noises; the labored breathing of the animals mostly, hacks and retchings and rasps from the hoary drivers. One of the rearmost elephants walked by me, and I stared bitterly at its enormous hindquarters, and if I did not speak the words, "What the hell," they were certainly on my tongue. I ran after the elephant, grabbed hold of its tail, kicked away up and scissored, and in that manner landed behind the grizzled pilot, albeit facing the other way.

"Help!" he screamed. "Help! I'm being attacked!"

I started to deny this, but then I noticed that the other old men had curled up upon their mammoth mules, cringing and whimpering. The animals came to a halt and stood around wondering what to do next. "Well," I said, "damned right!"

A hundred ancient fartbags begged for mercy.

"My friends and me," I called out, "only wish to be transported out of this desert! We want you to take us with you! All right?"

The men nodded, wiped tears away and cleared choked windpipes. Those nearest my companions touched their animals with silver riding crops, and three camels and an elephant laboriously dropped down onto their knees. My four naked friends climbed aboard, and the trek began.

I swung around and looked down upon the celestially emblazoned robe. "So," I asked, "where're we going, anyway?"

"California," was the answer.

You won't find anything about the Order of Ancient and Lucid Druids in the Encyclopedia Americana, and any number of reasonable people will tell you they don't exist, but why would I, alone in my cell and trying very earnestly to unburden my soul, why would I invent them? I mentioned the Druids at my trial a time or two, but the Judge tsked his tongue and told me to get back to the facts. Even as worldly a fellow as C.W. Willison put no credence in their existence.

"But," I once asked, "who the hell do you think is running the entire shooting match out here?"

"*Chews*," said Caspar savagely. "There is a great Zionist conspiracy. Mark my fugging words."

We were in the Salon upstairs at the White Owl Hotel, sitting on a red satin divan. Willison and I had large tumblers of cognac in our hands. "These Druids," the director yawned and stretched; veins marbled across the paper-thin skin of his forehead. "These Druids are but figlets of your imagination."

"That can't be right, Caspar," came a voice. "Thom lacks an imagination."

"That's true, ain't it. That's what I love best about him."

Jefferson Foote sat over in a corner, darkly brooding, his one hand full of drink, a black cigarette plugged between his lips. He was bored, intoxicated and restless, which is how he spent most of his time. During the day Foote would compose scenarios, and in the evenings he would sit around and sulk.

"Hey, Jeff," said I, "*you* tell them about the Druids."

Jefferson made a strange face, all of his morose shrikish features flowing together. "The Druids," he repeated, his voice thick with befuddlement.

"Foote don't count," I exclaimed, throwing a finger toward him. "His memory has been spotty ever since he was overcome by Tule Rooter Fever."

"Muss," snapped Willison, "you try our various patiences."

In another corner, his bulk teetering on a small chair (one of six around a felt-covered table) sat Jensen. He flipped out playing cards with his tiny sausage fingers. The other players, which included Mr. Boyle the Constructor, plucked them up grimly.

"Hey, Fat Man!"

"Yes, Thommy?"

"You must have heard of the Order of Ancient and Lucid Druids."

J.D.D. Jensen scowled, although I don't think too many people would have noticed. His visage was mostly moustache, grog-blossomed nose and tiny eyes made bleary by drink, so it took a fair acquaintance with the man to recognize mood shifts. But I saw him scowl, although I attributed it to his poker holdings. Jensen squeezed out three duckets and tossed them aside scornfully. "Ancient and Lucid Druids," he muttered. "Rings no bells."

"They are a very powerful organization of rich old men. They are running the show out here, and I know that for the very good reason that they told me so."

"They exist," said Thespa Doone, who was sitting on my other side. She was dressed in her regular evening wear, which consisted of oversized men's clothing, stuff that would have been disdained by many a farmboy back in The Confluence. Thespa drank distilled water, and not very much of that, because, she once told me, there was no process that could eradicate microzobes. Thespa would speak that way, and it had the effect of making me feel a little nervous. "They exist, all right," she repeated.

"Oh, Thespa," said C. W. Willison, "we all of us know that you lack any capacity for disbelief. It is my opinion that during the glory days of your whistling, dear gill, that you suffered a blow to the skell."

"I don't know how you could have failed to spot them," I said earnestly, and part of my earnestness stemmed from the fact that Thespa was now in this with me. "They wear peculiar outfits, blue robes with stars and moons and such all over them."

"Damn you, Jed," barked Mr. Boyle the Erector. "Swear to God, you're cheating."

"Harsh and hasty words, Boyle," said Jensen, and he gathered in a sizable amount of cash money from the center of the poker table. "And, may I remind you for the umpteenth time, my name is not *Jed*. Some believe it is so, but this misconception is based on a spectacularly inept reading of my name by none other than Buffalo Bill Cody, who gazed upon the cover of my first book concerning his adventures, *Hunter on the Plain*, and aloud rendered my name *Jed Jenkins*."

"Well," demanded Boyle, "what the hell is your name? If I'm going to accuse a man of being a cheat, I like to get his name right."

A gun appeared in Jensen's fat hand, a tiny thing with a pearl-inlaid handle, and he pointed this in the direction of Boyle's large head. "*Jensen* was taken from a dry-grocer's in Baltimore. The initials *J.D.D.* I chose for the sound, the rhythm, the mystery. I will not tell you the name my mother gave me."

Mr. Boyle the Builder was not as alarmed by the Derringer as you might have thought, so I surmised that this was not the first time it had been produced over ducats in the Salon. He gathered up the cards and tossed the deck toward the next dealer.

"I've attended their functions," said Thespa quietly. "I've whistled for them."

"Oh!" said Caspar. "Now *this* has the ringy-ding of authenticity. There is a secret society of old codgers, and Miss Doom is their whore."

"Prick," said Thespa.

"That is very ungentlemanly of you," said I.

Willison waved his hands before his eyes. "I see it now. Thespa stands before them nekkid. They kowtow and genuflect and tug at their wee-willy-woogies."

"Mr. Willison," I said, "you'd better get started on your apologizing."

"Listen, Miss, do me a favor? Lick the shit out of my arse-end."

"All right, I've had enough." I rose up on to my feet and adopted a pugilistic stance. Willison simply flicked the leg that lay draped across the other, and hoofed me in the pills. I gasped and my knees quivered, but I managed to remain standing.

Willison looked up at me, his blue eyes half-covered by dark and drunken lids. "All right, Messy-boy. If it is a tussle you want, it's a tussle you'll get." Willison rose to his feet, surveyed my pugilistic stance briefly, scratched the back of his head, and then smacked me lightly, almost gently, in the mouth. "Protect your face," he whispered. "Surrender your body, cede and relinquish your guts and your precious pearls, leave me at 'em. But don't let me mark up your beautiful face."

I swung wildly and connected with the side of Willison's head. For a fellow who went on so about protection, he didn't put up much. C. W. Willison reeled away, tripping over a divan upon which some people were knotted in goatish embrace. He rose up with his face twisted gruesomely — and this was especially gruesome, given how the thin flesh was stretched across to begin with, tight as a drumhead — and blood trickling from his nose. I did not understand how I'd bloodied his nose by connecting with his cheek. I did recognize that Willison's eyes belied fury and rage, that they remained still as a mountain lake in August. I did not have much time to reflect on this, howsoever, because Willison had reared up with an ugly-looking Mexican blade flowering out of his left hand. He commenced the herky-jerky gesticulation that had characterized his career as a movie actor, and I backed into the center of the room mostly so that the many onlookers wouldn't get stuck and poked because of me.

And as I wondered how best to proceed — there had to be some better route than the prissy leaping about I was doing — Willison whispered, "Knock the fugging thing out of my hand."

I did so even as he whispered the sentence, and to this day I don't know whether it was my idea or his, or if what he said was a command or a taunt, but I back-armed his knife hand and it sprang open. The blade arced high and landed in the middle of the poker table. Then I brought up a roundhouse from somewhere near the floor and my fist met Caspar Willison's pointed chin; to this day I believe he moaned, "Veddy gude," even as he slumped to the floor.

Chapter 9

"The city of Tenochtitlan," Thespa Doone said, "with a population of a quarter million, was one of the world's largest cities in the early sixteenth century." I nodded, because if I didn't keep my head moving at least a little I was gone to the realm of Morpheus. I sat on the wooden chair in Thespa's windowless room with my elbows digging into my knees, my hands laced into a studious little chin-cup. "Their civilization was very advanced. They were exquisite artisans with precious metals. They designed intricate and delicate feather ornaments. They composed poetry. At sites such as the Temple of Huitzilopochtli, architects raised some of the finest stone structures in the world."

I looked right at her lips, like a deaf man, hoping for facilitation.

I could write some about those lips, because although you might think you've seen them, you have not. You have seen Thespa Doone as she made herself for the Flickers. The Thespa Doone that stood before Billy Bittner's camera was a strange and other-worldly creature. The lips were black as pitch, and seemed to be made with a straight-rule. The face was chalk white, the only color coming from the eyes, and it was such a deep muddy brown that it hardly signified. And her hair was japanned, because

Thespa had her theories about photography, which as she would tell you (constantly) meant *writing with light*, so Thespa designed herself so she either sucked in all the light or cast it all away.

Each day, immediately after C.W. Willison had studied the sun and muttered sadly that the light was going yellow, Thespa would cleanse her face. Mrs. Moorcock, her mother, would hurry over with cold cream, a scrub-cloth, pumice stone and a basin of warm water. Thespa would work with fury, believing that she was rubbing away dead and contaminated skin cells. As she wiped the make-up from her neck she would tear away whatever garment covered her upper body, often whilst the cowboys stood nearby smoking cigarettes and laughing. To the credit of the fellows, they didn't as a rule gawk, except perhaps Bodnarchuk. A few times I asked Thespa about this propensity, and she fabricated an answer about the familial nature of thespianism, about how there was no need for modesty before your brothers and sisters. I knew that she had no idea there were carnival boys nearby, because Thespa's ability to block out the world was singular.

By the way, if I jerk away abruptly during this chapter, it is only because I am determined to write about Thespa Doone, and it is necessary to do some hard pulling at the reins or else I'll spend half the day lying down on the cot. So, the thing is, Thespa would scrape off the make-up, and the skin underneath would emerge, oddly colorful. Maybe this was just the contrast, maybe it was exaggerated by the harsh pumice, but Thespa's skin was splashed with freckles, and some things too large to be called freckles, but call them anything else around Thespa at your peril. And her skin was all sorts of reds and pinks; as much as she avoided sunlight, her skin seemed to drink it in. Once, we rented a cabin on a summer's day and went skinny-dipping at high noon. We were no more than fifteen minutes in the open air, yet Thespa managed to sunburn her bottom and that's it I'll be right back.

"Yet in other respects, the Aztecs were surprisingly backward. They had no alphabetic writing, only pictograms. No metal tools. Neither draft animals nor wheeled transport."

What I know of Thespa's early life comes mostly from Mrs. Moorcock. Thespa never spoke to me about anything that touched her life, she preferred to deliver second-hand stuff from various volumes of history that littered her room, the pages dog-eared, the covers scuffed and torn. Thespa was miserly with her true thoughts and feelings, and I only knew she was having them because she'd fall utterly silent and stare at shadows.

To gather the information from Thespa's mother, I had to spend many hours sitting in her tiny room at the White Owl Hotel. This was not a pleasant pastime. For one thing, Mrs. Moorcock seemed to have a perfumery operating out of her closet, and the chamber was rife with odor of such force that my eyes watered and my nose dripped like a broken faucet. Also, her little dogs attacked my ankles with yipping fury, and as many times as I hooked my boot under their bellies and flipped them away, they'd be back, their little teeth sharpened slightly.

All this I endured over and over again, because Mrs. Moorcock was not the most reliable narrator. My basic rule of thumb was, if I heard the same thing three times, it was likely to be true, regardless of how many conflicting and contradictory things I heard in the meantime.

Mrs. Moorcock was an actress in her youth. Coincidentally, she had once played Ophelia to Nolan Tweed's stooped and twisted Hamlet, although the experience did not drive her mad, as it did my mother. (My mother isn't crazy in that she should be strait-jacketed and locked in The Asylum, but she's gone away beyond eccentricity, and there are many rabid religious cranks who won't go anywhere near her.)

Thespa's father, Professor Moorcock, was, I believe, a man not unlike my own. They both spent much of their time envisioning the future, although my father walked a more theoretical path, confined to his porch chair because of temperament, also, his athletic bulk, which generally rendered him ham-fisted and clumsy. Professor Moorcock was a smaller man, and his fingers were long, thin and delicate. This is surely where Thespa gets her hands. It was also from her father that Thespa acquired some of her stranger notions, because Professor Moorcock (the "Professor" was auto-bestowed) was forever experimenting in the Realm of Science, searching for such wonders as the Shadow of Sound and Proof for the Corpuscular Theory of Light. Amongst many other things, Professor Moorcock was intrigued by the manner in which Icelandic

Crystal shattered light, spilling all the colors out its back-end, and it occurred to Moorcock that if that shattered spectrum could be re-ordered and then re-*assembled*, well, I amn't sure what he thought would happen, but he spent much of his time trying to create this Antiprism, and Thespa has in her possession an early attempt, something that looks like a lump of coal putting on airs.

Professor Moorcock was a huge New York Giants fan, his favorite player being Turkey Donlin, the fellow who larked about with showgirls and had a problem with the bottle but gave it all up for true love, marrying that Broadway belle, Mabel Hite. You can't say enough good things about true love, and that's from a fellow cooling his heels in a Federal Penitentiary, waiting about for an Eternity in the fiery pits. Anyway, also on that Giants Nine was Bonehead Merkle, he who forgot to touch second base in that famous pennant-deciding game, but also, it was Bonehead Merkle who fouled one off whilst Professor Moorcock sat in the front row behind the first base line with his seven-year-old daughter beside him. Thespa — I'll name her Gladys for a bit, as she was called back then — was bored, not especially baffled by the rules of the game, in that she had no reason to believe they made any sort of sense. If these men liked to toss about a ball, hit at it with a stick and then set off rather arbitrarily around a cinder-covered field, that was their business. However, Professor Moorcock spent a great deal of time explaining the intricacies of the game to Gladys, and he was doing so — perhaps it was the third strike rule, or some equally mystical bit of arcana — when Merkle line-drove a fouler, which smashed into the side of the Professor's head and killed him. The Professor emitted neither gasp nor grunt, just hushed up abruptly and for a time Gladys thought that he himself had become confused about the regulations, but then he made an odd whistling sound and slumped forward. A vendor misunderstood and threw a bag of peanuts at him.

Fred Merkle attended the funeral, so Mrs. Moorcock told me, a big gangly boy who wept throughout the service and then, invited back to the Moorcock household, singlehandedly devoured all of the foodstuffs.

"Commoners and slaves were given the honor of impersonating gods. They were lavished with care and attention. Then, with great ritual, their hearts were cut out. They were sometimes flayed, and the priest would don a coat of human skin."

Thespa had already discoursed upon the importance of public baths to the Romans and the British Monarchy, its Queens in particular. After the fracas with Caspar W. Willison — he had eventually reared up off the floor, bleary-eyed and contrite, kissing Thespa's fingertips and gripping my shoulder with his cold bony hands — Thespa and I had walked upstairs to her windowless room. She lit candles, saying, "Did you know Queen Victoria was only eighteen when she ascended to the throne?"

"No, ma'am," said I, and I sat on the one chair in the room, taking off my half-sprouted velveteen top hat and playing with the brim. Thespa sat down on the side of the bed, very erect, but as she droned on she reclined gradually, first throwing her arms behind her (the hands appearing to be wrenched painfully backwards), then going on to one elbow, twisted around so she could stare through the weak flickerlight at me, and by the time of the Aztecs she was lying down, her arms folded up behind her head, her boots toe-pried off and flung across the room. She had loosened her clothing.

Soon after Professor Moorcock's demise, Gladys discovered her singular talent. She learned to emit a whistle of such piercing purity that a Mason Jar would sing along. She soon began to imitate birdcalls, capturing perfectly the odd trills, the huge leaps between intervals — Thespa once said to me that anyone can whistle, but very few can negotiate the intervals. She could turn quite technical on the subject of whistling, as befits one of the great whistling prodigies of the age. Mrs. Moorcock avers that the young girl could actually draw birds to her, both wild and house-tamed. (This became part of the act, of course, Gladys would whistle center-stage and birds would fly to her and alight upon her; but they were trained pigeons, and birdseed was hidden upon her young body.) Then Gladys the Wonder Whistler began to whistle songs, at first little tunes and airs, but in a few months she was up to Bach and Beethoven and all those fellows.

When Gladys Moorcock was a teenager (her act had become somewhat rarified — the birds she imitated were extinct, the music she whistled was odd fare from Scandinavian and Russian drug addicts), Mrs. Moorcock re-married. The groom was Sam Crane, the former New York Giant, who had become a sportswriter with the New York *Journal*. It was Sam Crane who brought the women out to California, because Sam was a friend of Mr. Inge, the man that owns The World.

I suppose I should have mentioned Mr. Inge before now, but it is frightful hard to work in some pieces of information. Mr. Inge was ancient and so wrinkled that I cannot give a detailed physical description. He had about fourteen white hairs all told, half of which sprouted from his scalp, the others tumbling from his chin and nostrils. Mr. Inge bought The World some years before the turn of the century and had planned to raise beefalope, a cross between a cow and an antelope, which, being therefore agile and sure-footed, could graze on mountain-top and cragface. It was misguided thinking, and the only new creature that came from the interbreeding was a two-headed calf that lived four days before dying.

One day a Wild West Show, complete with horses and buffalo and trick riders and a long string of covered wagons, asked permission to winter on the land. Mr. Inge then had his one and only good idea — he hired the works, twenty-two hundred bucks for the season.

When the Flickers first got going, as you likely know, most of the cranking was done out in New Jersey. Inge let it be known that he had land, animals and good weather in abundance out in sunny California. The moviemen started to come, and it wasn't long before Mr. Inge was one of the richest men in the country.

From time to time, Mr. Inge hobbled his way up to the Salon. He enjoyed the company of young men, and regularly made advances upon me. During my career in the Flickers, I became worldly and sophisticated to the extent that I refrained from cold-cocking Mr. Inge, and once I even let him hold my hand as he drifted off into one of his fitful little naps, sitting in an easy chair and visited by bad dreams.

Sam Crane quit newspaper work and came out to California, to try his hand at writing scenarios, although he could not get his mind off baseball. The Cowboys and Indians always elected to decide their differences on the diamond. The Indians were given to dirty tactics, brush-back pitches and such, but it availed them naught, because the White Men had grit, fortitude and determination. They even turned a couple of these; Christy Mathewson came out here to appear in *Masterson on the Mound*. Apparently Christy did pretty well, all blond hair and good health, and while he pretended to be Bat Masterson, Bat Masterson (another friend of Mr. Inge's) stood beside the crankman watching carefully. Masterson was grey, wrinkled and fat, and mostly made his living as a boxing referee. He thought Mathewson did very well, although we'll never know because the picture burned up a couple of weeks later.

Sam Crane had his fill of Hollywoodland after a few months, and he went back to New York City and his beloved Giants. Mrs. Moorcock and her daughter remained behind, not so much due to the mother's wishes — Mrs. Moorcock doesn't seem to know, or care, where she is — but because Gladys needed to be near the sea. For this is when she first conceived of her notions of *al fresco* bathing, how the endless roiling ocean could peel off the patina of death that each day brings. At dawn, her arm held to the side with adolescent awkwardness, the naked Wonder Whistler would enter the water.

It was around this time that there showed up at The World a young man with an oddly shaped head, large and lumpy at the crown, pointed and hard at the chin. The man owned strange blue eyes. He had been both a player and an author for the stage, and when he first came to The World he had nothing but disdain for movies. He wore genteel riding clothes and spoke in an oddly civilized manner, that is, he seemed to come from a very odd civilization. He began to crank out two-reelers, and rapidly became the most important film director in The World. Mrs. Moorcock brought the sixteen-year-old Wonder Whistler to him.

"Doesn't that sound like a sweet deal?" Thespa asked in a manner which Hartrampf assures me was rhetorical and not requiring an answer, which is fortunate because I had none to give. "You get to impersonate a god. You get to wear a headdress made of feathers from the parrot, macaw and quetzal bird. All they want in return is your perfect flesh." Thespa laughs at this, a cruel laugh, such as when children laugh at the infirm or unsightly.

Mind you, Thespa Doone did not immediately assume the rank of primary female player. Lily Lavallée had that position locked up. Thespa began playing the Other Woman, the Temptress and Siren, in such films as *Flower of the Desert*. The story, penned by the Fat Man, goes something like this: a young fellow (portrayed by Manley Wessex) whose mother has recently passed over (and you can read the grief in Manley's eyes, except now we know what he likely was was so hung over that his eyes steamed like two little ingots dropped in the snow) who is affianced to a wholesome girl, played by Lily. She is so damn wholesome that the mere proximity of a man sends her into paroxysms and tizzies. So when Manley tries to give her a little kiss, she balks, and icily sends him forth to get his mind, and other bodily parts, right. He rides off into the desert, where a Being appears, a Medicine Man or Witch Doctor or something far more diabolical.

Our man Manley has Visions, which could have something to do with the drink the Shaman gives him, or might just be his brains on simmer underneath the sun. Amongst them is a Vision of Thespa Doone.

She comes with the descent of the sun, which sinks into the dunes behind her. The last dying rays scissor through the material of her robe. Thespa's body is silhouetted with a draughtsman's precision, all of the contours and hard edges. She is seen at a distance, briefly, and then suddenly her face fills the screen. The edges are darkened, forming a soft oval to hold her image. And it's just now come to me that Thespa *is* the Antiprism, that she gathers up the broken shards of the sun and throws them back in a new order.

In the tiny vaudeville houses and theatres, in the tents, *in the caves*, men squirmed and tried to find a more comfortable position. And although they all were resigned to going back to their dreary domiciles, they trained their eyes on poor befuddled Manley and screamed silently, *Listen, fella, there's no reason for you to hurry home.*

I watched this scene as it was being filmed. I was naked, except for a loincloth rendered out of feral pigskin. I was filthy and held no regard for personal hygiene. My hair was long, greasy and gnarled as old oak roots; my hands shook from rum-sickness. I watched from behind a great rock and when it was all over I crawled back to my cave.

"When the young woman came forward to be executed, she would be naked, wearing only a gold headband, fashioned into an eagle holding a serpent in its talons."

My left foot slipped from my right knee and hit the floor with a thud. My head jerked up, I hummed with evident interest and grinned at Thespa Doone.

"Tired, Thom?"

"Oh, no. Although, you know, I suppose I should get on back. The sun surely rises early."

"Have you read the new Scenario?"

"No, ma'am. Mr. Willison didn't give me one."

"We are newlyweds."

"Newlyweds, you say."

"We should look as though we've spent the evening in coition."

"Ma'am?"

"Don't call me *ma'am*."

"Thespa, then."

"Don't call me Thespa. Call me Gladys, the Wonder Whistler. Take off your clothes, Thom Moss."

Thespa — Gladys — pulled at her oversized newsboy's clothing, shook it off her body and was naked. She sat up with her back held unnaturally straight, which lent her breasts a certain, um, Old Man Hartrampf suggests *impudence*, but Hartrampf wasn't there, his five-dollar words are useless to me now. "Your turn," she said. "I want to see your body, Thom Moss. Why did you work at it so hard if you only want to keep it covered?"

I reminded myself of all those things Kingsley Palmer had told me about the God-Glory of the Unveiled Corpus, I recalled the evenings in the bunkhouse when I'd sat around in the buff-bare playing cribbage with the fellows. It didn't seem to help. When I'd removed my shirt the air felt too cold, I shivered and was covered with goosebumps. Then I pulled off my boots — Thespa lay back down, smiling at me — and then my trousers, and there was Jolly Roger all a-grin, much as he is now, and I'm going to have to take that little fellow in hand but I'll keep writing, even if the paper skitters about the desktop without my left arm pinning it down, so I arose, naked in the night, and I approached Thespa Doone, and she was suddenly all motion, and before I could lie down on the bed she swung her legs around and stopped me, her hands gently pressing on my hips, and she placed her dark lips to my, my, I have no hand with which to consult Mr. Hartrampf, this is none of his business anyway, *cock*. And I stared down and the image was seared into my memory, and then she rose up, standing on the bed, until her sex, alive and hungry, presented itself before my eyes, and I understood what I was to do although I had never done it and would have put mighty long odds on ever doing it. Thespa lazily swung one leg over my shoulder, and I felt carefully along the haunch and took the meat of her buttock into my hand. And then somehow she swung the other leg up and over, and I was buried in her, and we were reeling about the room, my fingers digging desperately into her backside, and I continued with my lover's labor until Thespa, panting above, gave forth a short cry and leaned back, which was a huge mistake, and we collapsed and missed the bed by just a few inches. I clambered up and eased into her, and though I was not a virgin, neither had I ever truly done it before, and she felt so perfect, my little fellow had found his true home and he never wanted to leave.

Chapter 10

After Thespa and I made love (which opened a hole in me, saddled me with a thirst I could not slake) and slept peacefully, albeit briefly, we left the White Owl and entered The World.

Directly across from the hotel, in the middle of the dirt street, Mr. Boyle the Builder had constructed the stage–set, which was basically a room except he'd left off half the roof and one of the walls, allowing the insides to be brightened by the sun. This particular room was a kitchen; there was a table, a sink over in the corner. The pipe from the stove rose into the air and connected with nothing.

Willison stood staring into this strange room. He waved at no one in particular and shouted, "I want a fire in that stoove!"

"Sure," said I, crossing over hand-in-hand with Thespa, "it's only about ninety degrees out here."

"Out here has nothing to do with in there, Mess," muttered Willison. "In there, dawn has just arrived and kicked Mother Night in her dimpled funny. So she has departed, leaving behind her bone-chattering chill." Caspar Willison spun on his heels and shrieked with fearful rancor. "Bittner! You have yet to set the marks!"

Billy Bittner, the ancient Georg and the young boy Welkin, were busy with their camera, checking the ground glass and pressure pad, and Bittner muttered a demurral to that effect. Willison grew quiet then, although he was just as easy, as painful, to hear. "Well, lookee, Bittner. I believe it was Galileo or some other ginny faggot who suggested that the sun remained constant whilst our little gloob flew around it. To this I say, goat–balls. The World stays still, I stand at the middle of it, the sun flies through the sky altogether too quickly and you waste my fugging time. Now set the sidelines."

Theo Welkin stepped into the strange kitchen holding a long stick with a piece of chalk attached to one end held gingerly between his thumb and forefinger. He moved about the kitchen, tripping over the furniture, whilst Bittner, crouched down behind his camera, shouted, "Right. Right. Forward. Back. Left. *Gone.*" And when Bill Bittner shouted *Gone*, Theo Welkin loosed his hold on the stick, dropping it to the floor where it left a chalk mark. They did this four times, at which point the ancient Georg mounted the stage, a hammer in one hand, his wrinkled mouth full of nails. I believe the way things worked in theory, Georg would simply espy each chalk mark and drive in a nail, but the way it turned out in actuality, he would wander blindly about for a bit, then Theo Welkin would call out helpful directions, which got muffled by Georg's ear-hair, and he would wander about just as blindly but a little more quickly, finally Theo would lead him by the hand to each mark, and Georg would drive in a nail, much of the downward hammer force being supplied by gravity. When, finally, there were four nails driven into the planks, Welkin stretched a string from one to the next, so that on the floor of the make-believe kitchen was a strangely shaped box.

Then Caspar Willison stepped forward, touched me lightly on the shoulder. "D'you see that, Mess? If you step outside that box, firstly, I shall murther you, secondly, and far worse, you will disappear from the camera's unblinky eye. All right! Let us begin. Scene One. Doomestic bliss. The young couple has spent the night rutting like pegs. They are naught but elbow sores and chafed bummies."

"Huh?"

"Mess. Sit down at that kitchen table. Rule the manly domain! Thespa, gill, get up there and scrub dushies."

"Dishes?"

"Those of us who eat use circular pieces of china to hold the fud. When they get too crumbly and besmirched, we toss 'em in a sinkful of suds. Now git!"

Thespa hiked her skirts, rolled up her sleeves and approached the sink as if she meant to do it damage. She had to pass young Welkin on the way. He screwed up his pimple-ravaged face into a leer; he winked a dark eye, and the front of his trousers began to roil. Thespa merely returned a brief but friendly smile.

"Mess," said Willison. "What ails you, Muss? You've gone all strange."

"Now," said I, collecting myself. "What exactly is it you want me to do?"

"Don't know yet."

"Shouldn't we figure that out?"

"Well..." Willison raised his hand, placed it to his pointed chin and pulled. I could see bones working beneath paper–thin skin. "I know! You could be rubbing your shin, trying to ease the pain—"

"You're about to kick me, aren't you?"

"Congrats, Muss! You've just become an actor."

So I mounted that stage, sat down at the kitchen table, and stared forward like an idiot.

"Veddy gude," said C. W. Willison.

"Hey," muttered Bittner, staring through the viewer of his camera. "Is that how Thespa's going to be standing?"

Thespa was busy at the sink, and while there were no dishes in the sink, nor water, she was sending up a lot of bang and clatter.

"If she was not going to be a-standing that way, Bully-boy, I would have told her elsewise."

"Yeah, but I can't see her face."

"Can't see that lovey face? Those dark eyes, those poutly lups, those succulent nares? Good."

Thespa muttered something, at least, I was at the time fairly certain that she'd done so, but here in the Cahuenga Federal Penitentiary, I am revising my opinion. I've noticed that several times in these pages I've written that, *Thespa muttered something,* but I amn't sure now that she ever did. After all, she was not one to mutter if she had something to say. My theory is now that when Thespa was angered her whole body would snap like a plucked guitar string, and produce a low growl.

"If we see her face," explained Caspar W. Willison, "it will be
Thespa Doone doing dushies. Yes? If we see unly her back and
arms, it will be every gill in the audience doing dushes. Right.
Mess, d'ya have a peep?"

"Hmm?"

"D'ya smuck a peep?"

"No, sir. I enjoy the occasional cigarette, but I try not to over-
indulge, so as not to impair my sense of smell or harm my capa-
bility for respiration. You should hear King Palmer on the subject,
Mr. Willison. God did not render the glorious fleshly bellows so
that they might be clogged and contaminated—"

"For fug's sake, Mess. Don't communicate with me. Answer my
question."

"I don't have a pipe."

"Get the biboon a peep."

It seemed like no sooner was the command given than someone
stuck a pipe in my hand; there were already licks of smoke curling out of the bowl. I placed it in my mouth, puffed on it, and as I
wondered what I was smoking, surely not tobacco, Billy Bittner
turned the crank and made the opening shot for that film, *A Fate
Worse Than Death.*

Caspar C. Willison was a physical culture faddist, his favored form
of physical activity being pugilism. Indeed, most days, immediately after calling the final fade-out, Willison would march over to
a boxing ring that Boyle the Constructor had made behind the
White Owl Hotel. There he would spar with various moon-faced
hulkers, as I shall relate in the pages to come. Whilst he was actually directing a motion picture, however, Willison had various
other activities. For example, he usually had two Indian clubs
nearby, and when he had a minute or two he often grabbed them
and commenced swinging. The clubs would fly over and about his
head, between his legs. He would turn huge opposing circles with
them, and delighted in seeing how closely he could fly the clubs
together without collision, how nearly he could force the two
objects to occupy the same small bit of space. There was also
shadow-boxing, and Caspar Willison beat up on more poor shadows than any man that ever lived.

Another thing he did was dance. On that morning, between

shots of Thespa toiling at the dishes and me turning various
shades of green (grey on the film, of course) Caspar would wheel
away, his little feet working like parts of a machine, tiny and precise movements which circled him around the dirt street. "D'you
know this one?" he screamed. "This is the latest latest! It's called
the *Très Moutarde!*" Willison stopped suddenly and stared at
Thespa and myself. "Oooh," he said quietly. "I am goose-
bumpled. I've had a little bit of genius blast into the noogin. You—
two—" His words came out this way, heavy and evenly spaced,
like soldiers marching off to their death. "You—two—shall—
dance."

I will bound ahead a bit if I may, and tell you about the Premiere,
which took place about a month after we filmed *A Fate Worse
Than Death.*

   This was in Hollywoodland itself, and afforded the opportunity
for my first visit to that strange place. We drove up from The
World in a fleet of fancy cars. Willison and Lily Lavallée rode
together in a Locomobile. There was a huge machine that held
the Fat Man and Foote, a Lanchester 28, specially imported from
England due to its size and subsequent ability to hold fat men.
There was an Italian Marchand that carried Mr. Inge and some
nameless catamite, a boy with a face of tallow and an overly complicated hair arrangement. Then there was a Marmon Landaulet
— "The Mechanical Masterpiece" — that carried me and Thespa
Doone. Up ahead sat a driver, but he was obscured behind a sheet
of pebbled glass, and stared steadfastly forward besides, so I got it
into my mind that perhaps Thespa and I might have some sport,
you understand. Thespa wore a satin dress that cascaded and
folded over her body, and there were few folds on the upper part,
and you could see her body when she leant forward, when she
raised her arms. I reached across and slipped my hand between
the pleats, I wrapped it around her breast and felt her nipple
stiffen, which I thought was a good sign, except when Thespa
turned to look at me she had turned to ice. I took my hand away
slowly.

   "Brother," I muttered, "are you moody."

   "I'm not moody," Thespa said. "I just don't feel like fucking in
the cab of an automobile. *Moody* is someone who has no control

over their emotions. I don't have many emotions, and those that I do have are under control, aren't they, Mess?"

"Look, my name is not *Mess*."

"Caspar calls you *Mess*, so that is your name."

"Caspar Willison is not God."

"Oh?"

"Well, this is going to be a pleasant little journey."

"Ride with Lily on the way back. She'll sex you."

"I don't want to ride with Lily."

"Ride with Mr. Inge. He's always in the mood."

"Let's just watch the scenery."

Thespa turned away rather regally, and we didn't speak another word.

I wasn't fond of going out in public with Thespa Doone, although I'm leaping ahead of myself somewhat, as it would take some months to develop into an abiding principle. She dressed oddly to go outside, donning a theatrical toque and various draperies, usually rendered from the thinnest and most sheer of fabrics. Thespa seemed to have two reasons for going out. One was, the smoking of cigarettes, the second was, the inspection of various lavatories. She certainly never went out to *eat*, although she liked to go to restaurants sometimes, always in Los Angeles proper. When people came up for autographs, Thespa would continue staring ahead like a deaf mute. I was always very eager, asking, "What's your name?" and "How do you spell that?"

Our caravan of fancy cars ascended a mountain, following one another around a series of bends and turns. The Locomobile was in the lead, Caspar Willison at the wheel, Lily sitting beside him, although she decided to have a little nap as the automobile crept up the side of the mountain. She slumped over toward Willison and then disappeared from view. The Locomobile had the canopy and windscreen removed, and Willison seemed to relish the breeze on his face. His head jerked and twisted, as though Willison were bathing it in the warm wind and wanted no part of it left untouched. At the top of the mountain his head twisted around so suddenly that I half expected it to complete a circle and come to a stop staring forward once more. Instead it stopped abruptly and was aimed back at the line of cars. Willison lifted a hand and

CALLS:

- Drive with the legs relax up the slide

"Drive, Relax"

- Everyone pulling into their marks. (This helps to balance the boat.)

- "Feel the run on the boat"
  "Excelerate"

- If the boat goes off balance for even 1 stroke demand to get it back this stroke
  "Next stroke, get it back"

- Watch the dip at the catch (with the hands) drop the blade right in.

waved daintily. Lily Lavallée woke up then, rising drowsily from the seat, wiping nap-spittle from the side of her mouth. She waved, too, and then Willison worked the long gear-changers, and the Locomobile — the fastest car in America, as you well know — flew from the mountain and vanished into the mist.

We were discharged onto Vine Street, and I was startled to hear a strange sound, namely, applause. There was a small crowd gathered on the sidewalk outside a theater — a revamped Masonic Lodge, I saw, a disembodied eye carved into the stonework above the entrance — and when I stepped out of the Marmon they had dutifully brought their hands together. They reminded me of the people that gathered round to hear my mother. Most of them were dough-faced and dull-eyed, and would have stopped to listen to anything. One or two were lunatics, dressed in rags, their skin diseased.

I extended a hand toward Thespa, and she leant forward to take it, and she might as well have been naked from the waist up. Thespa made no move to gather in the satin folds, and so she emerged from the Landaulet. Now the small crowd exploded with gasps and hand-claps, and the dull-eyed people were now touched alight with enthusiasm, and there were a few more lunatics mixed in.

Caspar Willison addressed the crowd, and he did what my mother always did, which was to speak more quietly than seemed logical. The crowd missed the first word or two and then hushed up immediately, shuffling forward to get closer to the source.

"—the primary players of my troupe. This is young Thom Moss! Perhaps you recognize the name. He had a long and illustrious career in the rodeo."

"I don't know about how *long* — "

"And this, of course, is Thespa Doone."

Thespa stiffened as Willison spoke her name. Her back went ramrod straight and her breasts pressed against the satin. She stared at the people on the sidewalk, especially deeply into the eyes of the madmen and madwomen.

Then the Fat Man got spit out of the Lanchester, and he bounced on the sidewalk — drunk as a sailor on shore leave — and commenced bellowing. "Do not be frightened, dear ones. Hold hands as you enter the cave. Look only ahead, do not turn around to stare into the bright light!"

"Ah," said Willison. "The scenarists. The hugely famous J.D.D. Jensen, and his young partner, Jefferson Foote."

Jeff followed the Fat Man out of the deep black car. He was wearing that hat, the wide-brimmed affair, and at the sight of the small crowd he blushed a deep red and lightly touched his fingers to the felt. Someone made a photograph then, I don't know who, but I came across the picture in a magazine not long ago. It was a story about Willison and the making of his "masterpiece" (how could they call it that, *Civilization* is not yet finished, Willison is travelling the globe searching for his fourth story) and there was Foote, looking like he'd got caught at something nasty. Across the spread was an image of Thespa, as she will appear in the Flicker, wearing a golden headband and a wash of shadow.

Just as we entered the theater, I noticed seven or eight lunatics who were different from the other lunatics. These held small placards. I managed to read only three: BAN THE FLYING W, said one, another announced THE SOCIETY FOR PEACEFUL SPECIATE CO-EXISTENCE, the last said something about Thom Moss being a heartless bastard.

Inside the theater, everyone was already settled in the seats; not the people from outside, no, there was a whole new breed inside the Masonic Temple, men and women exuding wealth and improbable posterity. Had my mother seen this bunch she would have set her jaw with fierce rigidity and given the Good Book a mighty double–thump. "A little that a righteous man hath is better than the riches of many wicked." Most of the men were very old indeed, and the auditorium hummed quietly, which was their collective and weak-lunged snoring. The women were many years younger than their escorts, and exuded a tawdry healthiness, as though they had been raised on cow's milk laced with gin.

A shaft of white light appeared, and Willison flew into it; he raised his hands for silence, and it was given. "Helloo," he said quietly. "Thanks so much for attending. It is my pleasure to show you some little Flickers we've made out at The World. I trust you find them a not unpleasant afternoon's diversion."

An old hunchbacked man sat down behind a huge organ. He worked the pedals hard and for a moment I thought the instrument was going to take off, like the flying bicycle imagined by my father. Then the hunchback placed his fingers on the keys and music blew throughout the Masonic Lodge.

First up was *A Wronged Man*, scenario by the Fat Man, based on the novella of the same name by the same Fat Man. It was a story about a young boy — portrayed by Manley Wessex, who looks especially bleary-eyed throughout — who is accused of cowardice by the local townfolk. He is accused of cowardice because there was a shoot–out with some banditos ("SHOOT-OUT!!" screams the title-card) in which our man did not participate, owing to a tree limb having fallen on his head in the preliminary stages. When he comes around all of his pals, including me, have been massacred. What I remembered most about turning that particular Flicker is, I won the five dollars, one of the few times I — or anybody else — beat Kingsley Palmer at the Death Game. Every time there was a shoot-out or similar massacre, Willison offered five dollars to the boy who could die in the most compelling and dramatic fashion. To win, it was usually necessary to hurl yourself off the horse, lard-plug guns blaring, and land in a convincingly excruciating crumple. King Palmer made far more money winning the Death Game than he did from his salary as a movie horseman.

But I have to tell you this much, I didn't care that I myself wasn't a bigger deal in *A Wronged Man*. I cared only that this young boy — I hadn't watched but two minutes before I ceased thinking of him as Manley — was ill-thought-of and unjustly so. So when the young boy got it into his head to do a little aveng- ing, I sat forward in my seat and nodded. And when he kicked down the door to the desperados' hide-out I squeezed Thespa Doone's hand, and I whispered "Duck," when Bodnarchuk snuck up with a two-by-four, and I clapped with everyone else as the young boy dealt out white-hot bullets of vengeance (that's what the title–card called them, and that's what I believed they were, even though I *knew* the bullets were only a combination of lard and candlewax fabricated by Mycroft the explosives man) and when a knife was plunged into his valiant heart I struggled with tears and choked on a stone in my throat.

Next up was *A Sound of Battle*, which featured Miss Lavallée as the virgin who gets bespoiled by a group of scurrilous carpetbaggers shortly after the war between the States. Whilst she lies upon her bed, her mind filled with fevered dreams, her brother — Manley once more — goes out to wreak some vengeance. He kills several people — many more than ever had at his sister — including King Palmer, although you mightn't recognize him all in black–face, his cheeks gleaming like the middle of night, his lips washed white and fashioned into a sloppy grin. Manley kills me as I am riding along a trail. There is a shot of me galloping along atop a grey horse. Suddenly, there is a puff of smoke from behind a nearby boulder, the horse crumples, and I fly away and land headfirst in some nearby rocks.

The story keeps shifting from Manley and his slaughter back to Lily twisting about in her bed, and a time or two we even see the dream she's having. In this dream she is tied to an oak tree, and looks to be wearing her costume from *War*, the tiny tunic that serves none of the functions of clothing, and she is being tormented by a man wearing only an animal pelt to hide his private parts. The creature is hornèd and sinewy, wearing a mask made of bird wings. I recognized the pointed chin, the broad forehead and tufted blond hair. I also recognized the title of the Flicker, because my mother often hollered this against the weather and the night: "A sound of battle is in the land, and of great destruction."

Next up was *Redemption*, and even though I knew it was coming, I was still surprised to see the credit for scenario, J.D.D. Jensen and Jefferson Foote. There was no mention of me on the players' card. It named Thespa, Manley and Lily Lavallée, who has a bit as a dead body. That's how the Flicker starts, Lily with a knife sticking out of her bosom. But there was no Thom Moss listed, and I was disappointed to discover that even as I charged into town — my heart bursting, my eyes afire with the glory of atonement — the audience seemed to care more about stupid Manley dangling over the side of the cliff. When he dropped to his doom they gasped. Many wept. When I was hanged, the people cheered and brought their trembling hands together.

At this point I was not overly optimistic about my future in the motion-picture industry. I sat scowling, my arms crossed, and I barely noticed as Thespa's hand snaked over the arm rest and into my lap.

The hunchbacked organist collapsed upon the keyboards and a huge chord thundered throughout the theater. *A Fate Worse Than*

Death began. There was Thespa doing the dishes, at least, there was Thespa's back, and her shoulders shook with what passed for industry, although I knew it was indignation. Then I snapped back in my seat, because I saw my face as large as the world. It filled the entire screen, and my eyes looked kindly and wise. The foul smoke from the pipe clouded around me. The organist drew out a few more chords, which sounded like God clearing his throat, trying to get our attention, and it was at this point that I realized that Thespa was working my shaft through the material of my pants. It was aching, bent up against my cummerbund. Her fingers were playful and light, yet Thespa directed all of her attention to the screen. The hunchback suddenly changed his tune, and a sea–shanty rolled out, as though squeezed from a hundred concertinas. In the Flicker, I stand up and pull Thespa away from the sink. In the theater that day, Thespa closed her fingers hard around me and I was filled with white heat. On the screen, Thespa and I danced, and when I reached across and lost my hand within the satin folds Thespa made no complaint, and my fingers kissed her nipples and then headed down below, and Thespa wore no underwear, and I worked my middle finger into her, and she tightened her hold upon me and my body spasmed, and hers did likewise, and we danced up there in the huge silver dream until Charles Wild Horse and assorted Indians came to commit heinous atrocities.

Chapter 11

I was surprised as hell to see old Charles Wild Horse, for the good reason that we had been separated some months back. There was no way you could have known that; the threads of the narrative here-in have become somewhat unravelled. This is a phrase I remember coming from the mouth of the Fat Man. J.D.D. Jensen often talked to me about authoring; talking about it seemed for him almost as worthwhile as doing it, which he almost never did. Sometimes, after a day of heralding another go at his typewriting machine — "I've got to finish up *The Satyrs of St. Louis*, or whatever the fuck it's called, Thommy" — Jensen and I would repair to his dingy little aerie at the White Owl. "Thom," he'd say, "crack open the rotgut, give us a suck at the witch's nipple." Before long he'd be too drunk to write anything, and he would spend the rest of the evening telling stories that were fanciful, to say the least. He'd lunge for those books of his, *An Encyclopedia of All Things Animate, Housed in Three Volumes.* Jensen would rip them apart and read aloud about some small lizard or bird. He'd keel over halfway through and no writing would be done that night, making it much like any other night in the Fat Man's room.

But it seems that J.D.D. Jensen taught me a few tricks despite himself, for instance, the sorting of narrative threads, and how not to keep them hanging.

The Order of Ancient and Lucid Druids stopped their westward trek at a place called Palm Springs, and the five of us walked away without so much as a thank–you or a fare–thee–well. We stole clothes from assorted washing lines. Some of us fared pretty well. I myself was able to find a nice white shirt and cotton pants; Kingsley Palmer ended up wearing a whale-bone corset and boxer shorts. Kingsley said he didn't mind, in fact, he strutted down the skids of Shantytown with his muscular rumpy sashay greatly exaggerated.

We presented ourselves at back doors and begged for work. We hoed and washed windows and such dismal chores. Wild Horse Charlie claimed that a woman had paid him five dollars for what he used to call the Royal Red Piggy Back, but that did not explain the callouses on his hand, nor the speed and determination with which he fell asleep, snores blasting through his hoof-crushed visage. We slept, by the way, in the shadows of mountains; the air was sweet and felt gentle.

But one morning I was awoken by a strange and terrible sound. I scrambled up on to my feet at the same time my friends did, and that was the moment we all first laid eyes on a tule rooter. Jefferson Foote, who I'm willing to allow was usually the most eloquent amongst us, said, "Holy fuckin' Hannah."

I did learn some Druidical lore on the westward trek. One thing the Ancient and Lucid Druids believe is this: at the beginning of time — which was a lot more recent than some claim, in fact, the Druids put it at October the fourteenth, 7,016 B.C. — all Life was the same. There were no geese, gophers, gazelles or graylings. There were only beautiful young men and women coupling with athletic abandonment. But there was Absolute Darkness on the one hand, and Absolute Light on the other, and rather than embrace one or the other, these lovely young men and women chose to live in the Shadow, and over time they were twisted and transmutated in the smoky netherworld.

And the longer a creature has spent in the shadow, the uglier and more hideous it became, the point I'm coming to being this: whatever transmogrified into a tule rooter was likely there at the get-go, and probably not the most sightly thing to begin with.

The best feature of a tule rooter is its hind legs, which are pretty standard porcine fare, a little bigger maybe, the hooves a little more covered with horny setae. These hind legs probably play some small part in a rooter's locomotion, but I swear I've seen a beast at full bore, his hinders turning like little paddle-wheels and never touching the ground. A tule rooter has a curly tail, too, situated over a sickly-grey slit, shit spilling out most of the time. Next, working toward the head, we have a pair of shoulders, from which sprout forelegs as thick as the boles of trees, and then all of a sudden we're at the head, and there is a damned lot of it. The snout is like the bell of a huge dented trumpet and capable of bone-chilling oinks, that render your bowels watery and bilious. A tule rooter's eyes are huge chunks of coal, thrown from a distance so that they bulge unevenly just above the tusks, which twist like a mountain road, meandering for a length of two feet and more. These great whorly arms of gristle — and this is the first thing the five of us noticed — come to a very sharp point.

A voice said, "You fellows want to grab that fuck-pig for me?" and thence issued forth a strange laugh. A man of improbable size stood nearby, holding a rusted firearm that Mr. Hartrampf might label a *blunderbuss.* It was a long-barrelled affair, heavily butted, and the man had a great deal of trouble handling it, seeing as he was a dwarf. It was the little fellow's apparent intention to level this weapon in our general direction. This seemed far more dangerous than the strange creature in our midst, who wasn't doing much other than blasting sharp gusts of snot-steam into the air.

Well, you know, it wasn't for nothing that I was a famous light-stock rider and rodeo roper. I saw right away that this animal's tusks, as fearsome as they looked, were also his weak point. They were too long, is what I calculated, so I grabbed them near the ends and fell to my right, twisting my shoulders as though executing a tumble-roll. Sure enough, my grip on the outgrown horns gave me enough leverage, and once that huge head got cranked, the rest of the body flipped over. The thing squealed in an ungodly fashion, as if trying to form words, and its legs flapped and beated upon the air. The belly was grub-white, naked pale leather flecked with spots and lesions, its private parts swollen and colored a bright pink.

Mind you, I am just reporting a fleeting impression, because I was at the time lying on the ground and contending with a ton of thrashing tusker. My companions now decided to help out, so Wild Horse Charlie clamped his foot down near where he figured the windpipe would be. Charles Wild Horse grabbed the rear legs, Jefferson Foote the fore, and that beast was taken. After a moment or two it even quieted down and resumed the dreadful puffing.

Then the tiny man came along, placed the end of his old gun on the tule rooter's head, and fired. We were sprayed with blood and little pieces of skull and brain.

Biggar U. Webb was the name of the man who killed that tule rooter, as nasty a little fellow as was ever turned out of Creation. I suspected he was nasty when he kept on firing his blunderbuss, long after the stilling of the pitiful death quivers. We stood some feet distant and wiped away gore and offal. Jefferson Foote said, after about the fifth gunshot echoed through the furzy hills, "Know what? I figure that animal's just about dead."

Biggar Webb stared up at us, Foote in particular.

"Is that what you think? Well, then, you haven't seen one of these fuck-pigs, its throat slit, its heart ripped out, all of a sudden rear up and start skewering. You haven't seen one of those tusks run through a man's belly." Webb fired once more; there was now no head to speak of. Biggar Webb gave what was left of the animal a very tentative nudge with the toe of his boot. I was alarmed to see the back legs, which had survived more-or-less intact, twitch violently. Biggar fumbled with his gun, pointed it at the tusker's hindquarters and blasted. He then seemed satisfied, waving to some nearby vultures as if giving them the all-clear. "God's little chambermaids," he said to us, and those birds descended upon the carcass and began ripping apart tendon and muscle, fighting amongst themselves for the privilege of drawing out the most disgusting bit.

Wild Horse Charlie now asked what we had all been wondering, "What the hell *was* that?"

"Tule rooter," was of course the answer, although Biggar only ever referred to them as "fuck-pigs."

"And," demanded Charles Wild Horse, "who are you?"

He gave his full name, "Biggar Ulysses Webb," and Jefferson

didn't subdue the chuckle quickly enough, and Webb's eyes flashed black.

"What I am is," said Biggar, and he elevated the pitch of his voice somewhat, trying to achieve a grander tone, "the local Wildlife Regulatory Agent. I have been engaged by a consortium of local farmers and landowners to rid the environs of the snorting fuck-pig, er, tule rooter. You men," said Biggar Webb, staring at me in particular, "look to be deft hands. I would gladly make you Wildlife Regulatory Sub-Agents. I would pay you, um, seventy-five cents fuck-pig taken."

"How much do *you* get per fuck-pig?" asked Foote.

"I do not serve on a per fuck-pig basis, sir," answered Webb tersely. "I am a salaried employee of said consortium."

"Do you have," asked Charles Wild Horse, "a place for us to live?"

"That I do," replied Webb. "Follow me to the Wildlife Regulatory Headquarters."

Headquarters turned out to be a cave about four miles away. It was there that I spent the worst of my days, although the Cahuenga Federal Penitentiary is no great joy, despite The Warden's dainty half-sandwiches and dry sherries.

Whilst I dwelt in the cave there was naught within me but desolation. *And they shall go into the holes of the rocks*, the Good Book tells us, *and into the caves of the earth, for fear of the Lord*. I took to drink in a grim and desperate manner, and not a night went by that I did not end passed out with black emptiness filling my heart and mind. Every one of us became an alcoholist, except Kingsley Palmer, who maintained his horribly cheerful ways even when he became a tule-rooter hunter. And I will now write that Kingsley Palmer did me a great service in those days, for as diseased as my spirit became, my body grew in strength. Kingsley insisted that we undergo the Rigors together, and even in the darkness of our cave we would get naked and stand side by side. Kingsley would whisper, "The essence of Corporeal Life is balance — between organ and function, between muscle and nerve, between assimilation and elimination."

What happened was, sometime near the beginning of the last

century, a ship full of wild swine ran high aground near Costa Mesa. The pigs got loose in the yam fields down there, and the sailors chased after them for a bit and then elected to head further south for a bit of Mexican debauch. They likely thought that the pigs would die off in time. The pigs, however, flourished on their diet of sweet potatoes. When the yam farmers went to kill the beasts that were chowing down on their cash crop, they encountered a strange and remarkable creature, fearsome and hard to dispose of, as likely to take off for the mountains as the sea. In open country, the damned thing could beat a horse every time on the gallop. Specialized skills were called for, and that's how come there was a demand for cowboys in that particular region of California.

A typical day of tule rooting went something like this: Biggar Webb would wake us up just before dawn, putting his face to yours, close as a lover's, his exhalation hot with stale alcohol. "Rise and shine," he'd whisper. "Time to slaughter fuck-pigs."

We would rise, dress ourselves in garments rendered out of tule-rooter hide. These garments tended to be of a utilitarian nature. Being as we were never in society, civilized or otherwise, it mattered little what we wore, so in hot weather we would wear loincloths, and on the few days that were not hot — therefore bitterly cold, California knowing no such thing as a happy medium — we would don skirts and singlets. Breakfast would consist of soft-boiled eggs. We never asked where Biggar got the eggs, but it was not from any chicken. They were very large, grey and spackled. It was not unusual for these eggs to have two, even three, yolks.

After breakfast we would go off in search of tule rooters. It would be overstating the case to call this *hunting*. We had no idea where the creatures were likely to be, we could discern no rhyme or reason to their habits. For that matter, we could discern no real habits.

The tule rooters used to find us. We'd be wandering around underneath the sun — our bodies brown and leathery, our lips blistered, our hair sun-bleached almost white as Jefferson's, except his hair had bleached as well and was now so radiant that to look upon it would blind a fellow — and finally Webb would anounce lunch time. Lunch was hard-boiled eggs, those strange eggs. The shells were so thick that sometimes you would have to break them apart using a fair-sized rock. One time Wild Horse Charlie cracked one and a tiny assemblage of bones fell out. They did not appear to constitute a bird-to-be. Charles Wild Horse quickly crushed them underfoot and it was not mentioned again.

Usually, while we would be eating strange eggs, we would hear the muffled grunting, we would feel the tiny blasts of fetid steam, we would meet the eyes of a feral fuck-pig. The beast would let out a terrible squeal and then scamper, and our daily activity seemed designed mostly for the creature's divertment, for we would leap up and the fuck-pig would scoot around the country-side for a while and then disappear. On occasion, occasions we celebrated with what little enthusiasm we could summon, we'd manage to rope or otherwise get a hold of one. Kingsley was fond of dropping aboard tule rooters from a tree or outcropping, I myself preferred the open ground pursuit. We'd pile on the fuck-pig and hold it until Biggar Ulysses Webb arrived with the blunderbuss to shoot its brains out.

We would hack off the skewers and head back to the cave, to a dinner of scrambled strange eggs and Distillate of Wildflower. It was a bitter drink that scraped away your throat and imparted the sort of drunkenness whereby you imagine tiny headless animals scurrying about.

We would lie down upon the ground and soon our hoary snores would explode into the cave, woeful testament to our life.

Toward the end of one day, I crept along the edge of some high-land, a scar that ripped through the world and separated a sea of dunes from pugnacious mountains. This eerie cleft was repeated in the sky above. On one side, black clouds brooded above the rocks, occasionally spitting down hailstones. They ended in a line as uniform as advancing militiamen. On the other side, the sky was empty except for the naked sun preparing to disappear into the sea, a grey-blue line as thick as a harlot's lipstick. I slithered over rocks and various outcroppings, hoping to flush some startled fuck-pig. I recall being particularly hung over that day, my skin beaded with foul sweat. I likely exuded a stench of such force that even tule rooters were keeping away. Because of my grogsickness, I did not immediately react when I heard a voice, the Distillate of Wildflower often giving you Blue Visions, so you might hear the odd voice or even see the Archfiend Lucifer, King of Hell.

"Hurry, hurry!" sang out this voice, although I could just as easily have set it down on paper as, "Hurrah, hurrah!" It is only with hard-earned knowledge that I know it was, "Hurry, hurry! The light is going yellow!" I threw myself behind a huge rock and peered out toward the dunes.

Some distance away stood a small clutch of men, their backs toward me, apparently worrying over a squat bird-feeder. Off to one side was a smallish figure clad in white, although his boots were black, also the thick belt around his waist, also the full holsters that dangled from his hips. He wore a Panama hat, and that's as much as I could see of the fellow, for he, too, had his back to me, staring at rolling waves of sand.

A girl rose up from the earth. She wore a muslin robe, crudely cut and stitched. Behind her, the sun deflated upon the distant ocean, and the last of its light danced through the robe, painting the girl's body black for me to see. She stood for a long time, absolutely motionless, except on one occasion she stumbled forward, perhaps shoved by the merest of breezes. She regained her posture and purchase, and I heard some soft laughter.

"Don't laugh, gill!" bellowed the man's voice, and the figure with the Panama hat pounded his fists into the air. "And stick out your bubs! You look positively boyish!"

The girl stiffened, pressing her breasts against the thinnest of materials.

I became squirmy and uncomfortable, and put a hand under the only garment I wore, a small loincloth rendered from the dried hide of a slaughtered tule rooter.

"Fade out," said the voice, as the ocean swallowed the sun.

Chapter 12

Sometimes we hunted in pairs: Jeff Foote and myself, Wild Horse Charlie and Charles Wild Horse, Kingsley Palmer and Biggar Webb. That last couple might seem unlikely, but in a strange way they enjoyed each other's company. Biggar listened to much of what Kingsley had to say vis-à-vis the human body. "You are stunted on account of cellular disharmony," Palmer might declare as they set off under the murderous sun, both bare-arsed, Palmer with a lariat wound round his rippled waist, Biggar with the blunderbuss slung over his shoulder.

"Do tell," said Biggar.

"God made us all giants. We have only to ingurgitate his Majestic Being."

"Uh-yeah." Webb pulled at his whiskers, removing loopy strands of dried yolk. "Know what, Palmer? I reckon that if I brought the butt of my gun down acrost your foot, it would shatter like a cheap mirror."

"*This* Heaven-wrought foot? Nay, nay!"

On one occasion, Jeff Foote and I wandered far from the cave. The day was especially hot; the sun was pasted to the front of the sky like a postage stamp. We sweated and were burned. On the few occasions that the clouds did drape and hide Phœbus, the bad liquor heaved up goosebumps and doubled us over with dry heaves.

Foote and I did not say much, but I know that we were filled with the same thought, that our adventuring had come to ruination. So we maintained a silence, although this was neither stoic nor philosophic. Our despair was merely too deep for regret.

We wandered the world all day, and as the sun began its descent, Jefferson waved wearily at nothing in particular and said, "Let's get on back, Thom."

Behind Jefferson the sun tore through the clouds, striking the earth in great heavy shafts. Something sat on the horizon, and the sight of it rendered me weak-kneed, and filled me with exultation and dread in equal measure. It is necessary now for me to write about the Frontispiece in my mother's Bible.

The Frontispiece was an illustration for the Temptations of Christ, and the artist had conceived of a single place that contained the desert, the exceedingly high mountain and the holy city. The city sat on top of the mountain, a distant and glorious place of pinnacles and turreted brickwork. The mountain was black stone, its faces sharp and flat. At its foot lay the desert. The sky above was black with clouds, but sunlight broke through in several places, and descending in these resplendent beams were angels. They came down to where Christ lay on the desert sands, there to minister unto Him.

The artist was not too skilled at depicting people, or whatever you choose to call Jesus and the angels. Christ our Lord was a frail man with a few chin-hairs and eyes much too large for his head. He more or less reclined on the ground, propped up on one elbow, his other hand occupied with keeping the corner of a sheet covering his private parts. He was naked, as were the angels. The angels were grown men and women, very muscular sorts, especially about the thigh, as if Kingsley Palmer had instructed them exclusively concerning the *vastus lateralis* and *medialis.* This makes a kind of sense, because the angels were not flying down from Heaven, they were jumping, their legs braced, their arms outstretched for equipoise. The women angels had the merest of breasts and vague shadows below their bellies. The men had tiny willies, small but bloated scrotal sacs. (I'll just mention that Old

Man Hartrampf knows more words for the manly bits and pieces
than I can credit.)

I was never much interested in looking at the angels, even if
they were naked. More's the point, it's not like you want to get
hot and prickly whilst gazing at the Holy Bible, so I always concentrated more on the background. The artist was better at rendering inanimata. He was very skilled at shading, darkening the
clouds and the mountain with dense and furious crosshatchings.

When Jefferson said, "Let's get on back, Thom," I did not
respond. I was staring out over his shoulder and would not be distracted. As a child I had understood that something was not right
about that Frontispiece. It dawned when I was perhaps ten, as I
stared at the modest twin peaks of Sariel and Uriel back in The
Confluence, Ohio. *Mountains did not spring out of barren sand.*
They were urged up, grown like hothouse flowers. From my bedroom window I could see meadow, foothills, forest that thinned
gradually — the Asylum, by the by, was nestled in that sylvan
bosom, far enough that we of The Confluence could pretend it did
not exist — and when it disappeared, the mountains were laden
with snow and draped with misty cloud. I mentioned this once to
my mother, stabbing a finger over her shoulder, pressing it to the
picture of the dark mountain.

"How could there be a mountain like that, in the middle of
nothing?"

My mother jerked in her chair and twisted her neck so that her
face was close to mine, her green eyes moving quickly, searching
my face, almost as though she wasn't sure who I was. My father,
at that exact moment, had a Vision of some force and clarity. I
heard his voice coming from the front porch, accompanied by the
dry creak of his rocking chair. "In the future," he proclaimed,
"men will have teats." My father's voice was clogged with Old
Bell's whiskey.

"God does," my mother whispered hoarsely, "as God wills."

That was my mother's standard answer to questions of this
nature, and did not make a great deal of sense. For one thing, God
hadn't made the picture, some anonymous artist had, some fellow
who thought that angels had bulging thighs and baby genitalia. I
dismissed the matter, or so I thought, but I suppose I'd made a bargain with myself, if not a very binding one. The bargain was: if I

ever saw such a scene, then I would truly know there was a God, for He would have done as He wilt.

And with Jefferson Foote urging me to return to the cave, his face shadowed, light burning all around him, I stared out at the desert. From it, stern, majestic and cut like a diamond, rose a naked mountain.

We had wandered into The World, specifically that section of it where Willison would turn his masterpiece, *Civilization*. The World — or, to give it its proper name, Inge's World Studios — was impossible to fence or mark off. In fact, no one really knew the true extent of the property. Mr. Inge was one of the richest man in California and, everyone agreed, could have as much of the state as he wanted, so long as he steered clear of the waterfront.

I had seen people come Unto the Fold many times. My mother would finish up her sermon, thumping on the cover of her Bible, wearing a hole in the leather until the Good Book looked as battered as an old baseball mitt. My mother's body would jerk back suddenly, convulsed by the Spirit, and then a man or woman would rise, blubbering with ecstasy, and come forward, often on hands and knees, and my mother would regard them, a little disdainfully I often thought, and lay her freckled hand upon their heads and they would be filled with holiness. That is what I prepared to do at that moment, to wail out *Hallelujah*, for I had seen the Hand of God and was consumed and conquered by Sin, but before I could wail out a *huzzah* or *hosannah*, Jefferson Foote sang out, "Holy—" and I thought that he too was about to be Saved, but then he said, "Shit."

The thin desert air was suddenly full of damp muskiness. From behind me came a grunted lament. I knew I was not to be Saved; indeed, judging from the look in Jefferson's eyes, I was about to be skewered like horsemeat.

"Big one?"

"Biggest I've ever seen," Jefferson answered. Foote shook free the rope looped over his shoulder, caught it in trembling hands, and slowly worked out the coils onto the sands. The beast behind me wailed quietly, in a peculiarly tuneful manner. I removed the knife from my loincloth, wiped it across the hide two or three times in a desperate attempt to lend it an edge. "At least," I whispered — Jefferson was working confoundedly slow, his rope had twisted up and he was trying to flick out the kinks — "at least it hasn't started pawing yet."

Naturally, the next sound I heard was cloven hoof upon baked desert. It sounded as though the monster was but inches away. "What's your plan, Jefferson?"

"What's yours?"

"My plan is to get a tusk up the backside. I'm willing to abandon it."

"All right." The rope was now lying at my friend's overgrown feet. "At the count of three, you start running. I'll take up the rope, and with any luck I'll get it shot and pulled just before he catches you."

"Bad plan."

"Yeah, well..." I watched my friends hands tighten around the rope. "It's the only plan we got."

"What if you miss?" I whispered.

"Look at the positive aspects. It's the largest rooter in Creation. Makes for a big target."

The largest rooter in Creation began to rake the ground with grim intensity.

"All right, Foote. I'll go along with your plan."

The tule rooter began to squeal, and I knew enough of the beast's behaviour to know they only squealed during a skewer or a rut. Either way I was off and running. I headed for the distant mountain as hard as I could, my legs and arms wheeling. From behind me came wet, slurpy grunts, the squeal and high-pitched rasp mixed in, so it sounded like a bone-chilling giggle.

Odd as it may seem, what filled my mind right then was the *other* picture I'd found in my mother's Bible. It was not attached to the Good Book like the Frontispiece; it tumbled out as I flipped through the pages looking for stories about Samson and the like, because I was not allowed to read, as was my friend Foote, the books of the fat man Jensen. (And a good thing too, I think, because Jefferson Foote possessed a degenerate imagination.) Out of the Holy Bible dropped a long rectangle of pasteboard. It landed face-down, I know that now, although at first I thought its freight was the small piece of paper glued there, tiny words printed on it:

But when Herod's birthday was kept,
the daughter of Herodias danced before
them, and pleased Herod.

I wondered at it, and it was not for some long moments that I had
a look on the other side. There was a photograph. Actually there
were two identical images side by side. It was a card for a stereoscope, a toy highly esteemed by C.W. Willison. Caspar had a vast
collection of cards, including this one, number 72 in the Grand
View Biblical Vistas Series, entitled *The Dance of Salome.* Did
you know that Salome was fat? Or as close as you can come to
being fat without people making pig-noises every time you take a
step? In the photograph(s) she has not dropped the last veil, it is
stretched too tightly around her waist, obscuring her pudenda. (I
did *not* consult Mr. Hartrampf for that word, at least not recently,
I simply recalled it from an innocent perusal of that particular section.) Salome's breasts are small, given her girth, and essentially
disappeared because her arms are raised high above her head as she
does her dance. On a nearby settee sits Herod, hunched forward,
his chin resting on a bed of knuckles. He appears to be brooding
over some matter of import, such as, why are her arms so short?
Herod is bare-chested and dressed in pantaloons, he has a goatee
and sabre-pointed moustaches.

Speaking of sabre-points, I'm going to get back to me being
chased by the vicious tule rooter. I am getting to be an adept at
this word-smithing, if I do say myself.

I shouted, "Throw your damn rope, Jeff!"

And came his doleful reply, "I did already."

I cut to my right, catching sight of the rooter's blurry hindquarters, so that I could charge back toward Foote. He was very calmly
collecting his limp rope from the desert floor. "You *missed?*" I
screamed.

"Well," he shrugged, all too conversational, "you shouldn't
have planted the insidious seeds of doubt."

The fuck-pig was snorting double-time now, I could feel the
snot-spray on the back of my legs.

"I'm a dead man, Foote. See you on the other side."

"Asooo-*wee!*" Foote dropped the lariat and cupped his boney
hands over his mouth. I didn't know Foote could hog-call, and the

truth of the matter is, he couldn't, but whatever he did it caused
a little ripple in the feral pig's gallop and I could suddenly sense a
little space between the monster and my pale behind. Jefferson
repeated his call and stopped the beast cold, turned him around
and had him charging. Foote's second hog-call went, "A-sooo-
wee—eeuh—uh—aagh!" I spun around and saw Foote turn to run,
and he pivoted and dropped his shoulder, and that's how the tule
rooter's tusk pierced the flesh just below his scrawny muscle.
Foote quickly turned back the other way, tearing his arm free. The
creature slowed to a canter then, turning its huge head this way
and that in search of more man-flesh. I was all of a sudden running
at him from behind, because I had half-baked a plan and only had
a short moment to execute it. I placed my knife between my teeth,
slicing open my tongue, and then I gained on the fuck-pig, dove
over the length of its back, and managed to grab hold of its tusks,
one in either hand. I drove downwards and the tule rooter somer-
saulted, which is what I'd planned, despite the fact that I was
therefore underneath it. It was perhaps not my best-made plan. I
spit the knife into a freed hand and blindly plunged it into the
monster's heart. Warm blood gushed up and geysered, some of it
ran down thick and hot into my eyes, blinding me. I stuck my
knife into the tule rooter, over and over again.

Jefferson's arm was pierced through, but the skewer seemed to
miss any bone or important muscle; Foote could still bend his arm
at the elbow, raise it above his head, and he reported sunnily that
it didn't really hurt. He was in truth rather pleased with his injury,
which seemed to be evidence of *bona fide* adventuring. As we
walked back to the cave, Foote would adjust the tourniquet (rendered with a fresh strip of rooter hide) and invent far more serious
mishaps which seemed to have come within an ace of happening.

"If I had of been two inches to the left and sort of crouched over,
that fuck-pig would have run me right through the brain."

"Yes, sir. You're damned lucky."

"Hey. Imagine if I'd have been standing over a bit and kind of
raised up in the air. I would have been pierced through the
gonads."

"How might you have been raised up in the air, Foote?"

"It's just imagining, Moss."

We were dragging the tusks behind us. Foote insisted on pulling the one with the tip dipped, as he put it, in his *life-juice*.

The only other injury we'd had was when a rooter, a smallish one, stomped on Wild Horse Charlie's toes. But I did remember one thing, namely, Charles Wild Horse had once pricked his forefinger on a tusk, not even attached to the pig at the time. The vultures had done their dance, nothing remained of the rooter but pinkish-with-blood bone, gore-flecked skull and the grizzled outgrowths. We went forward to claim the tusks, which we needed in order to claim the seventy-five cents. Charles Wild Horse scratched the tip of his finger. It but barely bled.

That night, Charles Wild Horse woke up all feverish. He stumbled out of the cave into the bitter chill of the desert night, delirious. He could not stop whispering, frantically, the signs that would mark the end of the world: trees would die from the top, the fish would perish in the lakes, people would huddle together in caves and gaze at shadows. Charles Wild Horse's forefinger puffed up like a party balloon. The end finally split open and the poison spilt out. He collapsed upon the ground and was better the next morning.

Biggar Webb looked at Foote's injury and shook his head mournfully. Webb had no great affection for Jefferson, yet the look in his demented face was truly saddened. "Tell you what," he said to me. "About four mile distant due east is a farmer name of, name of, name of, never mind what his name is. Go over there, steal a horse. Ride your friend into town, take him to see Dr., Dr., Dr. Whatever-the-fuck. Do it quick."

"You afraid something might happen to his arm?"

"His arm," responded Webb, "is buzzard grub. But if you hurry, you just might save his sorry life."

Chapter 13

Jefferson Foote went mad long before we got to the doctor's. At first, it resembled a kind of drunkenness. Foote was spread across Kingsley Palmer's wide shoulders, where he giggled and sang *Church in the Wildwood.* Soon he began puking, milky white bile that burned through his mouth and nostrils. Kingsley Palmer hushed and soothed him. We never did steal any farmer's horse. Palmer carried Jefferson Foote all the way to town, at a trot, no less, and the doctor later said that Kingsley likely saved Jeff's life. Anyway, Foote puked until there was no more, and then he was convulsed by the dry heaves. I convinced myself this was due to the Distillate of Wildflower, but I know now that a feral pig's tusk is just about as poisonous as a baby diamondback, that it carries every ill and affliction known upon the earth — *Sore sicknesses,* as my mother promised the disdainful passers-by if they failed to cleave unto the Word.

As Jefferson's arm puffed up and turned purplish, he grew calmer. It was then that his madness was at its worst. He started to babble, somehow trapped in the pages of his dime novels. *"Gunfire lit the azure sky,"* he whispered. *"It was the Doogan clan, godless men who knew no law save the law of the six-shooter!"*

"There, there," said I.

"The human body," announced Kingsley Palmer as he trotted along, "can resist every ailment, if aided by a Purity of spirit."

"He tore open her gingham dress and feasted his devil's eyes upon the alabaster whiteness of her cuneiform breasts. The fires of gross sensuality raged madly."

Gone was Foote's doleful expression. His eyes sparked with life, every so often he would grin in a horse-like manner, displaying all of his yellowed teeth. The wound in Jefferson's arms overflowed with poison and feculence. He passed in and out of wakefulness. The character of his voice changed, too; once he started up off Kingsley's shoulders, cocked his eyes at nothing in particular and gave forth a deep, husky howl. *"Conchita!"* he bellowed. *"Kneel before me. Wash my feet, dry them with your hair."* Then, a moment later, his voice came as quietly as a clergyman from another state. *"He was a tall, slab-sided individual, with a lean, leathery face and a grave and sardonic eye."*

The doctor didn't lose much time in deciding what to do. "Better to operate now, whilst he's out of touch. There's some liquor over on the side table. Try to get it down him, and have a drop yourselves. You'll both need to help. I'll go prepare."

I really had no idea what was going on. After the doctor had disappeared, I was alarmed to find Kingsley Palmer's chubby face slick with tears. "Now are we about to witness a miracle, Thom," he whimpered. "Oh, wonder most radiant!"

"Jefferson, have a little of the old Jameson's. It'll make you feel better."

"The man returned to the grave, and was about to resume his labor, when his eyes caught sight of a black object."

I put the bottle to Jefferson's lips, tipped it back. Foote was too busy talking to get much down. *"It was the upper part of the skull, with the long, dark hair of a woman still attached."*

"Oh, yea. For such is the Glory of the body that a Man does not need all of his appendages."

"What did you say?"

"Like a wall that has been constructed by a Master Engineer, the removal of a single brick does not weaken the construct. And who is the Most Masterly Engineer? The Engineer of the Cosmos."

The doctor entered with an ax cradled in his hands. "Hold him firm," he told us.

When the ax came down Jefferson looked more surprised than anything else. His eyes silently demanded to know what was going on. The first blow did not cut the bone cleanly, and the Doctor was forced to re-aim. Blood was everywhere. Foote passed out with the second strike; while his bloody stump was being cauterized he woke up long enough to let out a direful howl. My mother had often spoken of the fearsome moans that would come from the godless in Abaddon. I would have rather listened to them than to Jefferson, and now, of course, it looks like I'll get my chance.

The Warden snaps his long white fingers together. "That reminds me, Thom." He searches the pockets of his blue suit, sounding a tattoo up and down the length of his too large and hairless body.

"What reminds you, sir? The tale of how Jefferson came to be monodextrous?"

"My goodness. The improvement in your vocabulary is astounding."

"Improbable. Of eminent mark."

"That phrase you employed, *the godless in Abaddon.*"

"What about it?"

"That's what reminded me."

"Let us see if we can't get the horses of conversation hitched to the same wagon, sir."

"Ah!" The Warden withdraws a piece of paper from his trouser pocket. It has been neatly folded and my name, *Thom*, is written in a large and loopy script, what you might expect from a schoolmistress composing a love letter and nipping at the sherry bottle. At first I think it might be from Thespa, and that is why I tear it from The Warden's hands so eagerly, but then I realize I don't know what Thespa's damned handwriting looks like. She never wrote a letter to me, love or hate or any other variety. I pull it open a bit roughly, ripping the paper along some of the prissy folds.

Dear Thom, the note reads

How are you? I am very well indeed. I fear I made a poor impression the other day, and wish to correct that if

*at all possible. Therefore, I would like to invite you to
dinner. Any evening this week is fine. We must do this
soon, Thom, as I am to be hanged shortly.*

*Your fellow inmate,
J. Murtagh.*

We had, King Palmer, Foote and me, a small canvas gunnysack
that was filled with twenty-five- and fifty-cent pieces, because
that was how Biggar U. Webb paid us for our slaughter of tule
rooters. We used the money to rent a small hotel room in the
town of Crossed Palms, where Jefferson recuperated. The delir-
ium and fever did not end with the hacking off of his arm, but
stretched out into weeks. Jefferson lay naked on the bed, the mattress sopping with his bad sweat. He remained trapped in the bad
novels, whispering in a hoarse and ragged way. *"Hank Arm-
strong, the sturdy left fielder of the Resolutes, was the first at the
bat for his side, and with a vicious swing he hit the first ball
which Sam pitched to him. Squarely on the bat he caught it with
a resounding ping!"*

Crossed Palms rose out of the lifeless desert and looked, from a
distance, every bit as startling and odd as the Biblical mountain.
There were two small palm trees that struggled skyward and then
keeled drunkenly, one to the left, t'other to the right. Beside was
a huge sign upon which someone had painted a healthier version
of these trees, and subscripted a flowery *Crossed Palms — A Town
of Speculation.* There were three main buildings: a bath house, a
bank and a hotel. The bath house attendants were young Chinese
women who wore white shifts, damp thin cotton that clung to
their frail bodies. The bank, First Western, was robbed maybe
twice a day. The robbers would thunder out of the distant mountains with their guns drawn, firing into the clouds. I think they
had seen too many Flickers. From time to time the bank would be
filled with Pinkerton men, bored young mercenaries who would
kill the would-be robbers and leave the streets of Crossed Palms
littered with their bodies. At no point during any of this would the
Pinkerton boys seem less bored. Then there was the hotel, where
King, Foote and I shared a small and dingy room. The ground floor

of this building was given over to a casino. It was a huge room, finely upholstered and appointed, and drinks were conveyed from the bar to the patrons by young Chinese women, identical to the ones over in the bath house except these were altogether naked. They were there, I think, so that men would drink too much and become giddy. Kingsley Palmer thought that they signified a policy of Sanctified Nudism, so he would enter the casino naked, strutting from table to table with coins squeezing out of his hands. No one paid any attention, not even when Palmer had lost all of his money and was cheering himself up with a little of the old preaching: "Disproportionate development and strength causes food to not be equally distributed and consumed from cell to cell!" Palmer would strike a grinning pose; those days he favored a sideways stance, his knuckles resting lightly on his obliques. "Seek cellular disharmony here!" None of the gamblers took him up on it.

As Foote recovered, King and I would descend to the casino, and after Foote was fit enough to walk about, he'd join us. I don't suppose we had any plans. We lacked the ambition even to contemplate robbing the First Western, which seemed a dead easy way of getting money, providing you didn't get riddled by bullets in the process. The three of us merely gambled fecklessly, hoping (in a not very hopeful way) for a big pay-off, and when we lost a handful of change each one of us would merely shrug and retire to our dingy room.

Then one night, as I tossed quarters at the blackjack dealer, I heard a voice coming from behind me:

"I have had my fill of those Hollywoodland philistines. My gullet is stuffed with their cretinous jabber. Where on earth do these people get the notion that they have ideas? Hmm? I presume they awaken with a hangover, say to themselves, *My brain hurts, I must be having an idea, I had best go bother Jensen with it.* Oh, lookee. A pair of big-bubbied marms staring up at me. The pair of queens bets, oh, five dollars."

I rose, turned around, spoke quietly. "Fat Man."

Jensen sat with his walrus hands crossed over his waistcoated belly. The little bowler sat at a jaunty angle, his moustache bloomed even larger than the last time I'd seen him. "Do I know you?" he demanded snottily.

"No, I don't suppose you do. You brought about my Downfall, but you probably don't remember me."

"Well, I don't. So piss off."

I hauled him out of his seat, took my knife out of my back pocket and pressed it to his belly.

"B-b-b-but..." he stammered. Naked Chinese women were screaming and running every which way.

"Don't give me no buts, Fat Man. You stole my personal fortune and set me on the road to ruin. I am a penniless wretch, a drunken and lowly hunter of tule rooters. Look at poor Foote, my companion. He has been shot in the butt, he's got white hair, melted ears and he's lost one whole arm. You give me one good reason why I shouldn't push this blade into your stinking belly."

"Well..." Jensen's eyes darted back and forth, like a stage-frightened actor looking for a prompt. "Well, I could get you a job in the Flickers. I am a close personal friend of the renowned Caspar Willison."

"If he's a friend of yours, Fat Man, I want nothing to do with him."

"Opportunity!"

"What about it?"

"It is yours. Fortune beams down upon your fair head! Come on, son," he whimpered. "Don't stick me like a pig."

"You're fat as a pig, aren't you?" I grinned over at Kingsley and Foote, because I thought they might find that just a little bit humorous. They didn't seem to.

"Ah! It's come back to me now. We were on a train."

"That's right, Fat Man."

"And you won a great deal of money at the gaming table. Unfortunately, you also over-imbibed. You became shit-stinky. So, says I, *Jensen, this young fella might run afoul of verminous ne'er-do-wells.* There are many scurrilous knaves who pray upon young innocents."

"Yeah," I responded. "I believe I'm looking at one."

"Thusly, I — *temporarily* — relieved you of the lucre, with every intention of returning it in the morning. When I went to find you, I was informed that you and your friend had detrained."

"Detrained?! We got bounced off our heads into the wilderness."

"Don't kill me, son. Please."

I looked over at Jefferson and Kingsley Palmer. "What do you say, boys? Do we want a job in the Flickers?"

We arrived at Inge's World Studios, The World, well before dawn. ("We must get there before the light, boys," Jensen had whined. "Fuck with the light and Caspar will fuck with us in kind.") We were corralled toward a group of cowboys who milled around in the dark and smoked cigarettes.

By my side I found a short fellow with long hair falling into his eyes and a moustache that sprang out of his upper lip with enthusiasm and then dangled limply like dying vines. He also sported a goatee, although it merely looked like he had missed the same place shaving every day of his life. "Bodnarchuk," this man said. He tucked a roll-up under his moustache and lit it with a paper match.

"How's that?"

"That's my name."

"Oh. Good to meet you, Bodnarchuk. Thom Moss. Say, you wouldn't happen to have another of those cigarettes, would you?"

"I surely would. I am never without. It is a habit I developed whilst employed as a tobacco picker up in the Canadian province of Ontario."

"Uh-yeah."

He passed me the makings and then turned to Jeff. "Bodnarchuk," he said.

Foote nodded.

"I see that you have been visited by misfortune," said Bodnarchuk.

I handed a cigarette to Foote, lit it up for him, went to work on one for myself. King Palmer tsked lightly, it being his notion that smoking was deleterious to one's health. "Foote there had a run-in with a vicious tule rooter," I told Bodnarchuk. "Biggest fuck-pig there ever was."

"Indeed? I've done some tule-rooter killing," said Bodnarchuk. "It's gratifying employment. Although, one must be ever mindful of the venomous tusks."

"Shut the fug up."

Caspar Willison — God from *War* — stepped out of the night.

He stopped some feet away from our little clutch of carnival boys, throwing his hips away out to one side and buckling his hands at the waist. He wore riding breeches, a panama hat, a white shirt with a lot of pearly buttons, all done up, so that the cuffs wrapped tightly about the wrists, the collar closed across his Adam's apple which rendered his face pale and ashy. (As the day went on, Caspar Willison would free first his throat, then his wrists and hairless forearms, the white shirt would open and reveal his tiny nipples, dark as ink.) He wore a black Sam Browne, a thick gun belt held up by a chest strap, Bird's Head Colts sticking out the tops of the holsters.

"All right?" this man sang. "Let us continue the making of this cock-upright tale of thrulls," Willison said. His voice sat high for a man's, and he spoke softly, but it cut through the dewy night. "We await the fat slut Phœbus. When she arrives, no doubt hanged-over and fugged-out, we shall fillum the following: galoomping dash across the prairie, brave stalwarts pursued by nasties. Reciprocated bang-bang. Oh! One of you shall make me happy. Which one will make Mr. Willy happy?"

The strange little fellow Bodnarchuck stirred uneasily. "You wouldn't be talking about the Flying W, would you, Mr. Willison?"

"*Flying W?* You speak in riddles, man!"

"You know what I mean."

"Hmm." Caspar Willison nodded, removed his hat. The short blond hair pricked upwards. "If there was amongst you one brave and fearless soul, one who would rise up from the malodorous cess-pool of bummy-boys, a single and singular personage who would take a courageous step forward and say—"

"I'm your man."

"Uh-*huh!!*"

I pushed past Foote and Palmer. "What do you want me to do, pal?"

"Oooh!" Willison raised a finger and stabbed at the sternal portion of my pectorals, sending a thick little vein of pain through me.

"Come again?"

"Why so poofy and bloatish?"

"Oh. Bodily reconstruction. I undergo the Rigors."

Caspar Willison nodded and pulled at his pointy chin, but already I knew better than to figure he'd paid attention. What I know now is that he was sensing the arrival of the sun. He lifted his head, turned his blue eyes to the east. "Right. Bittner. You're away down *theah*. Bummy-boys, get on your neggs over *heah*."

An old man, his eyes silvered over by disease, picked up a square box mounted on three thin poles. He got about four feet and started to keel; both the ancient and the strange machine were caught by a gangly youth with an acne-plagued face, but then he fell over, too, and the pair went tumbling to the ground. The contraption was rescued by a sturdily built fellow, who proceeded onward, ignoring the flailing couple on the ground. That was my first experience of Bill Bittner working with his assistants, Georg and the young Theodore Welkin.

There were horses tethered some yards away, underfed and cold. I do not know why some people allow that horses can tolerate a chill, it's not as if they are furry. I fell in beside that little fellow Bodnarchuk, who told me, "There's nothing I enjoy quite so much as a good horse-ride. Mind you, I worked for a while as a jockey."

"Is that right?"

"This was in upstate New York. Unfortunately, I fell madly in love with a woman named Gross who owned a bakery. Battenburg cakes proved my undoing."

"Shut the fug up," said Caspar Willison.

I opted for a horse that seemed relatively free of disease, but Bodnarchuk shook his head dolefully. "Not that one, friend." He raised a finger and pointed toward the back of the pack. A frail and ancient mount stood there, four knees rattling together out of cold or timidity. It was just so much horsehide pulled across a skeleton that was about to turn to dust.

"That one?" I demanded. "You know, pal, I was the rodeo champion of three states."

"Do not think I am not impressed. I myself competed in many rodeos, my best finish being an inglorious sixth. However, if you are executing the Flying W, *that* is the horse."

"You! Hey!" roared Willison. "Here comes the fugging sun! Get up on your negg and let's do it!"

Foote grinned as I threw myself up into the saddle. "Which three states might that be, Thom?"

"Right," said Caspar C. Willison. "First shot. Ride down thet-away, pretend there is a pussy behind you, take out your six-shooters, beng-beng-beng."

I raised my hand, not high, either, just about even with my shoulder, and waggled my fingers a little bit toward God from *War*.

"Oh, it's skulltime! What is it?"

"Well... I thought you might want to let me in on this Flying W business."

"No, I don't. It works so exquisitely when the bummy is, ah, naïve."

"You want me just to ride down there, pretending to—"

"Pretend? *Nevah*. I want you to dream."

"You want me to *dream* that I'm firing at some folks behind me. At at some point I'm going to do something called a Flying W, which you won't tell me what it is."

"That's it." The sun rose over the plain, suddenly, just another employee of Caspar Willison's and late for work. "Bittner! Crank the contrumption. All right, boys, let's write with light! Go!"

The other cowboys immediately started whooping Indian-style, they kicked their horses into action and tore away. I heeled my ancient nag and it waddled forward; I kept digging my spurs into its side, and finally it was raising red dust, and we were drawing near Mr. Bittner and his strange machine, and I recalled that I was supposed to be firing at some murderous bastards behind me, and I further recalled that I didn't have a gun, so I pulled my knife and flung it away, and just as I was remarking to myself how foolish that must have looked, the horse vanished from beneath me. I was in an instant separated from that beast by a distance of ten feet and travelling. I hit the ground face-first, and to this day there is a small patch of skin on my upper right cheek that will not tan as well as the rest. I pulled myself up onto hands and knees — neither of which had escaped a grim skinning — but Caspar Willison sang out, "Yoohoo! You are deh-head!" so I lay back down, listened to the thunder of horsehooves on the belly of the earth, and began to weep.

Chapter 14

Jensen and I climbed the stairs to his little room in the attic of the White Owl Hotel. It was furnished with a Murphy bed, a small table that held a typewriting machine, two chairs that some engineering genius might have been able to combine into something a body could sit on, and books. My first thought was that every book in the country had been stuffed into Jensen's room. I realize that sounds foolish, but I was not used to seeing books whilst growing up. Oh, it's true, I'd all my life seen Foote with a greying nickel novel bent and twisted in his bony hands, but at my own home I saw only the Bible and a few thick illustrated instructional manuals about the care and upkeep of bicycles. There in the Fat Man's rooms there were thick romances and historicals with gaudy illustrations, novels both new and so old that the pages were turning to dust. There were huge atlases and lexicographies. I cannot recall specifically that Jensen owned an Old Man Hartrampf's, but I think it more than likely. The Fat Man's own books hid amongst the more dignified publications like addled children. Jensen's most prized possession was a three-volume collection, weighty and filled with the secrets of existence, *An Encyclopedia of All Things Animate.*

We had just been sitting in the Saloon, Jensen amusing himself by making various jokes at my expense. "I just *knew* you'd go far in the Flicker business, Thommy."

"Don't call me *Thommy*," I muttered, fingering the scab on my face and sucking raw whiskey. "Only my father calls me *Thommy*."

A young cowboy approached, his eyebrows flipping like fevered men on lumpy beds. He had his body cocked at us as though his privates wanted to join us for a beer. "I hear you like to play cards," he said to Jensen.

"I have been known to toss ducats," agreed Jensen, "although I do not like to gamble."

"Haw! Fat Man, *wah.*"

My shin was suddenly filled with white pain. It travelled up my body and shot through my eyeballs. I could not calculate how the Fat Man executed this kick, but he did and I hushed up.

"You young bucks," said Jensen, "like to play 'til the wee ones, much too late for an ancient wanderer such as myself. What I'll do, laddy-mine, is repair to my lair and have a little nap." The Fat Man waggled his arms in short circles, levitating himself into a standing position. "Then, sir," he announced, laboriously arisen, "*then* shall I play cards."

J.D.D. Jensen had no intention of napping. He went straight to the little table that held the typewriting machine, wrestled out a tiny drawer and removed a deck of playing cards. The Fat Man started playing with them, as he had done on that ill-fated train trip, cutting them one-handed, regular as a machine. He used his free flipper to indicate the chairs. "Sit down, young Moss. I'll tell you tales of tawdry wonder that will leave you drooling and slack-jawed." The Fat Man flipped each card onto the little table; his fingers, bloated and incapable of knuckling, worked so quickly that they blurred. The cards collected in an orderly pile. "I will weave little tapestries of eroticism that will drive your hands down into your trousers." Jensen picked up the pile, repeated the process, and then, shuffling and cutting all the while, told me a tale about a woman from New Orleans named Camilla St-Pierre who owned a parrot. While I did not abuse myself at the time, I may have done later that night. At any rate, the Fat Man spun a few of these stories (I drank sherry and listened, drooling and slack-jawed) and then suddenly the cards exploded out of his hand. They hit the four walls and ceiling with so much force that they made a sound like a Gatling gun. Some seemed to hover, spinning and topsy-turving before floating earthward. The Fat Man regarded the strewn ducats with evident pleasure, and left off his story-telling. "Ah," said he, "nap time has ended. I do feel refreshed. Let us go play cards."

I asked him about this one sweltering night, the two of us sitting in our underwear on the roof of the White Owl, drinking sherris sack and watching The World.

"Fat Man?"

"Yes, Thommy?"

"Before a poker game, you will sit in your room and play with your cards until such a time as they fly from your mitts."

J.D.D. Jensen held his hand up so that it was framed by the moon. It looked much like a beavertail with little stubs popping out of it. "These hands, Thommy, are not ideal for the manipulation of playing cards."

"No, sir. You would need fingers for that."

"Very droll, Moss. The reason I have never been found out is that no one can believe that I could actually be cheating."

"Aha! You admit you're a cheat."

"Of course I admit it, you pitiful shithead. I've admitted it to you ever since we met. As I see it, Thommy, if my Creator had seen fit to give me a normal pair of hands, I would be the best card doctor in the world. But I am not. I am fallible. On any given evening, I am going to lose control of them *once*. It's a very precise art, my buck. You must squeeze the cards with incredible force, yet your hand must look as relaxed as a powder puff on its way to a milky-white breast. So — once of an eve — they are going to escape my grip. *Once*. Well. I would sooner it happened away from the gaming table. Therefore, I remain in my room and wait until it happens. Then I play cards."

"Fat Man?"

"Yes, Thom?"

"First time we met, you peculated and diddled me out of my life savings. You engineered my Downfall, and brought upon me a long descent. I became a lowly drunken hunter of tule rooters."

"We've been through this."

"Now, you tell me everything I want to know."

"True. You are not the same boy I swindled." He raised a stub and pointed outward. Far away, the black mountain sat in the night's shadow and *insinuated*, as Hartrampf says, the existence of God, although the heavens above the World were empty and silent.

"That is what you are, Thom. A star."

"True enough."

"A tiny point of light."

In the middle of the night I awoke in my room on the third floor of the White Owl Hotel and saw Miss Justice near the end of the bed. She was holding her arms crookedly out to either side, her head turned and angled up slightly, so that she was profiled and staring at something far away and hard to see. The tunic was shifted and one breast was bared, all buttered by moonlight. Miss Justice was frozen like statuary, and I sat up in my bed and rubbed troubled sleep out of my eyes.

Miss Justice moved then, all in a twinkling, drawing her arms in, floating them back out again, going up on to her toes and settling down gently. Suddenly she was presenting her other profile. The tunic had fallen off the shoulder and now was simply a skirt, gathered and cinched by a belt of rustic hemp.

Lily Lavallée's stillness was so absolute that the moment froze and seemed somehow like a gift. I have not been terribly kind to Lily in these pages so far — I employ words like *puffy* and *bloated* — but her body had once been superlative, and she knew how to use the night and nakedness to her best advantage.

After that tableau (and I have no idea how much time the rest of the world counted then, one minute or sixty) Lily drew into herself. She became small, and her face and arms were disappeared into shadows.

Then her hands were buckled on her hips, and she was offering the three-quarter profile. Lily Lavallée was naked and a lot closer to the bed than I'd first thought. I pulled my sheet up as if I was the one with bosom bared.

"Requests?"

I did not see Lily's lips move. "Beg your pardon?"

Lily suddenly relaxed and her flesh fell. "Do you have any requests? Some men are partial to this sort of thing." She spun around and froze. Her hands framed her buttocks, the fingers bent to mirror the curve.

"Lily..."

Lily bent over.

"Lily..."

"Supine."

"Miss Lavallée," I said, which did sound a bit overly formal, as Miss Lavallée had rolled over onto her back with one leg lifted and the tiny foot elegantly extended toward me. "Lily, Thespa Doone is my one and only."

As if to prove the point to myself, I drew on my trousers and thundered upstairs, dove onto Thespa's bed and lay my head upon her bosom.

"*All aboard for Blanket Bay*," she sang to me, as she did upon occasion.

All aboard for Blanket Bay,
Won't come back till the break of day.
Roll him round in his little white sheet,
Till you can't see his little bare feet.
Then you tuck him up in his trundle bed,
Ship ahoy little sleepy-head,
Bless Mama and Papa and sail away,
All aboard for Blanket Bay.

The Warden enters my jail cell in a state of high agitation, which I've never seen before, and is really quite remarkable. His whole huge and hairless body has pinkened, and droplets of sweat have oozed out of him, but from strange places, his eyelids and the thick rims of his ears. The Warden has, finally, loosened his collar, torn it brutally away.

"Look out," he whispers.

I jerk my feet off the ground instinctively, wary of serpents from my days in the wilderness.

"Look out the window," The Warden instructs me, lifting his foot-long finger toward the shaft of daylight. It is alive with dust and sun mites.

To look out my window I have to leap up, wrap my fingers around the bars, and chin myself. I usually do this for Bodily Reconstruction exclusively, because there is not much worth seeing. Actually, I have been very negligent as regards undergoing the Rigors, and not only is the chinning a little painful, I have to leap up twice, as the first time my fingertips only brushed the iron. I rebound from the wall and find upon my belly a little crosshatching of blood from the brickwork.

The window faces the east, and frames foothills that give way to barrenness. Of the prison proper, I can see very little: a parapet, a watchtower, the backs of young guards.

But beyond the walls of the prison, a small crowd has gathered. They are the same people who assembled on the sidewalk to watch Thespa Doone and me alight from fancy automobiles; they have dull eyes and wear crude garments. They have been moved to anger; several curl their twisted hands into fists and raise them heavenward. Howsomever, their mood seems fey and half-hearted when compared to the towering fury of their leader. Her hands are small, but clenched in rage, they have the hardness of cut rock. These she shakes at the prison walls, and the people behind her do likewise, like incompetent musicians who cannot quite follow the maestro.

"What is she doing here?" I ask The Warden. My arms are trembling, which I attribute to a softening of the various muscles. I resolve to undergo the Rigors on a daily and continual basis. "What does she want?"

"She wants us not to execute John," that man replies.

Her face has been drawn downwards by the Great Weight of Being. She has jowls, and the corners of her mouth droop. Her eyelids are half-closed, except when she hauls them up like old theater curtains, the better to let her eyes glow like peridot. What were freckles in her younger days have melded together into a florid wash, webbed with fine broken veins.

"Her point being," The Warden continues, "that the Bible says, *Thou shalt not kill.*"

"Yeah, I seem to recall it saying something along those lines."

"She has taken up this vigil, you see. She hopes that like-minded people from around the nation will gather beside her."

My mother, who does have a sort of sixth sense, except I do not know if it is from motherhood or madness, suddenly jerks her head so that our eyes meet, and even though the distance between us is a hundred yards and more, our gazes lock. Her reaction is so subtle that I can but barely see it. Perhaps her mouth flattens out briefly, and perhaps later on tonight I'll be able to convince myself that this was some sort of smile. My reaction is more emphatic; I release the cold metal and fall back into the shadows of my cell.

Chapter 15

We have snuck back up on that moment that made me (and my one and only) so very celebrated. Which is to say, I am dancing with Thespa Doone in *A Fate Worse Than Death*. I have pulled her body to mine and can feel her breasts, the hard edges of her pelvic region (there, I was over to the cot and back before you even noticed I was gone) and all of a sudden my old friend Charles Wild Horse and other Indians surrounded the cabin, flapping their hands across rounded mouths and making sounds like giant birds from strange lands.

I ran out of the cabin with a rifle in my hands, but I was waylaid by an Indian who jumped off the roof and coldcocked me. Charles Wild Horse and the others then carted off Thespa Doone, which is *The Fate Worse Than Death* mentioned in the title.

They tied her to a tree and circled around her, a hopping shuffle where-in the Indians continued the odd practice of beating their hands across their opened mouths. They doubled themselves over as though afflicted by dyspepsia. Some Indians had stained their bodies with berry juice; they wore thick smears of war paint and had braided their hair into ceremonial plaits.

"The sun is going yellow," said Willison, staring at the western horizon.

Charles Wild Horse came over to me, offered his hand and said, "Let's go get some dinner, Thom."

There were two separate and notable things that happened that evening, but they happened at the same time, and I do not feel it would write down properly that way, going back and forth, so what I will do is, spell out one, then the other. I always assumed that, in the few books I have read, the author had made some sort of attempt to squeeze real life between the covers. Now I see that this is not so: life is made easier to handle — blinkered, tethered and hobbled — before it is whipped into words and bound between leather.

Charles Wild Horse and I located King Palmer who was with the rest of the cowboys over at the White Owl Hotel. They were generally a wild bunch, given to over-drinking and acts of foolish derring-do, and although Kingsley was as sober a man as I've ever met, he enjoyed their company. He exalted in the sinewy perfection of their young bodies. For their part, the carnival boys thought that King was unco, but he was the undisputed champion of the Death Game, which afforded him no little respect. The cowboys therefore refrained, most often, from goading Palmer into clubbing himself over the head and such-like, although they liked to see him consume disgusting things. It was his contention that the Human Body, designed by the Great Originator, could deal with all manner of foreign stuff, either by ingestion or regurgitation, an observation he made whilst Bodnarchuk was launching bad oysters across the bar-room. Subsequently, the fellows might proffer up dung-covered mushrooms with black devil's hoods. "Kill you dead," they'd say to Kingsley Palmer.

"Oh, yeah?" Palmer would pop them and grin, his bright eyes a-whirl with reverence.

Charles Wild Horse and I got King, and then we mounted the stairs to a room on the third floor. Through the door came the sharp *clack* of a typewriting machine. I know that it might more properly be *clack-clack* or even *clack-clack-clack*, but when Jefferson Foote worked it, you'd just hear the single clack and then there would be a longish pause as he hunted down the next letter with his one hand. We three pushed in and although Jefferson was pleased to see Charles Wild Horse, he made us wait as he finished up some changes to the scenario of the Flicker we were turning, *A Fate Worse Than Death.* I idly picked up a sheet of paper, much as The Warden does as he bumps throughout my cell, and read the words: "Our Hero is suddenly struck by an idea!" I read on and then said, "What the hell?"

"Don't read that," snapped Jefferson Foote. He lit up one of his black cigarettes, pulled his hand through the shoulder-length bone-white hair. He stared at the piece of paper in the machine before him and sighed heavily.

"I'm not gonna do this," I continued.

"Yes, you are, Thom."

We kept up this sort of bickering throughout the evening, the only change being the vitriol and foul language we each added to our stances. "Now, look, peckerhead. There is no way on God's green earth that I am about to do as you have written. And you can bank that between your arse-cheeks."

"You are a baboon. You shall do it. You have no choice. Caspar will make you."

"*Caspar*, is it? As if you two go away back?"

"His name is Caspar, so I call him Caspar. I don't even much like the man."

"Maybe you ought to call him *Mr. Willison* like the rest of us. You're a changed man, Jefferson Foote."

"I'm a changed man? Have you looked in a mirror lately, Moss? Wait, wait, I take that back. That's all you do, is look in mirrors."

At the end of the evening, after drinking too many glasses of scotch, I punched my friend in the face. I knocked out one of his front teeth, and I felt very bad about that, being as Jefferson's teeth, though bright yellow, were his best feature.

"It's ridiculous," Charles Wild Horse complained. "Just look. The war bonnet is, I believe, Blackfoot, this is a Crow necklace, an Arapaho pipe bag and this, of all things, is a Navajo chief's blanket. I do have a Sioux breastplate, but no shield."

"And who was it," I wondered, "painted your face so silly?"

Charles Wild Horse dropped his eyes bashfully, first one then the other. "I did that myself."

"Why? Is that traditional war paint?"

"No. I just thought it might look nice."

"So..." We were down in the Saloon now, drinking away, and although it was me who was building up to ask the question, my mind wasn't all on it. Some of my mind was on this silly idea that Jeff Foote had written into the scenario for *A Fate Worse Than Death*; much of my mind was wondering where Thespa Doone was, and if we were to share our bodies again that night. "Where's Wild Horse Charlie?"

One of Charles Wild Horse's eyes glanced at the cheap chandelier, the other seemed to ogle a nearby barmaid who was being harassed by a bunch of cowboys. Both got watery. "I don't know," Charles said.

"How's that?" asked Jefferson Foote. He had adopted a very prissy manner, his left leg crossed over his right and curling down like a vine, the toes hooked behind the polished heel of his boot. Foote puffed on his black cigarette in the middle of sentences, signifying that what he had to say was of uppermost importance and everyone should therefore just bide their time.

"The last I saw of him," Charles told us, "Charlie was being chased by a fuck-pig. They disappeared somewhere to the south of here. It was a very large fuck-pig," Charles added frettingly. He had a sip of whiskey and said no more about the subject.

What happens next, in *A Fate Worse Than Death*, is this: I come to, somehow already bandaged, and then race off to gather up the boys from the Saloon. I bang through the doors and shout something (the title card holds only the word "Revenge!" but my mouth moves as though I'm chewing on porcupine parts) and the boys, clustered together, follow me out to the Indian grounds. There was Bodnarchuk, Kincaid, Lonny Onley, Manley Wessex, a new fellow named Perry John, a few others I'm disremembering. We leap upon our mighty steeds and go racing across the wilderness, *but* — and Willison makes a cross-splice here, and a tiny flower of light opens up across the darkness of the screen — Charles Wild Horse is high in the hills, crouched behind a rock, and he has a Winchester which he no doubt purloined from some brutally slaughtered homesteaders. He rests the barrel across the stone and takes aim at me.

There I am, galloping valiantly along, when suddenly a boulder up on the hill explodes with a puff of smoke and down I go. More specifically, down goes my horse, felled by a Flying W. The beast rolls across my right leg and after I hear "Cut!" I test the ankle, seeing if it will bear my weight. It hurts but seems unbroken, so I limp about trying to ease out the pain.

"Veddy gude," says Caspar Willison. He struts over to the felled nag, takes a look at the rear leg. There is a sharp bend where the wire is attached, splinters of bone breaking through the fetlock. Caspar Willison unholsters a Bird's Head Colt. He places the barrel between the horse's eyes and pulls the trigger. When Biggar Webb killed tule rooters, pieces of skull and brain filled the air. Horses are either constructed differently or Willison is a whole other sort of killer, because the bullet seems to *calm* the poor creature. It quiets the twitches and takes away the look of fear in the huge eyes, leaving behind milky incomprehension.

Willison pulls his gun away. "Ambush," he whispers. "Fugging murdering bastids." Caspar turns away, places his hand over his eyes. "Let us see them descend the hills."

As I clamber to my feet, it seems like there's an Indian behind every rock. The murdering bastards rear up and come charging down, armed with bows and arrows, tomahawks, and purloined firearms. Willison called for the Death Game, to be followed by lunch.

It was at lunch that a young fellow from the Hollywoodland *Megaphone* sidled up next to me. I didn't know that's who he was, mind you, but there were many people about The World who I did not know. After all, at any one time there might be three or four scenarios being turned. Willison was merely the most famous of the movie-makers, but there was also Roald Nypes, Harry Joint, Bobby Hill and Oscar Delanoy. It was Delanoy who first broke away from Western High Drama, The World's stock in trade, and I'll never forget how shocked Bodnarchuk and I were when — in the midst of a Death Game, six-shooters blaring, fat/wax bullets flying, horses rearing — several men in green tights and little caps pranced by, bows and arrows at the ready. With *Robin Hood and the Merry Foresters*, The World immediately gained a reputation for Historical Romance. (The Fat Man took all his old scenarios, added a few *prithees* and *forsooths* to the title cards, made all the sheriffs Sheriffs of Salisbury, changed the murderous Indians to murderous Visigoths and re-sold them for bushels of clinkers.)

This fellow gave his name — *Oliver Howard* — and offered me a hand to shake.

"Do you think it hurts?"

"What's that now?"

Oliver Howard (or it might be Howard Oliver, I was always confused about that, which might be why he decided to precipitate my Downfall) said, "That horsey stunt." He had an English accent, which made me want to punch him in the face.

"The Flying W? Well, suppose you were running as fast as you could and didn't know you were attached by a piano wire to a rock or some similar immovable object. You reckon that might hurt?"

"You don't sound terribly *sympatico*."

I shrugged. "I don't suppose it matters much." What I meant was, I didn't suppose it mattered much to the poor horses whether I sounded *sympatico*, a word that was slobbered over by Howard Oliver's English accent and made me want to kick him in the shins. But when the *Megaphone* came out a week or so later, it read like I didn't suppose it mattered that horses were being killed by the Flying W. That article made it sound like I was responsible for the Flying W, whereas I was simply the buffoon most often along for the bumpy ride. The Society for Peaceful Speciate Co-existence began to mount a boycott against my motion pictures. The Society's leader, Apollo Greenling, gave testimony at my trial, for the Prosecution of course, to the effect that I was a sadistic young man who enjoyed mistreating animals. Don't get me started on those people because I'm like to tear apart this whole cell brick by brick. And what did they do to Caspar W. Willison? Not a fucking thing. And he was the man who killed Tragedy, and, well, don't get me started on those people.

Chapter 16

The cowboys truly enjoyed the Death Game, which is why several of them, although being ambushed by foul Red-dogs in *A Fate Worse Than Death*, are grinning like morons. Bodnarchuk especially grinned like a moron, although he never won the Death Game, by virtue of being overly dramatic. The new boy, Perry John, proved himself to be a worthy Death Game participant, executing a perfect cantle flip-out and landing flat on his back, which always earned high grades. Manley Wessex could get off a good one, especially when liquored up, his favored manœvre being a sidewise spill from the horse that landed him on his feet, where he could stagger around for many moments. Wessex liked to take two or three bullets before finally shucking the coil. The bullets we fired were composed of pigfat and candlewax. They'd come out of the gun and explode across your chest, the tallow and blubber spreading into the air like smoke. The stuff would harden in a couple of seconds, and you'd have to spend a good hour picking little globs of stuff off your outfit and skin.

Mind you, it was not as though any of these fellows came even close to Kingsley Palmer. Having received the mortal blow, Kingsley exploded from the seat into the air. He turned arse over teakettle about three times up there, began to fall, bounced off another fellow's horse and aligned himself so that his head was aimed for the ground. I believe his head sunk into the earth a good two or three inches, giving him enough purchase to stay standing that way for a moment or two, and then his body was sucked by Death into a cruel pile, limbs bent in every direction.

Willison stood at a distance with his shirt ripped off beneath the high sun. His upper body was slight and hairless, but, covered with sweat, showed itself to be a complex arrangement of muscle and fibrous tissue. Caspar Willison had very pronounced trapezius muscles angling from his shoulders to somewhere high on his neck. (His neck, by the by, was sunburnt, blistered by tiny whiteheads and usually ringed with grime, as if, like a schoolboy, he had simply not bothered to wash there.) As you may know, trapezius muscles are amongst the hardest to promote, since a man can find his way in life quite satisfactorily without them. Kingsley Palmer used to stand on his hands and execute push-offs, although they are the next thing to impossible. (I haven't attempted them in a while. I've definitely lost a lot of size from my various body parts, all except for the belly, which has puffed and swelled like that of a pregnant woman.) But Caspar Willison had these bold trapezius muscles, and they looked to be not promoted through bodily reconstruction, but rather granted by nature, which contributed to the overall effect of Willison's being not quite human.

He stood there, panting, and hissed at me as I drew near. "Messsssss..."

"I'd like to speak with you, sir."

"Tell me something, Miss. How long have you known Jeffie?"

"Foote? I've always known him, sir."

"Oooh, luvvy. Luvvy to have a bosom fiend."

"Yes, sir."

"Are you nancies?"

"Please?"

"Are you bungy nancy-boys? You and luvvy Jeffie?"

"Me and Jeff?"

"The World is full of 'em, Thom. It's nothing to be ashamed of."

"I am not ashamed — "

"Good for you!" Willison bent forward so that our foreheads

were almost touching. "Be a gud little boy and I'll let you have a run at me. I've seen you looking at my rock-hard buddy with its ebon nips."

"Just whoa up for a minute and listen, sir. All I came over to say is, it is my belief that this what is coming up is a very bad idea."

Willison inverted the little vee of his mouth and pointed at it with a forefinger. "A bad idea?"

"Yes. Sir."

"Ah!" The forefinger flew up into the air as though it had invented a Perpetual Motion Machine. "Because, if you do it, you fear people will discern your procluvities."

"Mr. Willison. We are having two separate conversations that you insist on running along the same track."

"You are not using the ol' noggin, Mess. The best defence? A bold offence. Once they see this, everyone'll say, *Muss can't be a bungy, because if he were a bungy, he would never do this.* Capiche?"

"Just try to forget this *bungy* business."

"If you *refuse* to do it, then any member of the popular press who knew of your refusal would put two and two together and conclude: bungy-boy. Cock-licking faggot. Your career would be stillborn."

"How would a member of the popular press know about my refusal?"

"Might forget myself whilst drunk and tell 'em." Willison smiled his sweetest smile.

I have never claimed to be the most intelligent man on earth, and it may well have taken me longer than most to comprehend all this. Willison studied me closely as I reflected, and he took the opportunity to reach down the front of his jodhpurs. I could see him work a long bulge. Then I nodded and he nodded.

"You and I, Mess," he whispered, "shall be fugging famous."

So I scramble around, desperately hiding behind the more-than-dead body of my felled horse. Cutthroat bastard Indians swarm around. Charles Wild Horse leaps from his steed, armed with a well-honed Bowie knife, and I know for a fact that the Oglala Sioux never owned such weapons traditionally, this was Charles's personal tule rooter sticker, and he comes scrambling

toward me with his misaligned eyes glowing red. Just as Wild
Horse is about to murder me, Bodnarchuk, risen from the dead,
pulls up alongside and says, "Hop up, Thom." Which I do.
Charles Wild Horse leaps over the body of the horse to get at me,
and the tip of his knife tears through the material of my pant leg
and leaves a straight line of dainty blood drops. "Calm down,
Wild Horse!"

"I'm acting!"

The white men make a narrow escape. Fortunately for us there
is a small log cabin nearby. We quickly tether our horses and file
inside. The Indians form a circle around the shack. Our faces now
blossom across the screen, large as God's. There is Bodnarchuk's,
all a-twitch, as though there is a mighty stench in the air. There
is mine. At first, as they made my image, I tried to look frightened,
at least concerned. Willison screamed, "Keep your face still, you
great biboon. We can't read anything if you keep moving the
pages." There is Charles Wild Horse. He has the eyes of a hawk.
The sunlight plays across his face like oil on a hot skillet. Then
comes a title. Jefferson Foote had written so many words they
would have required three full cards. The Fat Man replaced them
all with the simple, "Trapped!"

Trapped we are inside the little cabin. Which is when Our Hero
gets a brilliant idea — you can tell in the Flicker on account of a
sudden elevation of my eyebrows. Then the iris closes and the
screen goes to black.

It is a few hours later. The shadows of the Indians and their
horses inch toward the cabin. Suddenly, the door opens and out
comes a woman in a gingham dress and very ornate bonnet. She is
smiling, her mouth uplifted pleasantly, her large eyes cast as
though daydreaming. The woman carries two baskets, checked
tablecloths pulled across to contain steam, apparently from
freshly baked goods. She makes her way gingerly toward the Indians, who stare at her with befuddlement. They cock their heads
like hounds who hear farts at the Sunday dinner table. The
woman walks into their midst, sets one of her baskets on the
ground — pulling the cloth away to reveal black powder — and
then upsets the other over it. The second contains red-hot coals,
and when they meet the powder — the woman hikes her dress to
reveal legs, hairy and thick in the *vastus lateralis* as she scampers

back toward the little cabin — there is an explosion. It blows Charles Wild Horse off his horse, melts the war paint from his face, and takes away his eyebrows.

And in the theater that day, the day of the Premiere, the Day of Beginnings, Thespa Doone's hand began to work my shaft with more vigor when that explosion came, so I did likewise. The cheers of the ancient feebs and their milkmaids echoed throughout the Masonic Temple.

For now it was time for the Heathen Savages to play the Death Game. Our little gang stormed out of the cabin with six-shooters blaring. The Indians who had managed to remain aboard startled, and bucking horses made a vain attempt to resist us, but we had God on our side and more sophisticated weaponry. The pagans fell from their saddles, covered with pig-fat and candlewax. Charles Wild Horse raised himself off the ground, still clutching that huge knife, and the first thing he saw was me charging at him, still wearing the dress, waving handarms. "Oh, dear," he moaned.

I shot Charles Wild Horse through the heart. His body jerked as the pig-fat exploded, and there in the theater, so did Thespa Doone's. Perhaps I had hit upon some spot of great sensitivity. She made a sound now, Thespa Doone did, like her body was empty and being played like a flute; the grunted notes came one after another and without much expression. Up on the screen, I regard Charles Wild Horse with much compassion and pity, then race off to rescue Thespa Doone from her fate worse than death.

Thespa Doone is still tied to a post as near-naked savages shuffle around her, but I hide up in the rocks with a rifle, which I somehow acquired along the way, perhaps wherever I changed out of the dress into my regular clothes, and pick them off like so many tin cans on a fence. I thought I should kill the Indians more manfully, strangling the life from them, doffing my white hat and laying it across my chest before moving on to the next.

Thespa's dress has been reduced to tatters; the flesh shows through. There is soot smeared across her face. Thespa looks up at me and smiles weakly, then she faints dead away. Her body sags, and I can see a breast through a rent in her clothing, the nipple hard. In the theater my fingers come over all palsied, I abandon any control over them and let them do whatever they want. As I untie the ropes, Thespa wakes up briefly, looks up at me and mumbles. The title-cards claim she says, "My true love. I knew you would come." But she didn't say that, she said, "Take me to my room and make me come." And at the Premiere, she takes the reins away from her hand, and her fingers work my penis with a frenzy and, as we ride off into the sunset, Thespa Doone explodes, and so do I, ruining my fancy tuxedo.

"Oh, sorry!"

I leap up from the bed, adjusting my prison uniform. My uniform differs from other prisoners'. It is the same color and pattern, black stripes across white, but my uniform is tailored from silk. "Must get back to work," say I, and I leap on to the high stool behind the magnificent desk. There are papers everywhere, so I begin a little show of organization, gathering them together and making true the edges. "I must continue writing about *Civilization.*"

"And the part Thespa Doone played in it."

"The next thing I'm going to write about is very interesting, sir. It has to do with when the Johnston Brothers — that's right, *the* Johnstons, the notorious gamblers and thugs Lemuel and Samuel — came to The World."

"It can keep, Thom. You have an engagement." The Warden neatens some pages for me; his eyes move quickly over the words. The Warden seems even paler today than his usual complexion of a man recently deceased. "An engagement, Thom, is what you have. You are having dinner with your old friend Murtagh."

"He is not my old friend. I do not care for him. I do not see why you want to put us together, as if we shared a common interest in butterfly collecting."

"The man has but a short time to live. Surely you can spend *one* evening with him. I've made meatloaf."

"With baked beans on top?"

"Just so."

"You could bring me some meatloaf here, Warden."

"Could. Won't." The Warden smiles, his pale lips writhing like worms.

"How about this? I'll have dinner with Murtagh, but here in my cell."

"That would be unacceptable, Thom. John's spent all day cleaning."

"But, sir. I haven't been out of my cell since I arrived."

"High time, then, Thommy."

"Is he close by?"

"Oh, yes. It's just a little stroll. A constitutional. It's good for you. It benefits the blood!" The Warden shows me what excellent exercise walking can be. Keeping his legs ramrod straight he struts about the little cell, kicking over the occasional piece of furniture.

"Oh, all right." I pull on my bathrobe, look in the warped piece of silver metal that serves as a mirror. There are great pools of shadow where my cheeks once were, there are lines of worry growing like ivy from my eyes. I spend many moments smoothing down my hair. It has grown almost as long as Foote's was, and does not receive the care it requires. My beard hangs like seaweed from the face of a drowned man, and springs from the fount of cellular disharmony.

When I turn around, The Warden is dangling a pair of black iron handcuffs in the air.

"Warden?"

"Humor me."

"But, sir."

"One has regulations."

"When I came, I didn't have to wear any such things."

"Things were different when you came."

When I came, it was the dead of night. The Warden led the way through the hallways with a candle, and the shadows around us were filled with the sounds of troubled sleep. I was drunk, because the bailiffs at the courthouse had thrown a little party in my honor, a fine soirée in the Hollywoodland tradition. I have ragged tatters of memory: shrill laughter, nakedness and fornication. The Judge himself attended and rutted with a creature that was fabulously pink and obese. Women serviced me, in many and varied ways, they chewed and sucked upon me, and when I awoke in my cell it occurred to me that they had been feasting upon my Spirit and had left me nothing but scraps and gristly bits.

I meekly tender my wrists. The cuffs are too small, and the rough metal digs into the skin.

A key ring is chained to The Warden's belt, and he reaches for it as though it were a sidearm. Using a quick wrist action, The Warden makes the key ring flip circles around his huge index finger

"This should be fun." He lays a shoulder to the thick iron of my cell door, and it opens with a sound like when you first cut into the lid of a tin can. And — to continue what Old Geezer Hartrampf assures me is called an *analogy* — there is a sudden odor, as with a tin can, although I cannot imagine anyone canning Baked Shit.

The Warden takes two steps out into the hallway, but I hesitate at the threshold. I cock my head as though wondering about weather.

"Come along," snaps The Warden.

I am surprised to encounter a young man out there, all dressed in official blue, who puts me instantly in mind of Bodnarchuk, except that he lacks the limpid Chinese-style moustaches and goatee. This guy is standing rigidly just to the right of my door. "Good day, sir!" he barks at the Warden. "Good day, Thom!"

"This is Exley, Thom. He has been keeping an eye on you."

"He has?"

"Keeping track of your wants and needs. We like you to be comfortable."

The hallway is full of light and darkness, and only light and darkness. I am reminded of The Ancient and Lucid Druids, who believed that at the beginning of time, we were all beautiful and romped through fields of Absolute Light and Dark. Shadows are the bastard offspring of the unnatural forced union, and we will never be happy dwelling amongst them. But this hallway is naught but blackness cut by shafts of sunlight from barred windows high above.

There are no cells near mine, they begin about fifty feet down the hallway. The Warden stops as he reaches the first, much like a Tour Guide beside a museum artefact. "This," he speaks as I draw up, "is Kenelly. Shame on Kenelly. Kenelly killed an old man for eighteen dollars."

Kenelly sits on his haunches atop his crude bed, which is a warped board and a threadbare blanket. The largest piece of furniture in his cell is the commode, which has flies swarming about it and puts out steam.

"You mean he killed and robbed a fellow, and only profited eighteen dollars by this heinous crime?"

"No, Thom. He was offered eighteen dollars to kill a fellow, and Kenelly thought this ample."

Kenelly laughs at some portion of The Warden's answer, perhaps his own name.

The Warden takes a large step forward so that he stands in front of the next cell. "This brute," he points hard with his forefinger, "murdered an entire family. Including the family pet, a well-behaved Pyrenes. His name is Schmidt."

"Isn't Murtagh waiting on us, sir?" I do not wish to gaze upon Schmidt, but some part of me is unable to resist. Schmidt stands perhaps five–foot–two; his body seems to be covered with black down.

"I thought you would be interested, Thom."

"Why is that, Warden?"

The Warden raises his hands, holding them oddly, the fingers bent as though crippled with arthritis. The Warden laces the fingers together and raises this arrangement until the tips of his knuckles meet his chin. "Because I thought that perhaps you might understand, Thom."

I storm ahead of The Warden. The hallway bends to the left abruptly and is stopped by a huge iron door. The Warden flips his circle of keys, catches the largest, and feeds it to the lock mechanism. He pushes the door open, and I am alarmed as daylight bleeds through, first covering my feet and then claiming more and more of my body. "Sir?"

"Murtagh is across in the Death House."

"How nice. *Would you like to come to dinner?* All right, fine. *I'm having it in the Death House.* Peachy!"

"Shut up." The Warden pushes me outside, and I am blinded. "He killed his wife. He pushed the blade into her over and over again. So of course he's in the Death House."

And now instead of light cutting through darkness, the world is a ball of white fire in which shadows dwell. The first I see, standing upon the prison wall with her Bible raised toward eternity, is my mother. Or what used to be my mother, because she is now very far removed from the moon and the rare tender sentiments that resulted in yours truly. I hunch over (I am crippled anyway, by the sunlight) and scurry toward the black building across the courtyard.

"Hello, Mrs. Moss!" cries out The Warden. "Look! It's your boy Thom!"

"Thom?"

Her voice seems to contain real surprise and leaps, as a mother's voice should, into the heights of tender fragility. I walk into yet another door, I press my hands over my eyes and wait for the sounds of tumblers turning. The Warden's large finger prods me in the small of my back and I enter the Death House.

Chapter 17

"What has long perplexed me is this," says the doomed man, John Murtagh. "Where did the Hero get the dress?"

"I do not know." I pick at my food, which I have little appetite for, despite its being meatloaf, one of my favorites. The Warden makes it with baked beans on top, he covers his creation with strips of bacon.

Murtagh is eating as though he had recently wandered out of the barren wilderness, where there dwells neither fern nor fowl, where the last fuck-pig has been slaughtered and its deadly skewers traded in for seventy-five cents cash money. Flecks of meat and bean-mash cover his chin. Murtagh is a much more animated man this visit, he gestures with his fork, drags his hand through his hair, his legs beneath the table are vibrating quickly. "You don't know? How could *you* not know?"

The Warden has taken a seat in the corner on a wooden chair there, so tiny that it threatens to crumble beneath his huge stern. He sits very erectly, his forearms atop his thighs, his fingers resting peacefully upon his knees. "Thom knows surprisingly little," he says, and I nod emphatically. "He merely did as was demanded of him by Caspar Willison."

"Oh, yes," says Murtagh, somehow enlightened. "Still, a fine motion picture, was *A Fate Worse Than Death.* I enjoyed it almost as much as *Southern Honor.*"

"The thing I enjoyed most," says The Warden, sitting in the twilight, all aglow with hairlessness, "is that you can see Thespa Doone's breast."

"Can not."

"Can too, Thom. Her left breast. Through a rent in her clothing."

Murtagh takes up a huge serving spoon and ladles more meatloaf on to my plate. This is the fourth time he has done so, and as I haven't been eating much, he has created a cairn of ground chuck and Boston Blues. "I am not sure that you do," Murtagh says quietly, his eyebrows bumped up against each other. "It all happens so fast. It is light and shadow. There is a shape, but it is too quickly come and gone. I could not say definitely, *that was a breast.*"

"It was," says The Warden, "Thespa Doone's breast."

"Warden," say I, "I believe you are doing this to get my goat. I believe that you are in a foul mood today and are deriving an unseemly pleasure in tormenting me."

"I worry about the effect of this upon less disciplined men. What if this huge and perfect breast is seen by a deviate with little control over his gonadal impulses?" The Warden grins at me, curls his lips back from his teeth.

"Well, if you can see her, um, you know, and I'm not saying you can, it all happens in a trice."

"That's right," says John Murtagh. "You are left with only a fleeting impression. You ask yourself, *was that a breast?*"

"She is naked in *Civilization.*" The Warden drums upon his kneecaps with the thick fleshy pads of his fingers. "Stark naked. I fear total and utter chaos."

"But when you see the Flicker," wonders John Murtagh, "are you able to say, *yes, there is nakedness?*"

"Absolutely," avers The Warden.

"How would you know?" I demand. "No one has seen *Civilization.* It is not finished."

"True," says The Warden. "But soon, but soon, but very, very soon."

"Interestingly enough," begins Murtagh, and something in his tone sickens me, something in the way he realigns his posture indicates that he is about to launch into disturbing reminiscence, "she was not naked when I came upon them. The coupling was so wanton, unnatural really. And yet, she wore a nightshirt. It irked me, this pitiful claim to modesty. More than anything else, that precipitated the incident."

"When Murtagh says *incident*, Thom," announces The Warden, "he refers to the brutal murder of his wife."

"I *know*."

"I just don't like you men hiding behind words. I do not like *incident* substituted for *brutal murder*. I do not like to hear *manslaughter* when I should hear the word *fratricide*."

"Oh, now, Mr. Precision In Public Speaking, as an intimate of Old Man Hartrampf, I would have to say you have selected the wrong word there."

"I have not. *Civilization* is soon to be finished," he tells us. "And that is something we have to talk about."

I first heard of *Civilization* — as Willison bolted cognac and related the Vision — late one night in the Salon. I had heard mention of *Civilization* several times previous; often the word would slip through people's mouths, but I always let it scoot by. Amongst the first words Thespa Doone said to me were, "I am to be naked in *Civilization*, Mess." Even at the beginning of our relationship, those words tied half-hitches in my intestines.

And C.W. Willison spoke the word on more than one occasion. We were filming a scene in one of Willison's first six-reelers, *Zephyrs*. (It actually had only five reels, but all the long-lengths were called *six-reelers*.) I am of mixed opinion about this Flicker. What is good about it is, I play a young lightstock rider. What is bad about it is, Thespa portrays my sister.

In one scene, I chase a bastard who violated my sister. The bastard is portrayed by Bodnarchuk, who had hoped this meant some elevation of his reputation and status. Instead, he was so thoroughly vile as the Bastard, leering and drooling and twisting the ends of his tired Chinese moustache and goatee, that the audience would hiss and boo at the mere sight of him. In several cities, rotting vegetative matter was hurled against the silver screen. Bodnarchuk was cast forever back into the pool of background boys. Anyway, there I am in pursuit on horseback, and because I am portraying a rodeo rider, I draw up alongside Bastard Bodnarchuk's mount and leap aboard.

The problem being, you need ground to catch up on a horse, and in order to capture the whole sequence, Bittner had to set up his camera at quite a distance. Willison went berserk. "This is the time for testicular squeezes, Bittner. This is when I want tremblin's and fillips. Get closer!"

"I can't get clos—"

"*Fugya!* Fugya, Billy Bittner! You've ruint my career!"

The tall and gangly boy, Theo Welkin, snapped his body forward, the momentum threatening to hurl him to the ground. "Phantom Ride," he said. Theo used his arms to suggest what he meant, stretching them their oversized length and bouncing his hugely knuckled hands in the air. Fortunately, most of us knew what he was on about. A *phantom ride* was a type of Flicker popular in the tents, a panorama where a camera was installed in some vehicle — a train being most usual — and cranked as the journey was undertaken, so that the country bounced by in a blurred and sick-making fashion. "Put the camera in a motorcar."

Willison immediately fetched his own Locomobile. He tore away the rear — I suppose he was assisted by other people, but mostly I recall him stripped down, sweating, tearing savagely at the machine with his own thin hands — and constructed a crude platform in its stead, very large and tenuously attached to the frame of the car. The platform looked exceedingly dangerous to stand upon.

"Go stand upon it," Willison told Bittner and his assistants.

They did not demur, because Willison had that glow. When he was very excited his skin would mottle, his face assorted hues of fleshy reds and pinks. Water would bead up, it would almost hiss and sizzle and turn into steam. So the camera crew placed the contraption upon the platform and then gingerly stepped up themselves.

Willison then announced that he would do the driving himself. He cranked up the Locomobile, leapt into the vehicle without benefit of door-opening, and played with all the gear and brake levers. "Ooh," he whispered.

Bodnarchuk was hunched over his lunchbag atop a fairly twitchy horse, the beast made uneasy by the hacking combustible engine noises, the odd smell of gasoline. I was aboard Tragedy, my best and favorite, who never let anything rankle him whilst making a Flicker.

"Are you ready, Moss?" Willison demanded.

"I'm always ready."

"Bittner! Crank it!" he screamed, alarming Bodnarchuk, who was eating a banana (I've been wanting to work in that Bodnarchuk ate a lot of bananas, but you'd be surprised at how difficult some of these writerly tasks prove). Anyway, Willison screamed, "Bittner! Crank it!" and Bodnarchuk's little body spasmed, and a missile of bruised fruit blew out of his hand, and his legs convulsed and heeled the pony. The creature threw itself up on to its hind legs and frantically hooved the air.

"Love it ta pisses!" hollered Willison, and then Bodnarchuk was gone on the open gallop, and I lit out after him.

Willison worked his levers in a fury, and the Locomobile drew up even with Bodnarchuk. On the back platform, Bittner was cranking the camera, which had been cross-tied variously to the makeshift platform and what was left of the back of the car. Theo Welkin stood beside him placidly, his hands folded behind his back. When the motorcar hit a bump, Welkin would pop into the air, where he would remain for a moment, scanning the horizon, before returning to his position beside the camera. The ancient Georg knelt by the back of the platform, leaving a trail of vomit so that everyone might find their way back out of the wilderness.

Up ahead, Bodnarchuk took a hard left, for no apparent reason, but I of course took the left and Willison did likewise, so sharply that the whole automobile seemed to scream like a stuck tule rooter. Billy Bittner fell off with a rather graceful simplicity. The Locomobile hit a bump and Georg bounced high into the air, maintaining his wretching crouch. Whilst he was elevated the automobile gained some thirty feet. Georg landed on the baked ground and immediately christened it with pea soup.

Theo Welkin took a calm step to the side and started turning the camera crank. The boy grinned with such delighted force that trickles of pus leaked from his myriad pustules. "Faster, Mr. Willison!" he screamed, because Bodnarchuk was quickening. His horse was trying to evade and eclipse the Locomobile, and Bodnarchuk exerted little control. I spurred Tragedy, Willison worked gear levers frantically, and Theo Welkin giggled and worked the Wonderbox.

As I draw closer to Bodnarchuk — I'll admit that I did call out, "Will you slow the fuck up, Bodnarchuk?!" but without moving my lips — I pull my feet out of the stirrups and snap them onto the saddle seat. I crouch there, holding the reins in one hand, my other outstretched for balance, and Tragedy stretches out as though he was headed first for the gate at the Kentucky Derby.

Willison cranks the steering wheel, the Locomobile yaws and moves closer, too damn close, seeming to be screaming just a few inches away. Willison speaks quite calmly. "Get on with it, Moose. We haven't got all day."

All I have to say is "Okay," and Tragedy draws even with Bodnarchuk's horse. I let loose the reins and fling myself away. I almost miss, and frantically clutch at the cantle and rear-housing, but it looks smooth and heroic upon the silver screen.

Willison was ecstatic. He pranced about with his hands rigid and hovering around his brain, promoting it to inspiration. "We must use this," he cried, "in *Civilization*!"

"What's that?"

"In the Biblical sequences. You know the part, Mess."

"No, I do not," I tried to put in, but it was like trying to hand a flower to a passing freight train.

"*And it came to pass, that behold,*" said Willison, speaking the Good Book as if it were a nickel-novel written by the Fat Man, "*there came a chariot of fire, and horses of fire.*"

"And Elijah," I recalled, "*went up by a whirlwind into Heaven.*"

"*Civilization,*" said Caspar W. Willison, picking out each syllable very carefully, as if he were placing words on a satin pillow, "shall be comprised of four separate stories."

We were sitting upstairs in the White Owl Hotel, in the Salon, at a large round table. At the table were the following men: me and Willison, the long-faced Jefferson Foote (taking his poetical aspect out for a walk), and the Johnston Brothers.

The Johnston Brothers, Samuel and Lemuel, were identical
twins, although the sixty-odd years they'd toiled in the vale was
much harder on Lem. His face was cross-hatched with scars, and
did not have a nose. There was a bump with two hair-rimmed
punctures in it, but it was smaller than many of the boils and car-
buncles that puckered his visage. Lemuel was definitely lacking
an eye, and that I can set down with accuracy, for he neither
replaced it with a glass orb nor covered the hole with a patch.
Too often I looked up to meet Lemuel's glance and stared into the
center of his brain. Lem did have — as did his twin — beautiful
hair, which they wore shoulder-length, cascading waves of burnished silver. Samuel wore his to better effect, because he was a
rather handsome man, all of his features set with out-of-the-box
freshness.

Samuel sat in his chair draped with long-legged urbanity, his
arm crooked over the top of the chair, his right leg crossed over his
left and stuck out, where it interfered with his brother's left,
because his brother Lem aped the same sort of slouch. Every so
often the legs would clash like crossed swords, but neither of the
Johnston Brothers seemed willing to change over. A few times
they'd turned and spat at each other like tomcats meeting atop a
fence.

Here's how the Johnston Twins made their fortune. You may
have heard tales of the lawlessness in Nevada, which was geo-
graphically ideal for all sorts of crime. In order to get to California,
people were forced to venture through that desert land. Desperados would pop out of the Shoshones and descend with murderous
exhilaration. On the few occasions that lawmen were persuaded
to enter the state, their heads usually ended up on pikes, raised on
the outskirts of towns with deceptive names like Paradise and
Eureka. Then Lemuel and Samuel Johnston — hitherto feckless
gamblers — arrived and announced the creation of the Death Valley Equitable Life Assurance Company. In exchange for a substan-
tial amount of money, the Johnstons would ensure not only
whatever goods you were hoping to transport across the state, but
also your personal safety. In the beginning this was done by way
of escort. You would sit between the Johnston Brothers on your
conveyance of choice. Lemuel would remain perfectly motionless,
his good eye riveted forward, his other merely an empty pocket of

darkness. I've heard that Lem never spoke a word, was niggardly even with his grunts; the only sound he produced was a little whistle as air passed through the thing that wasn't his nose. Sam possessed an air of urbanity. He would join his charges in conversation, although he had some unconventional notions, chiefly regarding the discharge of bodily waste matter. The client was subjected to a lengthy and detailed description of a healthy bowel movement and warned against straining over the stool, which, according to Samuel, was a surefire way of exploding blood vessels in the brain. Soon the client would be praying for the intervention of murderous desperados. When the pig-dogs arrived, the Johnston Brothers would stand up slowly, pulling weapons from within their waistcoats. Samuel preferred firearms, Lemuel was partial to blades, which he honed to a fine, head-severing edge.

All that was long ago. The Death Valley Equitable Life Assurance Company was one of the richest in the land, and the Johnston Twins, very advanced in years, were trying hard to spend a dignified old age. Samuel was having an easier time of that, being churchgoing and sober. Lemuel still got into the occasional dust-up, as for instance when he kicked a fellow into a coma.

The Johnston Twins, being rich as Solomon, made the acquaintance of Mr. Inge (to whom Solomon no doubt owed money). They cruised upon Inge's yacht, the *Silver Dream*, and fished for mako. The Johnston Brothers went to fancy restaurants with Mr. Inge, who dined at only the finest eating establishments despite the fact that he lacked teeth. They went to nightclubs, where Samuel would sit, straight-backed and scowling, and Lemuel would pull off the waitress's thin clothing. And, of course, the Johnstons would attend the motion-picture theaters, because Mr. Inge was very proud of the Flickers turned out at The World, even if he himself failed to stay awake through them.

Lemuel and Samuel Johnston loved the Flickers. They always sat in the front row, their fingers wrapped around the armholds of their chairs, holding themselves back, as if they were both likely to hurl themselves forward, into the Flicker. Which in point of fact Lemuel did one time, so upset with some character's villainy that he drew the knife out his boot and rushed the screen, tearing the sheet into tatters.

Their favorite player was Thom Moss. The Johnstons saw all of my motion pictures, seventeen two-reelers and five long-lengths. They asked to meet me, and Mr. Inge brought them by the Salon. Samuel pumped my hand for a very long time, squeezing with friendly enthusiasm and nearly rendering the bones into dust. Lemuel seemed likely to kiss me on the mouth, he held my head between large calloused hands and gazed into my eyes.

Caspar Willison ignored this little scene, firstly because people held little interest for him (don't believe what you read in the Hollywood *Megaphone*, where Willison tends to spout off about Humanity), secondly because he was angry at Mr. Inge, as he had refused to give Willison the money to make *Civilization*. To his mind, Willison wanted to serve up *filet mignon*, and the common folk had been happily chowing down on horse meat, even horse shit. (Mr. Inge had been violently opposed to the Battle Scene in *Southern Honor*, which cost hundreds of thousands of dollars and only lasts a few minutes. When I say "violently opposed," I mean that his mouth opened and his tongue lolled out, he waved his liver-spotted claws around briefly and then went to sleep.) On this matter of *Civilization*, Inge was adamant. No money, particularly in the quantities Willison was demanding, a hundred-fold more than had ever been ponied up for a piece of entertainment. (And even that amount wouldn't have paid for the whole of *Civilization*, but this was a little secret that Caspar Willison kept to himself.) So Caspar sulked as the Johnstons enthused, and then some portion of his mind began to listen. And when the enthusing got to the point of asking what was coming up for me, and I said, "I'm not real sure..." because I was not, nor had I ever been, the director reared up to his hind legs. "I can answer thet question with one word," he told them, "and thet word is *Civilization*."

It was perhaps not the Johnston brothers' favorite word. Samuel's silver eyes hardened. Lemuel shuddered and felt about his person for hidden weaponry.

Jefferson Foote was over in the corner. He sat as though his limbs had been arranged by someone else, all awkward angles, knobby elbows and knees. His philosophic weariness was such that it was all he could do to hoist a glass to his thick, pale lips. There was a woman beside him, there always was since Jefferson had become famous, although I cannot recall Jefferson ever having intercourse with any of these women, even so much as asking,

"How about a pickled egg?" For a few weeks he squired around Miss Nola Hansen, and even she of the Perfect Bosom was treated with a disinterest that lived next door to disdain. Miss Nola left passers-by sucking for air (once I but glanced at her, and Thespa withheld her body from me that evening) but Jefferson may as well have been with my aunt Lacky.

Caspar Willison called over to my erstwhile companion, Foote rose wearily and adjusted his sombre weeds, and soon we were all sitting around one of the tables at the Salon.

"Four separate stories," Willison said, "that are as four rivers from four mountains. While each takes its own course, they come together in a grand, um…"

"Confluence."

Willison speared me with one of his looks. "Four civilizations," he continued, "distinct and disparate, yet, four civilizations damned and destroyed by human nature."

The Johnston Brothers brought up an index finger to pursed lips, as if to say *Now there's a fancy notion*, but when they saw that the other was beating them to it, they dropped their fingers fast and stared back at Caspar.

"One," Willison announced, "we travel to the fabled isle of Crete."

"The Cretan tale," said Jeff Foote, speaking on cue, he and Willison had planned this out, *orchestrated* it, "is somewhat light-hearted, but in it we first espy mankind's affinity for warfare and bloodsport."

"Uh-yeah,' said Lemuel.

"Two," said C. W. Willison, "is a stirring tale of the Aztec Sun Kingdom of Mexico!"

"Where-in we explore idolatry," said Foote, exhaling smoke from his black cigarette.

Lem commenced digging in his ear with a little finger, because when he did not understand a word he assumed it was because he had misheard it. He wasn't a stupid man, but had not nurtured a thoughtful, learnèd side, having gotten along with simple brutality.

"Three," announced Willison, fanning that number of bony fingers, so thin that the light behind illuminated the bones, "we plumb the Holy Bible."

"Largely," droned Jefferson Foote, "the Book of Kings."

"*And there were also Sodomites in the land,*" said Willison, smiling primly and satyric at the same moment, "*and they did according to all the abominations of the nations which the Lord cast out before the children of Israel.*"

Samuel bridled, his twin brother guffawed, spraying the table with spit shot over gap-toothed gums, Samuel smacked him in the head and the two grappled momentarily, albeit without rising from their seats.

"How much money do you want?" demanded Samuel and Lemuel together, their voices choir-like, Sam's sitting high and Lem's like a croupy bullfrog with a taste for cheap cigars.

"Oodles," said Willison, leaning forward and staring up at the Johnston boys through his paper-thin eyelids. "Money-wise, I want almost everything you've got. What I'm more worried about is your belief, your futh."

"Hmm?"

"Futh. I want your total and complete futh. Gentlemen." Willison's head snaked lower, closer to the Johnston boys, who regarded it with a measure of terror. Lemuel looked fairly close to pinning Caspar's head to the table with the stiletto in his boot top. Willison suddenly lay his head down on the table dreamily. "We are talking about the single greatest artist achievement of mankind."

The two Mr. Johnstons leaned back and chewed their nails.

"Thespa Doone is going to be naked," whispered Willison.

"I have been in communication with Caspar Willison," announces The Warden, putting the capper on what has been a dreadful evening. "He has almost finished his great masterpiece. That's why John wanted to speak to you."

"What?"

John bashfully rises from the table. "I was hoping you would share some of your... tricks."

"I'm sorry?"

"You are much more handsome in the Flickers than you are in real life," notes Murtagh. He squints and stares hard at my face, as if to make certain of this notion, then nods. "You could, for instance, help me with my make-up."

"What are you two going on about? Willison is going to film Murtagh?"

"Oh, yes," answers The Warden, nodding like an idiot child. Murtagh bats his eyelashes, something he learnt from watching me in the Flickers.

"He's going to come here and film you whilst you await your hanging?"

"Oh, no, no," answers The Warden. "He is going to film the hanging itself."

Chapter 18

Caspar Willison, as a young man, was employed by the Louisville *Herald*, given the sporting beat and dispatched to boxing matches, where he first made the acquaintance of the Fat Man. The organizers liked to have well-known personages as referees, almost always a largish over-stuffed man, as this seemed to lend the activity a certain respectability. Bat Masterson was frequently called upon, as was Teddy Roosevelt — although he gave it up upon becoming President of the United States — so, too, was the Fat Man, J.D.D. Jensen, the most famous novelist in America. ("In the *world*!!" he would have roared, causing the ends of his moustache to tremble with inebriated glee.)

Willison became intrigued with the squared circle, obsessed with it might be nearer to the mark, and he indulged in a good deal of shadow-boxing when there was nothing more tangible to be struck. There was a ring set up in The World, Mr. Boyle the Master Builder had constructed it behind the White Owl Hotel, and often after a day of cranking Flickers, Caspar would climb through the ropes, his shirt torn away, his pant legs rolled up above his tiny spade-like calves. He would flail away at nothingness, stabbing the air with right jabs and left hooks, and sometimes he would carry on until midnight before collapsing to the mat. Afterwards he'd ascend to The Salon, there to drink fine liquor.

One time, early on in my career as a Star Player of Motion Pictures, Caspar W. Willison looked up into the sky and muttered, "All right, all right. Enough. The light has gone yella." Willison always said this with disgust and frequently spat into the dirt afterwards.

Thespa and I had just finished kissing, which is the happy ending for that Flicker, *A Fate Worse Than Death.* Mrs. Moorcock came over with a small wash basin and the two women began to clean the make-up from Thespa's face. I believe I've attempted to describe the bridled fury with which Thespa did this, how her skin would come up prickled with irritation, the cheeks flushed by clownish circles. I hung about nearby, my hands tucked into my back pockets. Bodnarchuk hailed me on his way into the Saloon, but I ignored him, or rather, gave him a little two-fingered salute like he was the local greengrocer. Thespa unfastened her collar, worked the washcloth down the front of her dress, moved it across her breasts slowly. I rocked on the balls of my feet, which might seem an unimportant thing — *picayune,* suggests Old Man H. — but I am noting it because, had I not been rocking on the balls of my feet I might not have fallen forward into the street when Caspar W. Willison kicked me in the seat of the pants.

I slapped dirt from my clothes, and blew it out of my nostrils. "All right, Caspar," I snarled, "if you want another go at me..."

Willison peeled off his shirt, so I hammed up my fists and began to circle around him. Thespa and her mother moved away from us, not because of impending violence, which they didn't seem to apperceive, but because the make-up was off Thespa Doone, and her mother led her, mottled and red-eyed, her hair stuck up at peculiar angles, toward the privacy of her windowless bedchamber at the White Owl Hotel. So I lost enthusiasm about halfway through my first menacing fist-waving circle, but once you start, there's no giving up. Willison unhitched his pants and let them drop, stepping out wearing only his undershorts, which appeared to be rendered out of silk. "All right, Mess," he said. "Let's go."

I flew forward and delivered a mean cut and — being as Willison was no longer there, having sauntered off — I ended up back on the street. "Where the hell are you going?" I hollered.

"It's time for exertion." Caspar Willison headed down the alley-way that separated the White Owl from whatever building was its neighbour on that particular day.

Mr. Boyle was capable of erecting pyramids that fluttered in the breeze (indeed, Thespa stood naked on top of one) but his boxing ring was solid enough that Caspar was able to haul himself up by the ropes. Willison stretched by grabbing hold of one of the corners, leaning hard backwards; he flew to the center of the ring and jumped up and down, and he made not a sound.

"Come watch, Mess."

A young man stood in the far corner, a pale fellow wearing only boxing gloves and a leather pouch to contain his manly bits and pieces. He was reconstructed in an exaggerated way, particularly about the clavicular portion of the pectorals. Caspar tossed a pair of gloves over to me, stuck his hands through the ropes, wrists turned upwards, as if he wished to be manacled or to have his veins slit. I slipped the gloves on his hands and laced them up.

"That is young Jimmy Cook," Willison said to me, in a voice loud enough for the fellow to hear. "The Irish Rainstorm."

"*Hurricane*," adjusted Cook, his young dark eyes narrowing.

"Yes, yes!" Willison called over his shoulder. "I knew it was something climactic!" Willison winked at me, lowering one eye-lid without effect on the other blue orb, which remained absolutely motionless and aimed at me. "Watch this."

Willison's legs scissored with mechanical precision, and with each opening and closing he would advance about a half-inch, so that if he ever arrived at the far side of the ring, he would be spent and exhausted. Fortunately, this Irish Hurricane fellow came out of his corner to meet him, all hunched over with murderous intent. Willison raised himself up on to his toes and Jimmy Cook darted forward quickly and delivered an uppercut to Willison's belly. But when the blow arrived, Caspar's stomach was nothing but stria, eight little bricks of rectus, and the uppercut came to naught. Then Willison jabbed his left hand into Jimmy Cook's face, dancing backwards to escape the gushing nose-blood. Jimmy Cook returned to his corner.

"That was gude, wasn't it, Miss?"

"I don't know," I answered. "Might have been lucky."

"Nonsense." Willison stopped his dance and stood motionless in the center of the ring. "Hey, Cook," he sang out, "you fugging Irish wad-gobbler." Willison presented the point of his chin. "Have a bash."

Jimmy Cook, blood smeared across most of his near-naked body, moved forward with astounding quickness and delivered the punch all in the same blurred motion, but I do not believe it ever landed on Willison's chin, because Caspar snapped it back out of harm's way. Willison then returned a jab, and Cook's nose made more mushy sounds. The Irish Hurricane cupped his glove to catch the blood which flowed as from a pump-spigot. He returned to his corner.

"This," announced Willison, "is fun."

I crossed my arms on the apron, as though across a neighbourly fence. "I get the idea, Willison. But you know what? I think this is just more play-acting."

"Play-acting? I've just broken the faggot's nose!"

"I know what it is you're trying to demonstrate. But I took you that night up in the Salon —"

"You idiot. You *moron*."

"—and I can take you again." I turned around and left for the White Owl, Caspar's voice ringing in my ears.

"I'm not trying to demonstrate anything, Muss! I'm just having a good time! Come here, Jimmy Cook, you big beautiful thing, and I'll bash in your face for ya!"

I ascended to Thespa's room.

If the time has come for honesty (The Warden often barges into my cell and shuffles through my ink-spattered pages, intoning lowly that the time has come for honesty), I should relate the following story.

We were making *Dundee*, which is a very fine motion picture, although you've never seen it, because it auto-immolated in the canisters shortly after completion. I play Homer Dundee, Marshall of Circuit City, a town peopled entirely by heartless thugs and wide-legged women. This was the way the Fat Man perceived the world. All of the Fat Man's male characters married young and then had their wife and newborn child slaughtered by Indians.

This rendered them into murdering bastards or grim-faced law-men, although the ratio is about five hundred to one. Surprisingly, considering how many brides got killed, there was a goodly number of young women left over. They, too, shared a history. They were very pious, convent-reared, and they got raped a day or two after entering the Worldly Realm. Some became scarlet women with foul mouths, others became grim-faced schoolmarms, again, the harlots outnumbering the teachers by a wide margin. According to the Fat Man, the entire nation was peopled by creatures morally and spiritually bereft, although some were so because of unspeakable personal tragedy, others just for the fun of it.

Except Marshall Dundee, of course, who seems to step straight out of Sunday Prayer Meeting into this Gomorrah. I dress entirely in white, although my clothes soon become mud-spattered and dusty, because I march around Circuit City having various knock-downs and dust-ups. I tend to eschew the shooting irons hanging low on my hips, which is slightly foolish, because the entire populace is always aiming guns at me. This Flicker has an ironical ending. Marshall Dundee, try as he might, cannot tame the lawlessness. (A deputy or two would have helped, although this advice was not well-received by the Fat Man.) So he burns down the town. I do this at dawn, the sun struggling up into the sky. The townspeople run screaming into the hills, drunken men and women in their dingy underthings. I do not run into the hills; Marshall Homer Dundee wanders through the flame and smoke, I collapse upon the streets of the fiery Circuit City and that is the end of that particular motion picture.

Because Marshall Dundee was always dressed in white, Willison decided that I should have a white horse. Whoever was in charge of such matters found an Arabian steed. The first time I saw him, early one morning, fresh from making love to Thespa Doone (she was both more eager and more tender at dawn, a peculiarity I never understood) the horse was in the middle of the corral, carrying on, slapping hooves upon the earth and making thundering sounds. The other horses trembled in a clutch over by the railings.

"That," whispered Caspar Willison, appearing at my elbow, redolent of stale cognac, "is Tragedy."

"Good-looking horse."

"I love you, Muss," whispered Willison. "You want to fug *every-thing!!*"

My entry into the corral had a calming effect upon Tragedy, who watched my advent through an eye of inky blackness. He was suspicious, true, but intuited that I meant him no harm. I believe that Tragedy sensed our kinship: we both, the horse and I, distrusted and misunderstood people. Even Thespa Doone, my one and only, was a source of disquietude. And Willison, my goodness, the man's presence at even a distance would knot my stomach.

That's my opinion. The Fat Man adjudged that Tragedy and I got along so well because we had the same degree of intelligence. "You and that horse even have the same hobbies," said the Fat Man, filling his mouth with sherris sack. "Senseless whinnying and wanton shagging."

It's true, Tragedy did enjoy that. Not the whinnying so much (and what did Jensen mean by that, I have never let loose a *bona fide* whinny in all my days) as the latter, which Tragedy discharged with unseemly enthusiasm. I'd never heard a horse grunt until I spied Tragedy topping a grey mare. His tongue was flattened between huge white teeth, his crest and forechuck trembled, and he let loose loud and steamy grunts.

Tragedy, in common with myself, was a natural in the Flickers. I'll get back to that morning when we were making *Dundee*. (To tell the truth, I hadn't really realized I'd drifted away; this writing exacts great concentration from its disciples.) Tragedy calmed, as I was saying, and he remained placid as I saddled him, although he quivered as I cinched the flank billet, as if perhaps it tickled. I mounted and listened as Willison explained what was going on.

"Bad fellas," Willison muttered, pointing toward the south. "They went thetaway."

Tragedy seemed to think we were posing for a sculptor, such was his stillness.

"Dundee in pursuit. Got it?"

I nodded. Tragedy nodded as well, although perhaps he was just settling the bit.

Willison stepped away and raised his arms as if to conduct an orchestra. "Fade in," he said quietly — whereupon Tragedy emitted a mighty roar and threw himself up onto his hind legs. The horse took a step or two forward — I was pitching away up there,

plucking my hat out of the air and circling my free arm for balance, and for a moment I thought that we were going to walk all
the way. Then Tragedy dropped down to its forelegs, bucked the
hinders (just what I needed, poised as I was for the rear, the upshot
being that I dented my forehead on the saddlehorn) and lit out
after the imaginary desperado. I remained in my crumpled position, which I hoped looked like a canny crouch, and pulled out my
firearm. I pointed and pulled the trigger. A huge spray of wax and
tallow exploded into the air and blew back into my face.

"Cut," said Willison.

Tragedy stopped so suddenly that it was all I could do not to fly
off the horse. As it was, my dismount was rather undignified,
compounded by the lard hardening in my eyes.

I rode Tragedy in *Dundee*, and in the next three two-reelers:
Bald Mountain Men (I know what he meant, but I have to say
Jeffie mistitled that one), *The Sundowner*, and *Frontier Fury*.
These were the best Flickers that Willison and I made, and I wish
there were a few more like them. But Willison, you know, he was
changing. You could see him alter day by day. As he got new ideas
about the purpose and nature of motion pictures, his eyes
widened, the pale blue became surrounded by a latticework of spi-
der-webbed veins. His hair greyed and whitened, and bolted with
ever more energy, great swatches of it bolting clear of his head.
Willison lost weight, though he had none to spare. And as we
turned that last Flicker, he spent more and more time shadow-
boxing, less and less directing the proceedings.

"All right, all right," he'd bark out perfunctorily "Big thrulls
here. Mess and these bummies have a tussle. Bittner, crank the
wonder box. Fade in." One time some of the fellows and I had
orchestrated a wonderful fight, King Palmer taking a header off the
top of a building. No one else was fighting on the rooftops, but logic
doesn't pull much weight in the Dream Palaces. As Bittner cranked
his machine, Caspar Willison turned away, glancing at the sky. He
formed his bony hands into fists and pulled them through the air.
And then, just as Kingsley Palmer arced gracefully and headed
earthward, Caspar Willison wandered away. We kept up fighting for
a while, thinking that he might come back, but that was the last
we saw of him until the next morning, when he showed up with a
hangover of colossal proportions. Our director had the complexion

of a dead man, lifelessness belied only by wisps of odors and fumes that leaked from his clammy head. He could not even walk properly, stumbling and seeking anchorage every two or three feet. Despite all this, there was something serene about his aspect, a rare gentleness. The first words out of his mouth were, "Rig up Mess for the Flying W." Minions began to scurry around.

I looked about The World. "Where is it?"

"Where's what?" demanded Willison, whistling out some truly foul air.

"The horse."

"You, um..." Willison raised a crooked finger and waved it about in my direction. "You are a-settin' on it."

"No. The horse for the Flying W."

"You," he repeated evenly, "are a-settin' on it."

And that's when I noticed that his ugly little henchmen were attaching piano wire to Tragedy's rear leg.

"No way for that, pardner," said I, and the horse beneath me stirred, alarmed by something in my tone. Caspar Willison then threw my own voice back at me, "No way for that, pardner," and although it was dripping with sneering disdain, it was an uncanny imitation, enough to jerk up several heads and cause some nervous laughter.

I swung down off of Tragedy and marched over toward Willison, hitching up every article of clothing that could be hitched. "You can't do that." I spit and dragged the back of my sleeve across my mouth.

Willison kept his rum-fuzzy eyes aimed at me, but could not be bothered focusing, his little tongue darting out to wet his lips so that he could draw them up into the pursed little vee that he employed as a smile. He made no response, other than to cast a quick glance about The World. And I saw what Willison wanted me to see; that he *could* do that, it was in fact being done.

And that is when I grabbed hold of him, gathering material from his white shirt, slipping my fingers under the leather strap that crossed his bony chest. I leaned in close, though the air was putrescent, and I said, "I'll beat holy shit out of you, Willison."

"Hmm." Willison nodded once or twice, and then flew backwards out of my hands. I was left with a torn swatch of linen in my hand.

Willison had gone herky-jerky, his hands fisted and devoid of blood. He waved these in the air, challenging me, and anyone else in the general vicinity, to come at him. His feet moved incredibly quickly, forming a tiny box-step, dancing the Très Moutarde. "You shall, shall you?" Willison spoke as though we were sharing a congenial cognac up in The Salon. "I don't think so. I'll tell you what's going to happen, Muss. I'm going to uglify you. I'm going to flatten your nose and blacken your eyes and knock your teeth down into your belly. And then you won't be so pretty, hmm? Then the fillies won't squirm and wetten the benches. And you'll be through." Willison kept up his dancing as though he were a wind-up toy. "I shall pick another odorous bummy. Hasn't that dawned yet, Miss? It doesn't matter. *You* don't matter. I shall pick another boy, and what's more, I shall *still* destroy the horse. So put your perfect bottom back in the saddle."

"You're a true bastard, Willison."

He stopped all the commotion in an instant. "You know what, Thom? I am *so* sick of this shit."

"Yeah. Me, too." I avoided Tragedy's eyes as I mounted. That's all I'm going to write about that particular day.

Chapter 19

The Louisville *Daily Sun* also sent the young Caspar Willison to baseball games, so he was fairly knowledgeable regarding that pastime, although not especially enthusiastic. "Too fugging slow," was his opinion, voiced quite often, for many at The World were fanatics. Bodnarchuk had even played a few professional games, which makes sense because Bodnarchuk seemed to have worked most jobs at one time or another. "I played second base for the Sedalia Rose Blossoms. Ever hear of them, Thommy?"

"No. Ever hear of The Nine Men From The Confluence?"

"I'm afraid not. The Sedalia Rose Blossoms were a fine team, but I fear we were undermined by our name. A baseball nine should be called something fearsome."

"But..." It occurs to me that this conversation was had in the tavern of the White Owl, because here comes Robert F. Kincaid with an objection. He was a miserable fellow who liked to poke at your sentences and look for holes to plug objections. "But," it occurred to him, "what about the Red Stockings? What is so fearsome about the name Red Stockings?"

"Hey," said I, "just wait 'til Bodnarchuk pulls off his boots, you'll find out."

We all laughed, except for Bodnarchuk, not that he was hurt or insulted, mostly that he was still concentrated on constructing his own theory. "The underpinnings of the psyche," he said very carefully, which caused a number of carnival boys, including myself, to spew guffaws, "are affected by the coloration or the..." Bodnarchuk shaped his hands around emptiness, trying to mold thin air into a sphere "...or the *evocation* of nomenclature." The only point of that little story is this, that when we played that big charity game, our side was called The World Lightning Bolts.

The opposition, who lacked benefit of Bodnarchuk's unique mind, called themselves The Hollywood Stars, which was easy to understand, seeing as it consisted of people like Francis X. Bushman, Harold Lockwood, Doug Fairbanks, Carlyle Blackwell and Charlie Chaplin.

It was at this game that I met Ed Porter, he who turned *The Great Train Robbery*. I shook his hand and enthused about the Flicker for a minute or two, relating how much I'd enjoyed it as a boy. I got caught up in telling Porter about the travelling fair, the rodeo ("Bill Pickett himself was there, you know"), the faded tent that held the galloping tin-type. I turned to the benches behind the diamond. "Jeff!" I sang out. "Jeff, I want you to meet someone!"

Jefferson and I were not getting along those days, but it was hard to remember that all the time. Quite often I'd see him strolling through the set-stages, all dark and poetical in his cape and Spanish hat, and I'd wave and shout, "Ho, Foote!" Then he'd turn his eyes toward me, two little puddles of bitterness, and I'd recollect that Jefferson and I were on the outs.

I waved him over, and he stood up from within a little nest of blonde women, many of them wearing bathing costumes even though the ocean was miles away. Foote lit a cigarette in a slow and irritating manner, as if his cigarette-lighting was on a par with the sun coming up. "Jeff!" I called. "You'll never guess who the hell *this* is!"

And he never would, it's true, because Edwin Porter looked like a bank manager that even other bank managers would find bland. He perspired heavily and devoted much energy to mopping sweat from his brow. "This," I said to Jefferson, "is Edwin Porter."

Foote nodded, extended his hand, the cigarette clamped into the corner of his mouth by thick, fleshy lips. "Foote," he said.

"I was just telling Mr. Porter how much we enjoyed *The Great Train Robbery*."

"Yes, indeed." Foote smiled, puffed on his cigarette, nodded. "It was a charming little piece, although quite primitive."

Mr. Porter smiled like a fellow does when you inform him that his shoe is covered in dogdirt.

"No offence," said Foote. "It's just that I myself have been experimenting with form."

"Foote," said I, "you make it sound as if you got a room full of Icelandic Crystals and are trying to discredit the Undulatory Theory of Light."

Both Foote and Porter stared at me like I was a madman.

"Hey now," I pulled on my mitt, "we got a game to play."

We went to the heart of Los Angeles to play baseball, The World versus Hollywoodland, all proceeds from public admissions to go to a local orphanage. At least, that was the main purpose, but Caspar Willison rarely had just one reason for doing something. On this afternoon he had arrived with the Johnston twins, Samuel done up with brocaded immaculateness, Lemuel wearing the same fancy raiments, a velveteen jacket and ruffled shirt, to very ill effect. The brothers held fine suede hats in their hands, the better for the world to see their luxurious silver hair. The reporters thronged, but did not crowd too hard. They'd all heard how Lemuel, annoyed at being badgered, once took the pen out of a reporter's hand and very calmly drove it into the man's chest, burying the nib. Samuel was known to lash out with his formidable hams, despite the skin being white, soft and powdered.

When I came up to bat, leading off for the Lightning Bolts and looking resplendent in my uniform — upon the front was stitched the image of a storm-savaged globe — there was manly applause, some matronly cackle, and audible flutter from the younger girls, but much was drowned out by boos. I waved at the pitcher — it was Chaplin, the little fellow who is these days so popular everywhere — and stepped out of the box. The Society for Peaceful Speciate Co-Existence stood in a dense clutch just off third base.

Although, in their correspondence and circulars, the Society boasted upwards of eleven thousand members, I never saw more than about ten together at any one time. They were a uniformly unsightly Society, and I often wondered if they'd pushed this Speciate Co-Existence too far, if you see what I mean. (I'm not just saying that out of bitterness. Trying to dispel my bitterness, after all, is one of the tasks I've set for myself here in the Cahuenga Federal Penitentiary.) Whenever I looked upon them I was reminded of the lore of the Ancient and Lucid Druids. Recall, the Druids claim that at the beginning we were all beautiful, and frolicked in the Absolute Day and Absolute Night. But we could not choose between them and opted instead for the Shadows, and so began our devolution into assorted furry creatures. The members of the Society looked as though they were still undergoing the process, they had floppy ears, long snouts, eyes that seemed too far pushed to the side of the head.

Their leader, and the furriest of all, was Apollo Greenling. That was not his real name, which I heard at my trial but disremember, but the name this fellow put on a number of books of poetry. He wrote hymns and odes to the Animal Kingdom, long-winded and making much use of the exclamation mark. Apollo Greenling was a large man with a Biblical beard. His body was oddly twisted, his shoulders slumped, his back was humped, and his buttocks stuck away out like a baboon's. (I am not embittered, that is how the man looked.) At the moment I am relating — I'm still stepped out of the batter's box, Charlie is horsing about on the hill, winding up and pitching but failing to release the ball, in consequence flipping over in the air and landing on his butt, staring at the horsehide with confusion and contempt — Greenling cupped his gnarled hands in his beard and called out, "Shame on you, Thom Moss!"

C.W. Willison sat on our player's bench grinning at me, his pale blue eyes wider than usual. I searched in the stands for Thespa Doone, my true love, but she had fled the sun-beaten bleachers. I sliced my bat through the air. Jefferson Foote sat among the blonde-haired bevy and paid no attention to me. He puffed on his cigarette like he was trying to kiss bug-butts. Only the Fat Man seemed to care, his corpulent face worked with worry, although I think I knew deep down this had more to do with the bet he'd placed than with any concern for me. (Jensen had a little wager with the Johnston twins. Later that evening, the Fat Man wandered into the Saloon with frayed moustache hairs and empty pockets. No matter how many drinks I bought him, his foul mood did not improve.)

So I just hawked on the ground, kicked dirt over the oyster in a very bull-like manner, and stepped back into the box. "Come on, Charlie," I called. "Throw me one down the pipe here."

Chaplin assumed a very serious face and went into his wind-up. Ten seconds later he was still in that wind-up and the crowd was going wild, so I unshouldered my bat and laughed along. Naturally, as soon as I did that, the ball somehow shot forth. The umpire was a little ancient man, his face hidden behind a protective mask, shadowed by a cap, and wrinkled as an elephant's butt. He opened his mouth and a second later the word "Strike" crawled out, and I grinned, because this was, after all, a charity game, but that ball was nowhere near the plate.

"Good one, Charlie," I called, and the little fellow nodded, tipped his cap, and turned around on the mound. "Okay now," I hollered at his back, "let's see your best damn st—"

I held up on that sentence because Charlie had tossed the ball over his shoulder; it flew up like a fat pigeon and was now descending toward me, so I fumbled with my lumber and took a swipe at it. The ball landed softly in the catcher's glove. The catcher, Doug Fairbanks, laughed. That son-of-a-bitch was always laughing.

"Strike," croaked the umpire.

"Yeah, yeah, yeah. You don't have to call the ones I swing on, mister."

Chaplin made a big show of doing the little things a pitcher does before he hurls: hustling his beans, adjusting his cap, hiking up his trousers until they nestled just under his armpits. He spit, as many a fine pitcher does, but the spit landed on his toe, so Chaplin wiped the foot on the back of his other leg, and in doing so managed to trip himself. He was back up on his feet in a second, looking around to find the culprit who downed him. The people in the stands were dizzy with laughter.

I know, from the magazines and newspapers which the Warden fetches me, that these days Chaplin's fame is of an order we can but barely understand. When I myself was famous, it meant that occasionally someone would stop you in the street. Women would make themselves available, and men would either buy you a drink or start a fight, depending on their disposition. I meant nothing to the people with dead eyes, the hopeless and bedraggled, the people who have been given tears to drink in great measure. These are the people who follow my mother; even as she damns them for their inability to cleave unto the Word, they cling to her vague promises of Salvation. These are the people who love the Little Fellow. And Chaplin's fame is not, as mine was, confined to the United States of America. No, sir, he is renowned across the face of the earth, as if the world, now largely at war with itself, has also found a common delight.

The bastard struck me out. He did this not through swizzle and buffoonery, mind you, Chaplin did it by suddenly hurling a baseball toward the plate, and as I swung, the bottom fell out of it. I walked back to The World bench put out and befuddled.

Bodnarchuk was our best player, hitting a single every time he went up to bat, catching everything that came near him at the hot corner; however, his mind was not devoted to the game. Sometimes, at the end of an inning, as the rest of us trotted toward our bench, peeling off our mitts and waving at the fans, Bodnarchuk would remain standing near his base, staring off at the clouds with a particularly vacant look. And in the batter's box, it might take a called strike or two before Bodnarchuk would shake his head and address the plate with some conviction.

It was in the ninth inning that Bodnarchuk gave me some clue as to what was occupying his unlikely mind. He said to me, as we sat on the bench and awaited for our ups, "Thommy... you don't mind if I call you Thommy, do you?"

"No, Bodnarchuk, I do not mind."

"Only your father calls you Thommy. And your aunt Lacky upon occasion, I believe."

"That's so."

"Thommy, I believe you and I have become best friends."

Our side was losing by a couple of runs doing our damnedest to make it up. First to the plate, top of the ninth, was Kingsley Palmer. You'd think, with all his bodily reconstruction, that he'd be a crack batsman, but Kingsley's complex musculature interfered with his even holding the lumber properly. He somehow carried it out in front of him, and couldn't get it cocked back. His first few at-bats he'd struck out miserably, pushing the wood forward, emitting a mighty grunt, but failing to make ball and bat proximate. I'd have expected him to be downcast, but as he entered the box in the ninth, Palmer had an addled grin blooming across his chubby face, his eyes were tiny pools of ecstacy.

"What's with Kingsley?" I wondered aloud.

Caspar Willison, who sat on my other side, and was deeply, deeply involved with winning the game, said, "Palmer was unclear on some of the finer points of this pastime."

"What does that mean?"

"Watch."

Chaplin buckled the back of his hands on his hips (he continued tossing the ball up and down all the while, releasing it and catching it on his fingertips) and stared at Kingsley. Chaplin was a good pitcher, although he delivered the horsehide with a huge overhand (I decided this was because he'd maybe played cricket as a boy) that gave you a good read on the ball. Anyway, he reared back, hurled, and tossed a fast one right through the box. Kingsley joyously bent his head over, as if in prayer, and the ball connected with his skull. The sound was almost musical. The ancient umpire raised a bent finger and pointed Kingsley Palmer off toward first base.

"Well done!" sang out Willison, dancing over to the on-deck circle, while I heard Bodnarchuk ask, "What is it about me that you like most?"

"Hmmm?"

"Which of my qualities is most stellar, and binds us fast together?"

Manley Wessex was busy striking out, which he did in overtheatrical fashion, taking three huge swings that rendered him pretzelled and purplish. His third strike was especially dramatic, because Manley, pissed as a newt, spewed up a chicken sandwich along with an emphatic grunt.

"Well," I considered, "you're a good man to have a drink with."

"That is by nature of being a curse, Thommy. I am not proud that I'm bad to go to the bottle."

"Well, you don't put on airs, then. I like that about you. You're not all snooty-nosed."

"That's not it."

C. W. Willison, one hand thrust deep inside his pants to hustle his manly parts with vigor, took his place in the batter's box. He grinned at Chaplin, pulled his bat leisurely through the air.

"You're on deck, Bodnarchuk."

"It's my sense of humor."

"Come again?"

Willison laid down a bunt, and I think this was pretty savvy, because he knew how the battery, Chaplin and Fairbanks, would respond. They both bolted for the ball, their heads down, which they cracked together vigorously. Whilst Fairbanks and Chaplin rolled about on the ground, groping for the ball with their eyes pinched shut in pain, Caspar W. Willison almost strolled down the line to first base. Once there, he wagged one of his long pale fingers. "Charles," he said, "you've got to resist the chip and easy laughs."

"It is," persisted Bodnarchuk, although he was supposed to be on his way up to bat, "my sense of humor that you appreciate most."

"Well, it ain't the dog with the waggingest tail, Bodnarchuk."

He lifted a finger and placed it near my face, as though there was something on the tip he wanted me to see, something tiny but very important. "My sense of humor," Bodnarchuk repeated, as grave as an undertaker who's just buried his mother.

"You're up," I told him quietly, as the wizened umpire and half of the spectators told him the same thing at the same time. Bodnarchuk looked around slowly, placed his cap on his head, thereby squashing his limp brown hair over his eyes, and left for the batter's box.

He lined the first pitch into right field, where it was caught and then dropped by Crane Wilbur, the heroic sort from all those *Perils of Pauline* Flickers. That had the bases all loaded up, only one away, and I was up to bat.

I'd struck out twice and grounded out once (actually, as long as I'm coming clean about my life, I hit into a double play), but my attitude was that I'd do fine if Chaplin would ever just rear back and hurl one over the doorstep. The little fellow, I reasoned, was just about out of antics, so I entered the batter's box with my thoughts cleared and my attention devoted to the task

at hand. I stared forward, *toward* Chaplin but not *at* him, and I
ignored his little comicalities.

Just before the first pitch, Chaplin wandered off the mound, and
suddenly I was staring into the strange blue orbs of C.W. Willison,
who was standing on second base. There was nothing in those
eyes, and I fell into them, and I don't recall Chaplin finally pitching the ball, but I know he did so because I gave it a mighty smote
and sent it off toward heaven.

And at that same moment Jefferson shouted, "Hooray!" and
raised a hand toward the heavenly vault, but he chose the one
he'd left in the waste land swollen with tule-rooter bile. As I trotted round the bases I noticed him waving with his scarred stump.
I waved back and as soon as the game ended I gave him a friendly
swat on the back. Foote pitched forward, into the naked arms of
one of the blondes, a scantily clad girl who'd become lost on her
way to the sea. Foote giggled and pushed himself free. The boy
was exuberant and seemed to have become half-drunk in the last
few minutes.

"I gave that pill a shot, didn't I?"

Foote seemed not to know what I was talking about.

"The homer."

"Oh! Yeah, Moss. You gave it a shot."

"Right over the fence there." I pointed toward deepest center
field. Willison was standing on the pitcher's mound, surrounded
by a horde of newspaper and magazine reporters. His words floated
on the wind like paper boats on ditchwater. I could hear but few
of them. "Four separate stories," said Caspar Willison. The Johnston Twins stood on either side of him, their faces as full of clouds
as a moonrise in November.

"What's Mr. Willison on about now?" I wondered aloud.

"Do you mean to say," said Foote, and he let loose a quick bray,
"that Caspar didn't tell you?"

"You know, Foote, I see now why some people find that laugh
of yours so off-putting."

"*Civilization*," said Foote.

"What about it?"

"He's going to turn it."

Willison was now gesticulating at the Johnston Twins, who held their hands behind their backs and shuffled their feet, bashful as deacons at a church social.

"Caspar had a bet with the Johnstons," Jefferson Foote told me. "If we won the game, they'd pony up for the greatest motion picture of all time."

I took a few steps away from Jefferson, close enough that Willison's words linked up and started to make a bit of sense. "Flickers ain't all they're cracked up to be," he was telling the pack of newspapermen. "I am a little shamefaced to have been given such a great gift, and to have done so little with it. I mean, how many times can we watch Thom Moss jump on and off horses?"

I turned back to Foote, who was in the overly dramatic process of lighting a cigarette. "By the way," I told him. "I guess Bodnarchuk's my best friend now."

Jefferson only nodded, and slightly at that, absorbed as he was in holding the match flame to the end of his smoke.

"Yeah, me and Bodnarchuk are about as close as two people can be. You know what I like most about him, Foote?"

He shook his head slightly, drawing in his cheeks until his face was nothing but pools of shadow.

"His sense of humor."

Chapter 20

The Hollywood *Megaphone* made no mention of my game-winning circuit clout. The rag merely recorded that after a pleasant afternoon of playing at baseball, Caspar Willison unveiled plans for his latest project, a motion picture of epic breadth and scope, entitled *Civilization*. The paper went into some detail regarding the financing of this Flicker, how Mr. Inge was putting up only a portion, but the bulk of the money was coming from the coffers of the Death Valley Equitable Life Assurance Company. That company was also insuring the production against all sorts of possible mischief and destruction. "Protecting our investment," stated a laconic Samuel Johnston, whilst his twin offered a merry chuckle.

Samuel Johnston had many words of praise for the diminutive director. "Willison is a genius," he averred, whilst his twin agreed with a merry bark of laughter. "He made what we feel is the best motion picture of the age, Southern Honor." *His twin offered agreement via a contented chortle.*

This motion picture, *Southern Honor*, is the doomed John Murtagh's favorite. It is a very famous movie, but I am not overly fond of it, because I do not think Willison made the best use of my talents. My talents are seen to best advantage in *Dundee*, an excellent little Flicker that burned to ashes in the cannister.

Southern Honor takes place during the Civil War and the few months that follow. I play Maxwell Beaumont, a wealthy scion. Perry King portrays my best friend, Lex Hogarth, and Thespa Doone plays Bess Miller, the girl we both love. Bess is more fond of Lex, which is not surprising, seeing as I am an utter scoundrel. The first thing you see me do, in *Southern Honor*, is abandon all claim to such a thing, turning on my heels and heading for the hills during the Battle.

There was a section of The World, lying to the western extremity, where there was a huge depression, a concavity, bracketed to the north by a series of small hills, to the south by a dust-dry riverbed. It was at this hollow that I arrived one morning, sharing a Lanchester with the Fat Man. Jensen had been pressed into rare service by Willison, who needed every available hand for this, his most famous sequence.

Jensen did not look well, his cheeks flushed with either ague or cheap cognac. During my ascendency, the Fat Man fell out of favor with Willison. Jensen had problems coping with these long-lengths; his drinking and hangovers usually only allowed a few minutes of clearheadedness, so he was able to churn out two-reelers, but Willison had abandoned them. The Fat Man's novelistic career was also on the skids. His last books were so strange that he was fortunate not to be locked away in The Confluence Asylum. *The Lycanthrope of Lariat* pitted Billy the Kid against some werewolves. Billy was docile and law-abiding, the Werewolves ate live chickens (that's how the townspeople of Lariat knew something was up), and no female character seemed to be able to keep her clothes on for more than a minute.

The Hollow was surrounded by men, perhaps two thousand of them. They were derelicts, outcasts and bums, vagabonds and Ishmaels, all dressed in the most threadbare and tattered of rags. As we arrived, they stripped themselves naked, there in the moonlight. Scores of minions passed amongst them, distributing uniforms.

There were cannons in the earth-bowl, fully one hundred and

twenty, eighty of them lined out to the east (which was the Union position), forty of them to the West. These had been gathered from the townhall squares of every little burg in Los Angeles County. Trenches had been dug behind, looking like the work of some giant burrowing creature.

Caspar Willison stood in the center of all this, his hands on his hips as though posing for a statue. He wore, that day, a new hat, a huge white flat-brim. The Bird's Head Colts were holstered high, near his belly, which is where the truly murderous hang their weaponry. (In his Flickers, Willison insisted sidearms be worn low, over the hip.) He also had an old pistol, a strange antique that needed loading and tamping, and as I leapt out of the automobile and descended the hill toward him, Willison loaded this strange gun, and when I got to within twenty feet, he shot me in the heart.

"Ouch!" I was glad to not be dead, if only because I didn't want to leave "Ouch!" behind as my last spoken word.

It was bad enough that Willison had shot me, albeit non-fatally; worse was, it turned out that I had just happened to be in the way. He was most interested in the small cloud of smoke that lingered. He stared at it and remarked, "Still too grey, Mycroft."

Mycroft repeated, "Too grey," and nodded.

Willison canted his head so that his nares hovered near the smoke, he reached out a long hand and caressed the wispy mare's tails. "Too grey and too insubstantial."

"Oh." You and I have seen Mycroft before, of course, mostly hanging about the Saloon at the White Owl Hotel, invariably drunk and singing songs in the style of John McCormack, or what would be John McCormack's style if he were tone deaf. Mycroft bent over to pick up a long silver tube, but it kept falling out of his hands, back to the cold earth, and Willison ended up raising it himself.

"That's for the grape charge," said Mycroft, pointing at it, although not really, because Mycroft lacked fingers. There was one digit, the third on his left hand, that was long enough to be serviceable, otherwise Mycroft had only short stubs, the ends scarred and blackened.

I stood picking hardened globules of pig-fat and candle tallow off my shirtfront, so I didn't notice when Willison lit a punk on the end of the silver tube. A ball of white light flashed out the end, grazed my scalp and exploded in the starfield behind me.

"Not bad," judged C. W., "but too high."

"Ah, yes," Mycroft was reminded, and he fumbled in a small leather bag that he wore strapped around his neck. "Look at this." A few seconds later, Mycroft brought out a small hand grenade.

"Lovely!" chirped Willison, pulling the pin and lobbing the grenade at my feet. I turned to run, and then an explosion singed the hairs on the back of my neck and slammed me face-first into the clay.

"Mycroft," said Willison, "do you suppose that some of these bummies might be hurt by the little booms?"

Mycroft thought about that for a long moment. "Well, for god's sake, Caspar, it is a fucking *war*."

Willison nodded, and then turned on me. "Mass, why the fug aren't you in custoom?"

I nodded — at Willison, supposedly, although he had stormed away — and peeled off my own clothes. I stood naked in the night and waited for someone to bring me Confederate regimentals.

When the dawn arrived, Willison was stood on the edge of the crater with a megaphone clenched in his hand. Beside him, preparing to crank the camera, was Billy Bittner. His assistants were variously upon the field of battle: Georg was set up beside a small tree, and both he and his machine were disguised so as to be indistinguishable from the greenery. The old man — helpfully bone-thin — wore long underwear, dyed a deep verdure, and paper leaves had been pasted along the length of his frail and brittle body. The boy, Theo, was crouched behind a parapet, although his head kept poking up over the makeshift stonework. Theo's camera was aimed upwards in order to record the horses of the Union Cavalry leaping behind Confederate lines. The horses were of a whole other order than the ones we rode in the two-reelers. For one thing, regular horses were sorely needed for the slaughter over in Europe. So, these animals were blue-ribboned steeplechase jumpers, and the carnival boys, playing the opposing Cavalries, were ecstatic. Mostly my friends were playing Rebs, stuffed into ill-fitting grey suits, and Bodnarchuk had told me that they would be playing a grand Death Game during The Battle. They had even raised the winner's take, the cowboys ponying up extra, the winner claiming a ten-dollar bill.

Perry King and I stood side by side, near the front of the troops, because, being wealthy scions, we were lieutenants or corporals or some such thing. The men around me did not smell at all nice, many were drunk, some were having the blue terrors. There were a few actual veterans there, old men who were greatly alarmed to find themselves pressed back into action.

Perry King held the Old Glory, flying upon a golden standard. He wore a kerchief tied rather jauntily around his neck, which I wished I had, too. Perry King was a nice enough fellow (and I see his photograph often enough in the magazines to realize that he's making a go of it in the motion-picture business) but I still say I should have been playing *his* part, and he mine. Perry's hair was almost blue, and he needed to shave every half hour or so — that would have suited Maxwell Beaumont. I should have played the heroic Lex Hogarth, not that Perry didn't do it well, but because I have a more heroic aspect. At least, I *had*. These days my mien is shadow-filled and my eyes are hollow, but back then I was rosy-cheeked and sparky.

Willison spoke to us from the crest, his words loud through the megaphone, but mostly unintelligible. I'm confident it was encouragement and threats in equal dosage, such was his directorial manner. The only words that possessed clarity were the ones Caspar always used to begin a scene: "Fade in."

Bittner cranked and slowly opened the iris on the camera.

Beside me, Perry King yelled, "Forward!" hoisting the Confederate standard proudly. The men of the South began advancing toward the east, toward the Union encampments, toward their doom.

I turned around and saw my compatriots on their magnificent chargers, grinning from ear to ear — Bodnarchuk, Manley Wessex, especially Kingsley Palmer — and someone amongst them yelled, "Death Game!" because the Death Game always seemed to require an official commencement.

The fireworks began, Mycroft and various underlings firing sizzling light into the sky. Other underlings threw the grenades, which puffed white and magnificent wherever they hit the ground. Bodnarchuk took advantage of a grenade-landing to execute his special stunt back flip. His body lifted from the saddle and grace-fully revolved before being sucked into the ground. Bodnarchuk found his own efforts lacking. He sprang up, fresh and eager, remounted, and continued toward the Northern trenches.

All around the hole in the earth stood men with silver tubes and canvas bags full of hand-grenades. The Fat Man was one of them, and I went to stand beside him, because that was the extent of my involvement in the great Battle scene, I skulk shamefacedly off the field, a tallow-hearted coward. The Fat Man lobbed a grenade — rather feebly, I must say, even if he did give forth a grunt of con-siderable volume — and said, "You were wonderful, Thommy. I've rarely seen such a convincing portrayal of pusillanimity."

"Pass me a grenade, Fat Man. I'll show you some fancy tossing."

I watched Kingsley Palmer pretend to have been caught in the back by a bullet or shrapnel. Palmer pitched forward, over the pommel, sliding across the horse's face (which was suffused with a look of surprise, something you don't see that often on a horse). Kingsley dropped to the ground, convincingly bereft of life, and allowed the horse to continue over him. I swear to God I heard squishy and crunchy sounds. Many men, both Southerners and Union, stopped to appreciate Kingsley's play at the Death Game. He could have stopped there, winner for all time. Instead, Palmer got back up on to his feet, his eyes crazed with God-given inde-structibility. He leapt upon his horse and brought his heels into the horse's belly. "Ha!" he cried, and the steed reared before vault-ing forward.

Now, the Fat Man maintained that it was my grenade that landed at the feet of the ancient Georg, although there were many grenades flying about and it was not easy to keep track. If it was mine, it was a damned good throw. Georg, disguised as a tree, cranked a second camera on the far side of the field. He did not notice the grenade rolling to a stop at his feet, and judging from his reaction, he did not really notice when it exploded. Suddenly a little man, wearing green long underwear and paper leaves, was flying through the air, his mouth set grimly, his right hand still turning little circles in the air.

There was more excitement over in the trenches where the young Theo Welkin squatted, cranking his camera. It was Willi-son's notion that the horses should be filmed from underneath, so that all we see is the passing of their speckled bellies. One of the horses caught a hoof on the bricks of the parapet. Being as this was Mr. Boyle's handiwork, the entire construct exploded, all the way down the line. The horses — fine steeplechase jumpers, remember, and therefore unduly skittish — stampeded back across the field of battle, right through the line of advancing Rebs, giving the players an opportunity to harvest major scores in the Death Game.

Bodnarchuk pretended to receive a wound to the arm, and he clutched his bicep. He next began to sway slightly, there on horseback, and the swaying increased until he was turning huge moonish circles and then he disappeared. It is usually a poor idea for a Flicker Player to disappear from sight. In this case, howsoever, things worked out well, because he next shows up in the midst of the stampeding white chargers, still dazed and confused, one gathers, from the wound in his upper arm. He walks amongst the panic-stricken nags like a drunkard; he is buffeted and bounced and as the last horse goes by he teeters and expires. Now, let me be clear about one point: as the *last horse goes by*, I wrote, meaning the last of the stampeding Northern chargers, by this time mostly riderless. But when the horses met the other set of trenches and parapets they wheeled around, so that the last horse met the first horse of the second wave in a cyclone of confusion and whinnying terror. Kingsley Palmer spied an opportunity for immortality in the Death Game. First off, he received a wound, his selection being a bullet to the gut, which he represented by doubling over atop his mount. Kingsley clutched the pommel weakly, but life fled his body and he fell sideways. It was his great masterstroke to lie then bouncing across the backs of the equine vortex for fully a minute before being sucked down and out of sight.

Even this was not good enough. Kingsley leapt aboard another horse, kicked it into a warring stand, and shouted, "Ha!"

Theo Welkin had picked up the motion-picture camera and placed the tripod legs over his bony shoulders. Thus adorned, he walked onto the field of battle, one hand turning the crank with rhythmic equanimity. He stumbled about, unmindful of the horses and eruptions.

Whilst all this upheaval was on-going, little Perry King continued toward the Northern line with Old Glory held high. His rebel compatriots were biting the dust with great regularity, for so was it written in Foote's scenario, but Perry, the heroic Lex Hogarth, continued undeterred. It was as if the Union army couldn't draw a bead on that character. Perry even stepped on one of the grenades, which blew off one pant leg and all of the shin-hair, but he kept waving the Confederate banner.

As Perry drew ever nearer, C. W. Willison, standing on the crest, drew up his megaphone and exhorted his men, "Hand to hand! Mano-a-mano!" Union soldiers leapt from behind the stonework, grizzled old drunkards with palsied, liver-spotted hands. They were ready for a fight, those fellows, and they met their opposites with barbarous fury. The Confederates were largely slaughtered, except for Perry, who defiantly drove the rebel ensign into the ground at the Union lines.

There's fairness for you: Perry gets to perform this act of bravery so manifest that the enemy soldiers refrain from killing him, even though he's standing right in front of them. I, on the other hand, skulk away, and would not be in the scene at all were it not for a series of cross-splices, close views of my eyes, huge, and vibrating with cowardice.

Just a handful of Death Game participants remained in contention. Bodnarchuk, on foot by this time, threw himself upon a Northerner. They grappled briefly and then Bodnarchuk came away, mortally wounded. He was now going not for acrobatic tallies, but artistic ones. Bodnarchuk waltzed along the trench, and with every puff of white smoke, both Confederate and Union, he would spasm his body violently. After fully a minute of this, Bodnarchuk began to teeter and reel, and then he keeled into the trench and was through for the day.

At this point King Palmer appeared out of nowhere on a white charger, and as he neared the parapets he threw himself forward. (Theo Welkin happened to be nearby, still wearing the motion-picture camera, so Kingsley's final stunt is captured forever on celluloid.) Kingsley flew off the horse and turned a somersault, leisurely frolicking amidst the smoke. He timed his revolution so that he met the brickwork with his forehead. An observant Flicker-goer might think it unlikely that this blow could devastate ten linear feet, and improbable that the flying Confederate would pop up, refreshed as from a long night's slumber. Kingsley spied a riderless mount and leapt upon it, spurring the steed into a magnificent stand.

"Ha!" shouted Kingsley, and then his head snapped, just slightly. The horse settled back onto all fours. Kingsley remained with his mouth opened, white outlining his lips, and I realized that he'd been hit by a bullet made of wax and pig-fat. Apparently — this information came out after the fact — the little plug entered his mouth when he called out "Ha!", did a ricochet off his palate and then drove down and stopped up his windpipe.

Kingsley remained aboard the horse, his head jerking back to front and side to side, as he tried to cough it up and spit it loose, but the wax hardened within seconds. Kingsley's face emptied of color and filled with death-blue. I flew down the hill, Kingsley fell from his mount just as I arrived. He landed in my arms and I looked into his eyes, and I saw his belief in the Almighty fade. It disappeared like the white smoke around us, which was being driven away by a furious morning sun. I gathered Kingsley to me, embraced him, I hit him hard upon the back. I hit him with fury, and Kingsley's head jerked, but he made no sound. I kept this up until the other men gently stopped me.

They buried Kingsley Palmer with a ten-dollar bill stuck in his hand.

Chapter 21

Spliced in amongst the Battle scene footage is an image of my face, all a-twitch with cowardice. The photograph was made at the end of production, a week or so after the Battle scene. I was feeling better about the whole enterprise, and I'll tell you why, good old Maxwell Beaumont turned out to be not such a whey-faced poltroon after all. Sure, he skulked away from the Battle, but he was just a boy, really. His shameful flight remained a secret, because the Confederate army was destroyed in that battle, everyone dead except for Perry King/Lex Hogarth.

So, following the War, Beaumont and Hogarth return home, there to resume the rivalry over the pale hand of Bess Miller. She is undecided, even though I'm much taller than Perry. Then Bess is set upon by carpetbaggers and recently emancipated black men gone rabid with freedom, who ravish her in the night. Thespa — Bess — is saved by the unified forces of Hogarth and myself. I get killed during the fight, shot through the heart, and there's some fancy play-acting as I stumble about, clutching that recently swelled organ. Thespa kneels and I expire with my head in her lap. She kept touching my face with her fingers, which made acting dead a little tricky.

Willison whispered, "Fade out," and Billy Bittner closed up the lens iris slowly. I jumped to my feet, smacking away dirt from my Southern scion's apparel. "All right," said I. "What's next? I hope it's a good old Western two-reeler. I don't care for these historical melodramas. I think people like to see me doing simple things, standard avenging, horse-thief chasing, that sort of thing."

Mrs. Moorcock was standing beside Thespa with the wash basin. Thespa was drawing a cloth across her face harshly, ripping away the chalky make-up and leaving skin freckled by light and impassioned corpuscles.

"But we're not finished, Mess," said Willison.

"How so? You got the whole story, including a riveting death scene by yours truly."

"Moss, I decide when I've got the whole story. I need you — and only you — tomorrow."

"Fair enough."

Thespa and I ascended to her room. I was full of energy, so I tore off my clothes and began to undergo the Rigors. Thespa walked over to her bed and kicked away her garments, leaving on a small satiny thing called a *crêpe de chine envelope chemise*; it did not cover her in any significant way. She lay down on her bed and reached for a large volume of history which she thumbed through idly. I pretended not to see her, pressing my back against the wall and concentrating, because a river full of impurities is sluggish and slow. But it seemed somehow that the nature of her body was always changing and demanding to be looked at.

Thespa struck down at the pages with a finger and read aloud. "*On the day of an Aztec sacrifice, the nobles were seated and the prisoners were brought before them and made to dance. The victims were naked and smeared with plaster. White feathers were tied to their hair. Their eyelids were blackened and their lips painted red.*"

Thespa rolled over on to her back, wrestling the historical tome up into the air like it was a wild beast. "*The priests who would perform the sacrifice stood under an arbor atop a truncated pyramid. Each was disguised as a god and stationed according to rank and theogony.*" Thespa did not know this last word, so she cast the book aside. She arranged herself on the bed so that she could look at me. My buttocks pressed into the wall, my arms held out in front of me.

"Undergoing the *rigahs*," she snapped out playfully, imitating Willison's strange rendering of the word, the last syllable a coarse growl. "What's that one?"

"I imagine that I am pushing the wall back, expanding this room until it is limitless. I hold my hands thus and keep them still. I imagine small birds coming to land upon them, fearless. I stare straight ahead and imagine that no object interferes with my view, which is of the most distant stars."

But then Thespa was before me, and I could not imagine that she was not. My eyes fed upon her and Thespa twisted as if with electricity. She was before me, not touching, yet so close that the air that moved between us was warm and moist. I raised my hands but she shook her head gently and I stilled them. I continued to stare straight ahead, and Thespa disappeared from my view. I felt the smallest touch upon the end of my cock, then another, and I imagined small birds coming to land, fearless.

The next morning I left Thespa's bed, but did not wake her to say farewell. When she was given leave to sleep, Thespa did so with resolve, it being her contention that slumber encouraged the replenishment of natural fluids and luminous skin-cells. Thespa slept with her body curled up like a fiddlehead, naked, even though she never seemed to be warm enough. When I asked her about this, Thespa told me a story about a little girl strangling to death, the gown riding up and gathering around her neck during troubled sleep.

So I rose and went out into The World, where all was very peaceful and still. A spray of light to the east announced that the sun was shortly on its way, but the streets were deserted. I began to think that perhaps I'd misunderstood, there was no turning to be done that day. I wondered if perhaps it wasn't a National Holiday or something, and as I wondered along these lines Caspar Willison drove out of the shadows in his brand new lightning-white Wolverine.

I raised a hand to wave, and then I noticed that the lanterns were nearing with alarming speed. Willison had aimed the machine at me and had no apparent intention of working the brake lever. I threw myself out of the Wolverine's path and ended once more face-down in the dirt of the street.

"Well done, Mass!" I think I heard above the squeal of tires and the squawking of gears. The Wolverine had turned and was bearing down again. I rolled away, giving myself an even coating of dust, but the Wolverine stopped well short, and Willison lifted himself up off his seat. "Muss! What the hill are you doing? Yu'll get all fulthay!"

"Willison," I said, jumping up to my feet, "swear to God, you enjoy making me look like a fool."

Caspar Willison whipped his eyebrows up over his broad forehead, feigning great surprise at this accusation. He did not, however, deny it, merely threw open the door on the passenger's side and said, "Get in, Thom. We've got important things to do."

"Where is everybody?"

"We *are* everybody."

I got into the motor car. "But," I asked, "where's Mr. Bittner, for instance?"

"With a whore."

"Hmm?"

"Shagging a trolley. Dipping his wick." Willison spun around so that he could converse with me face to face. He was not at all concerned with his steering; he was headed east, and that was all that mattered, toward the sunrise. "Why? Do you think there is some mustery to working the wonder box? There is not. It is merely mechanical. I'll do it meself."

"Okay, sure."

We drove into the desert, past the lonely seguaros and rock nettles, toward the jagged mountain that rose from the sand in an unearthly and disturbing way. The sun now peeked out from behind the cliffsides, rendering the tors and precipices an inky, bottomless black.

The camera was set up on the plain, in the middle of The World. These wondrous machines were changing almost daily, and certainly no longer looked like children's toys, which they had when I first arrived. Back then I'd half-expected a little clown to spring out of the camera and interrupt Billy Bittner's cranking. The cameras were now rendered out of a cold black metal that gave forth no light.

✢ ✢ ✢

This afternoon, The Warden appeared in my cell with his usual array of treats; a cigar, two bottles of beer, and some daily newspapers. I should point out, though, that I used to get cigars from Havana (this one is stale and plain, something The Warden may have received from a new father, an impoverished and unenthusiastic one), the beer used to be nicely chilled, instead of warm as dog urine, and the newspapers are a couple of days old, read, reread, and sloppily reassembled.

"Hello, Thommy," he says, "how goes Chapter Twenty-one?"

I have not been keeping track as closely as the Warden, I am surprised to hear that I've worked my way into the twenties. "Fine," I adjudge, although I'm not being entirely honest there.

"Any idea," wonders The Warden, "when something might happen?"

"What do you mean?"

"An event. A narrative is, after all, a linking together of events."

"What the hell do you mean? There's nothing *but* events. I got baseball games, battles, and hey, look here..." I desperately search for a recently scribbled piece of paper. "An intimate encounter between Thespa Doone and myself."

"Is she a good fuck?"

"I beg your pardon?"

The Warden tosses his burden toward me, exhales deeply and walks away. "I'm sorry, Thom," he says, turning silver in the shadows. "I've been under a lot of strain."

"I can imagine. You are fixing to kill somebody."

"Oh. Yes, that's a little troubling. But Murtagh *did* butcher his wife, Thom."

"Well, sure."

"You certainly can't defend him."

"No, sir. He murdered his wife, that he did."

"I realize that you and Murtagh have become close, that you consider him a friend."

"Warden. I do *not* consider John a friend. I do not even much care for him."

"It's your mother."

"What's my mother?"

"That I find so upsetting."

"I see."

I open one of the beer bottles on the edge of the huge desk, leaving behind tiny bite-marks. I throw open the newspaper and focus my attention on the sea of ink.

"Lunatic *bitch*," snarls The Warden. "What business is it of hers? Society has demanded Murtagh's life, and meagre damned payment it is. But your *mother*—"

"Lookee, Warden, this is interesting. Seems like Harry Thaw has been whipping people again. This time, though, it was a young fellow instead of a girl. It says here that Thaw has become a fugitive from the law."

"And now, of course, there's politicians and clergymen and so-called intellectuals from the universities. *Intellectuals*." The Warden tries to give out a haughty snort, but a nose devoid of all hair produces more of a whistle. "This is not an intellectual matter. There is nothing intellectual, nothing *cerebral*, about knives and guns and raging infernos that consume everything in their paths."

"Buffalo Bill is dead."

"Hmmm?"

"Buffalo Bill Cody died. He suffered a nervous collapse and slipped away." I wonder at the slight tremor in my hand. "President Wilson has expressed sympathy on behalf of the American people."

"Cody killed by his own admission over four thousand buffalo. Imagine all their carcasses spread across the plain, Thom."

"His last words were *Let my show go on.*"

"At the Battle of War Bonnet Creek, he scalped — *scalped*, I'm saying — Yellow Hand, the great Cheyenne warrior."

"'Just before he died, Buffalo Bill was baptised and received into the Roman Catholic Church by Father Christopher V. Welsh of the Cathedral of the Immaculate Conception.'"

"Is that so? And will that be enough? Will it, Moss?"

"I'd better get back to work."

"Answer my question, you snivelling little bootlicking coward! *Answer the fucking question.*"

"No, sir. I don't suppose that it'll be enough."

The Warden marches over to the iron door, and he seems so calm that I half-think his rage was somehow in my imagination.

He turns back and smiles, his face now full of the little sunlight that has leaked into my cell. "Carry on," he says, "but don't forget. I'm waiting for something to happen."

"Go stand before the unblinky eye," said Caspar Willison, "and we'll wait for something to happen."

The mountain was rendered out of shadows, left over from the night, and the morning's first soft radiance. Whilst I gazed upon it, Willison looked through the eyepiece. "That's gude," he said. He reached forward, his wrist cocked awkwardly and his fingers spread like talons, to take hold of the crank. He worked it a few times, then stopped abruptly.

"Hey, Caspar, you let me know when you want me to start acting like a coward."

Willison nodded. "I'll let you know, Thommy. What's that?"

"Hmm?"

"When I said *Thommy*, I saw something."

"I don't think so. Hey, how about if I look something like this?" I allowed my face to quiver with dread, and I'm pretty sure my eyes bulged and my skin actually went clammy, which should count as good acting in anybody's books, except Willison just rested his chin upon the camera and smiled at me like a moonstruck schoolgirl.

"Come on," I said. "Work that thing or we'll be here all day."

"Yeah," he nodded. "You didn't have anything planned, did ya?"

"Not exactly. But, you know, me and Thespa."

"Yes?"

"Well, we could spend the day together, you know, doing all those things that lovers do."

"Lovers only do one thing, Miss. And they usually do it badly. B'sides, Gladys is buzzy."

"Busy?"

"She and Purry Kong are off to Hillywudland. There! Shut the fug up and don't say a blussèd word." Willison worked the crank. "The secret," he addressed me, "is in the rhythm. Know what the best training for a crankman is, Muss? Continual masty-bation. You do masty-bate, don't you, Miss? I thought so. We all do. I do it thrice nightly."

As soon as he stopped cranking I said, "What do you mean she's gone to Hollywoodland with Perry?"

Willison hunkered down on his haunches. He draped his elbows over his knees and appeared more comfortable than many a man on a satin pouffe. "I haven't confused you with convoluted syntux, haff I?" Willison met my eyes and then turned his head suddenly, so that he too was staring at the edges of The World. "What is it about the mountain, Miss?"

"Nothing," I answered, but Willison leapt to his feet and cranked the wonder box, grinding out a silver image of my face.

"To do what?" I asked. "They've gone to Hollywoodland to do what?"

"Shipping."

"Shopping?"

"Just so."

"I would have taken her shopping. I'm good at that sort of thing. An excellent driver, also, very patient whilst she peruses the stock and has trouble making decisions."

"I'm sure you are. You are a lovely man in every way."

"Because, you know, here's a thought which you might should have thought of, Caspar. While they're out shopping, somebody from *Silver Dreams* or the *Megaphone* might make their photograph together, and people will be confused."

"Well, I've been confused ever since you said 'might should have thought of.'"

"See, me and Thespa are a team. People see a notice for a Flicker, they read *Thespa Doone and Thom Moss*, they say, *Hell yes, I'm going to see that one, those two are true loves.* But if they see a photograph of Thespa and Perry King..."

Caspar Willison worked the camera.

Nothing happened for a good long while then, long enough that the local residents forgot that we were there. Beetles and side-blotched lizards crept over my feet. An Elf Owl lighted on the camera and craned its feathery neck, on the lookout for vermin.

Caspar Willison amused himself with dancing and shadow-boxing. Caspar would place his hands on his belly and his legs would scissor in and out, and in this manner he would skitter across the mudstones, his mouth pursed into a tiny whistle, although I never heard any of the tunes he was supplying for his feet. He would lift his arms and curl up his fists, or smack the thin air with the back of his hands. Then would come the grand loops, the buffets, pummels and rain blows, often as Willison danced in the shadow of the black mountain.

We ate no lunch, Willison never suggested I take a breather or have a cigarette. Around midday the sweat began to roll down my face, stinging my eyes and deforming my hair. I was never one to fuss much about my hair, but I was bothered to think it was all matted and turbulent.

"Don't be a bungy nancy-boy," Willison snarled.

"I amn't no bungy—"

"Hold it!" As Willison turned the crank, I watched his wrist-bones work beneath the pale and papery skin.

"I just think I could look a bit neater, is all."

"For fug's sake, Thommy. You *are* skulking off a field of buttle."

"You know, Willison, it's been some time since I've done any cowardly acting. If you didn't notice that, maybe you're losing your directing touch."

"What is it about the mountain?"

"Stop asking me about that."

"That's where I'm going to build the City."

"Uh-yeah," I nodded, not that I had any idea what he was talking about.

"Right up there!" Willison pointed a finger at the mountain-top, flat and veiled by clouds, although the high sun was burning them away. So I followed his finger and gazed at the dark height, and now I said, without Willison's having asked, which made it feel less personal and weighty, "It reminds me of the Frontispiece in my mother's old Bible."

Willison merely nodded and turned the camera-crank.

And being as the sun still floated slowly overhead, moving the shadows across my face, I told him about the angels, naked little footballers and floozies, how they leapt down upon the desert sands to comfort Jesus. Willison continued his nodding and crank-ing. "Hey, and one time..." I said, and Caspar had to ask me *what* a couple of times, because I chuckled it off and said it wasn't important, then I continued, "One time I found this stereoscope card in the Bible. One of Salome dancing before Herod."

"With her arms over her head?"

"Yes, sir."

"I *love* that one."

"You do?"

"Absolutely. D'you know, Miss, I am not at all gonoodally stimulated like other men."

"Pardon?"

"The go-noods. Don't respond like some feel they should. Look, I'm getting all personal and divulgent with you, Miss. We must be becoming friends!"

"Yes, sir, I expect we are!"

"Fast and precious fiends."

"So, tell me all about your gonads, Caspar."

"Ah. Yis. Well, it's just that they don't respond to..." Willison took his hands off the camera in order to search through the air for the correct word. "... the standard stimuli. Take a woman like Thelma."

"Thespa."

"Suppose she was standing right here, right now, stark nekkid. I can see those luvvy bubs, something almost winglike in the sweep of their soft and satiny underbellies. I can see her stomach, the gentle valley that leads to her beautious vaggy, all delicately adorned with hair."

"I'm missing the point, Caspar."

"*I don't like that.* You know what I like, Muss? I like a little fire hydrant, all thigh and fat buttooks. I like hairy bellies and hard little tits with nipples big enough to stop a milk bottle. Like Salome."

"You know what they say, each to his own."

"Oh, yeah, they *say* that, but they don't mean it."

"You want me to do some cowardly stuff now? You know, hold up my hands like this and let them tremble."

"Don't like hand-acting. Like face-acting."

"Fair enough."

"I guess your daddy put it in. Hoping to prod the old gill into peeny-vaggy contact."

"I expect that's *exactly* what happened."

"D'you luff him? D'you luff yer old daddy?"

"Sure."

"Tell me all about him." The hand snaked forward and wrapped itself slowly around the handle of the crank.

"Well, he's a fellow who likes to dream of a better world. He's a little disappointed with the one we've got. For example, he had high hopes of being a professional baseball player. But back in The Confluence, we never adopted the Cartwright Rules, we played our old Town Ball, so there's my old man, as good at the game as anyone ever was, except it's not the same game. The rules are different, and he can't quite get his mind wrapped around that one, and I understand that, because it's hard knowing what the rules are."

"Fug the rules."

"So, he imagines another world, one he understands better. It involves bicycles. He sits there on the porch and sips at his Old Bell's—"

"Pook-time."

"Hmm?"

"Old Bell's. Tastes like foul horse-piddle. The unly think it's gude for is gettin' drunk."

"Hey, now, he sure does that from time to time. Too much Old Bell's, that'd sure fog him up. Anybody got in his way—"

"Yes?"

"You know, he'd... Any man can get himself in a foul mood."

"He'd beat upon you?"

"He might slap me, or once in a while come at me with his fists up."

"Did he beat your mother?"

"I just have to ask you one thing, Caspar. Are we becoming friends? Because I don't want to talk about this if we're not. The only other person I ever talked to about any of this was Foote, and you know what Foote did? He was only twelve or thirteen, and he went marching over to my old man and he told him to lay off or he'd get a dose of the same, little Jeff sticking out that big fat lower lip of his like so. But my father was staring at the mountains and dreaming, and maybe he didn't even hear Jeff. I don't know."

"We're friends."

"Occasionally, then, I'd be lying in bed, and I'd hear my father out on the porch. There were little ways of telling that he'd had too much of the Old Bell's. His rocking chair would creak in different cadence, the songs he sang came in a different order. Then he'd rise and head off for bed, and sometimes you could tell he was in a foul mood — and anyone can get in a foul mood, right, Caspar, old buddy? And he'd head into the house, and I would just lie there thinking, come in *here*, old man. Come in here, come in here and beat on me, don't you *dare* go in there. And sometimes I would have to call out, *hey you fat drunk*, and divert him. Sorry, Caspar, I guess I'm ruining the shot here."

"No. No, don't wipe them away, Thommy."

"This was only occasional, Caspar. Otherwise, my father's about the nicest man you'd ever want to meet."

"I do want to meet him."

But it was only a day or so later that my father, raging out of a tavern back in The Confluence, climbed aboard his Columbia three-wheeler and collided head-on with a Hupmobile. The sheriff decided that my father hadn't seen the automble approaching, but I think it's just as likely that my father stared ahead and worked the bicycle pedals with greater fury.

I did not go back for the funeral, because we were turning another motion picture, my first and only modern-dress melodrama, *Go Ask The Mole.*

Chapter 22

There was an occurrence as we drove back toward the White Owl Hotel, and although I am a little uncertain as to both its significance and its gravity, I will set it down. At least then I will be able to wave some paper in The Warden's hairless face and proclaim, "There! Some-damn-thing happened!" I'm inclined to call him a bad name or two when I do this because, pressure and stress notwithstanding, The Warden is not treating me as nicely as he once did.

When the light began to turn yellow, Willison and I climbed into the white Wolverine and screeched away, toward where the sun was exploding upon the horizon, blackening the mountains and rendering the sky fiery. I was in a strange and giddy mood, so when Willison produced a pewter flask from underneath his seat, I drained a few inches into my mouth. I did not speak, because I had nothing to say, which I mean in the most literal way. I searched within and could find only emptiness, a big yawning ache. As on the motor-trip that morning, I imagine that Willison prattled and prated.

But I did say one thing. I grabbed the top of the windscreen and half-standing, my knees crushed against the dashboard, I yelled, "Fuck-pig!"

Willison was actually startled. His white-knuckled hands jerked and the Wolverine took a sudden bite toward the right, spitting up a plume of desert sand. I managed to hold on, but when Willison corrected, which he did angrily, I toppled over and landed more-or-less in his lap. I suspect he was surprised to find me giggling, seemingly piss-drunk after only a single tug at the witch's nipple.

"Fuck-pig," I repeated. "Tule rooter up ahead. We got him on the open trot, Caspie."

"Get off me, Mess," Willison said calmly. "I cannot pilot the motorcar."

I stood up again as far as I was able, extended my arm and sighted the beast. He was perhaps two hundred yards ahead, his hinders a frenzied blur, leaving behind a strange design on the belly of the world.

"Let's get that fuck-pig, Caspar!" I screamed, and when I almost toppled over, I realized that Willison had worked the gear lever and gas pedal. We began to close the gap. I did something that I'd never done in all my days as a rodeo boy, that is, I shouted, "Yahoo!"

The rooter suddenly cut hard to the left, and Willison turned with such sudden fury that the tires on one side of the automobile left the ground. We righted and bore down. Willison's nostrils were flared, and tears streamed out of the corners of his eyes. "Ya!" he roared, his jaw opening and closing mechanically, like those automatons you sometimes see at county fairs. Indeed, having got that similitude into my head, I never from that time forward could look at Willison and not think of one of those mechanized men, although I've also heard that the secret to those machines is that there is a real being, a dwarf or otherwise stunted fellow, hidden inside.

But be that as it may, it is a poor excuse for a diversion as we came up on the frantic tule rooter. While the creature was no giant, neither was he a suckling fuck-pig. "Hey, Caspie! I don't suppose you got a rope anywhere in this motorcar?"

Willison took one hand away from the steering wheel and extracted the Bird's Head Colt from its holster. He offered this to me, and I accepted it, but only to feel the cool ivory of the butt, intricately curved into wild-eyed, beakèd creatures. I handed it back and looked ahead at the scrambling monstrous oinker.

The air was filled with its almost sweet howling. "Naw," said I. "There's no sport in gunning down fuck-pigs. Draw me up alongside. I'll show you why I was the Rodeo Champion of— my flair for this sort of activity."

The rooter was terrorized, what with the mechanical noises right behind it, and it abandoned evasive turns and darts and made for the horizon with pitiful desperation. Willison drew the automobile up even, and I balanced myself with my hands on the windscreen and placed a foot on top of the door panel. Willison had the car parallel but about ten feet away, so I motioned him closer to the rooter, and when we were perhaps seven feet away I stood up erect, my arms held out to the sides like the Great Blondin traversing Niagara Falls. When there was six feet between me and the tule rooter, I let out another lusty "Yahooo!" The car moved a few inches closer and I jumped. I threw myself into the emptiness, and I believe I've mentioned how this moment feels as large and cold as an abandoned castle.

Then, my arms were suddenly full of bristly neck, as large as the bole of a tree. The rooter screamed and I had the impression that had I been paying attention I would have heard eloquent argument. I was not paying attention because I was busily hatching a plan. I am the first to admit, I have not led an exemplary life, and if you can draw any lesson from me, perhaps make it this: do not hatch plans as you are being dragged along by a vicious tule rooter. The plan I came up with was simple, although a bit tricky to execute. I pulled myself forward, slipped first one hand then the other away from the throat and on to the tusks. This was like grabbing handfuls of thorns and thistles and that evening my palms would be cross-hatched with tiny cuts, and I would have strange dreams, and Thespa would wipe away bad sweat with a cool sea-sponge.

Then the trick was leverage, and how I managed the throw was to kick my legs out and up over my head, and I imagine this was beautiful to see, that I was as graceful as a circus boy flying from one trapeze to the other, and when I was fully inverted I drove downwards and pegged the rooter, digging the tusks into the sand, and there was a roar that filled the world, because the rooter was suddenly stuck and I was flying free, though my landing lacked much of my previous elegance. Indeed, I bounced on my keester a time or two, landed in a creosote bush. With its tusks buried in the ground, the rooter sort of continued running, and its hinders were suddenly turning up in the air. Then the whole assemblage swayed, teetered, and collapsed, the rooter falling on to its back — although, because the tusks were pegged, this had the effect of breaking the beast's neck. It was a small sound, like breaking up tinder and kindling, and the creature's eyes turned milky and the terrible howls died abruptly.

"And that," I announced to the world at large, "is how we do business where I come from." I slapped my hands together, smacked dirt from my body, hustled my private parts although they didn't truly require it. I still cannot account for the oddness of my mood. "Know what, Willison? We can get seventy-five cents for those skewers there. We just need to wait whilst the vultures — nature's little chambermaids — do some cleaning up. Hey! Where's that Biggar Ulysses Webb when you goddam need him?"

I looked up and saw the most remarkable thing in all my life, and that is, Caspar Willison hastily wiping away tears from his face. He was also making odd convulsing sounds, as though his windpipe was filled with little stones. For a moment I thought this was a joke, for it looked like the kind of weeping you might see in a poorly acted melodrama, but the tears kept coming, along with huge streams of snot, which got laced up in his hands, so it looked like Willison was trying to knit the mucus into a pair of socks. I looked around The World to make sure no one else was watching.

"Hey," I said as gently as I could. "You all right, Mr. Willison?"

"Fugya, Thom Moss!"

"What are you so upset for?" I demanded. "It's not like you've never killed animals before."

"*I* didn't kill this one," he answered savagely.

From that day forward I have wondered at this. Was there something about just *watching* the death that bothered Caspar Willison, being a spectator and a witness, but having no control? Is it possible that Willison was simply overcome by grief, as fragile and sensitive as a choirboy? Or — and this is where I'd bet my money — was he distraught and angry because killing had been done, and he'd been allowed no part in it?

✢ ✢ ✢

One morning or afternoon or whenever we awoke in the window-less room, Thespa was sitting, naked, at the foot of the bed. She had one leg drawn up, the foot laid across her knee. Thespa's toe-nails were thick and yellowed, a quirky imperfection which caused her some distress. She took up a pair of scissors with which she meant to prune them down to a respectable size. "Don't look at me," she muttered, at almost the precise instant that my eyes managed to focus upon her.

"I can't think of many other things I'd sooner look at."

"Why? Because I'm naked?"

"Yes, ma'am."

"Soon you'll want to fuck."

"I wish you wouldn't speak like that."

"Like what?"

"You always use that word, *fuck*. Do you talk like that when you're with Perry?"

"Make sense, Mess."

"Do you say *fuck* all the time with Perry King?"

"I don't have any need to say *fuck* when I'm with Perry."

"I see."

"It's the air here in California. There is some chemical element in the air, I bet. I can smell it from time to time. Not exactly unpleasant."

"What's this now?"

"It affects my toenails, probably my inner organs as well. I bet my liver is about as tough as shoe-leather. Please stop staring at me."

"Why do you sit around naked all the time, like some cheap Chinese casino girl?"

"I'm sure that makes sense, somehow, in your little mind."

"I hate it when you say things like that, so calm and all."

"I am calm."

"What you are, Thespa, is *unemotional.*"

"Right."

"It's like you have no heart sometimes."

"I try."

"I wouldn't be surprised if you're, you know, him."

Thespa snapped upright then, although, you know, she was fairly upright to begin with, as she usually avoided postures which

she feared may weaken her spine. When she snapped further
upright it was like the plucking of a harp-string. Her flesh quivered for a moment before setting, hard as stone. "Who are you
accusing me of fucking?"

"Perry King."

"Is it not the case that Perry King is a Flicker Player, a carnival
boy?"

"You know he is."

"That's what you are, too, isn't it?"

"Kind of. I suppose."

"If *he's* what *you* are, why would I fuck him? I've got you to
fuck."

"I told you, I don't like such talk out of your mouth."

"You know what? I feel like fucking right now." She threw
down the scissors and stood in the corner, almost as if she was a
child who had misbehaved. "I wouldn't proceed along these lines
if I were you, Thom. You and I are lovers. I have no need for
another lover. And I do feel like fucking now. But I don't want to
look at you. Approach me quietly, so quietly that I cannot hear. I
may hear soft rustlings, but it won't be until I feel your cock
against me that I will understand it was your trousers falling down
around your ankles. And then your hands will come around and
hold my breasts, and they will be as tender as you can make them,
the great huge roughened hands of a young carnival boy, who
won't hear the word *fuck* but loves to fuck, oh *fuck...*"

We arose and put on satin bathrobes, and ate breakfast or dinner
or a midnight snack, ferried up from the kitchen below by an
albino Chinaman, ancient and stooped. He brought us grapefruit
and melon, huge mugs of steamy sweet coffee and glasses of
chilled orange juice. I pulled open the Hollywood *Megaphone*,
folded and pleated, laid the rag upon my knee and perused the
headlines. I did not know what to think of this business over in
Europe, which certainly seemed to lend credence to my mother's
roaring and finger-pointing.

   There was another article, written by Howard Oliver (perhaps
it's the reverse) but speaking mostly in the tongue of Apollo
Greenling, President of the Society for Peaceful Speciate Co-
existence.

When the Lord granted his First Son
Dominion over the Beasts and Fowls,
this did not extend to Adam's being
the Instrument of their End for reasons
of mere diversion. Thom Moss feels him-
self empowered beyond the indulgence
of the Almighty, for he slaughters only
so that a small segment of the population
— they that eschew the Blessings of the
Fair Nine — may experience a slight
titillatory consequent.

Then, of course, I glanced at the article about the man with the "skin condition" who drownded in a mud bath. I thought that had a certain amount of humor in itself, but when I read the name *Oglesby*, I had to laugh out loud. In doing so I startled Thespa Doone, who was sipping orange juice. Her hand trembled, juice spilt on to the front of her robe and stained the golden satin. She wiped at it angrily with her bare hand. I pointed at the newsprint and tried to tell her what was so amusing. She stared ahead as though trying to recall where she'd seen me before. "Bad news, Thom," she near-whispered. "Caspar told me yesterday. There is no part for you in *Civilization*."

Chapter 23

I stood atop the White Owl Hotel and surveyed the howling waste land.

The Santa Annas were blowing throughout The World that day. They came moist and cool off the Pacific, but got turned around in the mountains (much like a tule rooter, snorting and confused) and headed back. They dropped their water in the mountain passes and picked up heat on the barren desert floor. The winds roistered across the plain, filling the air with sand and tiny flakes of lichen. Tumbleweeds skittered across The World, and the occasional somersaulting kangaroo rat.

I do not know and cannot calculate how long Mr. Boyle and his boys had been at it. After all, it was just a chapter ago that Willison and I motored across the earth, and I did not see any of what now lay upon the horizon. Had Boyle the Erector managed it all in a day or two? Have I somehow misplaced time, time spent with Thespa in the windowless room, or time spent in the Saloon, arguing drunkenly with Bodnarchuk? I do not know. All I know is, they had almost finished the City.

It lay some two miles distant, but I could see it clear as Icelandic Crystal. The City sat atop the black mountain, the one that rose out of hardcake nothingness and proclaimed a sober-sided Majesty that ruled over us all. The wall surrounding it was huge and wide and bone-white, catching the morning light. Behind the rampart the city rose, square, squat buildings laced together by stairways and bridges. There was scaffolding throughout, and much evidence of Mr. Boyle (hoists, rigs, pulleys and steam-shovels), but other than that, it was in every detail the Citadel from the Frontispiece of my mother's Bible.

"Look, Mess, you have to understand," came the whispered hiss from behind me, "the Society for Peaceful Speciate Co-existence is breathing down my neck..."

"*What?*" I roared like the sea. "I'm your big star, Willison. Now you're telling me that I can't be in this Flicker..."

"It's not a fugging *Flicker*, that's the pint. It is something *new*. It is something thet the world ain't seen."

"Fair enough. Why isn't there a part for me?"

"World has seen you, Thommy."

The Warden has given me this news, that my mother wishes to see me. I dip my pen with a great flourish, and find myself imitating the Fat Man. "Good God," I mutter, and the words almost seem obscured by moustache-bristle, "do people think this tripe writes itself?"

"Hmm?" If I could give The Warden any gift, I would give him eyebrows, for without them his inquisitive expressions have the oddest effect.

"Tell my mother I'll see her another time."

"Thom! Is this any way to treat the woman from whose loins you emerged?"

"That is one *hell* of an awkwardly constructed sentence."

"Oh! Excuse me, Mr. Shakespeare." The Warden sulks in the shadows momentarily, but then he moves close, and speaks very lowly. "Thom," he says, coyly fingering a sheet of paper (words are barely legible, smudged loops and lopsided chicken tracks) "if you talked to her, Thommy, perhaps you could change her mind."

"How so?"

"You could persuade her to cease and desist this protest."

"I do not think so, sir. She has strong and heartfelt convictions."

"As do I! As do I!"

"The Word is in her heart as a burning fire shut up in her bones. *Thou shalt not kill.*"

"Murtagh deserves to die. Admit it, Moss. Picture the scene. He comes upon his wife and a stranger locked in carnal embrace..."

"I know the story."

"Do you? Have you really thought about it? I ask you, who amongst us has not rutted indiscriminately? I ask you further, is it reason to have the life dashed from your very body?"

"A man gets mad, you know, a man has a *temper*—"

"Aha! *I knew it!*"

"What's this now, sir?"

"You—" The Warden's finger pokes through the dingy air and into my distended grey belly. "You think we shouldn't execute Murtagh."

"I didn't say that."

"You namby-pamby little fuck."

"Now, Warden, your language has gone downhill something fierce."

"*An eye for an eye*—" The Warden lifted his finger, brushing the tips of my lashes. "*A tooth for a tooth.*"

"It doesn't ever say *a life for a life*, sir."

"Really? It *must.*"

"*Wound for wound*, it says. *Stripe for stripe. Burning for burning.*"

"*Burning for burning?* Now, *there's* an interesting one, eh, Thommy?"

I pick up my pen once more. "Go ahead and hang Murtagh," I say, burying myself in the act of writerly composition.

Willison stepped forward, staring at the City, bloodshot eyes boiling upon his face. "Thet, of curse," he said, "is for the Biblical Story. And it came to pass, blah blah blah, in the moth of Zif, which is the second month — I believe it was the thirteenth of Zif, to be precise, ha! — that he began to build the House of the Lord."

"I could play him, Caspar. I could play Solomon."

"*Solomon?*" Willison shrieked with laughter, at least, I'll call it laughter, but basically it was unadulterated shrieking. "If I remember correctly, Mass, he was the *wise* one."

"Well, how about, I don't know, King David?"

"King David's an old man, Muss. Ancient. I'm thenking of usin' Manley."

"Manley's not so old."

"He's too old. I'll gum on a beard, Manley will be perfect. His career, mind you, will be over, but he'll make a decent King David."

"You could do that to me. Stick on a beard, dye my hair—"

Willison suddenly pointed toward the City, his hand trembling, blue veins rising like tree-roots under the glossless skin. I followed the hand and saw that there was a shape stirring behind the dark mountain, trying to peek over its shoulder like a demented cousin, a geometrical shape which bled into the jagged darkness cast by the mountain.

"You can't see it from here," said Willison, "but that is Ancient Mexico."

"Is that where—?"

"Where Thespa peels off and shows us her stuff. *Yes.*" Willison swept his hand savagely across the edge of The World. "And yonder is ancient Crete."

In the foothills to the southwest, crude structures had popped up from the dry brown grass.

"That ain't so grand," said I.

"It's not finished," Willison snarled.

"What happens in the Crete story, anyway?"

Willison pinched at his lower jaw, pulled away the skin so that it tightened over his pointed chin and seemed in danger of splitting. "It's exciting."

"I could be in it."

"It's thrullin'."

"I am Mr. Thrills!"

"Death-defying deeds of derring-do!"

"Hey, now. When you called for a Flying W, who the hell stepped forward? Thom Moss, Matinee Idol and former rodeo star."

"It features Taurokathapsia."

"You're looking at your man!"

"You know what thet is?"

"No."

"*Taurokathapsia*," said Caspar W. Willison, "is frequently depicted in the frescoes of the Minoan age."

"Do tell." I crossed my arms over my chest and inclined the top of my head toward Caspar, so that the imparted knowledge might seep in more easily.

"Yiss," hissed Caspar. "Taurokathapsia. You could do that, Mess. You could perhaps do that."

I found J.D.D. Jensen sitting on a small wooden chair, dressed only in his underwear and socks. The Fat Man's body was alarmingly hirsute, most of his pulchritude covered by tiny white and golden curls, miniatures of his walrus moustache. His undergarments looked extremely formal, paisley shorts and a singlet that required doing up, thirty tiny buttons running over the expanse of Jensen's belly.

The Fat Man worked a deck of cards, breaking them, re-ordering them, fanning them into a huge half-circle. He watched, without much real interest, as I prowled near his bookcases. There was nothing in the *Encyclopedia Americana*, no listing under any of the various spellings I assayed.

"You don't want to be in *Civilization*," muttered Jensen. "It's going to make Caspie a laughing-stock. Moving pictures have gotten too big for their britches."

"Uh-huh." I came upon the three massive volumes, *An Encyclopedia of All Things Animate*. Each book stood well over a foot tall and was perhaps four inches thick; they were bound in leather, which had been worked until it shone a burnished gold. The Fat Man, even though he was busily disparaging the whole concept of *Civilization* ("It's like a young lad walking into a whorehouse with his little willy in hand. Truly laughable."), noticed my hovering and somewhere in the middle of that sentence in the brackets he threw in, "Check there, Thommy."

The three volumes stood shoulder to shoulder like forbidding sentries. "How do I do that?"

The Fat Man lifted up the deck of cards with his left flipper and sprayed them into his right. They made a soft whirring sound, like insects at dusk. "Well, take the one that says *Mammalia...*"

"Mamma-who?" The volumes were impressed with an ornate script, overly complicated and curlicued, which required some concentration. The first book, I finally discovered, was entitled *Avifauna.* Whatever that was, it wasn't *Mammalia,* as wasn't the next volume, *Piscatoria,* so that left Volume III, which I tore from the shelf.

"I fear for the future of humankind," moaned the Fat Man, leaving off his card manipulation long enough to have a drink of sherry, or whatever vile potation he'd decanted into the sherry bottle. "There shall they huddle, in the shadowed caves, their beady eyes trained upon the big screen. And what shall we show them, Thommy? Just such stuff as keeps them quiet. Give them the teat, as if they were mewling babies."

"Now what, sir?" I'd opened the book; there was an illustration of a mata-mata there, a huge tortoise with claws and fangs.

"I had thought," said Jensen philosophically, "that the Flickers were a harmless diversion. I see now that I've made a grave error."

"There's no listing under *taurokathapsia,*" I reported.

The Fat Man's head jerked up and he looked at me oddly, his head a-tilt, his eyes distant and watery. "Hmm?" The playing cards volcanoed out of his hand, shot straight upwards, collided off the ceiling; they landed spread out in an almost perfect circle. Jensen smiled and erected himself laboriously. He reached for the trousers of a cream-colored suit. "Of course there's nothing under *taurokathapsia,* my young moronic friend." Maybe in a whole other book, I'll write about how Jensen put on his pants, but I don't have the time right now. "You have been betrayed once again by your lack of education. As in all things, study the root, boy, study the root. *Tauro.* You're certainly familiar with the Spanish *toro.*"

"Sure." My fingers were already mauling the tops of the pages, peeling away letters toward the beginning of the book. "It means *bull.*"

In the Saloon downstairs, all hell was breaking loose, the carnival boys up to their several pursuits. Some played mumbleypeg, which is a good game except that every so often a fellow would end up with a knife in his foot, and there was one man, Joe Stump, who lost a whole toe. His opposition hurled and sliced it off cleanly. Joe Stump stared down drunkenly at his foot, noted the severed toe, and announced, "I win!" just before falling like rotten timber. There were several card games going, mostly poker, although there were a few fellows who couldn't figure the rules, and they played games like *Old Ma'am* and *Go Fishing*.

Lem and Sam Johnston were playing poker. They were keen enthusiasts of that game, and played it at every opportunity. The twins had disparate styles, as you might expect. Samuel breasted his cards, peeking suspiciously over the tops whenever anyone made a bet. He lifted his own chips with elegance, he formed stacks of immaculate order. Lemuel piled his stake like a trashheap. Sometimes Lem found it necessary to hold his cards at arm's length in order to focus his one eye upon them. At such times it was possible for many of the players to get a good gander, but they never did, because there was a story that Lemuel once caught a man doing just that, and with one brutal stab of thumb and forefinger, Lemuel plucked the eyes out of the fellow's skull. The Johnstons found it hard to find games (that's why they were in the Saloon and not the Salon), not just because of stories like these, mostly because they tended to bet like the rich bastards they were. "One dollar," someone would say. "Make it two." "Make it a hundred and seven!" Lemuel would cry, for some reason favoring these odd numbers. Samuel had the sense to keep the amounts even, although he could be even more flamboyant, and had been known to make a thousand-dollar bet on the fourth card of seven-card stud.

Mycroft, the explosives expert, sat upon a bar stool, although his balance and purchase seemed uncertain. Mycroft made noise on two accounts: for one, the beer steins and whiskey ponies kept falling through his lack of fingers — and for another, he had in his pocket some silvery dust, which he would every so often hurl on to the floor or into the air. It would explode there, making a tiny hole of light and a boom of improbable audibility. Mycroft was very drunk. He was befuddled and maudlin, singing songs in a crippled Irish tenor.

I myself was sitting at a little round table with Bodnarchuk, who said, "That sounds like a good way to get a bullhorn stuck in your belly."

"Hey, Bodnarchuk, where is this highly-touted sense of humor of yours?"

His little face furrowed up so that he looked like a water vole.

Bodnarchuk intended this as a display of High Philosophy, although he wore an identical expression when wondering what to eat next. "Thom," he said, "let us not deceive ourselves concerning the brutish nature of bulls."

"Hey, pal, you're looking at a famous lightstock rider and bulldogger here. I was the rodeo champion of four states, don't forget."

"You've competed again since first we met?"

I waved my hand and demanded more drinks. Bodnarchuk was having beer, which he poured down his throat as if his feet were on fire. Myself, I was drinking sherry, which I had grown fond of up in the Fat Man's room. Mycroft, weeping and caterwauling about a lost love, hurled some of the silver dust up into the air. It made a sound like God's cruel laughter. It filled the air with sparks and tiny Catherine Wheels were reflected upon his gleaming pate.

"I myself," announced Bodnarchuk, "competed in many a Round Up."

"Naturally," I muttered.

"Do not let my diminutive stature lead you to faulty conclusions," Bodnarchuk advised. "Knowledge overcomes all physical shortcomings."

"Now *that's* damn true."

Bodnarchuk chewed a fingernail, placing his forefinger through his limp goatee and munching on it like it was a carrot. "And Mr. Willison needs men to perform this *tauro*—"

"Bull-vaulting," I said. "Let's just call it bull-vaulting."

"And such deed, if performed well, would lead to our eventual stardom upon the silver screen?"

"I am already a *star.*"

"But I espy the door of opportunity creaking open for myself," said Bodnarchuk.

"I suppose. It's one hell of a stunt, that's for damn sure. Bound to impress. But Caspar never specifically said he wanted more than the one..."

"*Caspar?*"

"Hmm?"

"You refer to Mr. Willison as *Caspar?*"

"Surely. We're friends."

"That's not good, Thom. He is an unrighteous man."

"You don't understand him, Bodnarchuk."

"I most surely do not. He seems to have been born without a heart."

I shrugged and sipped at my sherry. Mycroft threw a handful of thunder and lightning at the shelves behind the long bar.

Bodnarchuk slapped the tabletop with both enthusiasm and solemnity. "I say, let's do 'er, Thom. Let's practise until we're bull-leaping fools. Then I shall join you upon the lofty crown of fame and fortune."

"That sounds just about right."

Mycroft, however, had drunkenly miscalculated this last charge, and several bottles of liquor exploded. The room was filled with tiny glass daggers. Bodnarchuk received one to the cheek; he slapped at it as if he were bee-stung, thereby burying the blade of bottle. His face would boil up over the next three days, the shard would flow out upon a tiny river of pus.

Chapter 24

"Exley," say I. "I need to talk to you."

His voice comes from the other side of the door, squeezing in through the iron bars of the tiny portal.

"What's the matter," Exley asks me, "have you had another bad dream?"

"No, no," say I. "Troubled sleep is indicative of an impurity of spirit."

"Exactly."

"Come again, Exley?"

"I have been positioned here long enough to know a few things, Thommy." His voice is almost a whisper; we share the soft belly of the night, and he is loath to disturb it. "You ofttimes have bad dreams. You ofttimes fall from your bed, especially when you have been drinking."

"What I have is *energetic* dreams. You know how a sleeping old hound-dog's legs will twitch, that's what happens to me. I would not say the dreams were *bad.*"

"Don't worry. I don't report to The Warden half of what goes on in there."

"What do you mean?"

"The Warden wants me to keep a log of every time you have a bad dream, to record any words that should tumble from your lips. But my attitude is, it is between you and your conscience. It is none of our business, that's what I say."

"Well, Exley, I agree with you on a theoretical basis, but where this entire discussion breaks down is, I haven't been having any fucking bad dreams."

"Uh-huh."

"Come in here, Exley. I want to talk to you face to face."

"I'm afraid not, Thom. It could mean my job."

"Exley, you don't want to be a damn prison guard the rest of your life."

"That's a true thing, Moss."

I grab hold of the iron bars, hoist myself upwards. This immediately brings some pain to what used to be my triceps. I have not been undergoing the Rigors, in fact, I would have to say my physical shape is pretty dire. My face is still thin, and looks even thinner — elongated — since I have stopped shaving. My beard is not full and luxurious; indeed, it dangles limp and straggly from various scattered patches. My hair hangs down to my shoulders. It is no longer golden brown, more a dull colorless shade, the only highlights coming from bone-white hairs scattered throughout. As for my body, I will be guided by Mr. Hartrampf here; if I was formerly reconstructed, I am presently deconstructed. I have the skin tone of a slug, erstwhile muscles hang with exhaustion. I have developed a paunch, despite the fact that I haven't been eating with anything like regularity. This is the drink, I suppose, whatever elixir The Warden brings along. Sherry is my favorite, you know, and I have horded the heels to many bottles under my bed. As long as I'm on this track here — I will soon return to my writerly task, for I am in such poor physical conditioning that I mustn't leave myself hanging by the bars in the cell door — I will report a couple of ailments. I haven't had a satisfying bowel movement in weeks, I strain upon the stool and drop tiny rabbit pellets. I've developed a cough that often fetches up ugly green things from my soul.

At any rate, here's what I say: "Exley. Come over here where I can see you."

I hear small shuffling sounds and he appears, his face shadowed by his offical blue guard's cap. Even though Exley's face is obscured, I give forth a little sound — part gasp, part sob, in large measure whooping cough — because I've forgotten to prepare myself for how much Exley resembles Bodnarchuk. Exley lacks the Chinese moustache and goatee, although perhaps he should cultivate the whiskers, they suited Bodnarchuk well enough.

"Exley, tell me about your dreams and aspirations."

"I'm shy to."

"Hell. You know a lot about me. I don't know the first damn thing about you."

"You know what I'd truly like to be?" Exley didn't take much persuading, his face had lit up before I'd finished speaking. "I'd like to be a Player in the Flickers. Like yourself."

"Is that so?"

"That's why I came out to California. To be in the moving pictures."

"Good luck to you."

"I have been in several theatrical productions," Exley barges on. "I always played the romantic lead. I realize that I am not handsome in a Classical sense, but my sister assures me that the Fairer Sex finds me oddly attractive."

"Okay, now look, Exley, I need a favor here."

"Did you know Manley Wessex personally?"

"Manley Wessex? Sure."

"Tell me about him."

"Look, Exley, I'm not prepared to hang up here and talk about Manley Wessex. Now, take your keys, unlock this damn door, and come inside."

Exley obeys, without hesitation, in fact, the door is swinging open before I have dropped from it, and I am slammed hard against the brick wall. I receive a nasty bump to the back of the head. Then I allow myself to drop down, but just as Exley pulls the door away, and I spill forward, giving myself a complementary swelling on my brow.

Exley is very amused by all this clowning. "You squandered your talents in Frontier Drama, Moss," he assures me. "You should have been in Comedy."

I pick myself up and smack away dust. "I was, Exley. I was."

"For me, he combines the following attributes: an evident

intelligence, an elegant yet masculine mien, and finely honed Classical thespian skills."

"Who's this now?"

"Why, Manley Wessex."

I tear the bottle out of my lips — I'd taken the opportunity for a smallish snort of sherry — and the stuff spills on to the front of the threadbare nightrobe and seeps throughout my limpid whiskers. "Manley Wessex is an ass in the lion's skin."

"What do you mean by that?"

"Oh..." say I, sitting down on my bed, "I am merely making reference to his wondrous acting skills."

"Uh-huh."

"The world has not seen his like since Nolan Tweed bestrode the globe."

Exley nods uncertainly and, having no clear notion of what to do next, snaps to attention.

"Care for a little tug at the witch's nipple?" I ask.

"I am on duty, Moss. Why don't you say to me whatever you were meaning to say to me?"

"Take me over to the Death House."

"No, sir."

"I have to talk to John. Murtagh, that is. It's very important."

"Moss, it is the dead of the night. Murtagh is fast asleep."

"Oh, for fuck's sake. We're fixing to kill the man, but we'd best not disturb his slumber?"

"This sort of thing has to be cleared by The Warden."

"Exley. The Warden is a crazy man. He's got some idea that Murtagh and I are kindred somehow."

"Oh! That *is* an interesting notion."

"The Warden will not let us talk in peace."

"Cruel and unusual punishment, to not let murderers have a nice little chitchat."

"I murdered no one. I was not found guilty of murder. *Mans laughter* means without malice aforethought. What Murtagh did was stick his own wife like so much meat for the spit. So *don't*—"

"It was just a joke."

"Take me on over to see Murtagh. Now."

Exley crosses his arms over his chest and stares at me. "Why would I?"

"Well," I say, licking my lips, which are always parched and peeling. "I'll write you a letter of introduction to Manley Wessex."

"Truly?"

The last I heard, Manley was wandering around from town to town and offering to mount any Shakespearian Tragedy of their choosing. "He and I are very close," I maintain.

Exley chews on a fingernail as he undergoes internal debate. He does this as did his compeer Bodnarchuk, like it was dinner. "Okay," he says, "but just for a few minutes."

Murtagh is not, in fact, asleep. Indeed, he is more active than I've ever seen him, although I could not say that he's actually doing anything. He is brooding in a grand sense, pacing like a caged lion, pirouetting gracefully whenever he nears the brickwork. The Warden has allowed Murtagh to exchange his prison-issues for more fashionable apparel. John wears a white shirt with a wide collar that droops almost morbidly. The shirt has not been buttoned with any thoroughness, and Murtagh's chest is bared, a pale dented chest that sprouts only the occasional hair. Murtagh wears velveteen trousers, far too tight. His manly bits and pieces are pressed up against the material, all thick and brutish. Anyone would think he was rehearsing for *Hamlet*, not his own death.

"Thom," he says, gesturing grandly at a wooden chair. "Please, sit."

I do so, because I was still shaking, for this reason: Exley and I went out into the blackened hallway, where there wasn't even moonlight to guide us. And as we proceeded along, I was all of a sudden grabbed by the throat and pulled hard into some iron bars. The hands squeezed with a fierceness beyond all humanness, the white anger of a crazed animal. However, I understood that the hands were human hands, if a little hairier than most, and it was a man's voice that said, "Caspar Willison is a *genius*." Exley was all of a sudden pounding at the hands with his cudgel, and with no great accuracy, either. "Schmidt. Let go! Schmidt!" I went light-headed and found myself agreeing with the dark voice. I produced some little gurgles and spit snail-trailed down my chin, but I was really saying, "He may be a genius. But he's a *bastard*." Finally, his fingers purpled and cracked by Exley's bludgeon (as was the bridge of my nose and my left eye), Schmidt loosed his hold and withdrew into his foul-smelling cave. I slumped down and fought to regain my breath. Exley dragged me to my feet and pulled me along the hallway.

Then we burst into the open air, and I looked up and saw my mother standing upon the prison wall, silver clouds draping her shoulders like ermine. My mother's head was bent in silent prayer, the Good Book clutched to her chest. The thought occurred that perhaps this was how she slept, which I would have thought impossible, except Bodnarchuk could sleep standing up. He could sleep standing, he could sleep whilst riding a horse, Bodnarchuk could sleep in the bathtub.

All these strange demons and ghosts (Schmidt, my mother and Bodnarchuk) have me somewhat agitated, so when Murtagh indicates the chair I accept gratefully.

"How are you, John?"

Murtagh knocks the hair from his brow with the back of a hand. "If I must die," he says, speaking toward the ceiling, his head turned and profiled nobly, "I will encounter darkness as a bride, and hug it in mine arms."

"Uh-yeah," I return. "I'm feeling pretty bobbish myself."

Exley is uncomfortable in the presence of the doomed man. He mills about, occasionally taking firm hold of an iron bar, as if checking Murtagh's cage for weaknesses. "Moss," he mutters, "why don't you do whatever you came to do?"

"Yes, Moss," agrees Murtagh. "I don't have all night."

"Your teeth," I say.

"Hmm?"

"Your teeth are bad."

Murtagh lightly touches his fingertips to his opened mouth. The teeth are tiny brown tombstones.

"The camera, which is to say, the unblinky eye, over-elaborates such imperfections. What is merely dingy becomes black. And your face will lighten and become ashen. You'll look like a clown, Murtagh."

I have caused the man great consternation. He spins around and faces Exley, hoping that the young guard will refute all this. Exley merely shrugs, and John Murtagh turns back to me.

"I know a secret," I whisper.

"Tell me."

"Suck lemons."

"Please, tell."

"That's the secret, man. Suck lemons. That's what Thespa Doone does, and her teeth could blind me in the middle of the night."

"Thank you, Moss."

"Her room was windowless, you know, and therefore as dark as dark could be, but her teeth would find light from somewhere. Her teeth, her eyes, the white surrounding the dark irises, that would be all I'd see of Thespa."

"Time to go, Moss," whispers Exley.

"Cool your heels. There's no place for impatient people in the Flickers. Some days is nothing but waiting."

"I'm patient enough," says Exley.

"I'm patient, too," says Murtagh.

"Hey, John, do you reckon you got a *career* in front of you?"

Murtagh kneels, as if I am a Queen and he a lordly supplicant. "What else, Thom?"

"Well, Johnny, I don't like to say this, but you're not in the best bloom."

"No?"

"You should exaggerate yourself. You should undergo the Rigors."

"All right." He thinks about that briefly. "How do I do that?"

"Gardening the physical plant, is what King Palmer used to call it," I remember. "*Gardening of a skillful sort may help the growth of a plant*, King would say, *but it cannot grow a beautiful and flourishing tree from a plant diseased at the root.*"

"Yes?"

"All right. Here's a good one. This one exaggerates the old anterior deltoids. Stay where you are, down on your bent knees like that. Now lean forward and put your forehead on the ground. Spread your fingers out, that's fine, Johnny. Now pick up your feet. Balance yourself there. Ideate solidity, John. Imagine igneous rock, volcanic extrusion hardened as it met the air. That's good. Johnny. That's real good."

"HowlonIdofer?"

"You have to do that for a *long* long time. You are undergoing the Rigors."

I myself undergo the Rigors, at least on a small scale. I place my fingertips together, press until they whiten. I ideate light corpuscles and their destruction within an Icelandic Crystal; I can almost see a rainbow form around my hands, the reworked shards of the broken spectrum.

"John, you know what occurred to me a little while back?"

"Uh?"

"You never mentioned her name."

Murtagh slowly keels over, letting out a long stream of air through his rotten teeth. "I beg your pardon?"

"Your wife's name. You've never said your wife's name. That's odd. Don't you agree, Exley?"

Exley is turned away; he shrugs his small shoulders and adjusts his cap.

"What's it to you, Moss?"

"A person's got a name, is all."

Murtagh climbs slowly to his feet, and I watch the anger wash through him. It is as though he is being struck by slow lightning; he stiffens and bristles and I half-expect licks of flame to shoot out of his ears.

"A name," I continue, draping one leg over the other, hooking an elbow over the chair back, "and idosyncracies. Partialities and annoying habits."

"Martha," snarls Murtagh. "Now fuck off out of here."

"Martha. So it was *Martha* you murdered."

Murtagh hooks his foot around one of the chair legs and pulls, and I topple, but it was not for nothing that I was the rodeo champion of five states. I roll and lunge and tackle him whilst he's still off-balance. Murtagh keels over and cracks his head on the floor, but his wrath is such that he continues to attack. Murtagh pulls some of the whiskers out of my face, he stabs a thumb into my eye, he wraps his hands around my throat and begins to squeeze. Exley rushes over to help, which he does by knocking my head hard with his nightstick. A flower of pain blooms within my brain, and as I haven't been doing much breathing for the past few moments, I decide to pass out. So it is only in some imaginary vaporous otherworld that The Warden steps forward, tsking his tongue like a schoolmarm. "Boys, boys," he whispers, "stop all this tomfoolery. I have bad news."

Murtagh vanishes from on top of me — in my dream he ascends toward Heaven — and Exley, or a clean-shaven Bodnarchuk, comes to see if I'm all right. I must be bull-thrown, and you can't let those beasts have the upper hand, even in a dream, so I scramble to get up on my feet, but none of my limbs are paying any attention.

"John," says The Warden, and these are the last words I hear before plummeting into a deep, dark hole, "I'm afraid they've stayed the execution."

When I come to, I'm back in my own cell, and I am startled because there Jefferson Foote is hovering above me. Actually, *startled* is what happens to an old dutch when you fart in Church. I am shocked and sickened, I am reduced to groans and shivers, even though I know Foote is just leftover dream, or memory, or whatever combination comes to visit me whilst I slumber. So I crawl up onto hands and knees. My head is pounding and my throat feels like rusted pipes, which I ascribe to my misadventures over at the Death House, although, truth to be told, I mostly feel this way upon awakening. This may well be nothing more than one of my blue-ribbon hangovers.

One time I did wake up to see Foote hovering above me, and I will now set that down, because as near as all this works out into a *story*, that was what happened next. I blinked open my eyes and there was Foote. He had a ghostly appearance, because it was night, he was hatless, and his bone-white hair was effulgent and glowing. "What happened?" he asked.

"That's what I was going to ask you, Foote." I lifted my head and saw dark shapes all about, but they made no sense. Though they towered high, the structures were skeletal and flimsy.

"You must have taken a tumble," reported Foote. He placed a black cigarette in his mouth and fired a match. His face lit up red and white, and tiny shadows played in all his pockmarks.

"I guess I must have."

"You're drunk as shit," noted Foote.

"That's true, pard." I raised myself up onto my elbows. I realized that I was looking at the City from inside its walls. From this secret vantage, the City lacked all substance; it consisted of a lumber framework that groaned, creaked and howled as it was beaten by the winds. The thin skin of the City was canvas covered by *papier-mâché*, whitewashed to resemble bleached brickwork. "Hey," I remembered. "I might be drunk, Foote. But that's not the reason I'm flat on my back here." I climbed up to my feet and found the opened doorway, the sheet of thin clapboard flapping some twenty feet above, singing horribly on cheap, rusted hinges.

I'd gone to the City — the Biblical Citadel that Boyle the Constructor had erected atop the black mountain — in the middle of a hot night, because I was a bit inebriated (as Foote had accurately somewhat sanctimoniously pointed out, as if he and Lucifer's Tea had never crossed paths). Thespa had turned me out of her rooms, citing her need for repose. Thespa claimed that only Slumber could return the luminescence to her exteriority. She would go to bed shortly after seven o'clock, some nights. She'd strip off naked and lay down upon the mattress, interlace her fingers over her breast. Sometimes she would have me read to her, usually from one of the thick historical volumes, sometimes poetry (she enjoyed the verse of Miss Emily Dickinson, who courted Death like a lickerish dowager) and the Bible. *Something hot and fiery*, is what she would ask for, squirming upon the bed.

The City was contained by a wall, a parapet, rising some forty feet into the air, a stark and sheer defence. It was a full forty feet wide and completed a circle, giving it about the same shape and dimensions as a horse racetrack. A gateway was cut through the wall, rough-edged and gaping. Beside this rose pillars, surmounted by strange and awful beasts; lions with wings, fowl with claws and hooves. Inside the great wall, the City was a busy mishmash of market stalls and hovels. Flags were festooned everywhere, blood-red fields crested with the same horrible creatures that guarded without.

The single greatest structure was the Temple, which rose with lopsided insistence. You might recall that Solomon sent fourscore thousand hewers to the mountains and they came back with broken backs and huge blocks of stone, which Solomon overlaid with pure gold. The plans for the construction are pretty much laid on in the Good Book — *the length thereof was threescore cubits* — but Boyle the Realizor opted instead to shoot the works upwards, more like you'd imagine the Tower of Babel. Each addition veered further off the mark, and the topmost spire pointed more toward the horizon than Paradise.

I lit a cigarette, had a small sip from the pewter flask from my back pocket, now considerably flattened from my tumble. When I didn't offer him a sip from mine, Foote pulled out his own little flask. He possessed an audible gulp, did Foote, an annoying, frog-like noise.

Inside the Temple were shadows, more banners, and crude drawings done upon the walls. There were paintings of creatures, black-eyed, scaly, owning the raptor's sharp hooked bill; their netherparts were unclothed and drooped with age.

I'd entered Solomon's Temple, drunkenly singing The Church in the Wildwood, the one hymn my father could abide, although I could not tell you why. I slammed the door behind me, which I report only because the building quivered like the feather in a piano-tuner's glass. I even rushed over to one of the walls and spread out my fingers upon it, hoping to forestall the collapse. But the structure finally steadied, I fortified myself with a sip of sherry, and continued my prowling around.

As you know, the most important part of Solomon's Temple, the reason he destroyed countless workers' lives and spent quite a hunk of money, was the Oracle. There-in would be an altar rendered of cedar. There-in would be two cherubim made of olive trees, their wings spanning one wall to the other, and there would be carved figures of palm trees and open flowers, within and without. That sounded like something worth seeing, so when I spied a broad golden doorway at the top of the staircase, I thought, *There's the damned Oracle.* I bounded up that staircase, through the door, and into nothingness. I flailed momentarily and then directed whatever portion of my brain was still sober to decide upon the least injurious position in which to land; it was still debating with the besotten majority when I met the ground. The air left my body like it had a train to catch. I looked up at the stars. I had time to think my thought (if there is a God, why can I not see His face?) but I am well-practised at thinking this thought, it does not take much time. Then the night sky peeled away white, and I was out.

When I awoke, Jefferson Foote was gazing down upon me.

"You're drunk as shit," he said, and I giggled and went like a puppy to the flask, but in truth I was all sobered up and found the world a chilly and troubling place.

We ended up on the ramparts, Foote and I, slowly walking circles around the City. "What are you doing here, anyway?" I asked, and Foote shrugged. This threw a limp hank of white hair into his eyes, which he tried to clear with a series of neck-snaps. He had been assaying this manœuvre ever since he was a boy, and had never had much success. In point of fact, the third head-flick did throw the hair back atop his head, but Foote executed about seven more, and so remained blinded. "I came for inspiration," he said.

"How's that?"

Like Caspar Willison might, Jefferson pulled his hands, bended as though by disease, through the empty air, trying to rake together thoughts. "It helps me to imagine," he said, words that were not worth much waiting for. "How about you?"

"How about me what?"

"What are you doing here?"

That was a stumper. Had I rampaged out of the White Owl with some sort of mischief in mind? I couldn't quite recall. I may well have been possessed by some moon-eyed poeticality myself. Or, I might have been simply out for a constitutional, because, as Kingsley Palmer was wont to say, pedestrianism is God-given and immanent. So I shrugged, and listened to the winds, and after many moments I said, "How've you been anyway, Foote?"

"Good," he nodded. "You?"

"Well, hell. I'm a big star."

"That's right."

"You're doing pretty good yourself, though, Jeff."

He nodded. The road we were walking on was made of wooden planks, covered by canvas and small stones. It squealed as it was trod upon.

"You fit in here," I went on. "You *belong* here." The Santa Annas picked up; the parapets begin to pitch slowly from side to side. "I don't, so much."

"That isn't necessarily a bad thing. This is a strange place."

As I write that down now, sitting in my cell, it seems a fairly innocent thing to say, maybe even good-hearted, but it snapped me upright and made me bilious.

I shook my head, spit onto the flimsy road. "You're a changed son-of-a-bitch, Jefferson Foote."

"*I'm* changed? Thom, you used to be —"

"Be what, Foote?"

"*Fun* is what you used to be. You're just a young man, yet. You shouldn't have that dark look in your eyes. Maybe we should, I don't know, maybe we should get out of here, Moss. What happened to all our adventuring?"

"This isn't a place for getting out of."

Suddenly the anger boiled over, and I spun around and grabbed hold of Foote's black lapels and drew him to mc so that wc wcrc nose-to-nose. He was so scrawny that his feet left the ground.

"Why the fuck didn't you write a part for me in *Civilization?*"

"What the hell are you talking about?"

"Willison said there's no part for me."

"What about Athos, the manly young Cretan?"

"Yeah! What about Athos, the manly young Cretan?" I set Foote back down, smoothed out his clothing for him. "Does this have anything to do with bull-vaulting?"

Jefferson nodded. "I suppose. Although I don't know how Willison thinks he's gonna film such a thing."

"You know what? That sly old bugger wants me to think I don't have a part so that I'll be inspired to stunts and derring-do that would daunt any other man! You reckon?"

"What are you talking about?"

"Athos, the manly young Cretan." I savored the words. "That sounds like a plum role for me."

By the time I'd finished that sentence, however, I was no longer talking to Jefferson Foote, he was gone. The ground beneath him had opened up and swallowed him, for it was only pretending to be stonework, it was but plankboard and two-penny nails, so it gave way and Jefferson was gone. The *thud* came a few seconds later. I dropped to my knees and peered through the ragged hole, but I could see nothing but blackness.

"Foote?" I said quietly.

"Lord," came a small voice, "that smarts."

Chapter 25

Outside the prison walls, they are exuberant. They give forth melodious hosannas, their prayers are full-throated and seem to contain indecorous grunts and lip-smackings. My mother struts along the parapet, marshalling the voices with her tiny hands. My mother has become a maestro of the human spirit, which oftentimes seems remarkable to me. After all, the citizens of The Confluence would parade by with uniformly impassive faces. I would be holding a sign, the Word from the Good Book written upon it. My mother's script was sloppy and childlike; the letters slanted and the circles were lopsided, although there was an attempt to clean things up with fastidiously dotted i's. *"If they speak not according to this Word, it is because there is no Light in them,"* said one sign. *"And they shall be driven to darkness."* My mother stood some feet away, braying and snorting. "They shall not see the rivers," she wailed, her head thrown forward like a dog giving up dinner, "the brooks of honey and butter." My mother had not learned the device of speaking lowly, of making the pedestrians falter in their tracks to hear, her whisper like the scratching of tiny claws upon a door. So they streamed by, and their indifference was such that no one even stepped forward to challenge her.

Somebody must have known a character like Caspar Willison, so wicked that the word lost shape and color, someone who thumbed his nose at God and was rewarded with vast fortune and eternal fame.

My mother was not discouraged, although a few weeks of this treatment did set her jaw with chiselled precision, and her green eyes hardened until they seemed made of peridot. Then she announced the first of her Missions. She left in the dead of winter upon one of my father's bicycles, a tall machine with a broad seat and high handlebars. There was a special carrying rack that held a carpetbag and the Good Book, lashed on with binder twine. My mother wore a heavy grey coat, because the world was clouded with grey snow. The coat had an ermine collar and some fancy bead-work upon the sleeve, and when my mother returned, seven days later, she was without that coat. She entered the house, shivering and so pale that her freckles had disappeared. She never mentioned what had happened to the coat; my father nor I never asked.

What turned the corner for my mother was the madhouse. The grounds were surrounded by earthworks, a gabled gate cut into them, "THE ASYLUM" incised with care and precision. The Asylum was actually The Confluence's single greatest employer, there were no businesses or industries to compete with it. (Dairy farming was pretty much the domain of Jefferson's uncle Maxwell; hard times and bankruptcy visited others who tried their hands at it.) So one day my mother and I walked to The Asylum, my sign for that day a passage from Jeremiah: *"Obey my Voice, and I will be your God."*

We mounted the earthworks and stared at The Asylum. It stood not many yards away, spired and turreted like a storybook Castle. There were all sorts of windows, but they were little more than a foot square. Inside the building there was nothing but shadow.

My mother stood on the rampart for a long time, clutching the Bible to her chest, much as a schoolgirl holds her primers. She cast her eyes about the world, and they lit upon most everything except The Asylum. I myself stared at it, trying to concentrate on all the windows at once, for I was pretty much convinced that monsters were likely to appear, goatmen and she-devils. I wasn't worried, mind you, I was looking forward to it.

Finally my mother began, lofting a small finger into the air as if to announce *point the first.* "Babylon," she began, and the wind groaned, at least, I believe it was the wind, although it sounded like the madhouse inhabitants protesting in unison, *Oh no, not that again.* "Babylon is fallen and destroyed," said my mother. Then, amazingly, she lost her place. My mother had not learned the entire Bible by rote, but she certainly knew huge great pieces of it, certainly whatever books and chapters she meant to hammer home, and although I had seen her falter a time or two, I'd never seen her like this. She turned bright-red and bit her tongue, her whole body swayed upon the earthworks, and the uplifted forefinger trembled so that it became invisible, like a hummingbird's wings.

And I will tell you something that my mother certainly never found out, which is: I knew what came next. I'd often rutted around in The Book of Jeremiah, which is more entertaining than a lot of the Good Book. And it was even more diverting because I'd concluded that Babylon was the name of a woman, mostly because they always say *her.* The line that had my mother sputtering, the edges of her ears flaming almost crimson, was "Howl for her." I imagined her wretched and vile, this Babylon creature (the Lord was certainly sore at her) with dark eyes and pale skin untouched by sunlight. I often imagined her naked — standing upon a precipice, because the nakedness was intended as effrontery to the Lord Almighty, and was full in His sight — and for this reason I didn't say anything to my mother, who had opened her mouth and was making small noises, spitting out tiny letters and consonants.

It was during this awful quietude — which extended for minutes, or so I remember it — that faces began to appear in the tiny windows. Much to my disappointment, they were not grotesque and mutilated, merely the faces of cave-dwellers, sallow and blinking. When there were perhaps three or four spotted about the stone edifice, my mother became more agitated, and her tongue shovelled out streams of spit along with the crippled stutters and mournful vowels. But when each window contained a face — and some two or three, crammed into the small square — my mother abruptly calmed. It was her finger, still raised and pointed, that stilled first, slowing in its vibrations, then stopping with dead certainty. "Howl for her," spoke my mother, with a gentleness I had never heard from her before.

The people in The Asylum applauded, and they did indeed howl.

"Take balm for her pain, if so she may be healed," said my mother, and she had found her way in life and was gone from me forever.

There was great activity throughout The World. Willison oversaw the construction of the three colossal stage-sets: the City, the Cretan village and the Aztec pyramid. These were erected all very near to one another, because it was Caspar's plan that transitional shots should contain disparate images. Therefore, as Thespa stood atop the pyramid, covered only in paint and serpentine jewelry, the camera would move away from her and, lo, we would be gazing at the cloud-shrouded City. Here is a map, although bear in mind I am not much of a draughtsman:

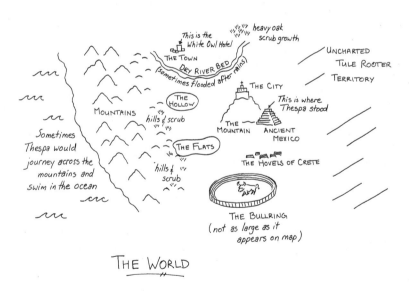

THE WORLD

I know all this because it was explained to the Johnston Brothers within my earshot. The Twins stood in the middle of the plain and surveyed all that had been wrought, most of which they had paid for. Samuel Johnston, his spats covered with dust, his walking stick skewering the dry earth, stared at the Creation. "That's an awfully big pyramid."

"Hmm," Willison nodded, as if Samuel had pointed out an oddity weather-wise. "They tended to be largish."

Lemuel stared up at the pinnacle, into the sunlight, wrinkling the skin around his eye and empty socket. "We won't be able to see much of her away up there."

"I shall ascend into Heaven in a hot-air balloon," said Willison, "cranking all the way."

The Johnston brothers nodded uncertainly, and despite their differences and constant bickering, some things — like this nodding — they did in perfect unison and rhythm, and when they had each nodded five or six times they fell into step and walked away.

Other activities at The World included Jefferson Foote appearing in public upon extremely rare occasions, looking more ashen than usual, which is going some. His tumble through the ramparts had left him with a twisted foot and pronounced limp, and he could walk only with a cane, which he would plunge into the ground as though it were a weapon, swinging his bad leg in a wide semi-circle, waving his stump in the air in order to facilitate this odd locomotion. Foote's fingers and lips were turned bright yellow by the black cigarettes; his eyes had been burnt red by drink and sleeplessness. Foote was still laboring over the scenario for *Civilization*, working all day and night at the White Owl Hotel, only emerging to haunt the stage-sets, searching for inspiration. All of which casts into doubt his claims to be a fine and masterful writer, because I now have some acquaintance with the trade and it is not all the rigorous toil Foote made out. Oh, sure, sometimes you get stuck, and you have to pace around the cell or maybe even have a nap, but then it hits you, *Hell yes, I better bung that down.* Foote made authoring out to be just this side of emptying a pond with a slotted spoon. The Fat Man was a further exemplar of this, but I believe Jensen claimed that writing was difficult so that he wouldn't have to admit what it really was, at least for him, *impossible.* Jensen had become an *Old* Fat Man, his brain a hotchpotch of bad liquor and dreams. The last book he wrote was entitled *Blood Money.* It featured a young carnival boy who gets a job in the Flicker business, becomes a star, has a hot romance, does some wicked things, and then gets killed at the end. It is a peculiar book in that Jensen petulantly murders off all of the characters, even the rotund gambler ("a fine figure of a man, far from overly-slender") who has become the boy's one true friend. After that, the Fat Man focused his attention on what he referred to as a *dignified retirement*. "But I need money, Thommy," he'd say, dribbling liqueur. "Must needs have much *gelt*." Thus the Fat Man conceived of his ultimate fleecing, playing poker with the Johnston Twins and relieving them of their vast fortune.

Thespa Doone had evolved her philosophy of slumber until she had the workings of the world turned upside-down. She now theorized that sleep was man's natural state, that waking was a necessary evil. At least, this is how things struck me, because she was in bed all of the time, naked and visited by dreams. Be the dreams gentle or troubled, she would writhe, pitching her body toward the shadows. When Thespa Doone did rise, it was to read books, crouched in the corner, the poetry and history opened before her. Thespa had decided at some point that chairs would warp and pervert the spinal column, so she would hunker down instead, her feet splayed and flat to the floor. Many times Thespa would look at me with indifference, but I was able to write this off to my being part of her life and therefore not worth noticing. Other times she'd come at me hungrily, her body taut and wet and hot to the touch.

One of the few happy stories I can tell about The World concerns my old friend Charles Wild Horse. After we turned *A Fate Worse Than Death*, Wild Horse stayed on, although the employment for a red man was occasional. Mostly he occupied a seat in the Saloon at the White Owl. He took up a cigar habit, his favored smoke being a huge torpedo that he'd puff on contentedly. Charles wouldn't remove the stogie, except to take genteel little sips at his drink or to tap the ash, so the smoke would curl up into his strange misaligned eyes and fire them with tics, spasms and blinks. This had rather a comical effect. One day Harry Joint, the famous director of comedies, came into the Saloon. Charles Wild Horse was minding his own business, sitting at a little table and smoking a cigar.

Harry Joint fell to the ground laughing. He was a broad-beamed chubby man, with a cleft in his chin and a dent in his forehead. His laugh was a bray that would have had donkeys telling him to pipe down. Tears spilt out of his eyes and he held on to his sides, much as if he was fearful of actual side-splitting. Charles Wild Horse merely stared at him with polite and uncertain interest.

Joint finally climbed to his feet, exhausted by his hilarity, and stumbled over toward Wild Horse. "I'm gonna make you a star!" he whispered, having used up all of his air, and that's how Charles Wild Horse came to be a comedian. You wouldn't know him as Charles Wild Horse, because Joint felt that no one would pay good money to see an Indian, so he greased back Wild Horse's hair, painted on a moustache that curled at the ends, and he gave him the name of Mickey Mungo. In the little biograph that was sent out to the *Megaphone* and *Silver Screen*, it said that Mickey Mungo was Corsican, because who the hell knows what a Corsican is supposed to look like?

Harry Joint rapidly cranked out a number of two-reelers. I don't recall the stories, other than they contrived to have Wild Horse — Mungo, that is — smoke a cigar. The cigar would explode, and his unsettling eyes would fly off in opposing orbits. People found that amusing enough, but those Flickers failed to fire the public imagination.

Joint decided that Mickey Mungo needed a partner, and he had the further inspiration that Mungo's partner should be ugly. So he ran a series of ads in the local papers, *Wanted, one unsightly fellow*, and they turned up in droves, men misshapen by nature, accident and the fury in Europe. They paraded by Joint, and he tittered and giggled, but he didn't truly laugh until there came a man whose face bore the impression of a horse's hoof, the depression shoving his features off to the sides much as a child might move peas on a plate. They gave this fellow a new name (he'd reported that his former one was Edgar LaChance, although he failed to respond to it) and that name was Pug O'Hara, it being Joint's opinion that anybody with a horse-crushed visage was likely Irish.

When they introduced Pug O'Hara to Mickey Mungo, the two men embraced. So that's the story of what happened to Charles Wild Horse and Wild Horse Charlie, and now I'm all out of stories with happy endings.

✧ ✧ ✧

They built a holding pen close by the Cretan village, one of the few instances of Mr. Boyle erecting something with substance. The fence was rendered out of thick timbers; the stanchions were sunk deep and set in cement, the crosspieces were dowelled and double-lashed. The enclosure measured a full seven feet high — Bodnarchuk and I sat on the top rail and stared down at the creature.

It stood in the center of the pen with its feet splayed. The legs seemed too thin for the monstrous body and were bent slightly by the weight. The body was muscle covered by shoeblack, polished and buffed. The head was a severely nostrilled affair, with prissy little ears and small eyes that spilled forth thick, runny tears. What Bodnarchuk and I noticed mostly, though, were the horns.

"Uh-yup," said Bodnarchuk, equal parts philosophic resignation and his breakfast repeating.

"Big son-of-a-bitch, ain't he?"

"You got to be big," noted Bodnarchuk, "you want to fuck a cow."

I grinned and turned to Bodnarchuk, but he wasn't smiling. His sense of humor was still nowhere to be seen.

Bodnarchuk cinched up his belt, adjusted the peak in his Stetson, tossed away his roll-up butt, and pushed himself forward. I caught him by the collar just before he dropped down into the corral.

"Where the hell are you going?"

"Taurokathapsia," Bodnarchuk said proudly.

I set him back on the railing and went back to staring at the bull. "First off, who says you're going first? Second, let's just think about this. I am a champion lightstock rider and rodeo boy—"

"How many states is it now, Thommy?"

"— and I am here to tell you that such stunts require forethought and planning."

"It seems rather straightforward," argued Bodnarchuk. "I take hold of the horns and flip acrost the back of him. I land on my feet behind him and I'm out of the pen before he gets turned around."

"Well," I admitted, "it does sound simple enough. But I'll bet there's something we're not thinking about. So let's just sit here for a while."

Bodnarchuk took out his makings and began to roll up a smoke.

"Well," he said quietly, "I thought we came out here to practise bull-vaulting."

"And who says you're going first, anyway?" I snapped petulantly, although in all God's truth I wasn't prepared to throw up much of an objection. "I'm the one with all the experience."

"I've got experience. I've done everything you have, Thom. I've worked with livestock and I've hunted tule rooters. I even have worked with bulls before, Thom, as a castrater, but they were not Brahmin, like this big fellow here, they were smaller and more docile. That bull is not even the largest animal I've encountered, Thom. I was employed for a time as an elephant handler—"

"You weren't."

"Gospel. For the Ringling Brothers. Mind you, I did not do any performing with the elephants, Thom. I merely wintered with them in Sarasota, one of the better jobs I've had. So, if you'll excuse me..."

I grabbed hold of his collar and pulled him up to the railing one more time.

"I just don't see why you're so keen to go first."

"Well, then, Mr. Moss, I'll tell you. It is no secret that you made a bigger splash around here than I did. You are a huge star, your admirers are legion, you end each day smothered by the womanly charms of Thespa Doone. I remain the lowest of the low, Thom. Now, we're both gonna do this stunt and everyone's gonna say, *You know what Thom fucking Moss did? Grabbed hold of an enraged bull's horns and vaulted the length of him.* But you know what I'm gonna say? I'm gonna say, *But I did it first.*"

This time when Bodnarchuk dropped I made no move to stop him, and he fell into the pen.

The bull cocked his head, as if it found it a fairly interesting thing to have a little fellow with an odd droopy moustache and goat-beard appear in the enclosure. The only snort it gave forth was small and likely due to the fact that Bodnarchuk smelt a bit oddly.

"What we have here," pronounced Bodnarchuk, "is a placid animal."

"That's good."

"Not particularly. The only way the thing works, the beast comes at you fast and he throws his head hard." Bodnarchuk took

off his hat and waved it in the air. The bull looked only briefly and
then dropped its black eyes, *No, sorry, that's not my hat.* Bodnarchuk took off his vest and worked it like he was a Mexican bull-
fighter, holding the shoulders daintily and draping it over the
breeze. The bull tentatively raised a foreleg and dropped it back
onto the ground,

"Oooie. You got him riled now," I noted.

"Shush." Bodnarchuk commenced walking about in a circle, his
fists knuckled upon his hips. He first did a broad sashay, the tip of
his tongue sticking out between a gap in his teeth. When that had
no effect he stuck out his arse-end and shuffled about baboonlike.
Bodnarchuk unhitched his drawers and displayed toward the bull
first a flaccid set of buttocks, next a long and gnarly root. Bodnarchuk pulled up his pants and wondered what to try next. He made
a tiny chicking sound with the side of his mouth, and the bull bore
down full upon him, bellowing like a steam engine.

Bodnarchuk immediately ran toward the creature, a course of
action which I counted as ill-conceived. My friend brought up his
hands and prepared them to receive bullhorn, spread at such a distance that I saw he meant to take hold at the outer extremities.
All of this had me pushing off the railing; I was falling to earth
when the actual encounter occurred. The bull dropped his head
immediately before reaching Bodnarchuk; and though Bodnarchuk's right hand took hold of a horn, the left hand missed, and
Bodnarchuk faltered sideways. The bull threw back his giant head.
Bodnarchuk, a stubborn little son-of-a-bitch, did not loose his hold
on the bullhorn, and was therefore lifted into the air, all so quickly
that I was just then landing on the ground. I braced myself so that
my legs wouldn't buckle, but they did, and I stumbled down and
had to right myself, which is all the time it took for the bull to
throw Bodnarchuk up into the air and skewer him neatly through
the belly on the return.

Bodnarchuk tore free, but did not make it far. The bull caught
him from behind and threw him up again. When Bodnarchuk fell
to earth the monster stomped on him like he was a cigarette butt.

If I'd been thinking clearly, or even at all, I'd never have done
what I did next, which was to punch the bull. I just hauled off and
administered a good old-fashioned haymaker, landing it on the
side of the thing's head. The bull took a step backwards and shook

his head vigorously, sending up a cloud of steam and snot. The dumb brute stared at me as though consumed with disbelief. Sobered and embarrassed, it wandered away to chew up grass.

I knelt beside Bodnarchuk, whose skin was already yellowed. His eyes appeared to be rendered out of glass, and his breath came in tiny drawn puffs. I could not bear to look at his belly, but I felt there with my hand and stuffed things back inside.

"Thom?" whispered Bodnarchuk.

"I think we're okay here, pal. This don't seem so bad." I think that perhaps these opinions were belied by the tears streaming down my face. Bodnarchuk looked at me, kindly and calm, and said, "Thom?"

"Yeah?"

He licked his lips then, and produced his last philosophical aspect. "Thom, I believe I know what I did wrong." Then Bodnarchuk grinned, and a huge thing tore out of my body, half-sob and half-laugh. Bodnarchuk giggled; his body convulsed, twitched and neared the brink. "Told you," he said, so softly that I had to touch my ear to the strange moustache/goatee.

"Told me what?"

"It is my most stellar quality. My sense of humor."

I agreed with him, but I shall never know if he heard me, because Bodnarchuk died as I spoke the words.

Chapter 26

Bodnarchuk had no family, so the little guy's death made but the barest ripple. Other than a small bit of reporting in the Hollywood *Megaphone* (which revealed the startling news that Bodnarchuk had the given name of *Horatio*) the only commentary on the mishap was written by Apollo Greenling, his point being, of course, that if one (Thom Moss, he meant) is going to mistreat animals, one is going to reap in kind (and there Greenling did some fancy skipping, to get around the fact that it was not Thom Moss who got killed). So, Bodnarchuk was laid into the cold ground, and the carnival boys retired to the White Owl Hotel and drank too much in his memory.

I then thundered upstairs to the windowless room of my one and only. I laid my head upon Thespa's breast and she lightly touched the back of my head, her fingers working like they were playing a slow and mournful tune upon a flute. I tore her shirt away and sucked Thespa's tit into my mouth. Thespa said that she needed her sleep, but as I protested she took my cock into her hand and worked it in a very businesslike way, spilling my seed upon the floor. Before I left Thespa's room I punched a hole in the wall, and cursed womankind with a vague howl.

Even the Fat Man offered no consolation, then again, I could not rouse him from his slumber upon the Murphy bed, the mattress and springs bent by his weight until they touched the ground like a fat dog's belly. Jensen slept upon his back, stripped naked, his body a mountain of tallow and blubber, adorned by tiny curlicues and elflocks.

I raced down to the Salon, and very carefully slipped my head serpentlike around the doorjamb. Willison sat on a settee, naked except for his leather belts and holsters. He held his pistols in the air, pulling a stick-up on the Lord Almighty, whilst before him knelt a young woman, chewing hungrily. Willison had his eyes raised and was moaning lowly, but for some reason his head jerked forward, and his pale blue eyes bounced and caught hold of me. Willison eagerly levelled the Bird's Head Colts, but I stumbled away before he could squeeze off a shot.

I was drunk and desperate enough to try Foote's room, but he was gone, no doubt searching for the Muse. It was my buddy Mr. Hartrampf who told me about the Muses, and there are illustrations, seven women with identical hairstyles, bedsheets draped artistically over their nakedness. They put me in mind of Miss Justice, as portrayed by Lily Lavallée, and speaking of that, when I was thundering about the White Owl, was Lily really standing in the shadowed hallway up on the fifth floor? I believe she was, naked, assuming a pose of classical elegance, her arms crooked like branches, her legs set wide, her feet carved into huge arches as she was raised up on to her toes. I believe I had the presence of mind to tip the velveteen top hat and blow out, "Good evening, Miss Lily," or something that approached it. Lily may then have said, "Fuck me, Thommy," but I cannot aver that with certainty. For one thing, I was even drunker than I was before, because when I could not rouse the Fat Man I stole a bottle of his sherris sack, and my storming about was accompanied by much sucking at the witch's nipple. For another, the Mistress of the Tableau did not move her lips, she remained as still as a painting. But some voice said, "Fuck me, Thommy," and I proclaimed my undying love for Thespa Doone as I mounted the stairs to the rooftop to gaze down upon The World. There was the Cretan village, a huddle of clay hovels. There was the moon-shadow of the Aztec pyramid, built as tribute to the great Flayed God, Xipes. And there was the City,

Solomon's Temple and the Oracle, atop the naked black mountain. I finished the liquor and threw the bottle toward it, with such force that I toppled backwards, and being as it was late, and being as I'd cracked the back of my head upon landing, that is where I decided to spend the night.

When I awoke it was still dark, but I had acquired the same knack as Mr. Willison, I could sense the arrival of day. It was almost as if I heard dawn huffing and puffing over the plains toward California. I arose, wetted my fingers with my tongue and drew the hair out of my face. I descended through the White Owl Hotel, and more or less ran all the way to the Cretan village.

The camera crew — Billy Bittner, Theo Welkin and the ancient Georg — busied themselves with photographic industry on the fence. Caspar Willison seemed to be expecting me, but the first words out of his mouth were, "Muss. What the fug are you doing here?"

I nodded toward the pen. "Tauro*goddam*kathapsia."

"Oooh," Caspar Willison trembled. "You're my boy, Miss. Let us go put on your costume."

This did not take long, because my costume consisted of a mask and a small leather pouch containing my manly bits and pieces; my rump was not contained at all. It was, however, the mask that concerned me. It was designed to cover my forehead and eyes, covered with bristly goat-hair and two horns, long and gleefully curved. The weight of these horns kept dragging the mask down over my eyes, obscuring my vision. I pointed this out to Willison, who tsk-tsked his tongue and snapped his fingers and thereby made a number of people run over to me. They affixed the mask with glues and adhesives.

"Okay," said I, walking back toward the bullpen. Thespa Doone stood there in a tiny white tunic, shivering in the near-dawn. Thespa smiled at me, but it was the oddest of smiles and quickly gone, as if she were afraid of creasing her face.

Caspar Willison strutted along the uppermost rail, grinned, popped a thumb into the air and said, "Good luck, Moss," as if we were collegiate footballers with a slim chance to win the big game.

There was a door cut through the barricade — Bodnarchuk and

I had not noticed it — and I pushed through and was alone with the bull.

He stood across the enclosure, placidly chewing on cud. He aimed his black eyes at me and his huge head tilted with the thought, *Now where have I seen this fellow before?* The bull could not place me, but did not dwell upon it.

"You about ready?" I called.

"Crank the wonder box," sang Caspar Willison. "Fade in."

I took a moment to compose myself, but all the moment did was churn up the stale liquor in my stomach and make my hands tremble. I made a small chicky sound.

The bull's head snapped up with indignation, *What bastard did that?* He snorted haughtily and when I made another small *chick* with the side of my mouth, the beast came toward me raging.

I braced, and that was enough to send the goat mask sliding down my face. The eye-holes slipped to the side, and my vision was limited to something the size of a pinprick. I could hear him, I could feel his cloven hooves upon the earth, but could only locate greens and blues and browns, the colors of this sad vale which, apparently, I would soon be leaving, carried away on blood-stained prongs.

Something flashed oily black, and I jerked my head hopelessly and saw a streak of vein-ribbed white that must have been an eye. I held out my hands and when they filled I closed them tight.

Then I went limp, because it was my theory that the actual vaulting would come courtesy of the bull. The monster jerked its head up and back with such force that my arms seemed to be seven or eight feet in the air before my feet left the ground. Then it was a simple matter of tucking into a roll and letting go of the horns — the bull bellowed, almost appreciatively, as I sailed over top of it — and when I landed on the other side the impact righted my goat mask, and I could see the far fence so I ran like the clappers and practically vaulted the thing.

I doubled over and started giggling, and it was some moments before I noticed I wasn't alone. Perry King stood nearby, dressed in the minuscule nether-harness and holding a goat mask in the crook of his arm. "Hey, Perry," said I.

"You cinched it, Thom!"

I heard the report of the Bird's Head Colt, I heard the muffled sounds of bull flesh tumbling onto sod.

"Well, hell," I muttered toward Perry King. "It wasn't for nothing I was the most famous rodeo boy in the nation."

Bittner and his camera were disappeared from the top railing, and now Thespa was perched there, naked legs draped lazily, the white tunic stretched tight, stained by her dark nipples. I heard Caspar say, "Fade in," and Thespa clapped her hands together and giggled like an idiot.

"It's my time," announced Perry King.

"Uh-yeah," said I, trying to be friendly, feeling right then that there were worse sons-of-bitches than Perry King. "Who are you playing, anyway?"

"Athos."

"The fuck you are, you son-of-a-bitch."

Willison's head appeared over top of the fence. It rose up, slow and easy as a hot air balloon, and appeared to hover there.

"Purry Kong!" hailed the director. "Hurry, hurry!"

Perry King hustled away, adjusting the goat mask over his face. I ran at the enclosure and leapt up; Willison's head vanished. My fingers lost their hold — actually, I was so angry right at that particular moment that I hadn't bothered to grab hold of anything — and I tumbled back to earth. When I arrived back at the pinnacle, this is what I saw: Billy Bittner cranking the wonder box, whilst Caspar Willison stood crookedly beside him, one hand down his jodhpurs to leisurely satisfy an itch. Thespa stood beside him, and she seemed to have caught his itch as though by airborne infection, except hers was on the butt, and she was scratching there, leaving behind thick red marks. She wore no underwear beneath her thin white tunic, and though I was sickened, I was not surprised, because Thespa Doone did not own any underwear. Perry King was strutting about like a rooster with a hard-on. Behind him, the dead bull was arranged artfully. Its eyes had glazed, but they held their last look of bewildered resentment, and I guess that Willison believed no one would pay much attention to the little red hole that sat between them.

Perry King pulled off the goat mask with exultation.

"Hey!" I screamed. "You think people will buy that?"

Willison hesitated, just long enough to make it clear that he really had much more important things to do than speak with me. "People don't have to *buy* it, Mess. I'm a'givin' it to 'em on a shovel."

"I'm massively reconstructed, Perry is slight and meagre. I am tall, Perry is short."

"You have a furrier arse, too, but no one shall notice."

"Are you crazy, Willison?"

Caspar laid his pale thin lips together and bent them upwards into a smile. "Fade in," he whispered. Billy Bittner turned the crank. Thespa ran over and embraced her hero, Perry King, the man who had vaulted the snorting bull.

"Where," I demanded, "is Miss Justice?"

I stood in the hallway of the White Owl Hotel, clutching a bottle of Jameson's from the Saloon downstairs. I'd marched up to the long bar and shoved between two brutish customers who had their chins in each other's faces and were barking things like, "I might have to kill you, Ned Kelly," and, "Mighty brave words for a yellowbelly, Sam Houston," and such foolishness. I pushed them apart and demanded redeye whiskey and a voice said, "Moss, what the hell are you doing?"

"Huh?"

Roald Nypes was, you know, the second most famous director of motion pictures in The World, one of those little fellows whose stature has rendered them pugnacious and bastardly.

"I'm having a fucking drink, Nypes. What does it look like?"

"It looks like you're ruining my shot!"

"Huh? Oh!" I blasted out a strange laugh. "Sorry about that, pardner!"

"You'd think you'd have learned," little Nypes muttered, "what is real and what is made up for the Flickers."

"Yeah," I agreed, "you'd think I would."

So now I stood in the hallway, clutching the bottle, and I'd drained enough that I was weaving slightly. "Miss Justice! Where are you, Miss Justice?"

She emerged naked from the shadows and assumed a classical pose, her legs braced for a little spree amongst sylvan sprites, her arms cocked behind her. Lily's breasts were thus presented forward, and I stumbled up and took hold.

"This had better be worth waiting for," said Lily Lavallée, without moving her lips.

"It will be," I snarled, although there wasn't a lot of variance in what I did under such circumstances. Mostly what I did that was different from normal was a great deal of huffing, puffing and grunting. When I was with Thespa Doone we tended to gasp lightly and sigh, because the night was always very fragile whenever we made love. So I made these noises, and they seemed to serve the hoggish act in much the same way as a piano player serves a Flicker.

Lily seemed satisfied. She put her arms around my neck and wrapped her fleshy legs around my back and clung on like I was a mustang fit to trample her to death. She moaned and spoke in tongues. Her body exploded inside, racked with spasms that continued for a good long while, aftershocks and tremors, as though compensating for her previous stillness.

"There," I said.

Lily writhed nakedly atop the bedsheets.

"I was wondering," I said, lighting up a cigarette (a habit of which I have rid myself, because I believe King Palmer was correct, smoking can pervert your olfactory system), "if you could maybe have a word with Caspar about—"

"I know, I know, yes, of course," she grumbled.

I nodded, took a puff, and made some genteel conversation. "How did you meet old Willison, anyway?"

She told me the whole story without ever letting up in her naked wriggling. Nolan Tweed had come into Guthrie, Kentucky, hunched over and stooped, to put forward his offer to the Chamber of Commerce. The Mayor and his cronies came up with *Hamlet*. (Seems like Shakespeare could have saved himself a lot of trouble and just written the one play.) Lily was the first citizen down to Town Hall. The little bleeder walked a circle around the girl, judging her as though she were a horse; he even took her small wrist and held it between his fingers, the thickness and feel of the bone telling him something. "*Nymph*," he whispered at last, "*in thy orisons be all my sins remember'd.*"

The town of Guthrie seemed none too keen on the whole idea, but all of the parts were eventually assigned. The *rôle* of Fortinbras was taken — without Lily noticing, although she was beside

Nolan Tweed from the very beginning — by a young man with an oddly triangular head. He was a distinctly unfriendly fellow. During breaks he would stand off to one side, his head bowed as though in prayer, his lips, taut and pale, silently spitting out his few lines. Other times the fellow would hunker down in various corners and produce huge leather-bound volumes, which he would read with astounding quickness, turning the pages so violently that many of them were torn away.

Once, Lily Lavallée (that was not her true family name, but she would not reveal any other, oddly secretive for a woman who told me this story as she tried to smooth out little bumps in her own naked flesh) allowed herself to drift near the man. "What are you reading?"

The fellow moved only the pale blue eyes until they bumped up to the eyelids. His answer was half-mutter, half-snarl. "Dickens." His eyes returned to the page.

Lily wheeled about and disappeared. She was not the sort of girl who found surliness and unsociability attractive, especially from runty fellows with oddly shaped heads. She had many admirers in the cast, not the least ardent of which was Nolan Tweed.

Now, the details become kind of vague, owing to a certain modesty on Lily's part, also an obvious embarrassment. She made no bones of the fact that she and Nolan Tweed made the beast with two backs. (That's how the Fat Man was wont to describe the deed, as in, *I can't remember the last time I made the beast with two backs*, whereupon I would guffaw and ask when he made the beast with several stomachs, and he would pitch an old shoe at me, which would overwhelm with odor, and remembering things of this foolish nature is about the only thing that gives me any pleasure these days.) Anyway, what Lily will not say is how, an hour before the curtain went up on Opening Night, Nolan Tweed was cut and started to bleed. I came away that evening with my back cross-hatched with scratches, so it's possible that Lily tore the fellow's back open with her fingernails. Lily also had the odd habit — should you be behind her, coupling in what Hartrampf says is an *animalistic* manner — of suddenly cranking her head backward and nipping at whatever was nearby. So, Nolan might have been unlucky enough to get his cheek or earlobe caught between Lily's teeth.

The blood poured forth and showed no sign of abatement. He reluctantly announced the cancellation of the play, as it did not seem fitting that the young Prince should drip blood all over the scenery props and other players.

This is when the odd young man stepped forward. He spoke without lifting his eyes, in a rough-edged mumble. "I shall play Hamlet."

He was, according to Lily, his bride-to-be, spectacularly bad. When he was not whispering his lines, he was bellowing them up into the rafters, as though his aim were to deafen the turtledoves that nested there. His physical gesturing was mystifying in its intent, as though he had come ashore amidst a tribe of aborigines and was desperately searching for some means of rudimentary communication. He was so terrible that the good people of Guthrie hurled abuse upon him when he was through, booing and pelting him with whatever came to hand. The young man stood center-stage, bowed deeply and made no move to protect himself. Indeed, he grinned as though the audience was up on its feet and cheering. He spun around and motioned for the rest of the cast to come forward, but they were scurrying for cover, except for the young Ophelia, who I wager could not have been the best Ophelia, being far too healthy and buoyant to ever drown. She flew forward and took his hand, and as the man with the odd head took deep bows, Lily folded herself into a series of pliant curtsies.

Lily told me how Caspar immediately abandoned his career in journalism and took up play-acting. As has been confirmed by Mrs. Moorcock, Willison's career was altogether ruinous. The couple was supported by Lily, who had discovered her talent for stillness. The Mistress of the Tableau became quite famous; men packed themselves into Masonic Temples to watch her representation of great works of art, *Venus on the Halfshell* and *Reclining Nude with Hand Mirror*, and that famous painting *September Morn*, which for some reason whipped up the male populace into an especially enthusiastic lather. Standing in what was basically an oversized footbath, Lily hunched over, her arms shielding her nakedness with frantic modesty, covering her belly and her left knee more than the interesting bits.

Willison first encountered the motion pictures when Ed Porter hired him as one of the desperados in *The Great Train Robbery*.

Although he'd seemed skittish and ineffectual when I first saw
that Flicker, I now held the opinion that Willison made a very fine
murderous scoundrel. "You know what," I said, raising myself up
onto one elbow, "I imagine Caspar would kill me if he caught
sight of me now."

"No, he wouldn't."

"You don't think so?"

Lily stretched upon the bed, and her whole body rippled. "I
know it for a fact, Thom."

"How so?"

"Well, he *didn't*."

I reached out to touch her pale-nippled breast, but I never did.
"Huh?"

"Caspie," she whispered, "stood in the doorway, grinning like
the maniacal shithead he is." The Mistress of the Tableau linked
her hands together and placed this ball of bony flesh between her
thighs. She began to rock upon the bed, she bit her bottom lip and
emitted a low hum.

"Let me get this straight," I said.

"Let *me* get *this* straight..." said she, and slipped her lips around
the head of my root, but I pushed her away, because that is an
abomination. "Stood in the doorway while we were...?"

"*Fugging*," said Lily Lavallée, in a voice that sat low in her chest
and did not seem to belong to her.

Chapter 27

"Thom," says The Warden, "your mother desperately wants to see you before she leaves."

I do not look up from my labors. "Where's she going?"

"Away, away, away." The Warden laughs in a spectacularly buffoonish way; I startle and my pen-nib rips through the paper.

"You tell her I was busy?"

"What did you say to Johnny Murtagh?" The Warden seems to have an innate disinclination to answer questions fired his way. "John was very upset."

"Is that so? That's a pity, isn't it? We do not like to upset fellows who've ripped apart their wives."

"Oh!" The Warden buckles his hands on his hips and waltzes around the cell, taking tiny, mincing steps. "Aren't we the sanctimonious one?"

"Warden," I heave out, along with an atrabilious sigh. "I do not understand you. I do not know what you want from me."

He climbs up on the chair I have set up beneath the high barred window. The Warden looks out upon the world and his hairless head glows with weak sunlight. "Her followers are slow to disperse," he informs me, not that I don't know it. They should be jubilant, but are not. They are lost and without purpose, they mill about sullenly.

"Is she out there now?" I ask.

"Yes," he answers. "Talking to another newspaper reporter. As a matter of fact, she's talking to an old friend of yours, Oliver Howard."

"Warden, that is by way of being a prank. She's not talking to Oliver Howard, whose name, I believe, is actually Howard Oliver. You are merely seeing what reaction you'll get out of me. It's very childish."

"Hello there, Mrs. Moss! Up here! Up here!"

I scurry underneath the huge desk, where I crouch and cower. The Warden jumps off the chair. When he lands the floor trembles.

"It *is* childish," he agrees. "But I get such wonderful reactions."

"I am undergoing the Rigors," I whisper.

"Indeed?"

"I ideate metamorphosis, as of a butterfly or moth. I have cocooned."

"You're an idiot, Moss."

"Sir?"

"You are a fraidy-cat and a moral imbecile."

"I do not hear you, sir, such is my concentration."

"Well," he says, "I have important things to do. Final arrangements have to be made. The seating plan, for one thing. And what I need to know from you, Thom Moss the sniveller, the mewler, the cowardly custard, is, are you going to be there or not?"

"Where's this now?"

"At the hanging."

"Execution's been stayed."

"Hmm." The Warden paces about my gloomy cell, I remain beneath the desk. Every so often the stiff blue of his trouser legs passes by. "Too true, too true. But, do you know what, Moss? That would not be in everyone's best interests."

"Aha!" I scramble out from under the desk. "I know whose interests it wouldn't be in. *In which it would not be.* The interests of Caspar W. Willison."

"Caspar Willison does not run the world, Thom."

"Oh, really? Who does?"

"The Order of Ancient and Lucid Druids, of course."

✣ ✣ ✣

"Moss! Moss!"

I was attempting to sneak past the Salon when a voice, a strange and strangled croak, rang throughout the building. Mr. Willison sat upon a silver divan, his arms and legs crossed primly, tightly, painfully. "Hello, Mass!" Willison called out. "Where y'all going?"

I realized, not without a certain clammy dread, that the man was drunker than I'd ever seen him. I knew we'd surpassed any previous benchmark by that uncultured drawl. He was too bibulous to maintain his disdain for proper pronunciation, the cruel twisting of vowel-sounds.

His inebriation accounted also for his strange posture upon the settee. Willison's arms wrapped around almost to the point where he could drum upon his own spine with his bony fingers. His legs were crossed so severely that he seemed in danger of pulverizing his bloated gonads. All this had to do with containment and control, the sort of thing Willison had never worried about before, confident in his ability to thumb his nose at God.

Willison blew out the strangled caw once more. "Muss! Come here and sit down, boy!"

I crossed over to the settee as though the carpeted floor were a pasture dotted with cow dung.

Willison kept his eyes upon me, although this seemed very strenuous. Harder yet was maintaining the smile; occasionally the corners would slip or heave with boozy spasms.

After I'd taken a seat, which I did with unnatural care, as though I had strange eggs in my back pockets, I took off my velveteen half-sprouted top hat and began to worry the brim. It wasn't long before I'd bent it completely out of shape. I replaced the misshapen thing upon my head and listened to Caspar Willison, who claimed to have made a mistake, but was a long time telling me what it may have been.

"I misjudged you," he concluded. "Because you were so well-suited to Western High Drama, I felt that you were *only* suited to Drestern High Wama." Willison grinned and had another slosh of brandy. "Lily," he said, coming at me suddenly, his body doubling over at the waist, "Lily is very fond of you."

"Uh-yeah."

"She is a tender-hearted woman. Did you notice?"

"Sir?"

"How tender and succulent her heart was?"

"She's very sweet."

"Sweet, no. Tart. *Ha!*" Because this was by way of being a joke, Willison attempted to slap my knee in a manner that Hartrampf maintains was designed to be *avuncular*. Willison missed by a broad margin, bringing down his hand in near-proximity to my testicles. He left it there, the fingertips bristling.

"So..."The word travelled throughout his body, reverberating in his empty chest cavity. "So, Thom Moss, I am offering you a plummy."

"A plummy, Mr. Willison?"

"Yummy-plum *rôle*."

"In *Civilization*?"

"Of course in *Civilization*, you giddy-headed mooncalf." His hand bumped up against my private parts. "The Tickbite."

"Is that in the Sun Kingdom story?"

"What do you want? Do you want to be the Priest who kills Thelma Doom, the naked virgin? Do you want to carve the heart out of her pale, lifeless body?"

I lit a cigarette so that I had a reason for saying nothing.

"Sometimes," Willison went on conversationally, "the female sacrifice was flayed, and her skin worn to temple by the officiating priest. Hmm! What will they think of next? So, Miss? Want to have a crack at playing the Tickbite?"

"Mr. Willison, I was led to believe that I would portray Athos, the manly Cretan. Instead, I risked my life jumping over a bull – "

"It was beautiful. Gave me a boner that could fell Redwoods."

"Uh-huh. The point is, Perry King was actually playing Athos, the manly Cretan, and will get credit for my astounding feat."

"People," he moaned, "are such idiots, aren't they?"

"How do I know you're not doing the same thing with this Tickbite?"

"Look. Perry is a nancy bungy wad-gobbler."

"Sir?"

"He's not a *man*. Not like you and me. I needed a fugging *man*."

"You could have just asked."

"I'm asking now. I need you to play the Tickbite."

"And I'm the *only* fellow playing this fellow?"

"Absolutely."

"And it's a big part?"

"Huge."

"Do I have to do anything dangerous?"

"No, no." He shook his head and tossed the snifter into one of the room's corners, where it shattered. "Just a little charioot driving."

When The Warden leaves, he takes the chair that sits beneath the window, tucking it under his arm like a folded gazette. But then The Warden usually takes something with him as he leaves, some small amenity. Often he'll aver, quite rightly, that I'm no longer using the item. The Warden long ago claimed my shaving gear, for example, my silver dish, walrus-hair brush, and gleaming blade. I now have a beard like the one sported by the milksop Jesus of the frontispiece in my mother's Bible. It is stained with grey hairs, and there is a large bald patch on my left cheek, the lingering result of my first Flying W.

The Warden has taken my ebony-handled hairbrush, my ivory combs, because I tend to gather my hair, now way past shoulder-length, into a horse's tail, to keep it out of my eyes and the ink-spattered pages. I have neglected my dental hygiene (The Warden has taken away the Rubifoam and gossamer powder) and my teeth have gone a mossy brown, except for my canines, which remain a startling white.

At any rate, The Warden takes the chair, and I begin to notice how altered my situation is at the Cahuenga Federal Penitentiary. For example, didn't I used to have a bed, a spring-bed with a fine mattress? Where did this thing come from, a smallish cot made out of wooden scraps, a tick-devoured pallet on top?

I suppose The Warden would claim that I no longer sleep, so why waste a comfortable arrangement upon me? I see his logic, and it's true, I don't sleep, although from time to time my eyes become teary from the trial of training them upon the pages. I will reel back from my huge desk, spin across the cell through the reams of paper, and collapse into a blackness where-in there is nei-ther peace nor comfort.

After I have completed my work, I intend to do more sleeping.

"Thom," said the Fat Man, "let us go for a constitutional."

"Don't feel much like it," I told him, lying upon the Murphy bed. I had it worked out so that I could balance the sherry upon my chest, the neck of the bottle propped up on my chin. If I ballooned my belly, small though it was in those days, liquor would trickle into my mouth. This freed up my hands, you see, although they had no pressing business, being folded up between my head and the yellowed pillow upon the Fat Man's bed.

"Do you know," demanded Jensen, "what a constitutional is?"

"Hey, Fat Man, it's all arranged."

"You told me. I've thanked you already."

"This Friday night. Me, you, Manley Wessex, Boyle the Erector, and the Johnston Boys."

"Yes, Thommy."

"A *walk*, that's what it means. You want to go for a walk."

"Very good, Thommy."

"Don't know why you want to go for a walk."

"Bath scene today. Over near the Aztec pyramid."

"Bath scene?"

"This is the scene where they bathe the sacrificial victim. In goat milk, I believe. Near-naked handmaidens scurrying about. Sounds like fun."

"Fat Man, you ought to hearken to my mother. *Abstain from fleshly lusts, which war against the soul.*"

"What rubbish. Lust is what flesh was made for."

"And this bath scene is what Foote scribbled down in his scenario, is it? This is what passes for employment in this strange land? He is a warped and twisted man, Jensen."

"Well, it *is* historically accurate. The Aztecs did used to pamper their sacrificial victims."

A thought came to me with considerable force, the impact reminiscent of those times in my bull-dogging days when I missed the steer altogether, leaping from my steed and crushing my skull against the ground. The thought was this, that if the Fat Man and I were considering wandering over to watch Thespa Doone bathe in goat milk, so were a good many other fellows, carnival boys who lacked even our meagre propriety. Then I leapt up from the bed — the sherry bottle hit the floor and rolled away, fortunately already drained — rammed on my hat and said, "Let's go." Then I flew down the stairs at the White Owl Hotel. I had a drink in the Saloon as I waited for the Fat Man to catch up.

Mycroft sat at the bar, fumbling with a stein of beer and a pony of whiskey, his blackened stubs a great hindrance to his career as alcoholist. Mycroft bemoaned the fact that there was not a great deal of exploding to be done in *Civilization*, nor mass warfare neither, that being his personal favorite. There was a Cretan Battle, waged against the Polynesians or something (I don't think Foote was quite the historian he fancied himself) but it was fought with clubs and maces and double-edged swords.

"Watch," Mycroft said. He placed his fingerless right hand into his jacket pocket and rooted about, coming out at last with what looked like a tiny piece of chalk. "Ethyl pyrate," he said, as if making introductions. He then tossed it on to the ground beside my bar stool.

The resultant explosion was, for one thing, so loud that the ringing in my ears persisted for the next two days, and for another, so powerful that it blew apart one of the legs on my stool. I toppled sideways and cracked my head on the saw-dusty floor. The Fat Man, wheezily walking by, muttered, "Quit dawdling, Thommy."

Caspar Willison and Thespa Doone were having an argument as we approached. Actually, Thespa was having the argument. Her arms were up in the air, bent awkwardly, her forefingers stabbing at Willison. Thespa had already made up, but such was her ire that her powder was pinkening, fired from underneath by her engorged corpuscles.

Willison merely stood there, his hands idly massaging his rump, watching her face intently, much as though he expected something interesting to come crawling out of her widened nostrils.

There were several handmaidens loitering nearby, wearing black satin underpants and, to cover their breasts, depictions of the sun, serpents and wild animals rendered out of tin. The Fat Man headed their way, which sent up a chorus of amiable hellos, the girls somehow failing to notice his steamy complexion, glassy-eyed leer and trembling moustache ends.

Lily Lavallée was there, her lower part covered by a small triangle of cloth, which was to modesty what Manley Wessex was to the Dramatic Arts. Her bubs were contained by coiled gold serpents, their cold tongues licking at her nipples. Lily wore a massive headdress that resembled a seashell covered with long feathers. I reckoned that Lily was the High Honcho Hand-maiden. When she saw me, Lily raised a hand and waggled her fingers in a small and listless manner. I returned the wave, even chicked my tongue against the side of my mouth and adopted a pose of what Hartrampf calls *insoucience*. Inwardly, of course, my heart filled with shame and tainted the blood that passed through it; that blood washed through my face and settled in all warm and mottled. I determined to resume drinking as soon as I returned to the White Owl Hotel.

Thespa's complaint had to do with bathing in the milk. She had not spent years eschewing tubs — searching out small playa lakes, journeying to the ocean in order to bathe, naked at dawn — only to climb into a vessel full of fetid microbes. "Bacterium," Thespa howled, "has festered and became a distillate of dead organisms." The husks of decayed microbes would infest her body. In order to add fuel to this argument, she pulled apart her robe and fleetingly displayed her body, pale and perfect and set a-thrimble by anger.

Willison took a few pulls at his pointy chin. "Jest climb in the tub," he said at last, "you silly cow."

"No."

"*Someone*," raged Willison, but in a quiet way, like a storm on the other side of the mountains, "someone has milked an awful lot of fugging goots here, Gladys. Or, I suppose it's possible that some unlucky nanny has given up the entire tubful from her own meagre teats. Either way, Gladys, *you* are fugging climbing in."

"Hey now, Caspar," said I, strolling forward.

"Oh, shit," he moaned.

"I don't think you should underestimate the destructiveness of microbes," I stated.

"Fug off, Moss. You don't want the world to see Thelma nekkid."

"That's not it, at all. I just don't think it's fair to pit her against the poisons of soured goat milk."

"Let *me* do it, Caspie," said Lily Lavallée, drifting near.

"Lil, *you'd* climb into a tub of rat piss."

"You really are ripe shit, Caspie," said Lily. "Anyway, I don't know why you're so keen on Miss Doom. She's all skin and bone, flat-chested. Isn't she, Thom?"

I grinned and shrugged. I strove to do this in as natural a manner as possible, but I have no doubt that I looked much like a baboon.

"I am womanly!" proclaimed Lily, striking a Miss Justice pose, her arm uplifted, a finger pointing toward Heaven. "Aren't I, Thommy?"

"Speak up, boy!" shouted Caspar Willison.

My tongue ventured forth to wet my lips, but I remained silent, not that this was elective.

"Thom," said Lily Lavallée, "like most men, appreciates a little meat on his bed mate's bones." She then dug her finger into my belly playfully. "So put me into the tub, Caspar. If Thelma Doom won't do it—"

"I'll do it."

Thespa dropped the robe and stood in resolute nakedness. "I'll do it," she said to Willison, her eyes frozen into black ice, her midnight lips moving only enough to vent the apathetic statement, which she repeated once more: "I'll do it."

Billy Bittner threw down his cigarette butt and walked to the wonder box. Theo Welkin, openly stunned by Thespa's manifest nudism, stumbled over to assist. The handmaidens came and crowded around the wooden tub. Caspar Willison muttered, "Fade in," and Lily Lavallée flew forward on her tip-toes, waving her hands in the air. Thespa slipped into the goat milk as though the stinking tub were a pleasure pool in sunny Hollywoodland. She dipped her body once, gently lowering and coming back up, so that the clotted cream ran over her breasts.

Thespa found my eyes with her own. She descended then, and disappeared from sight. A single bubble floated to the surface and popped without enthusiasm.

I run toward the far wall and loft myself heavenward, intending to catch hold of the iron bars up there, but I am too bloated and am repulsed emphatically as my belly meets brickwork. This is a poor end for young Thom Moss, who once performed stunts of manifest derring-do. Please recall that Flicker *Zephyrs*, where-in I launch myself from one charging mount on to the back of another, wrapping my arms around little Bodnarchuk who, although he was portraying Evil Incarnate, clucked his tongue appreciatively and whispered, "Good on you, Thommy Moss."

I take another run at the wall, already winded and gasping for breath. This time my jump is even less successful. In point of fact, it is hardly a jump at all. There's a vague twitching in my *gastrocnemii* but it affords no elevation. I plough into the wall. I have drawn my belly in and back, not wanting a repetition of my first bid, and thus do I ram my forehead into the wall, with sufficient force that the skin cracks and blood trickles forth. This is a poor end for young Thom Moss, who walked away unscathed from many a Flying W.

It's hard to believe that it was not such a long time ago that I draped from those bars by my feet, undergoing the Rigors, imagining myself to be a raindrop hanging from the petal of an oriental blossom. I have an inspiration: I imagine myself to be a great big dog turd that someone has kicked into the air. I meet the wall with a huge smacking thud, clench my fists and, miraculously, they are full of ice-cold iron bar. I grunt and exert, pain flaming the length of my arms. "Life is movement," I remind myself. "Death is stagnation." I manage perhaps eight inches before falling back, exhausted. My fingers have numbed, which is a good thing, because if I could feel their discomfort I'm certain I'd abandon the whole enterprise. Why am I doing this anyway? Not for Murtagh, certainly not for Johnny Murtagh, the heartless beast who took a knife to Martha's breast. Then again, I never held a knife in my trembling hands some of those times when Thespa would regard me with, with *disdain.* Oh, look, up I go, my eyes clear the sill and are filled with moonlight. My mother is alone, and has turned her back on the Cahuenga Federal Penitentiary. She has a small valise in her hand and is beginning the long march, the next step in her Grand Mission. And I shout, "Mother! Come back! It's a trick! They're going to hang Johnny Murtagh after all!" There are arms around my shins, I hear Exley say, "You're in the shitter for sure now, Moss."

"They're going to hang him, Ma!" She turns back, places her palm above her eyes as though blinded by moonlight. I believe she begins to wave, but there are more arms about my legs — The Warden's, I presume, because I hear a muffled whistle-snort — and I am yanked back into the shadows of my cell.

Chapter 28

There seemed to be no rhyme or reason to how Willison cranked his masterpiece *Civilization*. One day you would see everyone gathered at the foot of the Aztec pyramid, the next they would be skipping through the hills of ancient Crete, some days they would be gathered upon the Mountain, hidden within the walls of the City. I tended to keep my distance, being disdainful of the whole enterprise, also, sore angry at Caspar C. Willison, also, a little shame-faced regarding my own behavior. Occasionally I would sneak into the City and hide behind walls and pillars. I watched, for example, Manley Wessex's turn as the aging King David. Willison had allowed Wessex to do his own costuming, and the Tragedian showed up with a white beard that he appeared to have borrowed from a poodle, so heavily ringletted that Manley's back stooped under the weight. Neither was Manley about to let that "King" business skip by, and wore a regal bonnet that was bedaubed with fake jewels and cheap gold, and threw off so much light that one of the camera's magnifiers shattered. The reason that Manley had gone to all this trouble is that Willison had not allowed him, or anyone else, to do his making-up. His wrinkles and crow's-feet were displayed to the world.

"Caspie," Wessex exclaimed, for he exclaimed everything, but

there was an undeniable whine thrown in, "I thought I was supposed to look *old.*" Manley laughed; quite often he could get others to laugh at his jibes by dint of sheer force of guffaw. "Oh,
well, I suppose I shall just get on as best I can. I am, after all, an
actor!"

Manley lay down on the bed, and with Willison's terse "Fade
in," servants hurried over to cover him with bedclothes, but still
he gat no heat. Lonny Onley, portraying David's major-domo,
stepped forward and spoke. "Let there be sought for my Lord the
King a young Virgin!" words that would be scratched onto a
title-card.

Thespa Doone emerged from the shadows dressed —
undressed, really — as Abishag the Shunammite. She wore a
muslin robe, but it only obscured Thespa's nakedness to the same
extent as if, say, she was standing behind a window steamed up
from a hot bath.

I fled the City.

Look what wants to flow out of my pen now, a recollection of
some sweeter time with Thespa Doone. I see Thespa on the bed,
propped up on one elbow so that she can read a book, so that she
can lick the tips of her fingers and peel back the onion-skin.
Thespa moves her lips as she reads, and often drags a painted fingernail underneath the words. What is she reading about, by can-
dle-light in the windowless room? History, I'd wager. Or some
scientifical treatise on the Characteristics of Light, with words so
small that they required squinting, although Thespa would never
squint, of course. She would resolutely keep her eyes wide open,
until the little words swam in front of her, then she would close
the book and look at me. She might summarize what she'd been
reading, or she might select something from out of the blue,
which is what she does this time I am remembering. "Thom,"
she demands, "have you ever felt pain?"

"I'm feeling pain right now," I grunt, for I am undergoing the
Rigors, shirtless and shoeless in the corner. I have my palms
together and am ideating opposing universal forces.

"Stop," she says, with a sternness I haven't heard before. I pull
my hands apart and take a step toward the bed, optimistic that she
has stopped me so that I can fulfil my swainly duty.

"I want you to understand something," speaks Thespa. "I don't like pain."

"Hmm."

"A lot of what I do," she goes on, "I do to avoid pain."

"Like what, Thespa?"

She presses her lips together and pulls the mouth over toward one side of her face, as though to confuse any words that might be trying to find their way out.

"You know, when I was a carnival boy—"

"You still are a carnival boy, Muss," says Thespa. "You're *my* carnival boy."

"That sounds about right." I sit down on the edge of the bed. Thespa lies back now, folding up her arms beneath her head, stretching out her body so that it is as straight as a compass needle. I place a hand on her thigh, my forefinger lightly brushing the soft curly hair. "Anyway, we'd go to these Round Ups. Rodeos." I give the word the royal Spanish treatment, just as King Palmer might have. "They used to have these wild horses there, and the sport was to keep atop these creatures whilst they bucked and reared and unleashed their fury, without benefit of a saddle. There was a leather surcingle stretched across the withers, and you'd dig your fingers under that, and the horse would be let loose from a stock-pen. Sometimes I'd get thrown up, and my bones would rattle and my sinews would snap and my fingers felt like they were being torn off my hand. Then I'd come back down and crush my poor balls on the swells. And many times I wondered, *What the hell am I doing up here?*"

"What the hell," asks Thespa, "*were* you doing up there?"

"Well, getting thrown to the ground is no great treat, either. So I'd try to stay atop the horse, even though that necessitated some pain." As I have been speaking, my hand has been moving, my finger has found its way into her soft dampness, it is exploring, and Thespa is writhing, her eyes half-closed, her mouth half-open.

"This doesn't hurt, does it?" I ask.

She laughs, although a tear spills forth from her eye. "No, Moss," she whispers. "It doesn't hurt."

"Besides, getting thrown to the ground," I say, laying out my body beside hers, and Thespa undoes my trousers and frees my stiff cock, "is humiliating," guiding it into her, into its sweet home.

And now I will write of the last time I saw Thespa. The last time that I spoke with her, I mean, for I saw her one time subsequent to this occasion. But that was at a great distance. I was in a crowd of several hundred. Everyone else was costumed, loincloths and feathered headdresses, the women wearing small pieces of cloth to hide their breasts. I myself was naked, for that was how I was most inconspicuous, such is the perversity of Hollywoodland. I took off my clothes and mingled with the crowd, whilst the voice of Willison rained down from above, somehow made huge and hollow. "All right, you've been waiting *months* for this."

Willison spoke from the basket of a hot-air balloon. He held the megaphone to his pale lips and leaned so far out of the wicker that he appeared unmindful of falling, even eager to, although the balloon hovered some forty feet above the ground, tethered to iron spikes with thick ropes. The camera boys crowded behind him. Billy Bittner had his thick wrist cocked, his fingers already wrapped around the camera-crank. Theo Welkin seemed to be in charge of actually piloting the craft; he stood near a stovepipe with fire shooting out of it, frantically opening and closing the burners' drawers, adjusting the flame, making the massive balloon buckle and strain against its constraints. And, of course, there was the tiny ancient Georg, who had no actual job, unless we count turning green.

The hot-air balloon seemed to have been acquired second-hand from a circus or county fair, for it was painted red and covered with gaudy design. A theater in Hollywoodland was advertising itself: SEE CIVILIZATION, declaimed letters of near-illegible fanciness, AT THE GALAXY ODEON.

Before the crowd stood Mr. Boyle's handiwork, a massive temple, a broad stairway cut into the side. Huge blocks bore renditions of descending eagles, and serpents' heads wreathed in quetzal plumes. At the top there was a broad platform, raised and flanked by palm trees. Around it stood the priests, sombrely robed and bedecked with golden medallions and mandalas. The priests included Manley Wessex and Perry King. The High Priest wore golden underwear and a helmet that lent him the head of an eagle. I could not think then — and cannot think now, though I've devoted several long midnight hours to it — who it might have been.

Willison threw the megaphone aside and said, "Fade in." His voice did not seem at all diminished to me. Minions rushed forward, each with an ax raised high, and they struck mightily upon the thick ropes lashing the bucking balloon to the ground. The thing roared and groaned like the Fat Man roused from a deep slumber. It began to ascend toward the ether.

Thespa appeared from behind the platform, which she climbed aboard in a most no-nonsense manner, much like a carnival boy climbs aboard a wild horse. She was wearing a bathrobe, and for some reason spent several seconds cinching the belt and aligning the collars before pulling it off. Gladys Moorcock stood there, absolutely naked.

The High Priest produced a knife of obsidian, took a single step toward her.

From behind the crowd came a short, hoarse scream; I turned around in time to see Georg tumbling from the balloon, and although the withered little man survived uninjured, I believe the fellow he landed on is in the hospital yet.

So when I say the last time, I refer to the last time it was just me and her, although even yet I'm not being entirely accurate, because as I approached the windowless room the door whimpered open and young Theo Welkin stepped out into the hallway. I caught him in the act of lighting a cigarette, and the match flame illuminated and highlighted his blemishes and maculae. Welkin was shivering, as if he'd just stepped out of a deep freeze, his skin pale-white, although thrushed by washes of pink. His hair, which normally resided with such undefiled prissiness, was riotous.

Welkin smiled upon seeing me. "Hi, Thom," he said, his voice an adolescent toad croak.

"Now exactly what in the name of hell," I responded, "are you doing here?"

"Delivering, you know..." Welkin's hands described lopsided circles. "You know, Thom. The *scenario*."

This had a truthful ring about it, because Welkin had more-or-less become Willison's right-hand man, but that didn't stop me from gathering the young man's jacket lapels into my hands.

Mind you, I was raging drunk. I'll say one thing for Welkin, he was no coward. He neither flinched nor faded. "You stay away from her," I said bitterly, tasting bile. I propelled Theo Welkin down the hallway and then went into the room of my one and only.

The windowless room was wreathed in smoke, although it contained neither stove nor fireplace, far more smoke than young Welkin could have produced, even though he was perpetually drawing, hollow-cheeked, at his bent cigarettes. The smoke hung like lake-mist, clouding around the candle flames. There were many, many candle flames; Thespa had set up her entire supply. A strange acrid stink slapped me in the face.

Thespa Doone sat cross-legged in the middle of the descended Murphy bed. She was dressed in her ragamuffin attire, a cotton shirt misbuttoned where it was buttoned at all, corduroy trousers, her bare feet arched back so that Thespa could attend to the too-thick and yellowed nails with a heavy rasp. Her mind was only half on this activity. She also had all three volumes of *The Encyclopedia of All Things Animate* opened and spread out around her.

"What," I demanded, "was Theo doing here?"

"*The Sea Bear,*" Thespa read aloud, "*is a marvelously blatant animal. During the long nuptial season, the males will snort and roar, often in perfect harmony!*"

"I do not care about Sea Bears."

"*The females answer with loud bleatings, which excite the males to further magnification.*"

"Marry me."

Thespa waved the nail file in the air as though conducting an orchestra. "*The united cry of a large herd of Sea Bear,*" said Thespa, looking up at me, and I was deadened by the dark pitch of her eyes, "*is so deafening that human senses are stunned by the clangorous uproar.*"

Thespa then wetted her fingertips with her tongue and flipped through the pages of the *Encyclopedia.*

"*Carp,*" she subheaded. "*If we accept the year 310 B.C. as the Time of the Great Upheaval, it becomes evident that most members of* genus cyprinus *survived without Inosculation.*"

"It's a yes or no question."

Thespa pursed her mouth and moved it around her face, a sign of sure irritation. Not with me — I longed for her to be irritated with me — but with the last word that she'd read. *"In,"* she repeated lowly, *"osculation."*

"Say *no*, then. But say something to me."

Thespa pursed her mouth once more, making a knot of fine wrinkles in the middle of her face. Her tongue lashed delicately and briefly at the lips, and then departed, leaving behind a small dark hole. Thespa began to whistle. It was a sound unlike anything I'd ever heard, pitched like a scream, but pure and unwavering. I hear it still, here in my prison cell, and am haunted by it.

Chapter 29

I showed up well before dawn, chauffeur-driven onto the Plain. The hollow, the giant basin where-in we filmed the Battle, lay a quarter-mile to the south.

There was a chariot there, tethered to the ground like Willison's hot-air balloon. It was rendered out of clapboard, painted gold, strange designs scraped upon it with black paint. There were two white horses yoked and reined up ahead. Each horse had a blanket as though skirted for the saddle; these blankets were likewise white, and hard to spot at a distance.

Willison stood with his arms folded across his chest, his pointed chin lowered with brooding.

"What do you think of this ensemble here?" I was referring to my costume, which I'd taken the liberty of creating myself from the theatrical oddments that littered my little room at the White Owl Hotel. I had a tunic (it looked a lot like Lily Lavallée's Miss Justice outfit) which I'd sashed with a length of crimson silk. I'd taken a dainty tiara and entwined paper garlands about it, placing it upon my head in such a manner that I looked laurelled and dignified, although the tiara did dig into my temples and give me a headache of improbable dimension, but then my head ached most of the time back then.

"I don't think it's at all sitable," said Willison, although I cannot recall him actually looking up and regarding me.

"Well, I didn't know what a Tickbite dressed like," I whined.

"Take it off."

I unsashed the silk and shook the tunic away, so that I stood in my underwear. I was for some reason hoping that Willison would let me keep the wreath.

"Take off that silly little crown," said he. "And your shorts. Do you believe that Tishbites wore cotton skivvies?"

"Tishbites." Notice how I didn't throw in any ¿s as if I was greatly taken aback, neither did I mark down any !s of shock. Actually, what I felt most was a leaden stupidity for not thinking of it previously, for I knew the Book of Kings. Mind you, in my defence, it seems like every personage mentioned there comes from a different nation, what with the various Cherethites, Pelethites, Amorites, Perizzites and Jebusites, so it's not difficult to get confused.

A young female minion came along with my Tishbite costume. *He was an hairy man, and girt with a girdle of leather about his loins.*

"D'ya know the bit we're filming, Thommy?" asked Willison. He stood with his back to me, facing the east, awaiting the first golden flickers of the sun.

"I reckon I do." I spat onto the ground, except the spittle got caught up in the theatrical beard. "Elijah the Tishbite."

"That's the mook. Elijah the Tishbite." Willison took a few steps forward and fiddled with his zipper. He quoted from the Good Book even as he pissed upon the earth. *"And it came to pass that, behold, there appeared a chariot of fire, and horses of fire."*

"You thinking about lighting that thing on fire, huh?"

Willison turned around to face me. I jumped out of the way, lest he urinate all over my sandaled feet. "Got to, Thom," he said earnestly. "Says so in the Holy Bibble."

"How about the rest of that verse, Willison? How about, *And Elijah went up by a whirlwind into heaven?*"

"Hmm." Willison was stuffing himself rigorously back into the riding breeches. "Got a plan," he said.

I could hear the sounds of Boyle the Builder — the hollow thunder of a hammer, the wheezy grate of a cross-cut saw — coming from the south, from the giant hole in the earth. Willison was busy overseeing the loading of the camera onto the back-platform of the Locomobile. He and the young Theo Welkin had a series of rapid, intense conversations.

And as I stood there, my mind dull and fuzzy and about as close to empty as I could manage, Jefferson Foote limped up behind me and said, "You don't have to do this, Thom."

"Hell," I muttered, "you're the one put it in the damned scenario, Jeff. Who'd you figure was going to do it?"

Foote moved until he stood in my sight. His whole aspect was ghostly white. "I didn't put it in."

"Say, Foote, you know what I thought the other day? *Africa.*"

"Willison came up with the Bible cradled in his bony hands and he says, *Jeffie, you've missed the good bit.*"

"The Dark Continent."

"I said, *I didn't think you could film that.* And he says, *Foote, we can do whatever we want in the Dream Palace.*"

"See, *that's* where we should have headed off to do our adventuring. Just like Teddy R, gone over there and killed us some huge animals. We missed out on a golden opportunity, that's for damn sure."

Willison said, "We're ready," and Foote repeated, "You don't have to do this," at just about the same time.

I climbed aboard the chariot. It looked exactly like President Taft's Victoria. And, strange as it may seem, that's what I thought about as the minions busied themselves with the gasoline cans, how President Taft had ridden to his inauguration in a chariot, whereas Harding had gone in an automobile that coughed up smoke and noxious fumes all the way down Pennsylvania Avenue.

My own chariot was lit aflame, and the blankets on the horses' backs were lit aflame. I jerked the reins, although there was no need. The horses, screaming in terror, raced off for the edge of the world.

The Locomobile howled beside, Willison sitting behind the driving wheel, wearing little goggles and an oyster grey suit. The automobile spit up sand, spraying it into my eyes, into the horses'. On the rear platform, Theo Welkin very calmly turned the crank on the camera calling out, "Faster, Moss!"

"Hey, you manky little pisser!" I returned. "I reckon these blinded, burning horses are going just about as fast as they can!"

"Not fast enough!" screamed Welkin. "Not fucking fast enough!"

Willison suddenly cut hard to the left, avoiding a boulder, and the horses bucked in panic, and the chariot listed and keeled like a ship on a stormy sea. I fell to one side, burning all the hair off my left arm. When the chariot righted itself, I matched the right. Huge flaming sections of the sides fell away onto the sand. Then I did give out with a "Ha!" and lashed the reins across the horses, though I felt quite badly doing so. Amazingly, the horses found a bit of extra speed, and the chariot pulled up even with the Locomobile. Willison turned and grinned as a board suddenly disappeared from beneath my left foot, which brushed briefly against the hardcake earth. The sandal was sucked away, along with much of the skin, but somehow I managed to balance myself. I was too full of wrath right then for any extra freight, but I made a mental note to curse Boyle the Shoddy Workman in the future, assuming that I had one.

My remaining problem was aiming (through smoke-stung eyes) the flaming chariot (what was left of it) at the ramp that had been built down into the hole in the earth. For that was the plan, you see. I would ride the chariot down this ramp; the Locomobile would hold up at the Hollow's rim, and it would appear on the silver screen as if my chariot had disappeared from the earth. I didn't really see how it might resemble going up by a whirlwind into heaven, but I wasn't about to argue the point. So I squinted and stared ahead and saw the two little flags such as they use to indicate the holes on a golf course, and I steered the flaming nags, and almost collided with the Locomobile.

I pulled the other way (the remaining section of that side disappeared) and screamed, "Pull over, Willison!"

"Oh, I forgot to tell you! Change of plan!"

I looked ahead at the giant hole coming up — Thespa had a

theory that it was created by some satellite of the moon which had long ago plummeted to earth — and I said, "Fuck you!"

"Oh, come on, Thommy! You can do it!"

The thing is, you see, it would look like the chariot was going *up* if the camera was going *down*. That's the sort of thinking I could never wrap my sorry mind around, which is why I retired from the motion-picture business. It was Willison's intention to scream down Boyle's rickety ramp in the Locomobile; I was supposed to drive the chariot straight ahead, over the lip of the crater, and for some short time it would look like I was heavenbound.

It occurred to me right then that I was going to do it — if I wasn't, I likely would have pulled up on the reins, given out a few "whoas" and that would have been the end of it — and I had no better reason, unless you're willing to count the vague hope that the winds might suddenly pick up and ferry me on Elijah's glorious route.

I gave out a "Ha!" because, well, I'd become enough of a Flicker boy to think, *Better make this thing look good.* The kerosene-soaked blankets had been reduced to stringy ash on the horses' backs, my chariot consisted of a couple of floorboards and charred construct, and as I went over the edge I left behind a plume of sooty smoke.

I am not sure how long the horses and I were able to carry off the illusion of flight. The horses did their best, hoofing the air with whinnying frenzy. Beneath us, the Locomobile wailed down the ramp. Willison worked the brake and gear levers with both hands, leaving the actual steering to God. (Although he had no belief in God, Caspar was not above asking the occasional favor.) "Well done, Thommy!" he called out, and there was a moment when it felt like the horses and I were well and truly on our way, then the bottom fell out, in the most literal sense — the remaining boards disappeared. The descent was merciless, and quick enough that my ears filled with a huge whooshing, sucking noise. We hit in an odd silence, filled with the brittle snapping of bones, mostly the horses'. I fell on my ass, an undignified way to end such an impressive stunt, but what do you expect from young Thom Moss?

Willison unholstered the Bird's Head Colt and performed cold, cruel mercy upon the horses. I leapt up to my feet, at least, such was my intention, but my left leg buckled, owing to the fact that my ankle was purpled and about four times its usual size, and I re-fell on my keester.

"Hey, Caspar!" I howled. "Why don't you shoot *me*, you bas-tard?"

He slipped the revolver back into the pocket and smiled, and repeated what he'd said once before, although back then it had been a joke. "I wouldn't shoot you, Mess," he whispered. "At least, not until the climax."

Chapter 30

The Fat Man and I were in his room for hours, but the cards did not fly from his puffy pale hands.

For the first while, each of us was preoccupied with our own peculiar concernments.

"Sun Kingdom," I muttered, "ancient Crete, the City of David." I held up three fingers and stared at them, puzzled. I lay upon the Murphy bed in Jensen's room, drinking sherry and claiming to be a cripple. My ankle, although merely sprained, was splinted and bandaged tightly. I had several severe burns, mostly on my forearms, which I kept covered with grease. Throw in a couple of broken ribs and a black eye, and I felt more than justified in claiming invalid status. "What's the fourth story? Huh? You just tell me that, Fat Man."

Jensen manipulated the cards and waited for them to scatter as the Fat Man believed they would, once of a night. "Do you know what I'm a-gonna be, my lad?"

"No, sir."

The Fat Man executed a one-handed cut, so slowly that all of the engineering was plainly visible; I could see his flipper-fingers push a card out from the bottom and float it gently to the top of the deck. "*Rich* is what I'm a-gonna be."

Gradually the thimble-rigging speeded up; the Fat Man soon had it going where it was all smooth sound and soft motion. But the cards did not fly away like buzzards from a cleaned carcass. Jensen proceeded to "The Accordian." As the Fat Man drew his arms apart, the cards flew into the air between. They met, co-mingled, and collected into a perfect pile when they fell. He stared at the cards uncertainly, but elected to voice enthusiasm. "Oy-yoy!" exclaimed the Fat Man. "I'm in rare form tonight, Sonny Jim!"

"Yes, sir."

The Fat Man shuffled into the belly of the night. The cards remained as obedient as the outhouse line-up at a Sunday school picnic. In desperation, the Fat Man advanced to a grand exhibition of engineering, giving the deck a single shuffle so quick that you barely heard the ratchet, despite which, cards leapt out in various orders and regular processions, all of the face cards appearing, for example, or a sequence or flush.

Jensen stared at his little flippers with suspicion.

"We should going soon, Fat Man."

"But, but..." he stammered, fluttering the bristles beneath his little nose. "Something's wrong."

"*Wrong?* You're in fine form."

"What time is it?"

"I'll tell you what time it is, Mister Jensen. It's time for a little snort of the old sherris sack."

"You know, young Moss, I do believe you're right."

It is dawn and I have labored through the night. A few minutes back, I stumbled up from the desk and lay down upon the cot. I got myself naked and curled up upon the mattress. I played with myself briefly, but I toyed with my belly as much as with my John Thomas. In fact, given that my stomach has lately come to rival the Fat Man's, I find it ugglesome to even get hold of the little fellow. I did as much tickbite-scratching as self-abusing. I took the one-eyed snake in hand and ideated the naked Thespa Doone, but my root barely stiffened, and I abandoned the pursuit. I closed my eyes and prayed briefly for dreamlessness.

I almost managed slumber. Then, of course, a huge and mighty hammering sounded from without my barred window, from the yard below. I plugged my ears with my fingertips; the hammer blows sounded through. I cursed The Warden. My mother had resumed her post outside the Penitentiary, and her followers were flooding back with renewed fire in their eyes, so The Warden was defiantly erecting the scaffolding upon which he planned to hang John Murtagh until dead.

Sleep became impossible, so I have returned to my desk, I shall continue with my work even as the unholy thunder echoes about my cell.

It occurs to me that it's still some number of days — I cannot be sure how many — before John's hanging. Perhaps they are not rendering the scaffold, but if not, what the hell is going on out there? The Warden has apparently taken away anything that I might possibly stand upon. Even before I warned my mother of his treachery, I was rapidly losing favor with my Keeper. Remember when I complained about the outdatedness of my newspapers? Well, these days I receive no newspapers at all. I am served the same foodstuff for all of my meals (which are delivered by a glum Exley, who does not resemble Bodnarchuk as much as I'd first thought), a colorless compote.

But I have an inspiration, so what I do is, push the great desk over so that it squats below the barred window. This requires all of my strength and necessitates a small nap, four minutes of black numbness, which is about the longest stretch I can manage. Then I rise and gather up all the ink-spattered pages that litter my cell. Some places, I am knee-deep in paper. I occasionally scan the scrawled words, and have no recollection of their composition. *Thespa lazily swung one leg over my shoulder, and I felt carefully along the haunch* and my goodness, I didn't tell you that, did I?

I collect the pages into bundles, each about a foot high, and these I order upon the desk, below the window, so that they form a riser, a small set of stairs. And I carefully mount this oaken and papery construct, and gain just enough height so that my blood-shot eyes can peer over the edge.

Below me, his mouth full of nails, is Boyle the Builder.

The cards did not fly from the Fat Man's hands. Not even when he passed from prestidigitation to something that looked like true

Magic, aces leaping from the deck and re-entering it seemingly of
their own volition.

"I got it!" said I, snapping my fingers.

"Hmm?"

"Well, you've practised and practised, you know, like a damned
violin player, and now you just don't make mistakes."

"I've mastered the thing!" J.D.D. Jensen tried to get this out
with confidence, but he fell far short of the mark.

"Look. You know what all this business is, Fat Man? Super-god-
dam-*stition*."

"It is not. It is scientifical. *Once a night I'm going to lose control.*"

"Well, why don't you just throw the deck against the wall and
be done with it?"

"If I threw them against the wall, I would still be in control."

"Oh, for fuck's sake." I polished off our second bottle of sherry,
got up from the Murphy bed and limped across the room. "Look."
I spoke as gently as possible. I even placed my hand upon his knee.
It was cold to the touch, and I could sense a slight shivering. "Let's
face it, Fat Man, you are on the outs around here. Jeffie's writing
all the scenarios. You haven't been able to squeeze out a novel in
months. Now, you had a fine writing career, and you should be
proud of it, but I think we have to say, it is over. So what you need
is a grubstake, so you can move out to Arizona where you'll be
able to breathe —"

"Fuck off, boy, I can breathe—"

"Breathe without *wheezing*, breathe without bringing up a
bucket of old grog and last night's supper."

"But, Thommy..." The Fat Man was lost for words, or perhaps
out of them.

"The World is an evil and cruel place," I whispered. "You've got
a chance to get out. You better take it. Now let's get down there
and play poker."

Boyle the Erector is making a movie set-stage, a half-room in the
middle of the prison cloister. He works with gruff concentration,
spitting nails into cheap plywood, shoring up and steadying with
crudely hewn timbers. Boyle the Builder punches a hole in the
wall, inserts a small window, makes sure that the door swings

open unimpeded. He throws on a wash of dark stain. Minions scurry forward with furniture. They bring a small chest-of-drawers, which they position with care, they have a couple of small wooden chairs. They bring a large four-poster bed, with legs made of tree-boles, each carved like Indian totems. Boyle studies the work and nods.

Boyle the Wright lifts one of his huge hands and a small mole-like woman appears, toting a carpetbag so heavy that every two or three steps she has to rest it on the ground. The little mole woman grunts and hefts her way to the set-stage where she opens the bag and disappears inside, rooting around, sending up an improbable clatter. The mole woman produces a small oil painting, which she holds at arm's length and regards momentarily, but her eyes are small and mostly white, and I'm not convinced she isn't nearly blind. The mole woman hangs this on a large spike which Boyle left imbedded in the wall and returns to her carpetbag for one more prop. Boyle studies it, gives a nod and half-shrug. The mole lady holds up the knife, and breathes on to the blade, producing a hoary *haaaa* that fills the stillness. She wipes the blade across the material of her skirt and imparts to it a fine shine. Then she dartles up on to the set-stage — even her slight weight causes the construct to tremble — and delicately places this atop the chest-of-drawers.

And all this time later, I finally see what the fourth story of *Civilization* is to be, namely, the murder of Martha Murtagh.

Chapter 31

"Sorry we're late," I said.

The Fat Man plucked the little bowler from his head and executed a servile bow. Sweat was already rolling over his face and collecting on his shirtfront.

The poker game was played in the Salon, which was oddly empty. The Pianola sat in the corner, covered by a light layer of dust.

The players numbered six: the two Johnstons, the Fat Man and myself, Boyle the Builder and Manley Wessex. Wessex seemed to have aged many years in the past week, as though he had been keeping himself young through sheer will, now abandoned. His eyes were bloodshot and imbedded in purplish wrinkles, his face newly jowled and over-chinned; he wore a dour expression, and although he exclaimed the odd risqué theatrical anecdote, this was out of habit, and his heart was not in it. The Fat Man, as you know, was mournful, as was Boyle the Builder. Mind you, I never knew Boyle to be in good spirits.

The Johnston Brothers were, however, in gay moods. Samuel actually smiled a time or two, and when a young woman emerged from the shadows, dressed only in the white apron of a domestic,

Sam demanded a small glass of sweet wine. Lemuel's moods were harder to read, buried as they were in the unsightly morass that he used for a face, but he seemed rather buoyant. He demanded a bottle of whiskey from this young creature; he poked her in the ribcage and shivered with degenerate pleasure. When the girl left to get the libations, Lemuel winked, opening and closing the folds of skin that covered his empty socket.

The Warden and John Murtagh enter my cell, unannounced, unwelcome, and trailed, as though chaperoned, by the young guard Exley. I am sitting behind the great desk, covered with ink-blotches, because I am nearing the end of these pages. From outside, from beyond the prison walls, comes the sound of the melodian, a windy rendition of The Church In the Wildwood. My mother's followers sing furiously.

"Thom," says The Warden, "he'll be here tomorrow."

I lean back and lace my hands across my belly. "To whom do you refer?"

"Why, Caspar C. Willison, of course!"

"Caspie!" I exclaim. "How nice! We fiends, you know. Buzzum fiends."

Murtagh's hair is swept back, revealing a largish brow, covered, as is the rest of his face, with mortician's powder. His lips are rouged, his eyes outlined with the deepest black. Murtagh smiles at me, pulling back his lips to reveal his teeth. I realize he is demonstrating how successful he has been with his new regime of lemon sucking. Not very, although I nod appreciatively before lowering my head to my labors.

"Do you mind," says Murtagh, sounding his voice from deep down, rounding out the vowels, slapping the consonants with ridiculous precision, "if we rehearse?"

"What's this now?" I reach for Mister Hartrampf. I riffle through; some of the pages come away in my hand.

The Warden moves toward the desk, actually, he darts toward it, throwing me suddenly under his enormous shadow. "Come on, Moss. Don't play ignorant." He lofts a finger toward the window. "You've been watching."

"I've been working on my book."

"He was watching," says Exley, pulling a little notebook out of his back pocket. "Let me see here." Exley flips pages. "At six-fifteen A.M. he went over to his cot and tried, unsuccessfully, to masturbate."

"Hey, now, Exley!"

"He went back to his desk and tried to write. Then he looked out the window for a period of twenty-two minutes."

"Aha!" says The Warden.

"At seven-fifty-three A.M., he looked out for just over thirty-seven minutes."

"Good work, Exley!" enthuses The Warden. "All right, let's get down to work. For the purposes of this rehearsal, I shall play Mrs. Martha Murtagh." The Warden lays down on the cot, threatening to squash it like a bug underfoot. He raises his arms toward me. "Come, my lover," coos The Warden, batting his eyelashes, except that he has none.

Boyle the Erector lay down his winning hand, a straight flush to the eight, and raked in a smallish pile of money. Beside me, the Fat Man stirred and pawed his obeseness, searching for and finally locating a fine cigar. Jensen pulled this out from a fold in his body, bit off the end and spit it across the Salon. "Well done, Boyle," he said, but I read his true meaning, *Well done, Fat Man.*

Lemuel swung his head toward me. He had lost some money, but it did little to dampen his high spirits. "Thom Moss," he said, to which there was little response I could make.

"Thom Moss," added his twin brother. "Our favorite."

I smiled in thanks, busied myself with shuffling and dealing duties.

"You done good, Thom Moss," announced Lemuel, "in *Civilization.*"

"Yes, sir."

"*Very* good," added Samuel.

I flipped the cards about the table. "And I think Caspar's got something else planned for me. I do not believe I'm done yet, Mr. Johnstons."

I can't really write down that Lemuel went cross-eyed, but his one eye did start to spin like an alley in an empty milk-bottle. Samuel was arrested in the act of picking up his cards; he tilted his head and stared at me.

"Oh," said the Johnston twins in harmony, "yes, you are. Tomorrow is the end."

I dip my pen into the inkwell and scratch out words, even though they be illegible. My hand is swollen, twisted with discomfort; I have a writer's corn the size of a robin's egg on my middle finger.

"Come here, you great big *man* you!" sings The Warden.

"No, sir," say I. "I will not do that, sir."

"It's a plummy."

"A yum-plummy rôle?"

The Warden giggles, very unseemly conduct in a hairless giant.

"Let me guess," say I. "I'm supposed to play the interloper, the man in bed with Martha Murtagh?"

"Yes," says The Warden. "We need to see the murder first. Then the execution."

"You're not so special, Thom Moss," snarls Murtagh, so savagely that he has to spend a few moments re-aligning his hair.

"Never said I was."

"Oh, no." Murtagh's voice is laced with sarcasm. "Thom Moss, Famous Flicker Player. Famous Fucker of Thespa Doone. You sit in here writing your memoirs. You never come to visit. You're stuck-up and that's the truth."

"These are not my memoirs, Murtagh. This is the story of *Civilization.*"

"You're not the only one who can act. Watch this." Murtagh slowly turns toward the cot and his face fills with an improbable mixture of grief and horror. He picks up an imaginary knife and takes some halting steps toward the bed, picking up each foot as though it had been mired in a cowpie. The Warden whispers encouragement. Murtagh raises the knife away up in the air. He uses the other hand to pull away tears, and I'm surprised to see that he is truly crying.

"Plunge it into my heart," murmurs The Warden. "*Stick it in.*"

John Murtagh brings his hand down with tremulous deliberation. Exley claps his hands and Murtagh turns away from the cot, already bent in the first of many deep bows, graciously accepting the applause.

The Fat Man soon regained all of the confidence he lost upstairs in his book-choked room. He riffled the deck of cards with insouience and élan, all the time wrapping up a tale of tawdry delight. *"You see! said the Mandarin. That's what happen if you no drink milk!"* Jensen barked like a tickled sea lion. The Johnston Brothers howled, Lemuel maniacally, Samuel demurely. Even Boyle the Surly Assembler chuckled. Manley Wessex said, "I am reminded of this tale," and off he went, in grand oratorical style. The Fat Man strew cards about the table and puffed merrily on his Havana. So everyone was in a fine state of mind except for yours truly, still fairly stunned at the revelation that tomorrow was to be the last day of turning on Caspar Willison's masterwork, *Civilization*.

The Fat Man dealt me a full house, kings over threes. Trying to cheer me up, I supposed. I obligingly threw a twenty-dollar bill into the pot. "There you go," I mumbled.

"Ah, Thommy!" roared Jensen. "It's another of your damn bluffs!"

"But," said I, "he's only got *three* stories."

"Three, four, what's the difference?" said Lemuel. "I bet a hundred and forty-three dollars."

"Well, you know," I matched the bet, "he and Foote had these high-minded plans. Wasn't there something about modernity in there? You're seen."

"Modernity?" bombasted the Fat Man. "What care we for modernity?"

Lemuel gleefully unveiled his holdings, jacks and trays. "Sorry, Mr. Johnston." I flipped over the full house and reached for the pot.

"Not so fast, young Moss!" The Fat Man had given himself three aces and two queens. He lowered his enormous fat breast on to the table and gathered the lucre unto himself. Jensen caught my eye and flicked his eyebrows, so quickly that it used up none of the world's time. The Fat Man was on his way.

"If you gentlemen don't mind..." I gesture at my pages. "My Muse does not like to be kept waiting."

My words have no effect upon those three. Exley and Murtagh stand over on one side of the room. Murtagh is showing young Exley how to emote theatrically. The guard is particularly interested in the knife-wielding gait, which to my eyes would leave the intended victim time to pack up and move to another town. But this is what they are both doing, imaginary knives held high overhead. The Warden is still lying on my cot, his huge hands folded across his breast. "Thommy," he whispers.

I do not look up from my labors. "It's coming up, sir."

"Hmm?"

"What I did."

"I know what you did, Moss. It is, after all, what you got sent to prison for."

"Then why have you been riding me like a Columbia three-wheeler, sir?"

The Warden merely smiles.

"I am asking you a question."

"You ignorant little piss," returns The Warden. "It's my job. I don't have to explain my job to you."

"Your job is tormenting me?"

The Warden swings his legs around, sits bolt upright. "Someone's got to," he answers, then he, too, gets bitten by the acting bug. The Warden stands up, raises a fancy-bred knife, and begins a lead-footed march across my cell.

The Fat Man had to part the money amassed in front of him, shimming his hands into its middle and spreading it to either side. Then he commenced shuffling, the fresh Havana in his mouth moving like a conductor's baton.

"I just don't see," I said — and not for the first time, either — "how Willison could be finished."

This badgering, combined with the Fat Man's outlandish good fortune, had taken the sheen off the Johnston twins' celebration. Samuel didn't even bother turning his head. "He had better be. He's spent almost all of our money."

"And what Willison hasn't spent," said Lemuel, his words now inebriated diphthongs and spitballs, "Fatty's got piled up in front of him."

"Do not despair, good gentlemen," said Jensen, flipping out the cards. "I'm sure Lady Luck will soon weary of my company."

"What's he cranking tomorrow?" I demanded, looking down at my cards, a four-card flush. I was tempted not to discard the off-suit, because I was getting a little tired of having good hands trampled by the raging Fat Man. This was beginning to seem like a common thread in the tapestry of my life: give me something good to look at, then fuck me three shades of Royal Blue.

"Ah!" said Manley Wessex. "Tomorrow! Yes! Ahem. *And Ashibag the Shunammite ministered unto the king.*" Manley Wessex grinned with patent satyriasis. When I threw down my card for the draw, it was twisted all out of shape.

"Just the one, Thommy?" J.D.D. Jensen waved the deck in the air.

"Yeah, yeah, Fat Man. Just the one."

"Right you are. I hope it's a fine card. Erp." The Fat Man smiled weakly as playing cards rained down upon him.

The Johnston Twins spoke as one. "Clumsy, clumsy."

Jensen calmly gathered the cards together. "It's the wax I use to sharpen my moustache points. It gets on my fingertips, renders me graceless."

Boyle the Builder, who ordinarily never missed an opportunity to accuse Jensen of being a cheat, simply toyed with his dwindling pile of money and said, "Pass the deal, Jed."

"Yes, certainly." The Fat Man gently lay the cards to one side and tried to re-muster some mettle. "Although, for the umpteenth time, my name is not *Jed.*" The Fat Man smiled, his thick lips glistening wetly. "My name is Tom," he spoke quietly, searching out my eyes. "Didn't know that, did you? My name is Tom."

Lemuel spit like a cornered badger. "Let's get on with it."

"Hey..." I lay down my pen suddenly.

Those three are still doing the Knife-Wielding Slow Step. They stop abruptly and The Warden cocks what would be an eyebrow.

"Hmm?"

"Who is playing Martha Murtagh?"

"Who do you think?" The Warden raises his arm and turns to his companions. "Come on, girls!" He counts cadence and the three step in unison, lined out across my cell like vaudeville honeys.

"Get out of here."

"But it's time for rehearsal."

"Get out."

"But you have to play the interloper," whines Murtagh, whilst The Warden appends, "Caspar said so."

"What sort of man was this watched Johnny stab his bride to death? Who merely dressed himself and skulked off into the night whilst she screamed in mortal agony?"

"Oh," simpers The Warden, "aren't we too good for words? Yes, yes, let's condemn the man for saving his own skin. It's not as if he *killed anybody.*"

"Get on out of here now."

"Caspar won't be pleased."

"Yeah, well," I say, "fuck Caspar C. Willison."

The Fat Man meekly lost back the money; he even, by way of atonement, reached into a jacket pocket and withdrew a billfold, thin and creased. He pulled out a ten-dollar bill, faded with age, and allowed it to float across the table. Jensen pulled apart the wallet and demonstrated its manifest emptiness. "That's it for me," he said quietly. "I'm skint."

The Johnstons were arguing over that ten-dollar bill. Lemuel had hold of Samuel's nose and was trying to twist it into something unsightly; Samuel had driven his forefinger into his twin's empty eye socket. They seemed neither to notice nor care that the poker game was ending.

Manley Wessex was drunk, dreamily musing, in a very exclamatory fashion, "*Sleep rock thy brain; and never come mischance between us twain.*" Wessex then stood up, executed a stiff bow, and fell on his face.

I walked the Fat Man upstairs. His hands shook and his complexion was a step beyond ashen, as though the ashes in question had been pissed over by a drunkard.

"That was lucky," he muttered. "Thank God the Johnstons are not known for their penetrating intelligence." I wasn't sure to whom he was speaking.

"Yes, sir." I threw open the door to the room that smelt of cigars and liquor and the yellowing pages of antiquated books.

"Good night, Thommy." The Fat Man proffered one of his flipper-like hands, all puffed-up palm, the tiny little fingers clammy with stale sweat. I took the hand, shook it gently, and would not let go. "Here's my idea, Fat Man. You and I should do some adventuring. This ain't no place for us. How about *Africa*?"

"Africa sounds nice."

"Sure. Kill us something *big*."

"That sounds lovely, Thom." The Fat Man removed his hand, stepped into his room and quietly shut the door.

I raced down to the Saloon, and jumped aboard the long bar, eager to drink myself toward oblivion.

Wait, I'm missing something, because I did go to Thespa's room, at least, I stopped outside and raised my fist, which clenched and jerked as I resisted the impulse to pound on the door. The very best I could hope for was, Thespa would be sore angry at me for waking her. The worst is that she would be fucking another man, Perry King or the greasy Theo Welkin or Caspar Willison, God from *War*. The most likely thing is that she would stare at me with dark emptiness in her eyes, for I was no longer part of her life. On the morrow Thespa Doone would, for the benefit of the motion-picture camera, denude herself and climb into bed with Manley Wessex, who would gat no heat, but it would not be for want of Thespa's trying. I damned her for a whore, and turned away from the door.

And I'm missing something else, another small event, though nothing came out of it. I stopped outside Jeff Foote's room, pounded on his door, and called out, "Foote? Come on and get all liquored up with your best pal Moss!" But there was no response. I imagined that he was sleeping, for Jeffie was always a very sound sleeper. That thought was preferable to this one, that Foote was lying awake and listening to my uncontrolled hammering.

So then I was in the Saloon, sitting beside Mycroft. "Yes, sir," I exclaimed, "old Teddy bagged himself a Water Buffalo."

"Oxyliquit," said Mycroft, pulling his fingerless hands out of his pockets. He threw them heavenward and there came a dull thunderclap; sparks and fire rained down upon us.

"Now, I know what you're thinking. Water Buffalo, big and ungainly. Surely, you're asking yourself, there can be no sport in shooting them?"

Actually, Mycroft did not appear to be asking himself that. He appeared to be singing "Mother Machree" and conducting himself with charred stubs. Every time his hands swept across his face the air would be filled with efflorescences.

"But I am here to tell you this, Mycroft. The Water Buffalo is one of the deadliest creatures ever wrought by His Great Hand. Put that in your glass, add seltzer, and bolt it back, boy, because that is the truth. And Teddy, he bagged himself one."

The Johnston Brothers, walking in a curious single-file, Lemuel in the lead and Samuel behind, both with hands buried deeply in their overcoats, appeared at the bottom of the staircase, scuttled across the bar-room, and vanished through the front door of the White Owl Hotel.

"Hey, Mycroft, do you know this one? *All aboard for Blanket Bay, won't come back 'til the break of day...*"

I stopped singing abruptly. Mycroft produced a small black ball, shiny and speckled. "Philosopher's Egg," he whispered, waving a blackened nub in front of his lips, urging me to similar secrecy.

I jumped off my bar stool and bolted up the stairs.

Chapter 32

She is standing with her back to me, a man's overcoat draped over her shoulders. Her motionlessness is profound. She has grown out her hair and abandoned the merciless japanning; there is now some brown to it, and where the sunlight catches it, her hair shines almost red.

Her attention is fixed on the set-stage, where a young man holds, 'twixt thumb and forefinger, a long stick with a piece of chalk tied to the end. Setting the marks was, you'll recall, Theo Welkin's chore, but it has been given over to this new youth, who no doubt earned the job due to his gawky lankiness.

Theo Welkin is now the Crankman, it is he who stares through the eye of the wonder box (set in the center of the courtyard, aimed at Boyle the Builder's representation of the Murtagh bedroom) and croaks out, "Over. Right. Over." The youth moves about, the floorboards creaking with each step. "Gone." The young fellow looses his hold on the stick; it falls to the ground and leaves a ghostly mark.

When Theo Welkin straightens up to light a bent cigarette, I see that he is altered. His complexion has cleared up, which is to say, he has no fresh and oozing pustules, but his entire visage is pockled like the moon. His eyes have thick frames of smudgy black and Welkin no longer attends to his hair-styling. It is wild and unruly, and there is a great shock of white at the front, the hair as colorless as that of Jefferson Foote.

My mother's followers have gathered on the knolls and hillocks outside the stoneworks, the better to watch. They have abandoned their fierce hymns and are silent. My mother, full of righteous disdain, has turned her back on us all.

John Murtagh paces nervously in the shadow cast by the fortification. He has been dressed in a fancy black suit, with starched shirtfronts and collars, and a bow so intricately tied that it appears formless and cloudlike. As I remember the story, Murtagh was returning from his work as a forecaster of weather when he came upon his bride and her lover, but perhaps in Willison's reconstruction of events, Murtagh's job is walking out of operas or sneering at poor people.

Across the courtyard, as far away from Murtagh as possible, stands Exley. He wears underwear, but is otherwise naked. Exley does not seem at all embarrassed by this; he has assumed his workaday posture, hands clasped behind his back, feet set apart.

I stand upon my mountainous manuscript, balanced precariously upon the great desk, and watch through the iron bars.

The Fat Man was as I'd seen him so many, many times before, laid out upon the Murphy bed in dingy, paisley underwear, his hands camping out atop his huge belly. But that belly did not swell and sink, and the walrus moustache did not rustle.

There were cards strewn in every corner of the room, a few even settled amongst the dead flies in the overhead light fixture. I suspected that the Johnston Brothers had done this card-strewing irritably, and indeed, I suspect that's how the whole killing was done, *irritably*. My suspicions didn't carry much weight, mind you, especially with the law, which deemed Tom Delahanty (to give him his birthname) an old man, in debt to God to the tune of one death. Perhaps they are right, and the Fat Man was merely holding a deck of Bicycles, and when his Moment came, they exploded from his fingers one last time. This would not explain, however, the poker hand clenched between thumb and pointer, two pair, Aces and eights, which is what Wild Bill Hickok was holding

when he was shot in the back and called, henceforth, the Dead
Man's Hand.

Caspar W. Willison himself is altered. He seems healthy, if a bit
paler than a man should be. Willison has abandoned his tunics and
jodhpurs and Sam Browne. He is dressed now in a suit. The thin
lapels open high on the chest, almost nearing the throat; the
sleeves are too long, the cuffs bear a multitude of buttons. The
shirt is stiff with batens and studs. Willison wears a black wide-
brimmed hat that plunges his eyes into shadow, although they
manage to shine forth, those strange blue orbs. For a moment that
sears my guts like a branding iron, I'm convinced it is Jefferson
Foote's.

"All right," Caspar Willison says, and everyone quiets to listen,
everyone in the Prison courtyard and all the religious cranks gathered without the walls. "Let us begin."

She turns away in order to shed the man's greatcoat, out of modesty she turns away from the actors and movie-makers, she turns
away so that she stands full in my sight. She is wearing a muslin
robe, and I can see her nakedness, which is soft and full, and then
I tumble backwards, off my construct of ink-spattered papers, for
this is not Thespa Doone, my own true love.

I knew as soon as the Philosopher's Egg left my hand that Mycroft
had miscalculated once more, that the explosion was going to be
outsized and gargantuan, far greater than you'd expect from the
small speckled sphere. Mind you, I'd never really established what
the Philosopher's Egg was supposed to be capable of.

I'd returned to the Saloon, tears streaming down my cheeks, and
found Mycroft where I'd left him. He likewise had tears streaming
down his cheeks, which he tried to wipe away with charred stubs,
leaving thick runny streaks all over his face. While I'd been
upstairs, Mycroft had turned sentimental and blubbery. "*No place
is more dearer to my childhood,*" he sang, "*than the little church
in the wood.*" Mycroft saw my tears and experienced a spasm of
brotherhood, so he shook my hand. (If you let him, Mycroft would
shake your hand every couple of minutes, his little nubs tickling
your palm.)

"Give me that thing," I said, pointing at the Philosopher's Egg.

"This," pronounced Mycroft, "is not a toy. This is a Siphosover's, um, Egg."

"I don't want a toy. I want something that'll do damage."

Mycroft nodded sagely and pressed the thing into my hand.

But even as I heaved it I knew there'd been some serious mis-reckoning, both on Mycroft's part and on mine.

The Philosopher's Egg came to a stop at the base of the wall, and nothing happened, the inactivity utter and absolute. Then there came a giant ripping sound — God ripping the whole damn page out of the book — and a wall of fire.

If I'm being truthful, perhaps the charge was exactly right, for I cannot in any honesty aver that I meant merely to inconvenience Willison, to blast a small hole in his rickety construct. But I was still a little wonderstruck at the height of the flames, and truly alarmed by the speed with which the fire ate. And this much I swear to you was sheer stupidity on my part: I had failed to take into account the Santa Annas. Those winds, parched and sere, sucked in the sparks and embers and blew them throughout The World — the Aztec Pyramid, the small earthen hovels of ancient Crete, all the surrounding furzy gorse. Those of you who have not stood in the center of a holocaust mayn't have any idea how much noise it makes. The fire sucks and coughs and spews, and there is all around a raging, and something that sounds like screaming — and it was screaming, you know, and I knew whose screaming it was. I rushed at the City but was repulsed by the wall of flame, in the most literal way, turned back and deposited on my keester. The skin blistered upon my face, that's how close I was, but I could not get any closer.

From behind me, borne out of the smoke that now ruled the earth, rose the hot-air balloon. Theo Welkin worked the control pulleys, drawing in fire and bucking the wild currents of firestorm. Caspar Willison stood behind the black motion-picture camera, calmly turning the crank, photographing history, as first the City was eaten by flame, then The World.

The balloon kept going up and up, and I shook my fists at it and damned Willison to Hell, but ever the balloon ascended, and finally it was out of sight and likely through the Gates of Paradise. I collapsed and now my life has, in these pages, made its circle.

Chapter 33

They are building the scaffolding. Mr. Boyle the Great Begetter is overseeing the construction, which I feel is a bad idea. I have even bellowed this sentiment through the iron bars, but my voice is lost amidst the rumbustious song of Babel thrown up by mother and her followers. As the dawn nears, and with it Johnny's death, they clamor ever louder, for if previously they wanted governmental intervention, now they are demanding heavenly. This seems unlikely.

I have no doubt that John will be executed, because there are powers that seem to want this. Perhaps it is simply The Order of Ancient and Lucid Druids, but perhaps it is our Great Will, and we, like the Aztecs, must every now and again exact human sacrifice.

Given that Murtagh will die by the Hangman's rope, it is but a small and worthless mercy to scream at The Warden, "Hey! Take that hammer away from Mr. Boyle! His constructs have only the merest semblance of solidity!"

They filmed the Death of Martha Murtagh last evening, even as night fell, because they have lights now, great huge things the size of rain barrels, whose beams pierce the darkness.

Exley conferred briefly with Willison. I was surprised to note that the nearly naked Exley was reconstructed, at least to some extent. Exley kept one hand wrapped around his root, which bolted and pushed at the front of his drawers as if it, too, wanted a chance to be a Player in the Flickers. Exley then mounted the set-stage, which swayed and moaned, and lay down upon the bed.

The girl (for girl she is, no older than seventeen) threw herself into her rôle with alarming gusto. No sooner was Exley lying down than she hiked the diaphanous gown high on her thighs and mounted the stage. I half-expected her to spit on her hands and smack her buttocks, for in many respects she was behaving like a carnival boy at the Old Glory Round Up. She straddled Exley and was merrily heaving up and down long before Willison said, "Fade in."

The girl groaned and Exley turned brutishly carnal. He took hard hold of a breast, the other hand grabbed the girl's backside to assist in the pumping. They both made noises, beastlike incoherencies.

"Veddy gude," said Caspar Willison.

The door flew open and there stood Murtagh, his face cut by shadow. Murtagh's head tilted down, but his eyes bobbed like the bubble in a carpenter's level; he looked straight ahead through darkened lids and let loose a long sigh, full of philosophy and regret. It was a fine bit of acting, I suppose, although Murtagh had not yet actually looked at the wanton lovers, who continued their lively pumping unperturbed.

Heaving great sighs as though that were how he commonly took air, Murtagh lurched over toward the dresser, dragging heavy feet behind him. He picked up the knife, raised it up before his dark eyes. The blade caught the beams from the huge arc lights and suddenly glowed white hot. Murtagh was blinded, but did not avert his gaze, for he was heaving another sigh. (Murtagh had by this time heaved so many that he seemed merely bored, as if killing his wife was daily routine.) John Murtagh lofted the knife and advanced on the rutting pair.

Exley proved himself to be no slight play-actor. It was he who first caught sight of Murtagh, and he abruptly ended his frantic bub-rubbing. Exley's eyebrows vaulted high on to his forehead and he ejaculated, "What ho!?"

"Aha!" cried Murtagh, as if seeing them for the first time.

"Oh-oh!" sang the young girl, and she jumped off the bed and began to beetle madly about the room.

"Stand still," Murtagh muttered, through a mouth clenched so tightly that the lips had blanched.

The girl would not, and recoiled off walls, leapt over the sparse furnishings. She cowered in one corner and when Murtagh thought he had her cornered — beginning his lead-footed murderer's gait — she flew off toward another.

Meanwhile, Exley climbed calmly into street clothes, dressing with care and precision, even reknotting his tie when the end dangled too far over his belt buckle. Then he placed a fedora upon his head, nodded vaguely — at the girl, perhaps, thanking her for a lovely evening; at Murtagh, *pleased to make your acquaintance* — and left the room.

"Aha!" cried Johnny, as the young girl tumbled upon the bed once more. Her bosom was heaving, taunting the knifeblade. Murtagh fell upon her, and slowly lowered the weapon.

"Fade out," sang Caspar Willison.

When they place the noose around John Murtagh's neck, I expect to read something in his face. I know there will be neither fear nor anger, because Murtagh only thought in terms of something and nothingness, voids or bad weather. Defiance is for the man who cares something about his humanity, a characteristic I can't ascribe to John Murtagh, who might just as easily have been born a dog or newt.

They place the noose around his neck, and the clouds that darken his face do indeed lift, but what I am looking for is not there. Just before they drop the platform I see what is. Murtagh has enough information to make a prediction, and that knowledge lights his countenance with the smallest and most pitiable of smiles. Then he drops, and kicks and twitches, and he soils himself, the dark stain spreading throughout his prison-issues. The only sounds are a strangled gurgling and the machine noises of the motion-picture camera.

The Warden takes a step forward, removes his hat and covers his heart with it. "There is but a step," he chants, "between me and death."

"Could you come a bit closer to the cam-rah?"

"Hmm?"

"And take a step or two to your left, because you're blocking the view, and the fellow is still twitchy." Caspar Willison grins, and I descend from my pile of ink-stained yellowing pages and return to the gloom of my cell. The wind carries Willison's voice to my ears, even though he is speaking barely above a whisper. "Fade out," says Willison, and I know that John Murtagh is dead.

I fold up the piece of paper that bears this simple message, "EXLEY. COME IN HERE. MOSS." and slide it carefully under my cell door. It is some minutes later that the door swings open, and a very languid Exley takes a few disdainful steps into my dungeon. He has his guard's uniform on, but the collars are not fastened, the tunic not buttoned, and he has his cap tipped at a jaunty angle. "What do you want, Moss?" he demands testily.

"Return a favor, Exley."

"Favor? What favor might that be?"

"You ungrateful bastard."

"Hmmm?"

"Here I give you your in to the Flickers, your punched ticket to Hollywoodland, and you ask is *what favor!*"

"You didn't want to portray the Interloper. You implied you had some ethical difficulties."

"Oh, yeah, I *implied*. But do you think I give a rap if this fellow merely strode nonchalantly out of the place? Hell, that's what I'd do. I only *said* that so that no one would figure what was really up, namely, I was leaving the door open for you."

"Why would you do that?"

"Because, um, I like you."

"No, you don't."

"I like you well enough, Exley. I think you're a handsome and talented boy."

"Mr. Willison said I did well."

"And I could put the good word right in Caspar's ear."

"How might you do that, Moss?"

"Well, that's the thing. That's the favor. You tell Willison — *Caspie* — to come visit me. You bring him here in the middle of the night."

"*Caspie!*"

"He and I are fast friends."

"Why not ask The Warden?"

"I'm not talking to The Warden, that's why."

"I could get in trouble."

"Why should a future famous Flicker Player worry about getting in trouble at his stupid old job?"

"There's a point, Moss."

"Caspie was always asking my opinion, back there at The World. *Muss,* he'd say, because he liked to tease me, you know, call me peculiar names, *how am I going to do this Elijah business? Simple enough, Caspie,* I replied. *Light my chariot afire and send me over the cliff.*"

"Did you watch?"

"You were good, Exley. It was stirring."

"The little slut sure was lousy. She was very mannered, I felt, and lacked dramatic facility."

"Hey now! Listen to Mr. Actor talk!"

"And you'd tell Mr. Willison—"

"Caspie."

"—that you felt I had talent."

"Blue ribbon."

"All right, Moss, I'll do it."

"Done deal, Exley. And, hey, I've got a few bottles of sherry I've been saving. Which is to say, Caspar and I are going to have a couple of snorts, talk over the old times. Things might get a little rambunctious."

"Yeah? So?"

"The thing is this, Exley. No matter what you hear, or think you hear, please don't come in."

Chapter 34

At midnight the steel door swings open and Caspar Willison enters my cell. He affects a leisurely gait, his hands riding awkwardly upon his waist, turned so that the thumbs are aimed at his stomach. Willison's fingers are spread wide apart like the stays of a habit-back corset.

All this I see in a moment, returning my eyes almost immediately to the paper I have pinned down with my forearms. I dip my pen and scratch out a word with great care.

"Mess," he says quietly, "you're looking well."

I know how I look. I know that my face is white except for the darkness around my eyes, which is so deep that it resembles bruising. I know that my hair and beard dangles thin and colorless, influenced by profound cellular disharmony. I know that my belly balloons so that the top of my prison uniform rides up and reveals its pale grotesquerie. Willison cannot even see my feet, which have become miraculously deformed, bent and twisted, the toenails an inch long, thick and mysteriously yellow.

I do not respond to Caspar Willison, other than waving my pen vaguely in the air, indicating that he should bide a while as I finish up a most important sentence. *No matter what you hear*, I write, *or think you hear, please don't come in.*

I lay the pen aside, fold my hands upon my tummy, take a long look at the famous motion-picture director. "So are you, Caspar. So are you looking damn good." What I find especially pleasing is that he is dressed as I remember him, light-colored jodhpurs, spit-polished riding boots, his white shirt grimy-collared and insouciantly unbuttoned. He has the Sam Browne cinched tightly, the Bird's Head Colts peeking out from the holsters like hungry nestlings.

The cell seems to be a foot-deep with ink-spattered pages, and they have come unordered so that my Life is chaos and devoid of meaning, but Willison bends over and somehow deftly extracts Page One. He holds it at arm's length and reads, "*I am damned, all because I wanted to be in Civilization.* Not too shabby, Mess. Succinct."

"It explains what happened, how I ended up here in prison."

"In which, Moss?"

"Prison," I nod. "The Cahuenga Federal Penitentiary."

Willison raises his eyebrows, opens his hand, and lets the paper drift back to the ground slowly, like a piece of ash from a trash-fire.

"How's about," I say, slipping off my stool and scurrying over to the cot, "a little tug at the witch's nipple?"

Willison shrugs indifferently, which is what Caspar Willison uses for enthusiastic affirmation.

I pull out a bottle from underneath the cot, purse my lips and blow away dust and spider-webbing, a few actual spiders, and some creatures that God made in His spare time and never bothered to name. "A good sherris sack," say I, canting my head poetically, "hath a two-fold operation in it. It dries all the dull and cruddy vapors of the brain, and fills it full of nimble, fiery, and delectable shapes."

"Just as long as it gets us pissed," responds Willison. I hand him a tin cup, battered and green with tarnish. I myself drink from the bottle, but before I do, I swing it at Willison. He raises his cup to deflect the blow, and there is a dull clunk, and sherry stains our faces. "Cheers," say I, sticking the bottle in my mouth and pumping furiously.

Willison, his eyes narrow, has a small draught. This has the air of genteel refinement, even though his Adam's apple disappears into his chest and then bounces back, making a sound so loud that it fills the prison cell.

"So," I ask, and it does require steeling my nerves, more so than any other of my half-baked plans and schemes, "how's old Thespa?"

"Thelma Doom?"

"That's right."

"Gladys Moorcock, the Wonder Whistler?"

"How is she?"

"I do not know," he answers, but he is distracted. Willison climbs upon the stool behind the huge desk, a desk such as God must sit at as He plans our course, if indeed He does such a thing. Willison opens all of the bureau's secret drawers and compartments. "We've fallen out of touch."

"Once they turn twenty there's no room for them in the Flicker business, right, Willison? It has to be young skin, or the unblinking eye will not capture the incandescence."

"I don't know why you take this sunctimonious tone with me, Mass. I had not a thing to do with it. Thespa quit the busyness to have the baby —"

"Beg your pardon?"

"To be deliverèd of child."

"Whose child?"

"Ah." Willison continues poking around in the pigeonholes. "That's the question, ain't it?"

"How about this, huh? How about that was merely an aggressive thrust, a fabrication designed to throw me off balance and lend you the upper hand? What do you think of that?"

"How about this, Muss? How about that you are an imbecile who never understood the simplest things about that gill? What do you think of that?"

"Thespa is my true love. My one and only."

"Thelma Doom is a spoony mooncalf. Mind you, it's not her fault. It's the dregs."

"The what?"

"The dregs, you buffoon. Thespa is a dreg-addict."

"What sort of drugs?"

"Oriental stuporifics. I dunno. All's I know is, she takes 'em. And she's got young Welkin taking them ulso."

"Welkin? What's he got to do with any of this?"

Willison sighs heavily and sips prissily from his tin cup. I don't think the green stuff on the tin is mere tarnish; I suspect it may be lichen.

"By the way," I say, because Willison is a cunning fellow, and all this talk about drugs is designed merely to confuse and upset me, although I suppose it explains the strange scent that pervaded the windowless room, perhaps it even explains much of what Thespa was. "By the way, thanks kindly for coming to testify on my behalf."

"What could I say? *Yes, I had a hunch that Thommy might do such a thing!*"

"More than a hunch, I'd call it."

"More than a hunch."

"That's what you might have said in my defence. *Ladies and gentlemen, I knew Thom would burn down all the sets. I kind of put the idea in his head, what with giving him the rôle of Elijah the Tishbite and all. You recall that Biblical tale, don't you? You recollect it was Elijah who said,* If I be a man of God, let fire come down from Heaven."

"You over-esteem the extent of my Bublical knowledge, Mass."

"*You see, ladies and gentlemen of the jury, I had run out of money but I had not finished the movie. I didn't have the fourth story. So I needed Moss to burn down the sets so I could collect assurance money from the murderous Johnston Twins, two fuck-pigs who killed the Fat Man, I don't know how, but I know they did, and they should be hanged by their necks until dead but won't be, because there is no justice in this sorry, sorry world.*"

"Hold on, Muss. I wouldn't have said that last bit."

"No. I suppose you wouldn't have."

"There is a sort of justice, after all. Those with consciences are doomed to live with them."

"Why did you need the damned fourth story?"

"Oh, you know, simple narrative structure. A story needs an ending." Caspar Willison elects to turn a circle in the gloom. He holds his legs out as though they were wings and spins slowly. "You're lucky to be in here, where it's coozy. You should see it out there, Mess. Vast destruction. Chaos."

Willison leaks out the words and comes to a halt. "In years to come, men will find our abandoned temples. Our shrines full of comfy red velveteen chairs. An oversized bedsheet stretched across what should be the altar. Then they will watch *Civilization* and understand."

"Understand what?"

"How we destroyed ourselves, of course."

"Is that so?"

"How we worshipped ourselves. For that's what the Flickers are, Mass. Men render themselves giant creatures of light, they kowtow and genuflect and prostrate their pale fleshly beings before these new gods. Then, men do what they must always do to gods. Destroy them."

"You're crazy."

"You're a fine one to talk, Muss."

"At least I never thought I was anything more than a carnival boy in the Flicker trade."

"Oh, but you were, Miss. Much more. God, I loved you." Willison closes his eyes and draws his pale lips together, and it is the first time I've ever seen him bear a look of pleasure. "You should see the fiery chariot ascend to heaven. Fugging magnificent. People will look at it and say, Willison's a genius, this *looks* as though some poor fool has driven a blazing rickety carriage off a cliff and into the sky. *Ha!*"

"Glad I could be of some use."

"*Some* use? Thommy, I couldn't have done it without you. The Johnston Twats wouldn't have given me their money if they didn't have a bone-on for you. If you hadn't won the baseball game."

"I sure got a hold of that one, didn't I?"

"Yes, you surely did, Moss."

"We killed Jefferson Foote, Mr. Willison."

The director gestures toward himself and smiles meekly. "*I* had no way of knowing he was in there."

"You didn't know that Jeffie wandered through the City late at night? You didn't know that it helped him think up your fucking stupid little scenarios? How come you didn't know any of that shit?"

"If *you* knew that, why did you toss the Philosopher's Egg?"

My mind is suddenly full of bristling dreams that have the utterness of truth. I see Willison pressing the ebon jewel into Mycroft's fingerless hand, "Give him this," leaking out his mouth like a serpent's hiss.

I brush these thoughts away, for I must have my mind clear if I'm to do what I must do.

"Do you have a plan?" asks Willison.

"Hmm?"

"Do you have an actual plan here, or are you simply extemporizing?"

"What the hell are you talking about, Caspar? I just thought we'd have a little chat, is all. You're the first person who's come to visit me here at the Penitentiary."

Willison throws his eyes about my cell. "Moss, you are in no Penitentiary."

"Yeah? Then what the hell are those?" I indicate the iron bars that fall over the high window.

"You are back home in The Confluence, Ohio."

"Don't play your games with me, Mister."

"You are in The Asylum, Moss."

"Oh, that's rich. You fight like a little bulldog, Willison. You just keeping biting and keeping me off balance. But bulldogs, you know, they used to fight bears. And I'm a bear, big and balloon-bellied, and I don't think you're going to knock me down any time soon."

"Are you through? May I speak now, Miss?"

"Go ahead, Mr. Willison."

Willison cocks his arms awkwardly, his elbows in the air, his fingers pointed at the Bird's Head Colts riding upon his hips. "Do you think they'd let me into a Federal Penitentiary wearing pustules?"

"I expect they might if you, like The Warden, were a member of the Order of Ancient and Lucid Druids."

Caspar Willison shifts his eyebrows from side to side. "By the way," he demands gently, "have you figured out how to get your hands on these?"

"No, sir."

Caspar Willison flips the revolvers out of the holsters and lays them down upon the great desk. "There," he whispers. "That was easy, wasn't it?"

"What are you thinking, Willison?"

"I'm thenking you want to kill me, Thommy. I'm thenking I may give you the chance."

"How might you do that, Caspar?"

Willison steps forward and slaps my face hard, leaving his paw hovering momentarily in the air; then with a badminton-style backhand, he reddens the other cheek. "A duel, Thommy. "Let's have a duel."

"That sounds about right," I say, and suddenly my nose starts running, and my chest is convulsed with hoary graveyard coughs. I double over and hawk up an oyster onto the cell floor.

When I next stand erect, Willison's face is creased with distaste. "Are we ready now, Muss?"

"What's the rules?"

"Rules?"

"We need rules. What kind of duel would it be if we just stood here and started blasting at each other?"

"Oh, all right. If we must. We stand back to back—"

"Yes, sir."

"And then we count off five paces, turn and fire."

"Giant steps or baby steps?"

"Hyumm?"

"The five paces. Do we take great big steps or smallish steps?"

"You take a stride as befits a growed man, Miss."

"The challenged fellow gets choice of weapon."

Caspar Willison becomes suddenly irate. "Enough with the fugging rules and regalations. If you want to choose, *choose.*"

I curl my hand around the intricately-carved butt of a Bird's Head Colt. Willison smiles slightly, much like his thin lips are breeze-stirred, and then all traces are vanished. So I move my hand across the desk and take up the other revolver.

"Good choice," says Willison.

We stand back to back. Willison's shoulders cut across the middle of my back, my buttocks are mushed into the small of his, I had never before realized how little he is. Willison lacks substance, he is a mere vapor, when he is gone, no one shall notice.

"Ready?" says he, and as I consider my reply, he counts off, "One."

I take a step forward, a stride as befits a grown man, but what sort of man is what I'd like to know, a crippled fellow or hale? "Two." I suppose I should have a quick look at this pistol. If there is an art to firing it beyond pulling the trigger, I'm a dead man. "Three." Mind you, I'm a dead man any way you slice the pie. I'm off to the pits of Abaddon, because I destroyed my best and finest friend. "Four." And I have caused pain, I see that now. What I thought was just frivolous rampaging throughout The World was blind destruction.

"Five."

I do not turn around. I remain staring at the wall, which is all shadows. "See, Caspar? All I wanted to do was show that I *knew* you."

"Turn around, Miss."

"No, sir. Because as soon as I do, you're gonna shoot me. Because you have been standing there for the entire five-count with your pistol aimed at my back."

"If you know me so well, Muss, why amn't I shooting you now? Why don't I fire a slug into the back of your mealy head?"

"What I'd like to think is that some small part of you still believes in some small things, that deep down you know it's wrong to shoot a man in the back."

"Hmm. Any better theories?"

"Yeah. You're not shooting me in the back because the reason you want to shoot me is to see that look in my eyes."

"Brilly. Fair enough, Moss. You win."

"You know, you fellows in the Order of Ancient and Lucid Druids, you're full of horseshit. No offence. But this business about mankind's failure to decide between the Light and the Dark, I don't buy that for a second. I'm standing here looking at this wall, and it's covered with shadows. I'm watching them move. It's like water, you can let your mind go sailing. You start to see shapes. You can let the shapes become things, faces and such. But it's all shadows. That's what happens when you mix up night and moonlight, you get shadows. But there's nothing in Light *but* Light, unless you got an Icelandic Crystal —"

I pull away a few tears. "You ever hear of Icelandic Crystals,

Caspie?" I turn around now, but Willison is vanished. I am all alone in my cell. "They take in Light, you know, and they split it up into colors, and spit them out the other end. Thespa told me all about Icelandic Crystals."

I turn the Bird's Head Colt until it is aimed at my forehead. "Thespa was my one and only." I pull the trigger. My head snaps back, stung by a giant hornet. The hot wax and pig-fat dribbles down my face.

When John was executed, my mother's followers left: they were bored, mostly, but also disappointed with my mother, because for all her railing and impassioned Bible-thumping, a man had been hanged by the neck until dead. My mother stayed behind, a lone shadowy figure now, beyond the stone walls.

Sometimes I grab hold of my bars and pull myself upwards so that I can see her. I have begun undergoing the Rigors once more, but my arms are still weak, it is all I can do to remain hanging for a precious minute. When she sees me, my mother waves, but I cannot free a hand to return it. Sometimes I call out, but too often the voice is choked.

And one time my mother raised up her Good Book toward me and began to speak, and it was not a malediction, it was the twenty-third Psalm. *"The Lord is my shepherd, I shall not want..."*

There were a few men in the yard below me, men playing baseball with a broom handle and a ball of cloth bound tight with twine. They stopped, and stood upon their field, which was only pebbles and tufts of brown grass, and listened.

"Yea, though I walk through the valley of the shadow of death..."

I pressed my face against the bars (*between* them, as well as I was able) and I could just barely see that on either side of me, there were knuckles clenched around the bars across small windows, and men were pulled up in their cells and listening to the Psalm. The knuckles blanched, but hung on until the last words: *"Surely,"* said my mother, *"goodness and mercy shall follow me all the days of my life: and I will dwell in the house of the Lord for ever."*

I drop to the ground, there to mingle with the shadows.

I will throw myself upon His mercy.

For I am like Elijah the Tishbite, who started out with the roar of the whirlwind, and ended with the whisper of the still small voice.